THE RELUCTANT
MESSIAH

THE RELUCTANT
MESSIAH

An Historical Novel

SALAMON ESKINAZI

JASON ARONSON INC.
Northvale, New Jersey
Jerusalem

This book was set in 11 pt. Fairfield by Alpha Graphics of Pittsfield, NH, and printed and bound by Book-Mart Press, Inc. of North Berger, NJ.

10   9   8   7   6   5   4   3   2   1

Library of Congress Cataloging-in-Publication Data
Eskinazi, Salamon, 1922–
      The reluctant Messiah / Salamon Eskinazi.
        p. cm.
     ISBN: 978-0-7657-6168-2
     1. Shabbethai Tzevi, 1626–1676—Fiction.   2. Turkey—History—1453–1683—Fiction.   3. Jews—Turkey—Fiction.
4. Sabbathaians—Fiction.   I. Title.
  PS3555.S516 R45 2002
  813'.54—dc21   00–056935

Printed in the United States of America on acid-free paper. For information and catalog, write to Jason Aronson Inc., 230 Livingston Street, Northvale, NJ 07647-1726, or visit our website: www.aronson.com

To David and Michelle

"Tanto me lo quiero que me lo creo"
So much I want it, that I believe in it.

Acknowledgment

*T*he *Reluctant Messiah* is based on the historical accounts in the life of a seventeenth century Hebrew mystic who managed to stir up in the Balkans a messianic euphoria of intense proportions not only among his coreligionists but also among many European Protestants and Ottoman Moslems. To write and recreate many episodes in his private life required a comprehensive search of the historical facts of the time, and begged understanding of many convoluted and intricately interwoven concepts of Jewish mysticism so much an integral part of the canons of Judaism. To comprehend the unusual relationship between the spirituality and mysticism of this arch-religious person required a free and uninhibited state of mind able to separate the strange mix of intense faith, clairvoyance, etherealization, human compassion, and what some may call mental eccentricity.

An *intensive* effort was spent to dig up historical facts, not mentioning the enigma of comprehending the very unusual behavior of this mystic. I soon discovered that the task required an *extensive* ability of the mind to permit an impartial, or perhaps a sympathetic, attitude when examining the religious and mystical environment in which this man spent himself entirely and voluntarily to make good on a vision of a divine summons.

This book is an attempt to recreate the personal lives of those responsible in creating the events of a period that, to a large extent, remains missing in the historical accounts. While many of the personal details presented are created, the historical background is true. Many of the quotations abstracted from archival documents, private letters, religious tracts, etc., concerning the life of the main character are translations from Hebrew, French, German, and Dutch by the various authors listed. Much acknowledgment is owed to these publications. The spelling of a few words and names like *mashiah* (messiah), *Mordehay* (Mordecai), *Quran* (Koran) etc., although not conforming to accepted English or Hebrew spelling, have been intentionally adopted in the vernacular of the Sephardis[1], the mother tongue of the characters in the book.

Competent manuscript readers are hard to find. The availability of such readers, and more importantly, their willingness, becomes even more precarious when the manuscript is not what one might call 'light reading'. To Michelle and her husband, this book is dedicated with much indebtedness.

Among the many references consulted, most credit is given to the exhaustive work of G. Scholem (1975) in his *Sabbatai Sevi, The Mystical Messiah*, translated from Hebrew by R. J. Zwi Werblowsky. He, more than any other historian, has uncovered private letters and extant manuscripts of the time, permitting him to sort out true facts from reportings affected by the extreme euphoria that existed at the time. Significant information reported in Scholem's work comes from: T. Coenen, *Ydele verwachtinge der Joden*, published in Amsterdam in 1669, and from J. Saportas, *Kizzur sisat nobel Zevi*, 1693 archives. These manuscripts and many letters of the same period are not easy to find for in a number of cases they are the exclusive property of the *Dönmeh* sect Sabetay left after his death.

Forty years before Scholem, Joseph Kastein wrote "The Messiah of Ismir" in a book published by John Lane The Bodley Head Ltd.

---

1. Some authors have a tendency to use the Hebrew plural *Sephardim* and the adjective 'Sephardic'. This author prefers the western usage of the same.

London in 1931. The original publication in German, *Der Messias von Ismir*, was published in Berlin in 1930. He, more than anyone else, described the events as they affected the Jews of Eastern Europe and the European Protestants caught up in the excitement generated by the messianic hopeful. The small booklet by John Evelyn (1669), *The History of the Three Late Famous Imposters*, gave an excellent description of the manner in which the Puritans and the Quakers, during the rule of Charles I and Cromwell, reacted to the news of the likely revelation of a much awaited messiah born in Smyrna.

Much of the background in the history of the Ottoman Empire is detailed in E.S. Creasy's *History of the Ottoman Turks*.

Other works consulted are listed in the bibliography.

For readers not familiar with the Jewish era designation of C.E. and B.C.E., they are equivalent to A.D. and B.C.

Rockville, MD

Introduction

The story in this book is set in a historical background as it existed in the seventeenth century. Dates, major events, and many of the characters are true. The personal lives and details of many of the personalities, including that of the principal character, mostly missing in the historical accounts, have been recreated and perhaps dramatized in a manner thought to fit the circumstances of the time.

Mysticism is a philosophy of thought based on the doctrine that the ultimate nature of reality may be known through intuition, ecstasy, trance or other insights differing from the exact process of systematic reasoning. Taken in this broad sense, it is difficult to imagine that, when a lack of rational explanation confronts us, we have not succumbed to a contemplative self convincing meditation in order to extract a perception of truth about ourselves or about the world. Thus, subtle mysticism is inherent in the human soul and many of us find that it adds spice to life. Religious and fanatical mysticism is something else: it relies on direct communion with and knowledge of a supernatural spirit revealing to us abstract concepts unexplained by rational means.

Throughout history, societies have feared fanatical ideologies; nonetheless they have embraced them for fear of retribution arising from denial. Beginning with the Renaissance, the development of structured logic as a tool for rational thinking and the evolution of science have become an ever stronger weapon for combating fanaticism. True as this is, fanaticism has learned to become immune to rational rebuffs, much like viruses have grown to survive an increasing dosages of antibiotics. When a despondent society finds itself incapable of healing its ills by rational means, fanaticism never fails to emerge as a panacea. Then, the seed of fanaticism planted by a charismatic leader begins to grow and bloom in that fertile environment, sometimes uncontrollably and with devastating results.

The story in this novel is a case in point. It portrays one of the most intense social and political turmoils in recorded history. A frantic religious movement, driven by a seventeenth century religious mystic believing to be the messiah prophesied in the books of the bible, took universal dimensions in the Middle East and in Europe. Its leader, a Sephardi Jew, was enthusiastically acclaimed not only by Jews, but by many Christians swept away from Catholicism by the Reformation. So widespread was his influence that even Moslems were eventually affected by it.

Many messianic movements are mentioned in history, but only a handful reaping enormous successes swept large segments of population and left behind a permanent legacy. Many others had a modest success measured by the size of their following and the longevity of their influence, failing to solidify their doctrine. While the persuasion and zeal of the leading visionaries might have been as strong, it lacked the required chemistry between faith and the realities of life. As a result, leaders became either divine messengers or shunned fakes, frauds, hypocrites, or quacks.

The religious leader in this story, known as Sabetay Sevi, has only been judged posthumously as a messianic impostor. This of course implies that there are rational rules by which messianic contenders can be tested. The fact remains that the only test which has been applied in this respect is one of success or failure. As we enter the twenty-first century, Sabetay's movement that began in the middle of the seventeen century is alive today. Over fifteen thousand living followers in the Balkans await his resurrection and return to Earth. Was he the impostor some historians and traditional religious leaders would like us to believe? Or, was he an over-zealous arch-religious soul with intense imagination and illumination to have taken to his people every word in the holy books as supreme truth?

Before one decides on this question, one must ask: What is truth? Upon some reflection one finds that truth is not a unique concept. Truth to a scientist is the observable he calls reality. A concept derived through unfailing physical laws. For him the integrity of truth is in its ability to endure, test after test, and come out unchanged after scrutiny. In that physical sense, to quote a well known phrase, "the truth of the acorn is the oak tree." The visual observation of the acorn and the oak tree emerging from one another is always the same without a single exception.

Be that as it may, many concepts in life are not physical in nature nor can they be explained in physical terms. Therefore, one needs to allow a broader definition of truth. Philosophers like to speak of logical truth, ethical truth, divine truth and even mystical truth being transcendental verities not necessarily observable by our five physical senses. Many of the propositions in philosophy, and to a lesser extent in modern mathematics are said to be logically true without expecting them to be observably verified.

If one is willing to accept truth as a conformity of our mind compelling us to accept, by heredity, spirituality, emotion, and even limited experience what we perceive to be true, then *perception* must replace *observation* in determining what is truth. Then, truth leaves the exclusive realm of nature and encompasses the human soul. A simple fact of observing or perceiving, once or twice, an extraordinary euphoric moment, an ecstasy, is in itself capable of revealing for some persons the truth about divine intervention in their lives. In a mystical framework, the verity of the divine essence may come through a spontaneous apprehension, intuition, meditation, vision, or insight differing from ordinary sensation or rationalization.

Man is not all science; he is in part science and in part soul. In the domain of the soul dwells many forms of human emotions.

But understanding, defining, and characterizing the essence of the soul has not been as easy as comprehending the physics and chemistry of the body in which the soul is assumed to dwell. Philosophers, psychologists, and divinity scholars have yet to establish immutable laws governing the soul. Only when that has been accomplished can we expect to predict human emotions just as physicians predict many functions of the body. The soul appears to be free of restrictive laws. It remains elusive and unpredictable in the way it liberates emotions.

Not all religions permit personal or extrinsic mysticism to transcend the boundaries of their precepts. In modern Judaism and Christianity such liberties are viewed as a threat to the established dogma. It wasn't always this way. In Judaism and in past centuries of exile from the Holy Land, mysticism was not only permitted, it was nourished diligently. Mysticism allowed Jews to cope with the paradox and agony of living dispersed and as expatriates from the Holy Land. Cloistered in isolated pockets of the Diaspora and without a central spiritual authority, they deepened their knowledge of the Scriptures searching constantly for concealed reasons justifying their hapless dispersal. Their yearning for an ultimate gathering in the Holy Land became most intense at periods in history when oppression reached a climax. To avoid erosion of their ancestral faith and to increase their sensitivity at interpreting the divine laws, they corresponded faithfully with other Jewish centers of learning trapped in isolated regions governed by Christian or Islamic potentates. To test the validity and rigor of their faith they sought answers (*responsas*) and approvals to their philosophical and mystical interpretations of the broadly worded Scriptures and the Talmud.

A number of erudite schools in Europe emerged for the purpose of developing, testing, and publishing mystical propositions on divinity and religion similar to the axioms and theorems in mathematics. Only the extremely bright and mentally stable student was allowed to enroll in these schools, for it required a high level of maturity and intelligence for probing into matters within the domain of divine purview. They wrote instruction books and primers for the initiate in mysticism. The *Cabala* (Kabbalah), and later the *Zohar*, the living collections of tracts written about every aspect of man, his creation, and his Creator, became the mystical encyclopedias said to allow one to analyze the undefinable and explain the inexplicable in the grand union between man and his God. For Jews who never abandoned the yearning of returning to the Promised Land, one favorite subject in these writings was the messiah, the promised divine messenger who would gather the dispersed flock of God's chosen and return them to Palestine.

Until the fifth century C.E., Catholic scholars were permitted to dwell in the study and art of religious mysticism. But during the time of St. Augustine in the fourth century, when the Central Church became powerful, prosperous, and autonomous, it condemned all forms of personal interpretations of the New Testament, found the wisdom in the Old Testament stale, and declared prior mystical notions as 'old Jewish inventions'.

To understand the unusual behavior of the principal character in this story it behooves to understand the times in which he lived. At the end of the fifteenth century and beginning of the sixteenth century, 200,000 Spanish Jews were expelled by Catholic kings of Spain and Portugal from the Iberian Peninsula, a land Jews loved and in which they lived for more than a millennium. This was a time like no other in history when the spirit of the messiah was invoked more frequently and intensely. It took the expelled Jews another century to find safety and tranquillity in the Middle East and other European countries. The Holy Land, in the hands of an Islamic Sultan, permitted only very limited immigration of Jews, as it remained poor and barren since the time of the Romans. With the advent of the Reformation in the sixteenth century, new and freer spiritual ideas emerged; with them rose the need to reform the dogmatic Church autocratically dominated by a Pope, resulting in lessened reliance on the New Testament. The spirit of Protestant-ism broke out in many parts of Central and Northern Europe, seeking independence from Rome and a closer look at the teachings of the Old Testament. The Reformation did not come easily for the New Christians. For nearly a century, fighting in misery and oppression to gain freedom from Catholicism, they too put more reliance on the coming of a savior.

Early seventeenth century savage wars were unleashed by the revolt of peasants in the Ukraine and Poland against the Polish nobility who controlled these vast lands. Tens of thousands of Ashkenazi (Eastern European) Jews were slaughtered, while hundreds of thousands were left in dire misery. It appeared suddenly to all these oppressed people that the time was ripe to pray for and welcome any credible messianic contender who promised salvation. They had learned from the Scriptures and the *Cabala* that their misery was a direct result of an alienation from their Creator. Churches and synagogues preached that the divine substance of their soul had degenerated and fallen in the tentacles of the devil. God's spirit in the soul had become entangled in the impurity of matter. To restore good and communion with Him, evil had to be conquered and annihilated. Upon prayers of atonement, God would send to earth a messiah to cleanse all spirits and only then would grace descend upon the earth, restoring world order. All at once, rose crucial and urgent hope of a messiah whose sole purpose was returning the faithful to the Holy Land where he would serve Him in purity and piety forever.

Cabalistic schools in the Mediterranean Basin and their scholars were at their highest popularity in the seventeenth century. Unlike the suffering Ashkenazi Jew in Eastern Europe, the rich and educated Sephardi, or Spanish Jew, living in the Middle East, became attracted to mystical writings and seminars out of intellectual curiosity, boredom from affluence, and the love for a sporting debate. Before they could realize the power and magnetism of the freedom to interrogate and argue subjects of divine dimensions, they were swept into an extreme and fanatical form of religiosity claiming to have understood the nature of Deity.

Born and raised in this environment since childhood, Sabetay Sevi[1] was profoundly convinced that the prophesied divine salvation mentioned so frequently in the Torah, the Talmud and the Cabala would finally materialize in his lifetime. Consequently, he developed an intense desire to study and learn everything that was ever said or written about the blessed event since early biblical times.

But, the study and understanding of an abstract discipline demands a discriminating mental ability, devotion, and hard work. Study under the tutelage of masters obligates students to accept only what is basic and fundamental, that which has endured the scrutiny of the years, thus preventing them from going astray into irrelevant and even erroneous lines of thought. Accordingly, Hebrews in exile had their yeshivas, schools where they learned to read and write, and about their heritage glorified in the Torah, in the Talmud (civil and canonical laws), and in the Midrash (historical traditions and beliefs). When the bright pupils matured they were taught to analyze and expand on these writings, and thus enriching the existing recorded commentaries dealing with day-to-day living within the moral framework of the bible.

On the other hand, individualized studies without guidance—especially in profound subjects like the Cabala—while having the semblance of unbiased learning, runs the risk of leading the mind astray into misconceptions and falsehood. At nineteen, after his formal rabbinical schooling, Sabetay Sevi chose the road of self-reliance for his cabalistic studies. Many of the bizarre events in his life are a direct result of clashes between his home-grown maverick ideas and those of the establishment. At no time did he and his many disciples think of themselves as religious freaks or perpetrators of moral and civil laws, nor suffering from illusions or insanity. Quite the contrary, they considered themselves wise

---

1. The literature shows different appellations of the same name, among them: Shabattay, Sabbatai, Sabatay, Sabetay, Tsvi, Tsevi, Zevi, Sevi, etc. I chose that which was most commonly used in the Turkish community where I grew.

men like the patriarchs of the bible, and were prepared to become martyrs to fulfill the messianic prophecy of redemption. Throughout history the prevailing social and economic environment has always produced men with fitting qualities to suit the times. It will become clear, as one penetrates this story, that the world demanded of Sabetay, directly or indirectly, the fulfillment of the divine cause. Deeply believing it was time, he was more than willing to oblige, hoping that God would whisper a word of encouragement in his ear as He had done to biblical patriarchs.

Now, a comment about one of the titles of the book. I was asked by one of my readers how the subtitle of the book, *Harvester of Souls*, reflects the accomplishments of Sabetay Sevi when history portrays him as having little to do soliciting souls personally and aggressively like some of the television preachers we see today. As in most major messianic movements of the past, Sabetay was a religious revolutionary and a reformer who willingly portrayed his image as the much awaited messiah. He provided his charisma and at the same time assaulted the doctrines of the establishment. He promised changes when changes were expected by the oppressed population. His disciples did the field work. Jesus had little time in his short life to organize the new religion and the Church. Peter and Paul struggled through perilous years to accomplish that. The same is true about the Islamic and Mormon religions. In each case it was the power of the idealism that did most of the harvesting.

Finally and for the benefit of the reader, I would like to place into proper perspective the rationale used in blending what is recorded history and my perception of what had to be the personal and intimate life of the principal character in this book. To begin with, if all historical accounts on the life of Sabetay Sevi were known and documented, there would be no need to write this historical novel. It is generally true that when people achieve historical notoriety, details about life around them, family environment, friendships, and especially emotional beliefs and feelings during earlier years are often unrecorded, for no one could have predicted that eventual fame. Sabetay Sevi's case is no exception.

The geopolitical events and religious movements sweeping Europe and the Middle East in the seventeenth century are well known and documented. Generally speaking, all the major events and characters depicted in this book are authentic and can be found in the references cited in the Acknowledgment with few exceptions. For instance, in Chapter 6, the scene when Sabetay fainted on Solomon Molho's grave is imagined. Even though he made it a habit to visit cemeteries to bring himself in communion with the spirits of the dead, Molho's messianic zeal a century earlier was very much in Sabetay's mind. The existence of Molho's grave containing his ashes in the city of Smyrna is not known to be true. After Sabetay was banished from Smyrna, the passages, in Chapter 9, on board a ship with his friend Isaac Silveira is imagined. There is also no mention in history that Isaac accompanied him everywhere. I thought it to be important to make that supposition in order to maintain a living continuity of expression and sentiments through the many dialogues they carried. Historical documents make no mention of what must have been a heart breaking experience for him and his parents, when we know that, in spirit and dexterity, he wasn't able to provide for himself the simplest life–sustaining tasks. Someone like Isaac had to be with him at all times. Subsequently, history picks up with his life in Salonica as if the transition was of little significance.

Sabetay's dreams with damsels dancing around a burning flame, mentioned in Chapter 2, are historically documented. The damsels' connection to his trips to the Turkish bath are deductively imagined as a necessary justification for him to reject Alegra, his first short–lived wife. I drew that Middle Eastern experience from my childhood spent in the very same city of Smyrna. The sequence of narration of dreams among Yachini, Habillo, and Sabetay in Chapter 10 is factual. In Chapter 11, his visit to the ancient caves of Machpelah, and to Abraham's resting place in Hebron is also true. The scene in Chapter 8 when Sabetay nearly drowned in the Gulf of Smyrna is true, and that experience was taken to symbolize that of Jesus in the waters of the Jordan River. Other seemingly outlandish passages are true, such as the one describing Sarah's youthful life in Chapter 11; it is depicted, without editorializing, in Rabbi Saporta's archived letters to Raphaël Joseph.

In conclusion, it is fair to say that whenever dialogues or private scenes have been created, it was always for the purpose of connectivity between one historically described episode or behavior to another.

1

*M*ordehay Sevi was a poulterer in the Turkish city of Smyrna (Izmir). He rented a small shop across from the Spanish Sephardi synagogue, Neveh Shalom, to which he belonged. This was considered a good location for his business. After morning and afternoon services, men, who normally did the shopping for essential items in their household, stopped on their way home to buy slaughtered and plucked *quasher* (kosher) chickens and day-fresh eggs. When it came to buying fish, poultry, and meats, which needed to be bought very fresh and kosher, it was the men's responsibility. They had their favorite fish-monger, poulterer or butcher in the business district. Jews bought chickens no other way except live. They inspected the birds for polyps or other signs of sickness and had them slaughtered by a rabbi before their very own eyes. The vicinity of the synagogue was particularly convenient for Mordehay because he was able to hire one of the many young rabbis, yet without a parish, to slaughter the chickens he sold. From time to time these young graduates from the *yeshiva* also tended the store when Mordehay went on errands.

Women rarely went out shopping in this Middle Eastern culture, except for Thursday, market day, before the Moslem Sabbath. Then they took their young children and went to buy fresh produce at one of the market squares. On other days peddlers with donkeys carrying baskets full of dry goods, fabrics, mercery, kitchen utensils, etc., combed practically every street in town. This was the only time women stepped outside their front door to shop for provisions. Depending on the day of the week these ambulant peddlers also sold dry cereals, flour, sugar, spices, milk, and sewing materials and supplies. Also at seasonal intervals specialized peddlers made the rounds to repair household items like leaky pots and pans or broken furniture.

Sephardi Jews seldom ate other fowl except chicken. On rare occasions recent immigrants from Europe purchased a turkey. The dietary talmudic laws did not forbid eating other domesticated fowl, however chickens were considered safer because their feed was supervised more carefully while other fowl might have been allowed to forage freely.

Mordehay's shop wasn't very large. It was one in a series of cubicles extending the length of the street with walls built of stone and mortar and a common tile roof. The line of stores resembled the kind children built with playing cards. Only the fronts of these stores were plastered and washed in varying pastel colors. Difference in color was what distinguished one store from the other. The smelly nature of Mordehay's merchandise required special doors made of latticed wood placed in the front and back of the store for good ventilation. There was just enough room inside to stack two dozen wooden crates with open slats each containing a maximum of four live birds. Only before holidays were these crates ever filled to capacity. The hired young rabbi slaughtered the chickens over a sink outside the back door, holding the squirming bird for a few minutes until most of the blood poured out from its throat into a sink with a drain emptying into a cobblestone trough washed occasionally by rain.

At supper one night, Mordehay came home feeling discouraged about the state of his declining business. He tried hard to convince his second son Sabetay that it was in the interest of the family for him to begin thinking seriously about applying for a vacant position of parish rabbi at one of the many Sephardi communities in the city or in the neighboring towns. Mordehay was worried about his health and his inability to do more in his business. Sabetay's education for the priesthood had drained the family resources to an alarming state. This was not the first time he had brought up the subject. Each time, however, the final result was the same: Sabetay listened respectfully without uttering a single word.

Discouraged more than ever, as soon as he got into bed Mordehay pinched the wick of the candle and lay in the dark, tired and worried about his fate and finances at the age of 48 when new opportunities were not likely to come his way. Clara felt sorry for him even though she didn't share his disillusionment. Perhaps it was because women in the Middle East were kept totally out of their husbands' business. She wanted to cheer him up by giving him pleasure. She turned towards him, put her hand on his shoulder and turned him to face her. Then she grabbed his hand and placed it on her large bosom mostly out of the front of her nightgown. In a teasing tone of voice but half wishful she said: "I want a daughter! You gave me three wonderful boys, but I am getting tired of living in a house with four men. I have been wanting a daughter to hold and to spoil ever since I had Joseph. Make love to me now! Give me this wonderful gift!"

Mordehay was willing to make love, but when he heard she wanted another child, it must have been the right time in her monthly cycle to be pregnant. He pulled his hand away and pushed hers away from his body. Not another mouth to feed, he thought. Besides, girls cost a lot more to raise, and then there is the matter of a dowry! "No, my dear! not now. I don't want to have another child. I told you this many times. We can't feed another child! If you want to help me you should not insist at being pregnant again. Sorry, I must get some sleep. I am very tired." He turned around even more despondent, giving her his back.

She buttoned her nightgown and turned him around once again. "Why are you so discouraged, dear? I hate to see you so unhappy. Have faith in the Lord, and you will see things will turn around and improve. You'll see! Now hug me."

He did as she asked, but not for long. He released himself from the embrace and said: "How could I not worry? Inside me I burn from guilt. For the size of our Jewish community, there are too many poulterers in Smyrna. No matter how hard I work I can't seem to earn enough to provide fully for our family. I hate to see Eliyah and Joseph obligated to supplement my income. They need to think of themselves, get married and support their own family. If something better doesn't turn up soon, I won't be able to keep Sabetay studying at the yeshiva." An appropriate Sephardi proverb describing his dire financial state came to his mind: "*No tengo uñas para arrascarme!*" (I don't even have long enough finger nails to scratch myself.) Before Clara could respond, he added: "I truly feel awful for saying this! But why does Sabetay have to be so different than his brothers? He never seems interested in anything else except his books. There is no future in that! When I speak to him about life, as most people understand it, about what people must do to earn a living, to become part of the community that has kept us safe and alive for many years, he fails to understand me. In the end his attitude is always the same: He will never stop studying the Law of the Lord. You heard me say many times that the rest of the world is happily resigned to work for a living. Parish rabbis earn sufficient income to raise a family. He says this is not what he had in mind for his life's ambition. You and I are not going to live forever. How will he support himself when we are gone? His brothers will have their own families to provide for. My dear, how can we convince him that his selfish attitude to abandon everything we consider paramount for survival is very wrong? He says he wants nothing more than to be holy and pure. Well, he is not alone in this ambition. But you can't live on that single purpose! I venture to say that half the Israelite community in this town wishes it could afford to live the way he does, not having to work for a livelihood. Part of the blame is yours. You fail to support me when I speak to him. I am very discouraged, dear. What do you think we should do? As I ask this question, I have a gnawing feeling it may be too late for an answer. Is it so, dear?"

Clara didn't like to discuss anything having to do with pressuring Sabetay, who at thirteen had vowed to her he would spend his entire life studying divinity. Ever since then, she felt overwhelmed by his confession. She made it her duty to shield him from mundane concerns for in those days, two of the most honorable professions for a man were the clergy and the army. One was in the service of God and the other of the nation. Parents of children in these professions were treated with respect. But in the Ottoman Turkish Empire Jews were not allowed to serve in the military. The service of God was the only lofty and righteous choice for at least one of her three sons. She wasn't as concerned about Sabetay's future nor about his lack of interest in raising a family. She knew Sabetay's feelings and nature better than her husband. She didn't think his temperament fitted the business world. Her woman's intuition saw him married to a girl with wealthy parents providing for him the austere and puritanical life he desired. She answered her husband the way she had done it so many times before: "Have faith in the Lord and in our Sabetay. You'll see he'll make out."

Clara's optimism didn't reassure her husband. He had a realistic sense of his world. How could he think otherwise when Sephardis were leaving town for the big cities of Constantinople and Salonica because of the rampant economic recession in his city? His business was seasonal and not always dependable. The revenue from the sale of eggs was much dependent on the weather affecting the disposition of chickens. Although the climate of the city was mild during winters it was hot and humid during summers. Often during such stifling periods eggs and chicks were scarce, and so was his income. The cost of keeping Sabetay at the yeshiva was not free. Though he wished to keep him out of school, he knew well that Clara wouldn't let him. If it became necessary, she would return to providing maid services to supplement the family income as she had done before working for the Pinheiros, a rich expatriated Portuguese Jewish family. When her three sons were younger and in school, she had worked three days a week as a maid. Now that her elder Eliyah and younger Joseph worked as laborers, she cut her working days to holiday time cleaning only.

She raised herself in bed, searching in the dark for Mordehay's lips buried in his beard. She kissed them and said: "You'll see, things will work out, as always." She turned around and they fell asleep.

The next day was a Friday, a spring day in 1644. Sabetay came home from the yeshiva in a pouring rain. His clothes were drenched completely. He forgot to take an umbrella when he had gone out to the yeshiva, in spite of his mother's warning that it would be a rainy day. He wore a linen *caftan* (Middle Eastern robe) with long sleeves, a brown sash around his waist and a brown rolled head-dress resembling a turban. He entered the house still wearing a wet *taleth* (*tallit*, prayer shawl) over his shoulders dripping water on the floor from the hanging *tsitsim* (*tzitsim*, fringes at both ends of the shawl). His shoes were soaked and muddy.

"Sabetay! In heaven's name, you entered this house soaking wet! Look what you have done to my clean entrance hallway! It is flooded and soiled with dirty mud! Stop where you are! Don't walk any farther!" exclaimed his mother who had just finished mopping and had gone to the kitchen to prepare supper.

At eighteen, already absent minded and intensely preoccupied in his thoughts, he hadn't realized the mess he had made until his mother caught him at the doorway. Had he not been so absorbed by an unusual impediment concerning his graduation, he might have taken refuge in one of many doorways he passed along the way. Then too, he could have removed his shoes and the soaked *taleth*. His mother's reprimand made him realize he shouldn't have been wearing the prayer shawl anyway. His teachers reminded him countless of times that the shawl was to be worn only at prayer times. His excuse was he didn't know of any moment in his life when he wasn't praying, reciting psalms, or singing prayers to his Lord. In a manner of speaking this was true. Stunned by his mother's unhappiness and feeling guilty he said to her lovingly: "Oh, Mother I am sorry, I didn't realize . . ." He didn't finish the sentence when he saw his mother pointing to the floor. He looked where she was pointing and saw his muddy foot prints in a growing puddle of water.

"Must you be so absent minded and preoccupied? I have asked you this morning to carry your umbrella. Your father and your brothers never forget. You know it is springtime, and rain or sun-shine you must take your shoes off before you enter the house. I always keep a shoe tray outside the doorway just for this purpose. Since we bought the house I have never seen your shoes on that tray! It has been years! Same thing goes for your prayer shawl. Why are you wearing it in the middle of the day? Oh, what's the use! Stay where you are and don't move! I will go fetch a mop." As she walked to the kitchen she went on complaining: "I can't stop work-ing around the clock taking care of four grown men totally incon-siderate of a poor woman! It hasn't been my good fate to have a daughter to help me. You men are making sure I die before my age." Clara loved Sabetay in spite of his shortcomings. Her words were more intended to draw him to express his affection for her than a show of vexation.

Feeling shameful and scoffed he answered lovingly: "Don't say that Mamaritta. That isn't so. I love you very much and please don't talk about dying. I didn't realize . . ."

Clara was happy to hear those touching words, but she inter-rupted him while she mopped around where he stood on the toes of his shoes, afraid of taking another step. In a sweeter voice she asked without looking at him: "If you loved me you wouldn't make things harder for me, would you? Now, take off your shoes and *taleth* and move away from the doorway. You men always think women are made to serve you. To please me you say 'I love you' and you go on doing what you like anyway." She mopped furiously and before she sent him up to his room she made sure she drove an important point across: "Any moment your famished father and brothers will come home demanding supper before they take their shoes off. My work is never done. I don't have a moment to my-self. Don't you think I deserve it . . . ?"

Sabetay, who loved her dearly, hated to upset her. He interrupted her by reaching over her shoulders to extricate the mop from her hands: "Mamaritta," he called her affectionately. "Give me the mop! Let me do it!" He tried to free the mop from her hands but she would not let go of it. She knew he was totally clumsy in practical chores; he would make a bigger mess than it was.

"You haven't removed your wet prayer shawl and skull cap. Hang them on the coat rack standing near you. I will stretch them in the kitchen to dry in front of the stove. Leave your shoes there and run upstairs to your room. Go dear, it is all right. I didn't mean to shout at you."

Since the day he was born she remembered him to be a sweet and sensitive child. While the other men in the house loved her too, Sabetay never failed to demonstrate his affection towards the family, and especially towards her. The love he had for her was softer, warmer and closer, different than that of the others in the family. His was an idolatrous *cariño* (devoted fondness), demanding nothing in return.

He did as he was told. Walking up the wooden stairs, feeling reproached, he couldn't help but think remorsefully that family and friends were in the habit of discrediting him for lacking even the simplest physical dexterity. It was the same reason why children shunned him in the school yard and in the neighborhood. They made fun of him for being clumsy at games. As a result he withdrew from these challenges and never learned to relate to or enjoy outdoor activities, except swimming in the refreshing waters of the Gulf of Smyrna. For that he didn't need anyone to appreciate the delightful experience. Parents of rich schoolmates owned homes along the shoreline with detached bath houses extending into the sea. Because his mother cleaned many of these houses in the past, he had a long standing permission to use them. The Pinheiro bath house was where he liked to swim most of the time.

He entered his room and noticed it had been cleaned and straightened out. Since the day his brothers moved together into a newly built bedroom he enjoyed the solitude of his privacy for reading, writing, studying, and most frequently meditating and praying. In fact those were the sum total of activities he enjoyed. Being in company with people demanded listening and arguing boring subjects like politics, jobs, marriage, children, girls, etc. These topics not only didn't interest him, they took precious time away from what he liked to do best.

He shut his door and walked to his working table under the window. He wanted to finish reading a primer he had borrowed from the yeshiva library on how to be a serious cabalist (mystic). The author of the primer was Joseph Caro, a noted scholar of a century before, born in Toledo, Spain: In 1492, when Caro was four years old, he and his family were expelled from Spain to Portugal, and then expelled again four years later, reaching Turkey and finally the Holy Land. He taught talmudic Law and the wisdom of the *Zohar* at the famous school of Safed in the Holy Land. Sabetay had borrowed the primer in spite of strong warnings by his teacher that he was too young for such material. The warning was enough to stir in him a greater desire to prove otherwise. He sat down, opened the primer at a section he wanted to read most: a chapter on fasting. As he began reading, he became annoyed at feeling the onset of one of his chronic headaches which almost always disabled his vision, his alertness, and made him feel very sick.

Conscious of having upset his mother, his charismatic round pale face became spotted with red hives. A feeling of depression began to invade him, and invariably this would be accompanied by a throbbing headache. As a matter of fact, a pain over his entire face was beginning to intensify and he knew his vision would be blurred soon. The frequency of these headaches and depressive moods concerned him very much. Upon his mother's urging he had been to see the doctor who failed to discover anything medically wrong. The only remedy prescribed was the advice to study less and play more for relaxation and fun. Sabetay had turned resentful at that advice, saying to the doctor that the suggestion was totally contrary to his natural disposition. Studying, and not playing, was what he enjoyed most in life. He eventually resolved that his affliction, though painful and momentarily debilitating, could not be of a very serious nature. He stopped reading and decided to stretch out on his bed and take a nap.

Mordehay and his two working sons came home from work late in the afternoon before sundown on Fridays, the eve of their

Sabbath. Other days they worked from seven in the morning until
six in the evening. Clara made sure they washed and changed
clothes before they sat anywhere in the house and especially at
the table. She insisted on this rule for she possessed a formidable weapon for enforcing it: If they wanted to eat they had to
wash and put on clean clothes. Mordehay was the first to clean
up. He called Sabetay downstairs. It was time for prayers before supper. Sabetay was the one who chanted the blessings at
mealtime when he wasn't fasting.

Fasting was a recent habit he had acquired from his initiation
into the readings of the *Cabala*.[1] A few weeks earlier, when one
of his teacher introduced the subject of mysticism in Judaism,
predictably the topic fired his imagination and that of a few of
his classmates. Warnings by his teacher against dwelling in such
exotic philosophies of religion until they reached their age of
maturity (mid-twenties), only served to intensify Sabetay's curiosity. What fascinated him most was reading the captivating arguments about the origin of the cosmos, creation, attributes of
God and His angels assisting Him in ruling the universe. There
was an applied side to these studies as well; one which required
systematic fasting as a means of developing the right state of mind
and sensitivity to comprehend the wondrous works of God's realm.

---

1. The collection of mystical writings since antiquity. Mystical thoughts
are known to have existed in Judaism since the days of Abraham. Until
written records had began to surface, these theosophical theories and
arguments pertaining to God and His Creation were past on by word of
mouth. The first known organized compilation of these writings outside
the tenets preached in the Scriptures were found in *The Book of Formation* (*Sepher Yetzirah*) which is attributed to a number of different authors, among them: Abraham, Moses, Rabbi Akiba ben Joseph in the first
century C.E., Shimon ben Yohay in the second century C.E. Many tracts
were added to these occult discourses known as The *Cabala* up to the
thirteenth century C.E. when a Spanish Rabbi, Moses Shem Tob de León,
came up with a new and revolutionary book on mysticism we now call
the *Zohar*. Since then and up to the period of Sabetay Sevi many Cabalistic schools were created in Europe and in the Holy Land.

As a novice in fasting, he didn't eat Mondays and Wednesdays from sundown to sundown, the Hebrew day. His parents weren't sure how to react to this new fad. Sabetay hoped he would work his way to six fasting days a week in spite of the primer emphasizing that this limit is an extreme reached only by a few biblical arch-pious patriarchs.

The Sevis were a very close family. Heeding his father's call, Sabetay came down the staircase. He wore clean and dry clothes, a dry skull cap, and prayer shawl over his head and shoulders. From a distance he looked like an old rabbi. After a long nap, his headache had abated but had not completely gone. He felt very hungry smelling the cooking vapors from his mother's kitchen. When his elder brother Eliyah saw Sabetay on the stairway he said amusingly: "Here comes our rabbi in residence. Joseph we must behave! One should not underestimate the powers of a rabbinical spell!"

Loud laughs from his brothers followed, and then his younger brother added: "Amen. When he is finally ordained we will have our very own private rabbi. Perhaps we won't have to go to the synagogue anymore. Wouldn't that be great? Say Amen, Eliyah!"

Clara heard the teasing from the kitchen. She knew Sabetay wouldn't respond to those silly comments. She shouted: "Shush! Joseph, you know your brother's ordainment has nothing to do with attending services at the synagogue. You tease your brother because you know he takes your gibberish nonsense so seriously. I thank the Lord we don't have *minyan* (quorum of ten men to initiate services) in my house."

As Joseph said, Sabetay had not been ordained yet. He had completed all the requirements for the priesthood. The council of rabbis in the city had not agreed to ordain him *haham* (Rabbi) yet. That decision was still pending. His case was a controversial one, to put it mildly. The council of examiners spent hours discussing and arguing if they should approve Sabetay's ordainment. Most were against it in spite of the recommendation of the principal teacher. Sabetay, they argued was too young and immature to be ordained. He was still eighteen. Although there were no hard rules about age, ordinarily the title wasn't granted until the candidate was in his twenties, an age considered to be the threshold to maturity. Some members of the council went as far as questioning his mental and emotional disposition. Assuming age was the only reason for the delay, Sabetay objected to his teacher that if he was able to satisfy the academic and religious requirements, there were no reasons or official grounds to prevent him from deserving the title. In spite of his teacher's advice to wait a year or so, Sabetay insisted on demanding his rights.

He sat at the table between his two starving brothers who urged him to say the dinner blessings as swiftly as possible. He reached for his glass of wine and chanted the *quidush*, (the blessing of the fruit of the vine). This was one of his favorite chants because of its melodious composition with its *crescendi* and an extended *finale*. He enjoyed singing as much as praying. In fact he had an irresistible desire to chant all his prayers. If some prayers didn't have a traditional chant, he invented his own. When he finished singing the wine blessing, his younger brother complained: "Sabetay, must you take this long to finish the wine blessing? Please be briefer for the bread blessing! I am famished from a hard day's work. I want to start eating! Won't you please speed up your pace?"

Sabetay had always argued this point with Joseph. He repeated his argument to make his brother understand that singing gave blessings a heavenly destination. "Joseph, blessings without songs lose impact in the eyes of The All Merciful," he said, having hoped to be appreciated for his performance.

"I am not so sure," answered his spunky brother. "You say this because you have a good voice. Most men I know have a terrible voice. If I were God I would put my hands over my ears when they sing!"

"Joseph!" retorted his father, "don't use the name of the Lord in vain. Let your brother finish his Sabbath prayers!"

Sabetay didn't choose to respond to his brother's immature comment. His father had done it for him. He put his glass down and reached into the bread basket, picking the braided challah bread still warm from the Jewish bakery. Bread in one hand and the knife in the other he cut large morsels and passed them around. After he gave the last piece to his mother, taking turns, the family pressed the end of the morsel into a dish of salt and together they began singing the ancient blessing: "*Baruch ata adonay . . . amotsi lehem minaaretz.* (Blessed art thou, O Eternal, our God, King of the Universe, who bringest forth bread from the earth.)" He had a very melodious and vibrant voice. He exaggerated the emphasis he put in his *canto*. In spite of his younger brother's plea, he didn't stop at the bread blessing when it was customary to begin with supper. Fork in their hands, ready to eat, everyone waited for Clara to bring the first course. But Sabetay wasn't finished. He explained that many beautiful prayers in the liturgy didn't get the exposure they deserved. To prove his point he improvised singing a couple of his favorite prayers. He wasn't being fastidious, it was just that he loved to enlighten his family about the beauty of many forgotten prayers which he compared to madrigals, love poems set into music. He said: "As a lover expresses with songs his love to his beloved, I sing prayers of love to my Creator."

When everyone at the table thought he had finished he surprised them with yet another prayer from his large repertoire of chants in *ladino*[2]: "*Bendicho sea tu nombre Señor del mundo, y bendicha tu corona y tu trono.* (Blessed be your name, Lord of the universe. Blessed be your crown and your throne.")

Having heard this prayer before, the family returned in unison the required response: "*Sea o Tu voluntad de estar siempre con tu pueblo Israel para siempre. Amen.* (Oh, let it be Your will to remain with your people Israel for ever. Amen.")

Clara's meal waited to be served ever since they sat at the table. Fearful of another sequel of chants she stood up, went to the

---

2. Liturgical Spanish, frozen in its linguistic form when the Hebrew bible was first translated from Hebrew into Spanish. As the Hebrew language of the bible remained frozen for a few millennia, *ladino* remained frozen since the Lisbon Bible written by Samuel ha-Sofer in the fifteenth century and the Ferrara Bible by Joseph Athias in Sabetay's time.

kitchen, and brought the *sopa de fideos*, (chicken soup with very thin noodles). It was Sabetay's favorite. Everything in his life had a divine significance; upon seeing his soup bowl he exclaimed: "Ah! *cabellos de ángel*! (angel's hair)."

His two brothers weren't as pleased. They didn't like chicken in any shape or form. Clara cooked meals with chicken from her husband's store much too often during the week. It was the only way she could keep expenses down. When Joseph saw what was in his bowl he complained irritatingly: "Mother, I need substantial food, the kind that stays in my stomach longest. What is wrong with beef, rice, potatoes, or dumplings. I work hard all day lifting heavy sacks and crates . . . !" Realizing the sound in his words sounded harsh, he smiled and added jokingly: "Besides, Mother, I feel I am growing feathers eating chicken so many times a week."

Oldest Eliyah seized the opportunity to add his objection by imitating the sound of a rooster: "Coocooricoo!"

Encouraged by his brother's support, spunky Joseph pushed his bowl away and humorously added: "And I am ready to lay an egg." Sabetay was appalled. He was prepared to come to his mother's defense but Joseph wasn't finished: "Really Mother, what is wrong with beef or lamb? You know how much Eliyah and I love lamb. This is springtime. Lambs have to be plentiful."

Clara knew why her boys were rebelling. "Oh shush!" she retorted, "chicken is better for you. I know it is the season for lamb but we can't afford the prices Menahem the butcher asks for red meat these days." She pointed her wooden serving spoon at Joseph and warned: "Why do you complain about my cooking? You know very well what we can and cannot afford. I am doing my very best to stay within our budget and I expect you two to help me. Instead of using your heads, you are thinking with your stomachs. All this greasy food with meat dishes the *Turcos* (Turks) eat is not good for you. Now, eat your soup and be quiet!"

To change the subject, picking this propitious moment, Clara signaled her husband about something important he was supposed to say. She nodded her head and Mordehay understood. He put his spoon down and addressed Sabetay: "Sabetay, my son, you are eighteen and according to tradition you should be thinking of marriage . . ."

A loud sound interrupted Mordehay. Sabetay had dropped the spoon over his bowl and splashed broth on the table and on his clean prayer shawl. He nearly choked from the piece of bread he was about to swallow. Joseph and Eliyah rapidly reached their napkins to wipe the mess he made. Only for that short moment Clara felt relieved that her husband had mustered the courage to bring up the subject of marriage. But staring at Sabetay's second mess of the day her mood changed instantly: "Sabetay, you did it again! You messed up another prayer shawl! It is the second to-day! Now you don't have another clean one to wear! Why must you be so. . . .Oh!, never mind. You have to wait until the one you wore this morning is dry."

Sensing she was changing the subject, she remained quiet. Totally surprised at their father's remark, Sabetay's brothers appeared delighted. Eliyah was already engaged and waited for a better financial situation before planning his wedding. Joseph, the youngest, had been thinking about asking his parents' permission to propose to a girl down the street. But, according to tradition, he had to wait his turn to marry until his two older brothers married first. The moment they finished cleaning Sabetay's mess, Mordehay scratched his bald head, brushed his long beard and continued with what he started to say before Sabetay dropped his spoon: "Yes, Sabetay I didn't finish what I was saying. You know very well many young men your age are already married and some have children. You are about to be ordained soon. The salary of a *haham* assigned to a parish is substantial and definitely more dependable than mine. You can have a comfortable life raising a family larger than ours. Your mother and I have been talking about this for some time. Your older brother is engaged and we all hope to celebrate his wedding very soon. Then it will be your turn. You know you can't wait too long even, if just for the sake of your younger brother." He paused for a second to detect an interest on Sabetay's face. It was totally blank. Mordehay resumed: "Son, have you given some thoughts to marriage? Would you like to share your feelings with us? Maybe you know a young girl who has caught your interest. If we know who she is your mother and I are pre-pared to engage a marriage broker. They do wonders extricating maximum dowries from your future father-in-law, you know."

Clara was eager to hear Sabetay speak on the subject. She shook her head and frowned at Mordehay when he looked her way. In-terrupted by her gestures, he stopped and asked: "I would like to hear what you have to say, son."

All eyes fell on Sabetay. His face turned white, almost as pale as the color of his silk *taleth* he wore. The red blotches he had on his face earlier when he had a headache began to reappear. Sheep-ishly he asked: "Do we have to discuss this now? To tell you the truth, the question hadn't entered my mind."

He lowered his face, staring at his bowl of soup hinting he wanted to resume eating. Clara suspected that much. But Mordehay refused to accept that absurd attitude. Annoyed, he scratched his long and kinky beard again and demanded, pounding lightly on the table: "But you must think of marriage! I don't want to hear this nonsense about you not thinking about it! Every man and woman thinks about marriage at your age. Your younger brother I am sure has already ideas about it. He hasn't talked to us, but I am sure he will when the time comes! This is ridiculous."

Clara, with a softer tone of voice, resumed the conversation. She approached the subject from a different angle, an approach that played an important part in his life: Hebrew mysticism. She said: "Son, you must begin to think of marriage. Do you know why? It was you who told me that you read in the *Cabala* the only time the messiah would come and take us to the Holy Land was after all unborn souls were born. You remember telling me this, don't you?" He shook his head but didn't say anything. "Doesn't this mean it is our commandment to seek marriage and have as many children as we are able to support to speed up the much awaited arrival of our *mashiah*?" Again she waited for a reaction but Sabetay only nodded again. Clara resumed: "Like everyone else you must do your share too. Aside from this, your father and I believe in the sacrament of marriage. I know a man cannot be fully happy and satisfied unless he has a woman to share his life with. This is the way the Lord willed it since Adam and Eve, and that is the way it has been since then." She paused. Now she was ready to make her bid. "Your father and I have been searching for a good mate for you, and we think we have found that person." Eliyah and Joseph stopped eating instantly waiting to hear who that person was. All eyes turned towards their mother. "She comes from a very good family and she appears to be a young girl who would honor and love you." As she spoke Clara looked to see if she was making any impression on Sabetay. Alas! he looked totally disinterested. She changed her tone of voice and resumed with a categorical statement: "Son, we want the very best for you. I know you will not disappoint us and you will be happy with our choice. I want to hear you tell me of your approval."

Everyone at the table waited for a response. He lifted his head and looked at his mother with his expressive and loving eyes. He said to her: "Mamaritta, you know I love you very much. You also know that I wouldn't do anything to hurt or disappoint you. While it is true that haven't given any thought to marriage, I will honor my parent's wishes if they so desire. This is a more important commandment to me than marriage itself."

Eliyah and Joseph didn't know what to make of his answer. Was it an approval or a delay tactic? But Clara understood him well. She uttered the final decision: "Very well, son, it is our wish! I am happy to know that you are ready to accept our decision. Father will start making the arrangements. In time you will bless us all the days of your life. You will be very happy with Alegra, you will see. You know her, she is the youngest daughter of Baruch Mizrahi."

It was the first time his brothers had heard the name of the girl they had chosen for Sabetay. They knew who she was because she lived in the neighborhood and her parents attended the same synagogue. Sabetay had seen her many times, but not always under pleasant circumstances. When Clara mentioned Alegra, all at the table saw him twitch his eyes as if he tried to erase unpleasant memories. Clara continued: "Señor Mizrahi is getting old. He told me before he dies he wants to see his last daughter married to a respectable man of God. He has been following your progress at the yeshiva and inquiring about you. Last week, he visited your father and me and told us he will be delighted to have you as his son-in-law. Who wouldn't?" she remarked proudly. "I want you to know that Alegra's father is a rich man. In recent years he has accumulated a large fortune from the growing shipping trade. His other daughters married well and I happen to know their husbands were given generous dowries. This being his last daughter, I imagine he will outshine his previous commitments. Your father and I are delighted with the choice we made. Don't you think we picked well, son?"

What was unfortunate about this seemingly marvelous news was that everyone knew Sabetay's heart belonged elsewhere: to an invisible realm of spiritualism. To this point in his life there had been no other partner except his small library of books of prayer and companion books probing into the fathomless attributes of Divinity. He felt happily married to his books, and to the noble purpose of becoming holy in the eyes of the Lord. His total devotion was to Him, to know Him as many prophets in antiquity had known Him and even spoke to Him. Clara knew all this but she hoped to change her son's lonesome and egotistic vision of life without destroying his ambition in the priesthood. She waited for his reaction on the choice she had made while the rest of the family remained silent. Sabetay picked his empty bowl and extended it to her: "Mamaritta, is there more chicken soup? I would like to have another bowlful." That unexpected and inconsiderate reaction drew his father's ire. Sabetay realized immediately he had blundered. Before his father could spill his irritation on him, he answered quickly: "If you desire to see me married to this girl, then so be it. You may arrange the wedding any time and in any way you like. Now may I have more chicken soup, please?"

Clara signaled Mordehay to let the matter rest. She got as much commitment out of her son as she knew she was going to get. She refilled Sabetay's bowl and as soon as he finished his dinner he went directly to his room joyless.

CHAPTER

2

$\mathcal{ح}$

There were three separate Jewish communities in the city. Their separation was voluntary and on the basis of cultural affiliation. Two of the most recent immigrants in the Middle East were Sephardis, descendants of Jews from Spain and Portugal who were expelled one hundred years earlier. Most Portuguese Jews were immigrants from an earlier Spanish exile who thought they could find permanent refuge in Portugal. The Spanish and Portuguese groups each had their own quarters and synagogues. The third group, known as the Romaniote Jews, were native of the Balkans and Asia Minor and were descendants and long time residents of those lands when they were under Roman occupation. They had their own distinct community. The Sevi's lived in the Spanish district, west of the city known as Karatash.

Young and eligible girls in that community who knew Sabetay, including Alegra Mizrahi, considered him to be a handsome and attractive young man of eighteen with an enviable future. Sabetay's physical appeal came mostly from the soft facial features around his eyes, nose and mouth. His lips were round and fleshy with a coloration distinctly feminine, giving them a look of sensuality. When he spoke his velvety voice was warm and inviting. Anyone fortunate enough to have heard him sing Sephardi ballads always came out rewarded. Sabetay was very artful in his speech and knew how to combine voice quality and poetic metaphors to capture the interest of the listener. When he didn't suffer from headaches his puffy brown eyes possessed a rare moist brilliance betraying a state of deep thought and illumination. His eyes had such an vivid sparkle that people who faced him felt drawn towards him with an uneasy feeling of intimidation. At his age he was already taller than his father but not much thinner. He had none of his father's strong facial features. He drew his resemblance from his mother, inheriting her white, almost transparent skin. At seventeen he had begun to grow a short oriental and well groomed beard and mustache combination, making him look more masculine and less like his beautiful mother. He dressed neatly in a vestment resembling a cassock of the French ecclesiasts. It was an oriental adaptation of the French *soutane* made with lighter weight textiles which Middle Eastern rabbis preferred to wear. His clothing reached to his ankles, and was fastened with tightly spaced handmade buttons down to his shoes. He always wore a skull cap, but when he went out he placed on top of it a round yellow headdress and a sash of a different color around his waist. His attire blended well with the garments of lay Sephardis who partially imitated the costumes of Moslems. Though the headdress was an imitation of the turban, the genuine white Turkish turban was not only a headdress, it was a symbol of Islam. Therefore, non-Moslems were careful to make a distinction. To say explicitly that one wore a turban meant he had been converted to Islam.

The fine physical attributes of Sabetay failed to match his withdrawn personality. He was very shy, distant, temperamental, and to say the least, eccentric. He was seldom seen with young men or women his age. Eligible young ladies, including Alegra, viewed these personal shortcomings as a challenge, but definitely improvable.

Stunned from his mother's wish that he marry Alegra Mizrahi, Sabetay lay in bed with his eyes wide open fearful of falling asleep. Sleep after an unhappy event almost always meant bad dreams would occur. Ever since he was nine years of age he began to have intense and disturbing dreams, dreams beyond his comprehension that left him totally confused. As he grew older, their substance grew in detail, intensity, and frequency. Their occurrence seemed to coincide with periods of unhappy moments, excessive exhilaration, and day dreaming. Recently, because of his constant preoccupation with his graduation, he had been free of such unhappy occurrences. In fact, he had temporarily forgotten about them. But now, with the mention of Alegra Mizrahi he was sure the dreams would return. Oh, how he wished his mother hadn't brought up the subject of marriage, more specifically marriage to Alegra.

Laying in bed and reminiscing, he traced the origins of his dreams to his youth when his mother took him to the public bath. Private baths in residences was a luxury; only the rich afforded them. The daily sponge baths in the washroom sufficed only for a few days, but Clara took her children to the *hamam* (public bath) for women once a week until they reached the age of thirteen. All mothers of middle class and poor families did likewise. After his bar mitzvah, Sabetay was no longer allowed to go with his mother. It became Mordehay's responsibility to take him in the evenings when the *hamam* was used by men only. These baths were like a large community reunion. Mothers and children from the neighborhood paraded naked in this immense heated marble room. Sitting alone and away from his mother and young brother he felt totally privileged examining and analyzing without inhibition or reproach young girls and women down to the smallest details of their bodies. All other children splashed water at each other and played silly games, except Sabetay.

The bathing area was a very large heated circular room with marble walls and floors and a sweating platform above ground at its center. Individual marble washing pedestals and wash basins spaced a few feet apart were set against the entire wall. Each basin had two brass spigots with cold and hot running water. Families sat around a basin, and adults took turns washing the children and themselves; but Sabetay preferred to wash himself. A shallow brass bowl was provided to scoop clean water from the basin to soap and rinse several times. The waste water ran down into an intricate array of open troughs crisscrossing the entire floor space and finally draining outside the building into the city's open water sewer system.

Completely absorbed, Sabetay loved to watch the esthetic
beauty of the young girls' bodies in constant motion. They didn't
seem to follow a pattern in the moves or games they considered
fun. Some paraded freely, enjoying the warm and wet feeling of
condensing steam rolling down their delicate skins. Others preferred to run, playing catch for a while; then, for some mysterious reason they grouped together imitating oriental dancing. But
in the end their play turned to teasing and splashing boys, who
then chased them until the girls began screaming while avoiding
being caught, wrestled and pinched. This was when mothers put
an end to that play. Sabetay never took part in these games. Among
the many vivid memories he recollected were the giggles and
laughters that filled the echoing space of the *hamam*.

On his return home the remembrance of what he had seen did
not go away immediately. For a day or two he would be driven by
incomprehensible desires to want a repeat of that experience.
Young as he was and inexperienced in talks about girls with other
boys, he remained confused about this urge to return to the *hamam*
and observe children at play when he knew well that he hated to
join them. Alas! He also knew he paid a severe price for that enjoyment. He loathed the ensuing dreams that night brought. They
left him terrified when he woke, and he believed the dreams were
a major cause of his headaches and insomnia.

Stretched on his bed, he wished he had the courage to tell his
mother how he really felt about Alegra, the young girl down the
street he was to marry. Shivers ran down his spine. How was he to
explain the reason why he couldn't marry Alegra? It was not the
kind of confession he could make to anyone, except to his Creator
when he begged many times to relieve him from that anguish.

Invariably, the nights following his visit to the *hamam* he dreamt
of sitting naked while the young girls in the neighborhood, including Alegra, danced around him, while he sang lovely Sephardi ballads. In the dreams there were no one except him and the few girls
in the neighborhood. As long as he kept singing they kept dancing
gracefully and invitingly. Every so often one of them, usually Alegra,
broke away from the group and came close enough for him to ad-

mire how much prettier her silky body was compared to his. Her skin was soft white without a single blemish, wart, or pimple. The perspiration from the heat gave that skin a brilliant silky shine. Eventually, she would come closer motioning with her hands the contour of her firm little breasts in the shape of large strawberries. Coming even closer she would brush her body against his. Instantly he would pull back and stop singing out of fear. "What is the matter Sabetay?" she would say surreptitiously. "Why are you fearful of me?" He would pull his body back even further against the marble wall and would not answer her. As she repeated the scene a few times, he never failed to have an erection. It seemed to him that she waited for that moment to happen. Then, she would scold him immediately: "Oh, look! Look between your legs! Shame on you! I am going to tell your mother about this."

Ashamed and drenched in perspiration he would look where she pointed. Teasingly, all the other girls would burst into laughter. As soon as he raised his head Alegra and the girls faded away but the laughter remained long after they were gone. Quickly, he would resume his singing to make them come back, but to no avail. They would not return no matter how long he remained singing. Finding himself sad and alone, he woke up feeling awful with sweat all over his body and a firm penis, and his nightgown soiled between his legs with a strange fluid smelling distinctly different than his urine. Disturbed and in shame, he attributed these dreams to an evil spirit trying to lead him away from purity into sin.

The worse dreams occurred when the girls failed to appear some nights. He found himself sitting in his night gown all alone waiting in the *hamam*. He sang and sang but no one came. Suddenly a flame appeared in front of him and danced, imitating the motions of the young girls. Perplexed, he stopped singing so that the flame would go away. Instead, unexpectedly the flame thrust itself towards his nightgown and burned it completely, leaving him naked and unprotected. At that instant he would scream in terror wondering about the flame's next move. The flame spoke to him and reproached him for having desires of innocent naked girls just to satisfy his carnal pleasures. Sitting in fear and ignorant of what his dream meant, the flame warned him that it was a sin and, to punish him, the flame jumped towards his groin and burned his penis. He screamed again at the top of his voice while covering his aching penis with his hands. Laughing as the girls did, the flame warned him it would return with more punishment if he persisted in having such dreams. His two brothers, who then shared the same bedroom, would wake up and comfort him, not knowing the cause of his nightmares. Frightened, he would run to the washroom, light a candle, and inspect between his legs. Relieved to find there were no burns or ache anywhere on his body, he would return to his bed totally confused and concerned.

At thirteen, after his bar mitzvah, he no longer went to the *hamam* with his mother. He went with his father and older brother. The contrast of being among naked men utterly disgusted him. Nonetheless his dreams with the damsels continued on, leaving him utterly joyful at nights and terribly fearful and remorseful in the mornings. For a long time the significance of the recurrence of these dreams troubled him and escaped comprehension. Only recently he had found comforting explanations about them in the *Zohar*. To his great surprise he discovered that he wasn't alone in having experienced such sexual temptations accompanied by extreme distress and misery from nightmarish dreams. An anthology on dreams compiled by an anonymous rabbi at the Cabalistic School of Leghorn (Livorno) in Italy, explained Sabetay's consternation. The rabbi wrote that seemingly sinful visitations from the queen of whoredom, Naamah, who dwelt in the abysses of hell, were not uncommon among intellectual men and especially among boys. The author had been accosted several times by the sons of whoredom whom he described as scourges of the children of men. These were demons born of masturbation and were ordered by Naamah[1], the

---

1. The mystical books of the *Cabala* and *Zohar* contain descriptions of many allegoric characters representing angels as well as demons and mothers of demons. Naamah was one such mother. There were three others: Lilith, Ogeret, and Mahalath, each with special attributes.

queen of demons, who seduced men by lascivious fantasies, haunting highly intelligent and righteous men and women and driving them to experience the pleasures of sin. This curse, the writer of the *Zohar* concluded:

> ... was an important and ceaseless divine testing of men who hoped to attain the highest level of purity and holiness. The dreams simply constituted the manner in which the willpower and fortitude to resist sinful temptations were tested. Their occurrence was without consequence. Behavior in the conscious state was what really mattered. The judgment of sin did not encompass acts committed in the subconscious state of dreams. Resisting temptations or abstenance from sexual pleasures were meaningful only if exercised in the conscious state. . . .

This discovery made considerable sense to impressionable Sabetay, who would never in his life forget how these profound explanations applied to him perfectly. Laying in bed thinking, he couldn't fall asleep until he resolved how he would cope with the agreement he had made with his parents to marry Alegra. What if she shared the same dreams? What if she knew of his struggles and the pleasure he derived from admiring her body? What if she became angry and disgusted? What if the flame came back when he would make love to her as his wife? The fear of sharing his life with a woman who became, since early puberty, a symbol of demonic temptations intensified his headache. Massaging the side of his face that hurt the most, he came up with a thought so comforting that it began to release his tension: He would go through the wedding ceremony for he had given his word to his parents. Marriage ceremonies, he reasoned, were only important to parents of the bride and the groom. What happened afterwards was the couple's private affair and did not concern most parents. So, why deny them the joy and fulfillment they wanted to experience from his wedding? On that basis he conceived a plan which gave him the confidence of being able to control the events after the wedding. He closed his eyes and fell asleep.

꒳

The wedding was scheduled for Sunday, a day of the new moon
in the Hebrew month of Heshvan 5404 (1644). According to tradition, the day of the new moon was a most favorable time to initiate any event of great importance. It was considered to be a day
of rebirth, a renewal, and the beginning of an event sure to succeed. Alegra's wealthy parents set in motion very lavish preparations. Before the blessed day, at two separate receptions organized
by the Sevis and then by the Mizrahis, the young couple was brought
together to become more intimate. The engagement parties proved
to be fulfilling and rewarding for the parents, but did nothing to
stir warm feelings in the couple. Alegra, under the watchful eye of
an older married sister, tried to be friendly and sweet. Sabetay,
though proper and courteous, did nothing to improve his image of
a removed person. This didn't bother Alegra, for she knew him to
be shy and interested only in subjects most people didn't dwell on.
She accepted the fact that, like most women in her community,
she lacked the level of enlightenment of men. She came to these
receptions resigned that she would have to make up in love what
she lacked in scholarship.

Three months before the wedding, Alegra's father walked into
Mordehay's store with a mood of great urgency. Before shaking
hands, he stared at the young rabbi waiting to slaughter a chicken
and told Mordehay he wanted to talk to him in private. Mordehay
became concerned that something had gone wrong with the wedding plans. "We can't talk here!" blurted Baruch Mizrahi as he looked
with disdain inside the shop. Mordehay dropped his preoccupation.
His small and smelly poultry shop was hardly the place to discuss
important matters. He dismissed the young rabbi sitting on a wicker
chair outside the store and asked him to return in two hours. He
pulled down the shop's roll-up door and invited Baruch for coffee
at the Turkish coffee shop down the street. They walked the short
distance without saying a word. The coffee shop was crowded with
men shouting with excitement, some playing dominoes, others back-
gammon, and a group playing cards while they smoked their water

pipes. Mordehay approached a waiter and murmured a few words in his ear slipping a few coins into his hand. The waiter showed them a quiet corner inside a small alcove. Baruch ordered a cup of Turkish coffee with sugar, and Mordehay ordered his plain.

Baruch was in his late sixties, twenty years Mordehay's senior. He was a descendant of an Romaniote Jewish family with roots in Smyrna long before the Sephardis arrived in Asia Minor. The Spanish and Portuguese Sephardis were so self-confident of their superior Western European education and wealth that they instantly became the major communal influence in the Middle East. Oriental Jews, including Mizrahi's parents, quickly assimilated into the Sephardi fold for economic advantages. They learned Spanish and lived by Sephardi customs. Waiting for their coffees, Baruch finally opened the subject about which he came to see Mordehay. "Mordehay, I have the most important and wonderful news. Could I count on you to keep it confidential for a while? It is to your advantage to do so." The words 'wonderful news' were a welcome signal to Mordehay who had misjudged the purpose of Baruch's visit. Pleased that nothing had gone wrong, he forgot that he had been asked a question. Baruch sat impatiently waiting for his response. Finally he said: "Well? Mordehay you haven't answered me. You don't seem to be responsive to the importance of my visit. Is there something wrong?"

The age, the economic and social status difference between the two men made it mandatory for Mordehay to show consideration in the way he addressed Baruch. "Oh, excuse me Tchelebi[2] Mizrahi. No. There is nothing wrong. My mind was elsewhere momentarily. Forgive me. Please repeat the question." Baruch repeated his question about confidentiality and Mordehay replied: "Oh, yes, Tchelebi Mizrahi, you may count on me for sure. I will not discuss what you are about to tell me."

---

2. The social etiquette of the time demanded of a younger person or one with lower financial status to address the other with the honorific title of Señor in Spanish or Tchelebi in Turkish.

"Very well, then. I have news of colossal importance, the kind that will make us, I mean you and me, rich beyond our wildest imagination. . . ." He stopped when he saw the waiter bring the two cups of coffee. Mordehay wondered what he really meant by 'you and me.' The thought of becoming rich beyond his 'wildest imagination' also stuck firmly in his mind. As soon as the waiter left, Baruch signaled Mordehay to bend over the table and bring his ears closer to him. Mordehay obliged but Baruch, attracted by the smell of freshly brewed coffee under his nose, took a sip of it and made an unhappy face. "Eeh! The waiter must have made a mistake. He served me the wrong coffee. This is terribly bitter! I must have the wrong cup." They exchanged their cups. He took a new sip and with a joyful face, he said: "This coffee shop makes a much better brew than the one near my office. I wonder how they brew it?"

Mordehay couldn't care less about his evaluation of coffee shops, especially when it became obvious that it wasn't the coffee Baruch liked, it was the sweetness of the sugar that made the difference. His feet began to ache from the fast walk on the cobblestone street to the coffee shop. He wished Baruch would tell him what he had to say so he could go back to the store and soak his feet in a mineral salt solution. "You were saying, Tchelebi Mizrahi, something about news of colossal importance."

Taking a second noisy slurp of his sweetened coffee Baruch responded: "Yes, yes! Let me ask you: Why do you suppose the Jewish congregations in Constantinople and Salonica are considerably wealthier than ours?"

Puzzled by what seemed to him to be a totally irrelevant question, Mordehay shrugged his shoulders and replied: "I don't really know. Why do you ask? You tell me."

As most Mediterranean people, Baruch relied extensively on the motion of his arms and hands to express himself. Pulling himself back from the table, he lifted his hands and, pressing them against his cheeks, he said in disbelief: "Ay! I am surprised you don't know. But then selling chickens doesn't exactly bring you into contact with the outside world." Mordehay didn't like this disparaging remark, but he let him go on. "By far the greatest

majority of foreign trade between this country and the wealthy
Europeans is in the hands of the Jews of Constantinople and
Salonica.[3] The greedy and extravagant Europeans can't stop buying products from us, from Persia, and Central Asia where all the
silks, spices, hides, dyes, and handcrafted merchandise, like oriental rugs and jewelry are at bargain prices. Regardless of the
countries of origin, the flow of trade to Europe must pass through
our country. It is of colossal proportions and very little passes
through Smyrna. It represents the biggest revenue of our nation."
Baruch was enjoying his lecturing of uninformed Mordehay who,
to this point, hadn't touched his coffee. While Baruch took a few
more sips, Mordehay wondered how he fitted in Baruch's yet
unrevealed scheme. So far all he had heard were statements about
rich Jews in other cities. While Baruch slurped, Mordehay asked:
"How does this concern me? Would you care to explain?" He
waited patiently for an explanation.

"Haven't you heard the news that he Republic of Venice and the
Ottoman Turks are ready to declare war against each other? The
news broke a couple of weeks ago. Do you know what this means,
Mordehay?" Instead of answering he rubbed his bushy beard with
a few nervous stokes, a gesture which always meant he was turning nervous or impatient. He shook his head in a negative sense
knowing an explanation from Baruch would be forthcoming. "I am
telling you, this means good news for us. I suppose you are wondering why I am saying this. Well it is very simple! I have learned
from reliable sources that our government intends to ban international trade from the cities of Constantinople and Salonica. They
intend to shift the trade to Smyrna. Now do you see why I am excited? The government has demanded foreign merchants to deal
with shipping agents in our city, the way it always was. This means
with us, Mordehay! The decision was made for national security
reasons. Constantinople and Salonica are too close to the fortified

---

3. Sephardis used the Spanish alphabet. Since there was no 'k' in that
alphabet, they substituted 'qu' or 'c' for the sound of 'k' in foreign words
as in Salonika and Cabala.

Straits of Dardanelles, which are the doorway to our capital. The mighty Ottoman fleet is in the Aegean and Mediterranean Seas and believes it can defend Smyrna swifter and easier if Venetians become too adventurous." He stopped long enough to catch his breath and added: "Need I say more, Mordehay?"

Though Mordehay began to understand Baruch's justifiable excitement for his potential profits, he failed to see how his little poultry shop was of interest to Europeans. Annoyed, he pressed him on this point: "Tchelebi Mizrahi, how does this affect me and my business, or does it? You seemed to have implied that; or am I mistaken?"

With a grin on his face Baruch expected the question. "I am coming to that, Mordehay. Don't be so impatient! My daughter Alegra tells me that you have studied English in school. Is this correct?"

"Yes, but . . . ."

"Excellent. Most foreign trade representatives now in Constantinople and Salonica are in the process of moving their offices to Smyrna. The commerce with the East has been so profitable they don't want to lose it if Sultan Ibrahim announces the embargo of trade from the northern cities. Under Turkish law, only agents of Turkish nationality are permitted to deal with our Commerce and Mercantile Department. Do you see what I am driving at Mordehay? People like you and me who know foreign languages will be picked quickly as agents. A few foreign firms have already done so. I have signed so many contracts that I am not able to take on anymore." He paused, feeling it was time to impress Mordehay with his generous offer. "As my daughter's future father-in-law, I thought it to be my duty to ask if you wish to be involved in this new surge of commerce. Now hear this! I don't want you to ever forget the favor I am about to extend to you!" He said this slowly and deliberately. "I turned down an English agent working for the British Eastern Trade Company. This is a big account! I would have liked to sign him on, but he came too late and I can't handle more accounts. Dutch businessmen arrived earlier and I committed myself to them. The Dutch are smart, they speak many languages, including Spanish, which they told me they learned during the Spanish occupation of their land. How strange! I wasn't aware the Spaniards had occupied Flanders. Besides, I didn't learn English in school and no one in my office speaks the language."

Mordehay couldn't stand listening to what appeared to him bragging on the part of his visitor. There was nothing Baruch said that was remotely connected with his business. His feet were killing him. Tensed and resentful, he rubbed his beard once again and demanded to know how he fitted into all this. "Señor Mizrahi, it is all very interesting but I must get back to my shop. Customers will be looking for me. If I am not there they will go to my competitor. I beg you to come to the point and explain how all this affects my business in poultry?"

Baruch was surprised at Mordehay's impatience and lack of perceptiveness. He thought he had already hinted at an important role for him, but apparently not. "I thought I've already told you. The agent who approached me and whom I had to turn down asked me to recommend someone else. Do you want me to talk to this Englishman about you?" To add a little humor he added, "By the way his name is *Rico* (rich in Sephardi Spanish) but he spells it the English way: R. Y. C. A. U. T."

Mordehay didn't react at his punt. He insisted: "I am still confused. Why would this Englishman be interested in me or my chickens?" he blurted in annoyance.

"Mordehay, you haven't been listening!" Baruch shouted so loud, card players outside the cove turned their faces towards them. "Nobody wants your chickens, for heaven's sake. I thought I explained that this man wants to meet someone already in business who can speak English. He does not seem to require previous knowledge in international trade. He will train that person in his field." He slowed his speech, brought his voice down, and enunciated the next sentence word by word: "He wants a Turkish agent speaking his language and willing to deal with government offices. Is that so hard to understand? He knows the only sources of English speaking people in this land are the Sephardis and the Greeks. For some reason we all seem to have chosen French in school and you happened to be an unusual sort of person who studied English. Why is it so hard for you to have understood this?" Now, angrily, again Mizrahi blurted: "The man couldn't care less about your stupid chickens!"

Mordehay felt insulted at the snobbish remark about the product which provided his livelihood. Resentfully he replied: "Excuse me Tchelebi Mizrahi. I am not as hard at understanding as you have implied twice already. Forgive me if I make this point bluntly. You have not been straightforward from the start. I am not afraid of meeting the Englishman. But before I talk to anyone about an employment I know nothing about, I want to be sure I don't waste his time or mine. If I am not mistaken you want me to portray myself as a trade agent. You know very well I know nothing about the business. I am a poor poulterer who sells . . ." He hesitated and said defiantly: "chickens you think are stupid." He asked to be excused.

Baruch grabbed his sleeve and pulled him back. "Please sit down Mordehay. I am sorry if I annoyed you. I am simply surprised that you haven't jumped at this unusual and once in a lifetime opportunity. Ambitious men don't wait to decide until they have all the assurances you seem to be seeking. The Englishman simply wants a man like you, honest and hard working who understands English. Period! How many times should I repeat this! I know for a fact that you are honest and hard working, and that you know English. Isn't that enough justification for me to have taken the time to speak to him about you . . . ?" He rubbed his hands solicitously and continued: "You know I did this because we are about to become related. When I spoke to him through an interpreter about you, he asked me to arrange a meeting. Now tell me: Didn't I do well? Wouldn't it be wise for you to meet him?" he asked in a fatherly manner.

"Forgive me. I didn't know you had already spoken to him. Yes, I am grateful, but . . ."

He didn't let him finish. He turned authoritative once again and interrupted Mordehay: "Good! I will arrange for you to meet him at my office. The Good Lord is turning things around for us, for a change. I recommend you take a more heartened and positive attitude during this interview. I hate to say this, but since the thought crossed my mind I must tell you the truth. I don't know if you know the reason why poor people are poor." He stopped and enunciated the rest of his advice slowly and affirmatively. "I maintain they are poor because they think like poor people. Don't let this happen to you." With that impertinent and patronizing remark Baruch stood up. He sipped noisily the brew above the coffee grounds settled at the bottom of his cup. They shook hands and before leaving he warned: "Mordehay, don't let me down. I will arrange the interview and send someone to notify you. I want my youngest daughter's future father-in-law to become a respected man in our community."

With this garish comment he left the coffee house. Mordehay hadn't even touched his coffee. He too stood up and could hardly walk back to his shop. He unlocked the roll-up door and raised it. He rushed to feed his chickens before he gave himself a foot bath. For a long time he sat with his feet in a pail of medicated water incredulous about the turn of events in his otherwise uneventful life. Perhaps, he thought, Baruch wasn't wrong about his characterization of the poor. Though it bothered him, he saw some truth in it. Was he poor because all these years he thought and acted like a poor man? How many opportunities had he missed that would have lifted him from poverty? He couldn't think of one. Well, it didn't matter. Now a seemingly wonderful opportunity appeared to knock at his door. Perhaps the hand of The Lord had finally touched him as a reward for the sacrifice he had made in dedicating one son to His service.

That evening when he went home he didn't mention his encounter with Baruch to his family. He had a good reason. He wasn't sure about the final outcome of the promised interview. Two days later he was summoned to Baruch's office by a messenger. He had been dressing well for work expecting to be called in. Clara suspected something important was in the making. She kept quiet and waited to be told. He was ushered into a small office where Baruch and a European gentleman sat in silence. The foreigner was dressed in black Van Dyck style clothing with a pleated white linen collar around his neck. He was neatly groomed and looked very distinguished. He wore a sculptured pointed beard which attracted Mordehay's attention. He thought what a difference a stylish beard made in the personal appeal of an individual. He wore black short breeches fitting loosely and gathered at the knees. Long and tightly fitting black socks reached over and covered the end of the breeches. The black and ornate silk blouse complemented the rest of his clothing so perfectly. He had seen pictures of such distinguished Europeans in books, but it was the first time he was in the company of one.

Baruch's office looked as if it had been rearranged and cleaned. Once before Mordehay visited that office when Baruch had proposed the marriage of his daughter. Then, piles of papers cluttered his desk and armoires. Now everything was stacked neatly in the corner of the room and painted portraits of European men of distinction were hastily purchased and hung on the walls. Baruch was a foxy businessman. He had redecorated his office, Western style, when he learned European executives were moving to Smyrna. Jews and Moslems never hung portraits on walls, except that of the Sultan and only in government offices. Mordehay was struck by this craftiness, yet he saw nothing dishonest in the act of persuasion. He smiled and bowed as he entered the office. He made sure to walk straight and conceal any sign of a problem with his feet. Baruch introduced him in Turkish. During the four years in Constantinople, Sir Paul Rycaut learned a few Turkish sentences adequate enough for bare necessities. The Englishman extended his right hand and, to test Mordehay's skill in his language, he greeted him in English. Mordehay trembled on his aching feet. In turn Mordehay extended his hand and, in a rehearsed manner, said: "Pleased to meet you, Sire."

This was the first sentence he had learned in school. Now he hoped the rest of the conversation would flow smoothly and without embarrassment.

"Won't you please sit down Tchelebi Sevi?" asked the Englishman haughtily.

He was happy to oblige. This was the first time he had spoken to an Englishman and also the only time anyone addressed him by the title. After a few introductory polite questions from Rycaut and answers from Mordehay, looking pleased, Rycaut came to the point: "Given the superb recommendations from Tchelebi Mizrahi about your personal qualities, and having had the pleasure of attesting the adequacy of your English, I would like to know your intentions regarding the possibility of your working for me in the capacity of a Turkish agent. I need a man to deal with Turkish government personnel and to seek approval of all the paperwork related to exporting goods to His Majesty King Charles' Kingdom. Your lack of training in the business should not be of concern to you. I will provide whatever is necessary for that assignment and for negotiating on my behalf with the Turkish laborer which I intend to hire for packing and shipping a variety of products to Britain. Are you willing to work for me, and in that case would you, perhaps, have any questions to ask me regarding the assignment?"

He stopped and waited for Mordehay to respond to his proposal. It was a good thing that Baruch had prepared him two days earlier about the nature of the new job. Never in his life had Mordehay heard such long sentences spoken in any language, much less in English classes taught by a Greek instructor. With his eyes squinted, a frown on his forehead, and lips tight, he had listened attentively. But just when he thought he was following the gist of Rycaut's statement, he would lose the thread of thought from one clause to the next only to pick up disjointed meanings. He thanked God for catching the meaning of Rycaut's final question. He answered hesitatingly in comprehensible but broken English: "I am pleased, Sire. I work in your business if you want. . . . My store I must close . . . . Hmmm! How do you say, I have family, Señora and three sons. . . . Hmmm! You tell me what you pay, please." He asked what he thought was most important.

It was fortunate Baruch did not understand English. He would have had a fit at Mordehay's brash bluntness soliciting about the pay at this early stage of the deliberations. Mordehay wasn't taking any chances. In his cruel world losing the poultry business on account of a misunderstanding, even though he hated his business, was tantamount to disaster for him and his family. There were no jobs out there to help him recover from the mistake.

Rycaut laughed heartily, understanding very well that Mordehay wasn't about to give up his store unless his pay was better. He liked his gauche but frank attitude and felt their working relationship would be honest and in a forthright spirit. "Of course, dear gentleman, you have the right to know," he answered. In a very English and methodical manner, he gave details of Mordehay's responsibilities, the working hours, the training program, dress code, beginning salary as well as advancement opportunities. Mordehay couldn't believe his ears listening to the lucrative proposal. Baruch had been right. This was a once in a lifetime opportunity which wouldn't have surfaced had it not been for the threat of a Venetian war. His city had been poor all these years. Constantinople and Salonica had been reaping all the economic advantages from exports. With God's help now it looked as if it was his turn to benefit from others' misfortune. During the brief dialogue Baruch sat baffled, curiously observing a conversation he didn't comprehend. He had no idea at what stage of the negotiations they were. He tried to pick moods only from the facial expressions.

"Pleased to work for you," answered Mordehay with a glow on his face.

"Splendid!" said the Englishman. "Here is my business card. Tchelebi Sevi, it will give me great pleasure to see you at my office tomorrow at ten in the morning. As you will see from the card, my office is located at the corner building of Istiklal and Banka streets. I look forward seeing you then."

The Englishman stood up, shook Mordehay's hand and said to him: "Good day." He turned to Baruch, shook his hand and thanked him in Turkish. "*Teshekür, Mizrahi Efendi.*" In turn they bowed and the Englishman put on his Robin Hood-like hat adorned with a long ostrich feather and left the office. Before Rycaut was out of site, Baruch, who had been kept in total suspense, threw his arms in the air and asked in *espagnol*:

"*En el nombre del Dió* (In the name of God), what happened Mordehay? What did he tell you? What did you tell him?" He spoke as fast as he could.

Mordehay, filled with surprise and satisfaction, answered: "I guess he hired me!"

Relieved, Baruch pointed his forefinger at Mordehay, as a gesture of warning, and reminded him, as he had done before: "Good! Wonderful! Don't you ever forget who made it all possible. I may need a returned favor someday." Rendering reciprocal favors was a legitimate form of bartering in eastern countries.

Mordehay reached for Baruch's two hands and shook them tightly as a sign of deep gratitude and respect. He thanked him in *espagnol*[4] saying: "*Que los Diós de los cielos bendigan tu corazón! No me olvidare nunca tu favor!* (May God bless your heart! I shall never forget your favor!) He walked straight home as fast as he could to inform his family about the providential news. This time he wasn't concerned about his duck-like wobbling nor the pain in his aching feet. The only one who didn't congratulate him was Sabetay. He saw in this blessed event a misgiving. His father had to feel beholden to his future father-in-law. That concerned Sabetay because he didn't know how much of that obligation would fall upon him, personally. That evening Sabetay retired to his room after dinner, but the rest of the family celebrated joyously, making daring plans for the coming days.

Mordehay sold his poultry business to the father of the young rabbi who slaughtered his chickens. Now he could count on a

---

4. It was the popular Spanish language Sephardis brought from Spain. In exile, the language was allowed to evolve with time and was influenced by the introduction of new words about new concepts borrowed from host countries. The bitterness of Sephardis against Spain was so deep after the expulsion that there was hardly any form of contact between them. In spite of the linguistic distinction, *espagnol* remained amazingly close to Spanish after centuries of nearly total isolation from Spain. Spelling of words mostly eroded the similarity with Spanish. Also, in different regions of Europe the initially Castilian Spanish succumbed to different influences.

secure salary many times greater than the best of his monthly income. As Baruch indicated at the meeting in the coffee shop, Mordehay expected his appointment to induce other foreign representatives to seek him.

With Eliyah and Joseph they formed their own company on the waterfront where the exporting agencies were located. With a loan from Baruch he bought a new house in a wealthier district. Clara was beyond herself. The house she now owned was of the quality of those of the rich people she had been cleaning all these years. Mordehay decided to make a wedding gift of the old house to Sabetay and Alegra. Joseph began his training as a buyer of goods from the interior. Baruch's master buyer took Joseph along to show the location of the suppliers and the manner in which Turkish artisans and farmers did business. Eliyah supervised the warehousing and shipment of goods to be sent abroad. Mordehay showed to be very capable of managing the paper work involved in shipping manifestos that were taken for approval to the government authorities. It was a perfect arrangement. The only person who remained unaffected and unconcerned by all this was Sabetay. His mind and heart remained in the final resolution of his ordainment.

Mordehay wasn't a physically able man. His health and size did not permit him to engage in difficult jobs with better pay. He was small and paunchy. He had a very distinct way of walking. He shuffled, taking short steps at a time, swaying from side to side on account of the pain from the gout. The joints in his feet and especially his toes were constantly inflamed and swollen, making it very painful to stand on his feet for long periods of time or to walk the way most people did. Doctors had no cure for an ailment he had inherited from his father, who had become debilitated at the age of forty. The only solace the doctor gave him was a pat on the back and the consoling statement: "You have the illness of kings." Mordehay didn't take comfort in that compliment. He wondered if he would succumb to the fate of his father in a few more years.

Mordehay was born in 1606 in the port city of Patras, situated in Northern Morea on the Gulf of Corinth. The waterway separated the Peloponnesus from Central Greece. Grecian lands were under Ottoman occupation. Mordehay's father had also been in the poultry business. That was how Mordehay learned the trade. After his father died, there wasn't sufficient income to support his brother's large family and the one he planned for himself. He had fallen in love with Clara, an orphan adopted by a pious Sephardi neighbor. Mordehay and Clara were engaged before his father passed away. Like many other engaged couples, they waited to be married until Mordehay could support a family. It wasn't unusual for engaged couples to wait as long as ten years before they married. It was unthinkable for parents to permit their children to go into matrimony before they had proven financial independence. Anxious to wed his beloved Clara he decided to move to the larger city of Smyrna, in Asia Minor, on the eastern shore of the Aegean Sea, where economic conditions were more favorable but not outstanding. Mordehay's parents were originally Romaniote Jews. In the dominant Sephardi Diaspora of Patras they adapted to the Sephardi way of life to feel more at ease in that Spanish community. They learned to speak Spanish and even changed their family name from the harsh sounding *Tzvi* to the softer Spanish appellation of Sevi. His given name also underwent a latinized transformation from the biblical Mordecai to Mordehay. After signing a matrimonial agreement and registering it in the record book of the synagogue, he married Clara and soon after they booked passage to Smyrna to begin a new life.

At the time of this story Smyrna was not the only city in the Ottoman Empire where Sephardis settled. Constantinople on the Bosphorus, Salonica in northern Greece, Cairo in Egypt, and to a lesser extent, Jerusalem, had many Sephardi communities. There were other smaller towns, always near the sea, in Asia Minor and Greece, that experienced the same influx. For the most part Spanish Jews resided in the lands of the Mediterranean Basin. Centuries after they were jolted by the Spanish expulsion they seldom ventured into the interior lands, away from the sea. The roads to the interior were poorly maintained and difficult to travel. In the event of hostilities by fanatical Moslems who never accepted the concept of religious tolerance, they feared they would be trapped inland. The proximity of the sea was a great feeling of security at all times.

In his new community of Smyrna, the five-year elementary education was free. It was provided for all Sephardi children at the *Cal* (school of the synagogue) and financed entirely by the wealthy members. The secondary school, available only to boys, prepared them for three more years in a variety of subjects strictly relevant to the business world. Parents had to pay for this education according to their income. For Spanish-speaking Sephardis, French, a romance language, was understandably the more popular choice for a foreign language. After having enrolled in French, Mordehay found the grammar much too difficult. He switched to English, not knowing the benefits he would reap later on account of it. At home and among friends they spoke *espagnol*. They made little or no effort to learn Turkish. One would assume erroneously that illiteracy in Turkish or Arabic,[5] for these sons of immigrants would have been a handicap in their local commerce and when dealing with the civilian authorities. The facts pointed to the contrary. Because of their superior European education and of the wealth brought by their immigrant ancestors, they commanded a high degree of influence, controlled the local and foreign trade, and hired sympathetic Turks to do their bidding in Turkish or Arabic. They kept their children in private schools and never in the inferior Turkish state schools. As a result, the well-to-do young generations didn't learn Turkish. Aware of their distinct advantage in a Moslem land which granted them only partial civil rights and citizenship, they made sure to maintain and nurse diligently the superior legacy of their grandfathers.

Sabetay, who had demonstrated superior aptitudes for learning and a fervent desire to become a rabbi, remained at the *yeshiva* after

---

5. Many of the people in the lands occupied by the Turks spoke Arabic, an influence from the *Quran*. The literature and science of the Arabs were so rich and advanced that Arabic had a considerable level of penetration into the Turkish language.

secondary school. That education was not free; it cost as much as sending a child to a special trade school. Clara was determined to keep him in school for as long as he wished. She had learned to appreciate the value of higher education from her parents, whose Spanish ancestors valued scholarship highly when they resided in Spain. Sending a son to the ministry was considered a mitzvah (act of redemption). Clara's encouragement shielded Sabetay[6] from the responsibility of earning a living.

6. A favorite name for boys born on the Sabbath. The idea is analogous to naming Spanish children 'Domingo' if they were born on Sunday.

3

$\mathcal{M}$ordehay no longer felt inferior in social standing to the father of the bride. He was not a poor poulterer anymore; he was a commercial agent for foreign institutions, the same title as Baruch's but with considerable less wealth. That didn't matter now. The day of Sabetay's wedding arrived. The marriage was celebrated with great pomp, and the parents on both sides appeared supremely happy. Alegra's mother spared neither detail nor expense at arranging the wedding of her youngest daughter. The nuptial party didn't break up until past midnight. The exhausted and tensed couple occupied the Sevi's old house, arranged to suit Alegra's opulent taste.

Tradition demanded that the morning after the wedding the bride's mother visited the newlyweds. Though this visit was given the appearance of a social call, the principle intent was to pick up the blood-stained sheet or panties of her daughter, as proof of her virginity. When that happened, another celebration was arranged, at which time the substantive proof of virginity was displayed proudly to a group of invited women. But the day after the wedding Alegra's mother left empty handed and disappointed. In her wisdom she rationalized that some young couples, out of excitement or fear, weren't always successful in their first attempt to make love. She waited patiently for succeeding days when she would be rewarded. Alas! Eight weeks

went by without the proof of honor. Unkind and damaging rumors had begun to spread. Alegra had not delivered the important evidence. Baruch was alerted by his wife that something
had to be wrong and needed intervention. Perhaps, Mrs. Mizrahi
thought, her daughter needed advice on how things were supposed to have happened. Distressed and unwilling to wait any
longer, Baruch took matters in his own hands and with his wife
went to interrogate Alegra. To their great surprise they were
shocked to learn that the problem was not with her. It was
Sabetay's lack of interest in bringing her to his bed. She assured
her parents she tried every fickle trick and enticement she could
think of. Baruch became furious. He was more concerned about
his perceived new image in the community than the anxiety it
was causing his daughter. He advised her to seek an audience
before the Rabbinical Council demanding to bear pressure on
Sabetay to consummate the marriage even if he had to be ordered to have intercourse with her. He could not allow his daughter to live with a man while she remained an innocent virgin girl.
That would be deviant and disgraceful.

Terribly embarrassed, she followed her father's advice and
appeared before the Council. She complained that while by religious marriage she was Sabetay's wife, she could not consider
herself a wife, yet. Perplexed, the rabbis asked for clarification.
Alegra explained with great difficulty that the marriage hadn't been
consummated in eight weeks in spite of the number of induce-
ments she tried as recommended by her married older sisters. But
Sabetay remained aloof from ever touching her. At the end of her
testimony, Baruch demanded swift intervention by the Council
or an annulment. The judging rabbis were sympathetic with the
Mizrahis' problem. They were astonished but not totally surprised,
for they knew Sabetay's strange personality from varying degrees
of contact at the yeshiva. Granting a divorce was one of the most
difficult of rabbinical judgments. The Council didn't accommodate married couples as easily as they wished. The grounds for
annulment had to be of extraordinary nature and only when the
reason in itself was a violation of talmudic laws. The Council

wanted to hear Sabetay's side of the story. The Mizrahis returned to their home and waited for things to improve after the Council questioned and advised their son-in-law, who appeared willingly before the court.

Honestly and comfortably he admitted to the truthfulness of Alegra's charges. Dumbfounded, the judges wanted to know the reason for refusing to take Alegra into his bed. He said he had none. They assumed at first Sabetay might have felt shy telling the truth about Alegra. They even went as far as suggesting the possibility of a number of reasons often given by troubled couples. Was she cold or perhaps unwilling? Was she pervert or distasteful? Did she keep her body clean, etc.? An affirmative answer to any of these questions would have turned the blame in Alegra's direction. In a man's world he could have taken the easy way out and agreed to any of these reasons. He would have been exonerated. The Council would have ordered Alegra to be more submissive, proper, or clean. They sat waiting for an answer from Sabetay. He answered calmly that she was none of those terrible things. What Alegra had told them was the truth.

The judging rabbis thought of Sabetay as an eccentric, but none could have accused him of being a liar. In total disbelief they retired in the back room to decide on a verdict. A few minutes later they returned where Sabetay waited for a ruling. The senior rabbi asked him to approach the bench and addressed him with the following order: "The court decided to order you, Sabetay Sevi, to obey to one of the following of two options: You may go home and fulfill your duties as a husband or present your wife with a deed of divorcement, as you are not permitted to live side by side with Alegra unless you decide to consummate the marriage. Is that clear?" he asked.

"Yes," answered Sabetay showing no emotion.

But the question required of him to make a choice. The senior rabbi stressed: "You haven't told us which option you plan to follow!"

Calmly Sabetay responded: "I agree with your verdict and I will give Alegra a deed of divorcement."

The incredulous rabbis shook their heads in disbelief. Never in their lives had they seen such a strange behavior eight weeks after the wedding. As soon as the news of the verdict became known, people began to talk in uncomplimentary ways, mostly about Sabetay. Men accused him of being impotent and possibly a homosexual for his refusal to make love to beautiful Alegra. Women, and especially the eligible young girls, accused Alegra of being a cold fish, unworthy of marrying a handsome and smart Sabetay. Sabetay didn't care what people said. He deemed it his personal business to sleep with Alegra or not. He had already concluded the night his parents proposed the marriage that she wasn't the right woman for him. He was fully acquainted with the biblical laws pertaining to matrimony. From the day he had agreed to marry Alegra, he knew exactly what the council would decide. His devious yet respectful scheme permitted him to obey his parents without having to rekindle bad dreams for the rest of his life when Alegra exposed herself in the nude with dancing flames scheduled not far behind.

Since men have a propensity to react emotionally to anything discrediting their manhood, Mordehay turned angry and furious at his son for allowing his name to be soiled with filthy rumors about sexual inclinations. Back in his mind was also the financial covenant he had made with Alegra's father. The scandal and the return of the dowry and loan to get his business started would damage his personal credibility. He, and Clara by his side, de-manded an explanation from their son. They weren't going to take the cold shoulder he had given the Council. Realizing how dis-tressed his parents were, Sabetay chose to answer them in the following manner: "Dearest ones, I know I deceived you but not intentionally. I have a good reason for doing what I did. I had dreams which I believe were brought by angels that Alegra was not the mate destined for me. These dreams were so vivid I am convinced they were ordered by God. Please don't ask me for more details. I beg you to accept my reasons and respect my convic-tion. Rest assured that the time will come when the right person will be revealed to me in the days ahead."

Clara accepted his judgment immediately, knowing her son strived with all his heart to be excessively pure and godly. She convinced her husband that it had to be Alegra who failed to understand their innocent son, for she did not know how to entice him to want her. They made a commitment to search for another compatible wife. Clara closed the matter by quoting a Sephardi proverb: *"Mas de boda que de novia.* (More about the wedding than the bride.)"

Sabetay moved into his parent's new home and Mordehay sold the old house to pay his debt to Baruch. While family and friends continued to wonder about the broken marriage, Sabetay had only one thought in mind: receiving his deserved title of rabbi. He was totally obsessed with that. He continued pressing his teacher on the right to be ordained at eighteen. He demanded to know why he should be penalized for having completed his studies sooner than his classmates. He had passed all his examinations flawlessly. He couldn't care less about the contrived reason of immaturity the members of his examining committee had brought up. His teacher promised another review of his case.

During the stressful days in waiting for his confirmation, he prayed with his own words, speaking silently to his God and promising to become his eternal and devoted servant for the rest of his life. He vowed to be not just an ordinary rabbi like his teachers and student colleagues, but a special rabbi probing into the deepest recesses of his soul in search for Him, to find Him, to understand Him, and to do His will. He also promised to make every effort to harvest thousands of lost and errant souls and return them to Him. Being in the habit of writing in a special notebook thoughts and ideas of great importance to him, he wrote during those stressful days a quotation from the Talmud:

> "Like an ox bearing a yoke and an ass bearing a burden will I make myself to serve You, Almighty God, King of the universe! May this cause be thy will, O cause of All Causes.[1]"

---

1. J. Saportas (see Acknowledgment) as reported by Scholem.

He accelerated his practice of meditation in solitude, his acts of penitence, increased the number of fasting days in the week, and abstained from many of the things he liked. He plunged every day in the cold sea of the Gulf of Smyrna as acts of ablution and penitence. These acts of mortification were recommended in his primer book on practical mysticism as effective means to atone for past sins. Emotionally and physically immature, Sabetay intentionally ignored the strict warnings in the primer and of his teachers that young and inexperienced persons should not attempt these severe forms of penances without professional guidance and before the age of twenty-four.

Moses Pinheiro and Isaac Silveira, both twenty years of age and sons of wealthy Portuguese Sephardis were his classmates and the only friends he had. But friendship in the normal sense of the word was not one of Sabetay's import. He neither felt the need for a close kinship nor the desire to nourish intimacy. Clara had always regretted this side of her son's personality. She liked Moses for his open personality and for striving to be close to Sabetay. He belonged to a nice family she knew and had served as a maid. Two years older, Moses was a compassionate young man who admired Sabetay's depth of knowledge on subjects they studied at the yeshiva. He admired Sabetay most for his precise and accurate memorization of texts in the bible, the Talmud, and the Midrash, and especially his ability to retrieve what he read at will and without errors. These were vast and profound writings. Since biblical times these were collections of Hebrew history, rabbinical decisions, legends, codes of law, literary critiques, traditions, stories, parables, customs, and everything falling under Jewish folklore. Sabetay knew them all. From childhood Moses tried to be much closer to Sabetay, but it wasn't in Sabetay's nature to allow anyone close enough to bring to the open his thoughts and feelings. Isaac Silveira, on the other hand, enjoyed being with Sabetay only because he represented for him the ultimate challenge in debating and provoking him on biblical knowledge and especially his global understanding of the foundations of Judaism. He loved to challenge him only to sharpen his ability to argue. No one else in the class, except Sabetay, dared confront Isaac in a debate on talmudic writings.

Moses was a good looking young man with dark complexion and dark black eyes. Even though he was two years older than Sabetay, he had not yet completed his studies simply because he studied to become a rabbi and a physician at the same time. The dual profession was not unusual for gifted children of rich families. Before the Portuguese expulsion of 1497 his great-grandfather held a faculty position of medicine at the prestigious University of Coimbra north of Lisbon. When the Edict of Expulsion was announced in Portugal, refusing to leave his position, he was arrested and imprisoned with other wealthy Jews who had fled Spain five years earlier. His family was among six hundred others that were granted permanent residence paying a large gift tax to the government but unaware that their residency would eventually be revoked. After many attempts by the Church to convert Moses' great-grandfather, he died in a dungeon from sickness and starvation. His grandfather accepted expatriation and, one struggle after another, he managed to cross desert lands of North Africa under Ottoman rule and settled in Smyrna. Proud of the family heritage, the Pinheiros constantly reminded their children of their responsibility to live up to the standard of achievement and dignity of their scholarly great-grandfather.

One Thursday morning in the spring of 1645 Moses was called into the office of Rabbi Escapha. "Where is Sabetay? He is not in the yeshiva. We have looked all over for him. Where is he? I need to talk to him. It is urgent. Go fetch him. You are his friend, you should know where to find him. I don't intend to sit in my office all day, waiting for him either. Go!" He ordered without any explanation or reason. However, rumors had circulated that the commission of rabbis who were to pass a final decision on Sabetay's ordainment had met again upon the urging of his mentor Escapha, and the commission had arrived at a final decision.

Moses ran as fast as he could to Sabetay's home and knocked at his door, first gently and, when no one answered, he pounded with his fists loudly and yelled: "Sabetay open the door! It is me, Moses, Moses Pinheiro!" Still no one answered his call. He was certain his mother would have answered if she was home. Since Sabetay seldom went out except to the yeshiva and religious services, he was convinced he was in his room, oblivious to the world, immersed reading, meditating, or praying. He ran around the building and knocked at the back door repeating his call. Still no one answered or peaked through the windows. As he was about to leave the lady next door came out to tell him that Señora Sevi went out shopping with a basket under her arm about an hour ago. She didn't know if anyone was in the house. Moses thanked her and remembered it was Thursday, market day. He sat on the marble front steps waiting for Clara to return. The thought that Escapha wasn't going to wait for Sabetay haunted him, especially when he was certain Sabetay was in his room.

He sat for an hour on the front steps worrying their teacher would become impatient and leave. As he debated if he should wait longer, he recognized Clara coming down the street with a basket full of fresh produce and a loaded shopping net. He rushed to help her. "Good morning Señora Sevi. Let me have the basket. It must be heavy for you. I can carry the shopping net too."

Pleased to see Moses and to be relieved of the heavy burden, she said: "Good morning Moses. Thank you. You are a thoughtful young man and I am sure your parents must be very proud of you. Why aren't you with Sabetay?"

Surprised, Moses asked: "Where is he?"

Clara realized that Moses had been unable to move her son away from his books. She had left him in his room before she went to market. Angry she complained: "What is he doing in his room? You must have knocked at the door and called him, I am sure. Is he ignoring you? I worry about him, Moses. He has a bad habit of ignoring people. You must forgive him. He doesn't mean to be unfriendly. I left him feeling terribly depressed and with a severe headache.[2] I will fetch him and have him come downstairs immediately." She unlocked the front door and shook her head in disapproval of her son's indifference.

"Is he home? I knocked so many times . . . . "

She interrupted him. "Sure he is home. He is buried in his books. That was where I left him. I don't know Moses, he worries me. He is also probably faint from all the fasting he does." She paused, looked at Moses in the eye and asked: "Do you fast too?"

Caught by surprise, Moses answered with a blush on his face: "Sometimes, when I feel like it."

Clara knew he wasn't telling the whole truth. All the young rabbis in town were afflicted by this new fasting fad encouraged by modern cabalists. "I know he likes you, Moses. He would have come down if he knew it was you. It hasn't been easy for him waiting for a decision from the Grand Rabbi. No, it hasn't been easy, I feel . . . ."

"Excuse me, Señora Sevi. I don't mean to interrupt you. But I think I have important news for him. That is the reason I came to find him. I think it is about what you just said. He is expected at the yeshiva at once by orders of Rabbi Escapha. You know how demanding and difficult he can be. I am not absolutely sure but I suspect it is about his ordainment. It is very important that he comes with me right away. Otherwise Rabbi Escapha will be tired of waiting and he will leave. Then for sure we will both be in trouble."

Anxious to know if Moses knew the final decision, she asked in a choked tone of voice: "What is the final decision? Tell me quickly." She waited hoping Moses had a positive answer.

"I don't know Señora. I have not been told anything. They wouldn't tell me anyway. All I know is he must come with me at once."

---

2. Only recently psychiatrists were able to diagnose Sabetay's cycles of depression and headaches as manic depression; a recurring psychosis marked with nervous excitement, delusion, hallucination, followed by headaches, depressive mood, and ultimately reverting to normal behavior. Author is indebted to Dr. Barry Morenz, Jr., psychiatrist, for this confirmation.

Standing by the stairway while Moses placed her purchases on the kitchen table, Clara shouted at the top of her voice to make sure Sabetay heard her. She had to repeat her call twice. They heard footsteps upstairs, and they waited patiently for him to appear. Finally they saw him on the landing outside his room. He looked very pale and held his head with his right hand. He didn't say a word nor did he recognized Moses standing besides his mother. He wore his *taleth* over his head and shoulders. His left shirt sleeve was rolled up above the elbow and on his bare hairy left arm he had wrapped tightly one of the two phylacteries. The cube of the second phylactery hung crooked on his forehead and the one leather straps attached to that cube dropped from the back of his head to the front of his body while the other dropped straight down on his back almost to his shoes.

"Sabetay! My dear son! You look awful! You haven't eaten for two days. You cannot live like a hermit in a cave! You cannot go on like this anymore! You know you are not supposed to wear philacteries[3] all day, and wrapped so tight around your arm, blocking your circulation . . ." She paused with a discouraged look on her face. ". . . . Oh, what's the use! I must have said this a hundred times! Your friend Moses has been knocking at the door for an hour. You are summoned at the yeshiva at once. For the love of the Lord, come down and eat something before you go!"

Hearing the name of his friend, he recognized Moses at the bottom of the stairs. He didn't have the strength to greet him. He hadn't shaved in days. He stared at Moses waiting to be told why he had been summoned. Moses understood from his emaciated look and said swiftly:

---

3. Black leather thongs, half inch wide and about eight-to-ten ft. in length, one end terminating into a black leather cube containing passages from the Scriptures. According to Deuteronomy they should be worn during week day morning prayers. Symbolically, they are reminders of the obligation to keep the Mosaic laws and to remember the most frequent prayer: the *Shema*, proclaiming the uniqueness of God. The faithful binds this message upon his hand, arm, and places it for 'frontlets between thine eyes' (*Deuteronomy* Vi. 8 and Xi. 18).

"Sabetay, Rabbi Escapha asked me to fetch you as quickly as possible. It appears that the commission has reviewed your case again and they might have reached a decision. I am not privileged to know what they decided. Nobody knows except they. Rabbi Escapha wants to talk to you personally. He told me he won't wait all day. Come down please. We must rush."

He did as he was told and came down the stairs. His worried mother looked at him up and down, wishing he would groom himself and put on clean clothes. "Aren't you removing your prayer shawl and the phylacteries? You can't go like this. Dear, could you at least change before you go?" begged his concerned mother.

Sabetay didn't pay attention to her pleas. "Hello Moses," he said, squinting his eyes in the bright light of the living room. It was obvious that he was in great pain. He placed his right hand over Moses' shoulder as if he expected to be guided to his fate, and they both walked to the front door.

"You look sick, Sabetay! Are you sure you feel up to it?" questioned his friend with great concern.

"I am all right. I wish I could get rid of these headaches. I get so sick from them that I cannot see clearly enough to read. Don't worry, eventually they go away and I feel as if I come out of the darkest abyss on my way to paradise." He put on a faint smile knowing that Moses knew the source he paraphrased, and added: "I will be fine, Moses. Let's go, I am ready to face Rabbi Escapha."

They left the house and didn't say another word until they entered the heavy wooden door to the courtyard of the yeshiva. Sabetay, knowing he had failed to convince the council before, didn't want to be disappointed again in the presence of his friend. He said to Moses: "I am going to the office alone. I want to face this judgment alone."

Moses put his two arms around Sabetay, hugged him tightly to show his love and support. He wished him success and went down the hallway. Sabetay, holding his aching head, walked to the office of Master Rabbi Escapha. He knocked gently to avoid aggravating the pounding headache.

"Come in," said the voice inside.

Escapha had always been in favor of Sabetay's early ordainment. He argued with his colleagues that their indecision was totally misguided and cruel. He maintained that Sabetay deserved to be ordained on the basis of his proof of scholarship and devotion to the faith. Age had nothing to do with the decision. He charged the commission of yielding to criticism from the community of rabbis that Sabetay's ordainment would deflate the value of the prestigious title. He even went as far as calling their reluctance cowardly and unjust.

Sabetay entered the office and shut the door behind him. Before he had a chance to turn around and face Escapha, he was scolded: "Oh! Finally, here you are! Where were you all this time? Your classmates were here all morning. . . ." He paused a moment then added a little sarcasm to his admonition. ". . . . Oh, yes I forgot. You don't attend classes anymore. Didn't you know we had a meeting of the Commission early this morning? Everyone seems to have known it except you of course. You are impossible, Sabetay. For someone so concerned about his ordainment you should have been here sitting in front of my door long before the meeting. The Commission might have wanted to ask you questions. I had to send Pinheiro to fetch you and for some reason I had to be the one waiting two hours for your personage to show up. If it weren't for the importance of what I have to tell you, I would have left my office long ago. I have important duties to attend." He took one sad look at him and said: "You look awful! How dare you come to my office wearing philacteries at this late time of the day?" Sabetay remained quiet. Escapha lifted his arms in despair and shrugged his shoulders as if he had been talking to a stone wall. Then he added: "This is not the first time I find myself reprimanding you about your personal attire."

Sabetay was listening with glassy eyes focused far past his master. He was going to take all what Escapha was capable of dishing out until he came to the point for which he was summoned. There was a moment of silence while Escapha collected his thoughts. "It was no surprise to me that the Commission remained very adamant conferring you the title of rabbi. You knew that, didn't you? They didn't want to deviate from that opinion, insisting there was no precedence in this community to rush and make an exception in granting you the title at eighteen. They wanted to wait at least another year." He paused, looked over Sabetay's discombobulated attire once again and continued: "At this very moment as I look at you, you are demonstrating to me the very reason why some of my colleagues were opposed. Personally, you don't make a good impression. You are a loner, undependable, and far too selfish to serve a parish. At times I have my doubts, too; like this very moment." Escapha, who was also a physician, realized Sabetay was suffering badly. He wanted to bring his lecturing to an end: "You are very fortunate that I happen to be compassionate towards you. You have completed your studies with distinction. It is my feeling that if you remain in the diligent pursuit of excellence in your piousness and scholarship you will have a bright and fulfilling future as a pundit and a thinker, brighter than any other we have seen in this congregation. I emphasize the word **if** because your personal qualities need much improvement. Your worst qualities are unfriendliness and lack of realism. I am hoping that with age you will overcome them. . . ."

Sabetay's eyes rolled a few times and he collapsed to the floor. Alarmed, Escapha opened the door to his office and called for help. To his surprise, Sabetay's classmates were standing close to the door waiting to catch a few words. He summoned them inside quickly. They lifted his body from the floor and stretched him on the divan. After Escapha administered first aid, Sabetay came to his senses not knowing what had happened to him. He tried to make a move to get up but his master ordered him to remain on his back for a few more minutes.

"You worry me, Sabetay. I determined from your pulse rate that you must have been fasting longer than you should. I recall warning you once before about this. I don't understand your purpose unless you have decided to become a biblical recluse!" He enunciated the last sentence angrily. But he drew a boisterous laughter from the other students. To put an end to his agony, Escapha blurted out quickly what Sabetay wanted to hear: "Anyway, you interrupted me by fainting in front of my eyes. As a result of my insistence about your rights to have the title of rabbi, the Commission gave me the authority to proclaim you Rabbi Sabetay Sevi in their absence. Now go home and celebrate."

Escapha asked him to sit up. Never in his life had he conferred the title of rabbi under such unusual and painful circumstances. He quickly pronounced the Hebrew oath for ordainment. He blessed him and shook Sabetay's limber hand, wishing him well. There was a short but loud shriek of approval from his classmates. Escapha turned his head around towards the cheering students to show his displeasure at rowdiness. He ordered Moses to walk him home and Sabetay to come the following morning at ten to be congratulated by the other members of the Commission. He left the office in a hurry.

Sabetay was still numb and unsure about what he had heard. This was not the way he had imagined his graduation ceremony. It was supposed to have been joyous with lots of guests, singing choir, and sumptuous food. Instead he felt terribly sick. After the students congratulated him one by one, Isaac Silveira asked Sabetay if he could come along and help Moses take him home. Sabetay didn't understand why Isaac had to ask that question. He was in great pain.

They walked slowly to the Sevis' home. Isaac wasn't as elated about Sabetay's success as Moses was. On the contrary, he felt envious and jealous not only because Sabetay was the first in his class to be ordained, but because he was the youngest ever. His thoughts turned inward in jealousy, comparing Sabetay's abilities to his. Instead of being objective and recognizing Sabetay's performance as a model seminarian, his mind turned towards his shortcomings. Why was it necessary for school officials to break a long standing tradition? Did he possess extraordinary personal qualities to overlook the rules? Teachers, colleagues, friends, and acquaintances all reckoned that he was an odd and unfriendly sort of fellow, hardly fitting the description of a parish rabbi. What then prompted the fathers of the *Cal* (community) to agree to a precipitous decision? It had to be

Escapha's biased opinion and influence. Whatever it was there was nothing he could do about it!

That afternoon, Sabetay did not heed to his teacher's advice. He had no strength or desire to celebrate. He locked himself in his room after telling his mother what transpired at Escapha's office. His excruciating headache had not abated. He went to bed and didn't reappear until the next morning. When he woke up he felt much better. Still in bed, his first recollection was being in Escapha's office learning about his crowning success. He was so full of gratitude he had a great urge to thank his Lord for making it possible. He recalled making promises in his room the day before, that he would devote his life fully and unconditionally to His glory if He judged him to be worthy of the title. Surely, his ensuing success was a direct result of his pleas as well as his accelerated acts of mortification to atone his sins. Now, for the first time he sensed a sweet feeling of the divine spirit residing in his small room. He became overwhelmed with the awesome thought that perhaps from now on he would no longer be alone in that room. Totally overwhelmed, with tears in his eyes he was gratified that this was the beginning of a close communion with his Creator.

$\mathcal{S}$

Sephardi Jews are culturally very different from Ashkenazi Jews. The former were Jews who never left the Mediterranean culture. The continuity in their customs, habits, mores, temperament, attitude and philosophy of life remained nearly unchanged from biblical days. The Ashkenazi Jew, starting from the same cultural environment, was temperamentally transformed by a more ascertive and dominant 'Germanic' culture. For them the art of compromise, sentimentality and shrewdness, dominant in the Mediterranean way of life gave way to dogmatism, rationalization and expediency.

In Sabetay's case, his Romaniote lineage of a generation before had been totally effaced living and learning in an exclusive Sephardi society. His customs, habits, temperament, attitude, and outlook on life were thoroughly Sephardi and rooted in two of its unique characteristics: sentimentality and fatalism. His fickle and elusive soul ran freely since childhood and was nurtured by a freedom to explore self serving interpretations of the Scriptures, the Talmud, the *Cabala* and the *Zohar*. He became absorbed by the poetic imagery of what he read during the years at the yeshiva, instilling in him a profound spiritualism full of allegorical imageries. This special kind of faith in his early development left him with an insatiable thirst for knowledge of the Deity, trusting that it alone could lead him to an understanding of the Maker of his soul. The works of the cabalists drove him intensely to become the living link between all human souls and the divine Creator of those lost souls. To bridge that vast metaphysical realm of complexity, he pledged to become an elite interpreter as his idol Isaac Luria was. Only *Cabala* masters like Luria were able to assure themselves the sublime confidence of having been able to reach and feel the communion with God.

4

ﶀ

*I*t was mid-afternoon Friday, the day after Sabetay's ordainment. The family planned a special dinner to celebrate the great event. They couldn't do it the day before because Sabetay had one of his bouts of headache and depression. Also, knowing it was the day to brake fast, Clara prepared a special meal. The family waited to take their places at the dining table. He emerged from his room with a lighted candle in his hand singing a love ballad in *espagnol* at the top of his beautiful voice.

> To the mountain I ascended
> To the river I descended
> My Mamaritta[1] I met there,
> The king's daughter bright and fair.
> There I saw the shining lass
> As she came up from the bath.
> Her arched brow dark as the night
> Her face a gleaming sword of light
> Her lips like coral red and bright
> Her flesh as milk so fair and white.

---

1. Original source Thomas Coenen. The woman's name in the poem was Meliselda. Sabetay liked to pretend that the composer mistakenly used the name of Meliselda instead of the nickname he gave his mother: Mamaritta (little mother).

The song was very popular in Sephardi communities throughout Europe and the Middle East. It was one of many brought from Spain two centuries before. This particular song had a special significance for Clara. At happy times he sang it to tell her she was the most beautiful woman in all the world. It never failed; each time he sang it, it drew tears to her brown eyes. This time her tears had a special significance. She was happy for him for having received the honor he sought so resolutely. Deep in her heart, however, she harbored a sad feeling that this reward had a severe price attached to it. She dreaded to see him drift slowly into a world of profound and somber religious complexity incompatible with the simple and happy life she aspired for him. Comparing him to her other sons and to other men his age, she questioned herself sadly: What feelings resided in his soul making him so very different than other young men? How was it that marriage, family, spiritual leadership in a parish became unattractive to him?

He walked down the steps wearing a happy smile. It had been months since his family had seen him so happy. His change of mood from the day before pleased everyone waiting for him. Now more happy tears began to emerge in Clara's eyes for it was so unlike him to act silly but human as he walked down the stairs singing. She stood by the dining room door watching his performance. At the bottom of the stairs she rushed to him and kissed him lovingly. He responded affectionately, almost dropping the burning candle he held. With his left arm he engaged her under her right arm and the two walked to the dining room table where the others were seated and waited.

"Sabetay, you must be feeling better," exclaimed his father in an ebullient tone of voice.

His two brothers had invited their girlfriends to celebrate the onset of this special Sabbath after graduation. Sabetay's difficult accomplishments at the precocious age of eighteen was a feat worthy of pride and respect. The dining room was lit brightly with two large candelabra hanging over the table, each holding six candles. Judging from the shine on his face and the rosy luster on his cheeks it was obvious that he had washed before coming down.

His beard and mustache were neatly trimmed. He wore a clean skull cap, the white silk vestment he wore on holidays, and a clean raw silk *taleth* over his shoulders. Clapping her hands Clara announced:

"Here comes Rabbi Sevi!"

Seeing how happy his mother was, he let out a rare laughter of pleasure and fulfillment. This was the first time they had addressed him legitimately as rabbi. In the past his brothers used the title to tease him. He took a deep breath of relief and exclaimed giggling: "Hey, I surprised everyone, didn't I?" Quickly, he added: "Everyone but the Lord above. He knew it all along, and He wouldn't divulge His secret to me until the very last minute."

Though his remark had a strange bent to it, it went unnoticed. There was seldom any time when Sabetay didn't invoke the name of God in his conversation. It seemed that everything and anything had a divine significance. It was evident to everyone that he was exceedingly happy. It was a special kind of happiness that poured out after having removed a choking grip from his heart.

"Here, here, my son. Come, sit by me this time," said his father, pulling a chair next to him. "We've got lots of things to talk about; don't we?" Sabetay did as his father asked. Finding him in an unusually happy mood Mordehay wanted to deliver all the advices he was unable to pass on and that had waited until this day. "You know, as you get older, my son, it seems we have less and less time to talk . . . to talk like I talk to your brothers and to your mother. You always seem so deeply involved with rabbinical studies, with prayers, meditations . . . activities that keep you away from us."

Sabetay listened but had a good notion what his father was about to tell him. It had to be a repetition of the kind of life he aspired for him. But how could he make his father understand that he was born with feelings and desires different than those of most people, and, as such, he had no appreciation for the ordinary life of the multitudes. Willingly and happily he had already pledged his life not to the community or to a family of his own, but to the service of God. He wished he could make his parents understand, once and for all, the divine goal he had chosen. His mother knew it, why wouldn't his father understand it?

"You know, Son, you lock yourself in your room for long hours as days go by, and we see less and less of you. You can't imagine the deep longing we have for conversing with you about ourselves . . . just ourselves. That isn't necessarily bad is it?" Sabetay felt embarrassed for being lectured like a school child in front of company. He glanced shyly at the two girls sitting side by side at the table, but quickly lowered his eyes, fixing them on the plate in front of him. His father wasn't finished: "It is a strong human desire to want to talk about one's self. Don't misunderstand me, Son, we are extremely proud of what you have accomplished. But being humans and wanting to act like humans, we may at times want to make small talk, to act silly, and even a bit sinful. That is what ordinary humans are supposed to do." He thought he should use words familiar to him. "If there is no sin, there would be no need for prayers, now would it? . . . And if there were no prayers there would be no need for rabbis." He laughed following his reasoning, looking at him to see if his advisement meant anything to him. But Sabetay remained expressionless; his eyes were still fixed at the table. Disappointed, Mordehay brushed his beard and expanded on the subject: "Tell me. What purpose would atonement prayers serve if nobody sinned? Huh! Am I right? Just now when you came down the stairs singing with a candle in your hand you acted . . . ," he stopped and hesitated a moment. He was about to say: "like a human," but that wouldn't have sounded kindly. Instead, he said: "The way most people act all the time. Your mother and I want to see you this way more often now that you have accomplished your goal. Let us seize the moment and enjoy it! I hope with all my heart this is the beginning of a new and pleasant chapter in your life, and ours. Is that a bad wish my son?"

Mordehay choked with that question. He wanted to say a lot more and hug him but instead he patted him in the back. Sabetay, too, felt an anguish in his heart. He understood perfectly well what his father wanted of him. He wasn't offended by his near slip of the tongue. He had no desire to be the ordinary person his father wanted him to be. Instead, he considered himself privileged for being touched by a blessed sensitivity that he hoped would draw him closer to a divine mission not yet clearly defined. He was confident that in time this mission would fashion itself into a real and magnificent design. No, he wasn't destined to live the stolid life of most men: earning a living, caring for a family, fighting and loving, suffering and rejoicing, sinning and atoning, and, in the end, wondering if all that was worth living for. Instead, he was determined to rise above the ordinary and, with divine help, remove apathy and sin from the souls of his brotherhood and show his fellow men the way to communion with the Creator. Yes, this was what he wished to tell his father and all the people in the community who unjustly judged him as an eccentric with little or no interest in the human race. He knew he had to be patient and wait for the day when he will prove his worth to humanity, even if the road to success was a long one.

His mother sensing his discomfort on account of her husband's lengthy advice. She changed the subject: "Sabetay! you must be starved. You haven't eaten in four days. Ever since you started fasting I make sure I keep on hand, at all times, the meals you like. I never know when you will decide to break fast. I cooked especially for you three of your favorite dishes. We will start with *fritada de prasa*[2] (tart of leeks au gratin). I know how much you love it. You may commence with the Sabbath prayers. I will go fetch the first course."

---

2. The Turks borrowed many words from the Greeks, the Arabs, the Slavic languages, and from the Sephardis to supplement their own limited Turkic vocabulary. The word *praseo* in Spanish, and *prasios* in Greek entered the Turkish vocabulary as *prasa*. Similarly, the word *barbunya* was borrowed from the Greek name for mullet. Other words borrowed from *espagnol* and fashioned into the Turkish language were: *pandispanya* from *pan de España*, a sponge cake Sephardis brought from Spain; *fasulya* from *faséoles*, French beans; *pantalón* for pants; *caket* from *jaqueta*; *baul* from *baúl*, trunk in Spanish, etc. These words were foreign in the original Turkic language brought by the Turks from Central Asia.

During Mordehay's lecturing the two brothers and their girl-friends where busy whispering and teasing each other quietly. When Clara asked Sabetay to recite the blessings, experienced in how long it took Sabetay to go through them, Joseph begged him to be reasonable. Sabetay didn't argue this time; he, too, was famished. Clara returned from the kitchen and cut the first large wedge of the tart and placed it in front of Sabetay. She said to him: "You may start eating, my son, you don't have to wait until I serve the others."

As Clara began serving the others, Sabetay was eating hurriedly and with a mouth full he said: "This is delicious Mamaritta!" Before finishing his first course he asked to know what the main dish was. Somewhat embarrassed at his brashness in front of company, his father politely asked him to wait until everyone finished with the tart. But Clara answer him anyway:

"I cooked special *barbunya con salsa y avicas*. Figuring you might break fast this afternoon, your father bought fresh red mullets early in the day and sent them with one of his employees. I cooked the fish with beans in a tomato sauce. I also cooked *pasteles de carne* (ground meat tarts). Be happy my boy; eat all you want to your heart's content." As she said that she remebered an appropriate proverb: "*Shabat sin pastel es como una madre sin ija* (Sabbath without pie is like a mother without a daughter.)" Then she added quickly: "I ought to know the meaning of this yearning for a daughter, living all these years with four men in the house."

The men didn't react to her comment, but the two girls nodded their heads in a gesture of sympathy and support.

Mordehay remembered suddenly he had something very important to ask Sabetay. He had been meaning to confer with him about a controversial conversation he had been having with his employer. "Son, I don't know how much attention you pay to world news. . . ." He had to stop in the middle of his sentence because his introductory beginning drew a loud laughter from the other two brothers. The apparent tease was unintended. It was general knowledge that Sabetay didn't dwell on such mundane activity as world news. Mordehay erased the sneer off his face and continued: "Why did I say that? Of course I know you don't. You don't read the newspaper nor frequent coffee shops. I thought maybe Moses Pinheiro or Isaac Silveira might have mentioned what I am about to tell you. Anyway, for some time now the major preoccupation of our weekly Jewish newspaper, *La Semana*, has been about the recent war of our nation with the Republic of Venice. This war has affected us in good and bad ways. Because Jews are excluded from the military, you might say that the good news is Jews have not been mobilized to go and fight. We have also benefited from the shift of trade from Constantinople and Salonica to our city. The newspaper writes that Europeans are getting tired of this unending war between Christians and Moslems. If you think about it, it has been off and on for nearly one hundred years, ever since the Turks conquered Byzantium, that clashes between religions brought armed conflicts. Now we read that Christians are also fighting each other over what the paper calls a Reformation. I don't know exactly what the conflict there is all about. The paper says that the average European is yearning desperately for freedom of religion and a betterment of world conditions." Mordehay stopped to get a mouthful of food. Eating his delicious mullets and dunking large pieces of bread into the sauce, Sabetay heard nothing that interested him yet. His father continued. "The most recent issue of our weekly paper has printed a story so fantastic that I thought you will be interested in hearing. True or false I want to ask you about it. It says that newspapers from many parts of Europe claim sightings of a messiah at various locations in the continent. As every reader, I suppose, I am curious to know how much truth there is in these reports. We Jews have been waiting for the messiah since the beginning of time. What surprises me even more is that these reports have not originated from Jews; Christians are spreading them. I had no idea they waited for a messiah. I always assumed that their messiah had come in the embodiment of Yeshua (Jesus). Why would they be waiting for him again? I don't understand it. . . ." He stopped to dwell on what he had just said and continued: "For that matter I don't understand why Jews wait for the messiah either, if it weren't because the good books say so. But then not long ago a Jew like Molho shows up declaring himself as the Son of God. Some people believed in him, others cursed him. Well, in the end he couldn't have been the messiah; could he? He ended up burned at the stake by Christians. This time the paper appears very serious about a messianic appearance. Have you read anything about this, Sabetay?"

Mordehay had more to say but he waited for a reaction from his son, before he mentioned that he had troubling conversations at the office with his employer, Rycaut, and also at the coffee shop with his friends. In particular, Rycaut, who was also a reporter for English newspapers, had been questioning him about the Jewish biblical understanding of the messiah and how Jewish prophecies related to these reports.

Sabetay didn't answer his question. He had plenty to say on the subject. Before he reacted he wanted to hear more details about what his father had read in *La Semana*, considered to be a reliable weekly paper. Waiting to be answered, Mordehay took a large morsel of bread, dunked it into the sauce, and managed to fit it into his hairy mouth without the slightest drip on his beard. He chewed and swallowed until he could speak again. Repeating his consternation he said: "What puzzles and stirs me at the same time, Son, is that Christians should be concerned with this topic. Didn't they have their messiah already? You are not answering me!"

From the other end of the table Joseph interrupted with a crude joke to be funny in front of his girlfriend. "Maybe they didn't like the first one," he blurted and laughed loudly. The rest of the family ignored him. The girlfriend bumped him sharply with her elbow reminding him to behave. That was when Sabetay felt he had to respond to keep the conversation serious. He asked: "Where does Señor Rycaut get his information?"

"From English papers. He tells me he is of the Puritan Christian faith. I didn't know there was such a faith, all I know is he is a Christian." He shrugged his shoulders in a gesture displaying ignorance. "To me a Christian is a Christian. I have been to his home frequently to talk about our business. Lately it seems all he

wants to talk about is the eminent coming of a messiah. How is it
that all of a sudden this subject has become as important or even
more important, I should say, than the war? Nothing of the sort
is being discussed in sermons at the synagogue. Yet, he seems to
leave no doubt that the messiah has already been born and lives
somewhere in the Ottoman Empire; but he doesn't know exactly
where. Do you know how vast this empire is? To find this messiah it would be like *buscar una aguja en un pajar* (searching for a
needle in a hay stack). He told me the blessed event could have
taken place anywhere from Central Europe to Asia Minor, the
Holy Land, and even North Africa. Sabetay! He seems to know a
lot about this. He confuses me even more when he says that proof
of the birth of this messiah had been predicted in the New Testament. Eventually, this messenger of God will make himself
known in the year 1666. Why don't Jews talk about that! It goes
to show how poorly informed I am about other religions. I have
always thought that the *mashiah* was strictly Jewish." This drew a
smile from Sabetay. "What is this New Testament anyway? . . ."
He paused in a confused state of mind and continued: "Oh! Yes,
he has asked me if Jews have a definite calendar date for his arrival? Is there any truth to all this? He appears to know more about
our bible than I know about his. I am totally confused. It is difficult for me to disbelieve him, for he is a very serious and well-edu-
cated person. In the time I have known him, he has never permitted himself to fantasize or fabricate stories . . ." He paused again
and concluded: "Heavens! If he is right about the date, we don't
have much time to prepare ourselves for the blessed event. When
I said this to him, he laughed and told me that many people in
England—you know he comes from England—are already preparing for the day, atoning and selling all their belongings. The last
time I visited him, he went to his desk and handed me copies of
published reports from England and Germany to read and reassure
myself. He insisted that I pass them on to you. He knows all about
your ordainment and your profound knowledge on religion. Sabetay,
don't keep me in the dark! You are constantly reading about religious matters; you must know the answers to all my questions."

Clara interrupted Mordehay's captive state of mind. She was concerned about Sabetay who had stopped eating his favorite meal. She said: "This is no time to discuss serious matters. Dear, put aside worldly news before the fish gets cold."

Eliyah and Joseph had finished the second course and wanted a serving of the tiny meat pies. They agreed with their mother and both said: "*Si, Papá! Básta!* (Yes, Father! Enough!)." That was when Mordehay resumed eating; but Sabetay was so engrossed in the topic that, for once, he found this mother's preoccupation with food very distracting. He wanted to hear more about the reports from England and Germany. He was about to ask his father about the reports but Clara, upon seeing her two other sons devouring the meat pies, said in a teasing voice: "Joseph! and you Eliyah! I want you to notice in front of company that I don't always serve chicken. I don't see any feathers on the fish, the meat pies, or on you for that matter. You could at least say something nice to me."

The girls had no idea what she meant, assuming Clara was begging for a compliment they said: "It is delicious Señora Sevi." Eliyah's girlfriend added: "This is the first time I ate mullets prepared this way. It is delicious."

Clara waited to hear the same from Joseph and Eliyah but Sabetay responded: "Mamaritta! You prepared a very fine supper. I love it, and I also love your chicken too." Holding a morsel of bread ready to dunk into the rich sauce, interested Sabetay turned to his father calmly and said: "Do you have them, here?"

The question went unnoticed. No one understood what he was referring to. While his brothers enjoyed their little pies, Clara assured them: "Boys! There is plenty of fish or pies. You don't have to eat so fast." She had heard Sabetay's question. She turned her face towards him and asked: "What is it you want to know if we have here, Son? Your father and brothers are more interested in their stomachs than in your question."

He gave his mother a loving smile, then turned his face to his father and elaborated. "Father, you were telling me about Señor Rycaut's papers, then suddenly you stopped."

Mordehay, busy cleaning the bones of his second mullet remembered that he had not finished retelling his conversation with Rycaut. "What was it that I said about those papers?"

"I believe you spoke of published English and German reports that Señor Rycaut gave you. Didn't you?"

"Oh, yes. Rycaut had a German report translated into English. I read both reports, not very carefully I might add, for they appeared to me to be strange and far fetched. They seem to be the kind of fictional stories written to inject suspense and horror. They fail to make sense to me. I brought them for you to read. They speak of a town in the empire were the messiah was born, a town whose name I don't even recognize. I am not as educated as you are to verify if this town exists or not." He shoved into his mouth half of the mullet filet he had been stripping and he was barely able to speak: "And this brings me to another point I wanted to make. Señor Rycaut is pressing me for a reaction to the contents of the reports. He wants a Jewish reaction, he says. He wants to know how the expected event of our messiah differs from what is written in the reports. I forgot to tell you, he is not only the English Consul General and trade representative in Smyrna, he is also a journalist reporting regularly to English news agencies about aspects of Turkish life and politics. English publishers are pressing him for a comprehensive article on Sephardi beliefs about the coming of the messiah. He surprised me when he said Jews predict the same event to take place at a slightly different date than 1666. I didn't know that! And how would he know this? Is it true? If it is true, then because there are two different dates we must expect a Jewish and Christian messiah." He let out a forced laughter after that sentence and said: "Now I told you everything I know."

He looked at his son's plate and saw the mullets were untouched. He ordered: "You haven't touched your fish, Sabetay!" In a joking mood he added: "I hope I didn't spoil your appetite. I want to see you dig into your meal. You need sustenance after a long fasting. Anyway, Rycaut won't be questioning me until this coming week. We have time. I want you to help me. I haven't the faintest idea what to tell him. Could you read the articles and return them to me by Sunday morning? Give me your thoughts and I will pass them to him. I think he will be pleased about that."

The truth of the matter was, Rycaut had given him the articles with the explicit instruction for his rabbi son to read and give his expert opinion. Mordehay put it differently because he didn't want to appear as if he was just a messenger. It seemed strange to Sabetay that people thousands of miles away would have similar premonitions as he had been having, a feeling that a divine revelation was about to be announced. The conviction he harbored about the imminence of the messiah didn't come from hearsay or his father's story. He had felt it recently within himself. His faith, his knowledge of the Scriptures, and particularly the *Zohar*, reinforced the written warnings that strange things were to happen before the messiah's revelation. Then there were those mysterious and miraculous events he had been observing lately in his life and had attributed to heavenly messages trying to link him with a divine force. He had been attempting so hard in his prayers and meditations to seek that linkage and be able to understand clearly what those divine messages meant. The news his father brought pleased him but didn't exactly surprise him. Now he was anxious to read what others thought of the divine redemption. He couldn't wait to finish his supper and withdraw to his room where he would spend the evening examining the foreign reports. Sabbath began at six that evening and his religion forbid lighting a candle after that hour. He ate the rest of his meal in a hurry without enjoyment.

He excused himself, much to the chagrin of his mother. He took the reports from his father, apologized to the guests, and retired to his room saying it had been a difficult week and he needed rest. He went upstairs and locked his door. His bookshelves and work table filled most of the space in the room. The austere but freshly made up single bed occupied a small corner. Once a week, on Fridays, his mother cleaned his room, changed his sheets, and made the bed. The rest of the days he left his bed unmade. An hour of sunlight still remained. The bed was so inviting he undressed quickly, crawled under the freshly pressed sheets with the two reports and an English-Hebrew dictionary in his hands. He chose to read first the paper written by a Protestant minister in Nuremberg, Germany, dated September 24, 1642. The translation into English at the Consulate was hand written in beautiful calligraphy. He leaned back on his plush pillow and began to read:

> "Our ambassador from Constantinople writes about a new messiah born to a Jewess in the Turkish town of Ossa. He has conquered many cities, among them Aleppo in Syria and Alexandria in Egypt. . . . To the king of Persia, he sent his sword, implying he should deliver his kingdom to him on his free will. He sent another sword to the Turkish emperor in Constantinople demanding that he deliver to him Jerusalem and Damascus. He declared both kingdoms as his for he is of the seed of the kings of Judah. The Sultan was greatly perturbed and is said to plan to move his capital to Mecca . . . . He calls himself Joshua El Kam, the God of heaven and earth. His mother's name is Gamaritta[3]. . . ."

Stunned as he read that name, he stopped and reread the name of the reported messiah's mother. How strange, he thought: except for the first letter 'G' it was exactly the nickname he had given his mother. His endearing way of addressing his mother couldn't have been known to the outside world. He focused outside the window with dreamy eyes at the lowering sun, asking himself was this a coincidence or another divine message with providential import? Did this revelation apply to him? Was this another clue originating from heaven and whose specific meaning was to be taken suggestively. From the day he entered the rabbinical studies he had become impressed by so many miracles in the bible. He formed a general notion that God spoke to every human being, not just to prophets and patriarchs. The reason why most people didn't hear the voice of the Creator was because they lacked the purity of soul that made them sensitized to His words and actions. As he read

---

3. From Buchenroeder's *Eilende Messias Juden-Post*, Nuremberg, 1666, quoted by Scholem.

this first paragraph in the German report a hint of his mother's name appeared as the mother of a messiah **born in Turkey**. Eager for more discoveries, he returned to reading.

".... His mother's name is Gamaritta, a beautiful woman not of noble descent. The day he was born the sun became dark in the middle of the day.... A mighty voice was heard miles away calling out: 'Repent ye sons of men, for today the messiah was born'. Many fiery dragons and devils were seen in the air. On the eighth day after birth he was circumcised ... and he began to speak. He says he is the son of God, God, and the true messiah. His birth was a marvel, for a few months later he grewn into the stature of a young man of twenty-four or twenty-five.... He has a thick neck and a pointed head. His face is like that of a Turk. His brow is wrinkled, his eyes terrible, his ears long, his genital organ big, and his teeth are sharp. Those who refused to obey him fell down and died on the spot.... Reports tell us that he raised the dead, and healed the sick just by his look.... He plans to conquer the whole world and make all the kings his servants. Those who believe in him receive in return kingdoms and distinctions.... He has chosen twelve apostles who preach that only in his name is eternal life. They condemn the state of matrimony. He has about four hundred wives and owns seven hundred virgins.... Fifty thousand Jews from around the world have joined him and he has provided them with weapons. He has already conquered Damascus, killing the inhabitants that refused to believe in him...."

He stopped this time just before the last paragraph and frowned in disbelief. He found this description of the messiah by the Protestant minister far-fetched as his father claimed. This was not the way he envisaged him to look or act, nor did it correspond to the descriptions by Maïmonides, the *Zohar*, the Talmud, or the Mishnah. How can a God-loving person in his right mind accept the holy messiah to have four hundred wives and seven hundred virgins? That description was more of a monster than a heavenly being. The accounts sounded more like a horror story than a news chronicle. None of its details fitted the Hebrew concept. Disgusted, he rejected the Nuremberg report and concluded the writer must have had a wild imagination or, more likely, the mind of a pervert. He read quickly the final paragraph.

"All Christians should take this revelation to their hearts and begin repenting, for it is evident that the end of all flesh is not far away, and that he is the Antichrist prophesied by Daniel, John, and Paul in their epistles."

This was the only part in the article that seemed credible because it was taken from the New Testament. Sabetay was familiar with the prophecies of Daniel and St. John but he had never heard nor read one by St. Paul. He wondered if the minister got mixed up in his references. Except for the surprising mention of the misspelled name of his mother there was nothing else trustworthy. He put it away. Anxious about what the English article said, he picked it up. He recognized the author's name for he was a prolific writer on a diversity of subjects from agriculture to religion. His name was John Evelyn. The information for his articles was provided by correspondents in every important city of the world. They fed him reports on a regular basis on unusual subjects which he rewrote in his own provocative style for a wide English readership. Sabetay fluffed up his pillow, pushed his body backwards and leaned towards the light. He hoped this one would be more serious and in harmony with accepted biblical concepts.

"According to the Predictions of several Christian Writers, especially of such who Comment on the Apocalypse, or Revelations, the year 1666 is to prove a Year of Wonders, of strange Revolutions in the World, and particularly of Blessing to the Jewes, either in respect of their Conversion to the Christian Faith, or of their Restoration to their Temporal kingdome: this Opinion was so dilated, and fixt in the Countreys of the Reformed Religion, and in the Heads of Phanatical Enthusiasts, who Dreamed of a Fifth[4] Monarchy, the downfall of the Pope, and Antichrist, and the Greatness of the Jewes: In so much, that this subtile People judged this Year the time to stir,

---

4. This was the kingdom of the saints which would succeed the four kingdoms of the four beasts in the Book of Daniel.

and to fit their Motion according to the season of the Modern Prophecies; whereupon strange Reports flew from place to place, of the March of Multitudes of People from unknown parts into the remote Deserts of Arabia, supposed to be the Ten Tribes and halfe,[5] lost for so many Ages. That a Ship has arrived in the Northern parts of Scotland with her Sailes and Cordage of Silke, Navigated by Mariners who spoke nothing but Hebrew; with this Motto on their Sailes, The Twelve Tribes of Israel. These Reportes, agreeing thus near the former Predictions, put the World into an expectation of strange Accidents, this year should produce in reference to the Jewish Monarchy.

In this manner Millions of People are possessed when a Messiah publishes himself to the Jewes, relating the greatness of their approaching Kingdome, the strong hand whereby God was about to deliver them from Bondage, and gather them from all partes of the World. . . ."

"This is more like it," Sabetay said, excited with what he read. Evelyn's article was quite long. It went on explaining the nature of St. John's prophecy. He was familiar with that prophecy; his liberal teacher Rabbi Escapha insisted his students read and discuss parts of the New Testament, in particular John's prophecy in the Book of Revelation, because it borrowed its concept from the Book of Daniel in the Old Testament. Also, Moses Pinheiro had an uncle in the famous cabalistic school in Livorno, Italy, who maintained contact with leaders of the Protestant churches in Holland and Germany. Because Moses Pinheiro was studying to be a rabbi, his uncle kept him abreast of his extra-religious activities. Encouraged by what he read in Evelyn's article, Sabetay looked out the window to ponder and review in his mind some of these notions on the Christian prophecy.

The Reformation movements which had sprung in many cities of Europe from within Catholicism was only a century old. Mar-

---

5. J. Evelyn, *The History of the Three Late Famous Imposters* (Savoy, London, 1669). Spelling, grammar, and the indiscriminate use of capital letters are reproduced as they appeared in the original text of the seventeenth century.

tin Luther, considered the father of the Reformation, posted in 1517 on the door of the Wittenberg Castle Church his 95 Theses of theological disagreements with the Church. Since then many Protestant movements, striving for religious and moral freedom, denied by the autocratic Catholic Church, manifested themselves as revolutionary changes within Christianity, then known as Catholicism. There were a number of such revolts with different objectives and under different leaderships, yet all rejecting the strict dogmatic interpretation of Christianity by the Holy See. They went seeking Hebrew and Greek Scriptures as a truer source of Christian religiosity. With it came an estrangement from a total dependence on the New Testament. They sought a balanced wisdom that included the New and Old Testaments. To this point in history the Old Testament had been the sole bible of the Jews.

One of the consequences that surged from the Reformation was the revival of the old prophecy of the *millennium* and a presumed date when the messiah would appear. During the early days of Catholicism the messianic advent was very much a part of the Christian credo, but in the fifth century the Church, feeling itself powerful and prosperous, condemned the use of mystical interpretations of the New Testament. The *millennium* notion was declared to be an old Jewish invention, even though the Book of Revelation, the last canonical book of the New Testament attributed to St. John, contained such a prophecy. St. Augustine was responsible for propounding this ban, recommending that the Church take an official position declaring the writings in the Book of Revelation merely as a spiritual allegory, and insisted that the *millennium* began with the birth of Christianity and was fully realized by the founding of the most powerful Church on earth. In spite of this, the utopian concept of the messiah remained very popular among the poor and the dejected who found themselves outside the realm of the success and prosperity the Church claimed. For Jews and Christians alike the *millennium* idea meant the same thing: that a messenger of God, or God himself, will come upon the earth a thousand years (millennium) after a reference date or event fixed, *a priori*, in biblical times. While the meaning of *millennium* was clear and precise, the reference date from which to count one thousand years was vague and dependent on a variety of convoluted interpretations and prophecies, thereby generating strong controversies among biblical scholars. Of great interest to Judaism was that Protestants believed and defended in public the right of the Jews to proclaim the restoration of the kingdom of Israel. Many Protestant clergy began to establish contact with local Jewish scholars, and that was how Moses Pinheiro's uncle had been sought in that respect by these New-Christian leaders.

At this point in his thinking Sabetay smiled as his thoughts turned to Moses Pinheiro, who argued strongly that the Reformation was the historical event most friendly to Judaism. He used for a metaphoric argument that the Reformation was the 'pin which someday would deflate the bag of antagonism' between Judaism and Catholicism. Sabetay hadn't agreed with that forecast. He had laughed at Moses' naivete. His response was: "Just because someone is an enemy of our enemy, it doesn't make him our friend." As these thoughts crossed Sabetay's mind he noticed that at the bottom of Evelyn's article was a hand written note he thought must have been put there by Paul Rycaut. He presumed it was to attract his father's attention to the level of interest people in England were all worked up about the coming of the messiah. The note read:

> There are many English sportsmen, including myself, who actually have placed bets that the messiah would be crowned King of Jerusalem in the next twenty years. The lesser the years for his appearance the higher the odds. In any case, that the event will take place is not in doubt, the only uncertainty is the accuracy the English bookies placed on the odds.

The two articles added fuel to the fire already burning inside Sabetay, a fire he had kindled steadily through the years and which lately grew in intensity. He believed that the hand of God had been searching for a wise and pious Son to save Israel from misery, sin, and bondage. For the first time, the two foreign articles demonstrated he hadn't been alone in his belief.

The sun was about to set. He got out of bed and placed the papers on his work table. He lit the candle in his silver candle holder and walked towards the book shelves. He searched for a personal notebook in which he had written important but scattered fragments of thoughts and ideas. He pulled it out and returned to his bed. He placed the candle on his night table, opened the notebook, and searched for a section in which to enter his thoughts of the moment. The section of the notebook he opened was entitled *chilias*, written in Greek characters to elude the curiosity of someone accidentally stumbling into it. The Greek word meant thousand or millennium. He flipped the first page, and saw an entry with a Hebrew date: 9th of Av 5386. He stared at the date reminiscing his original intent for writing it. It was his birth date. There was an important reason why it belonged in this part of the notebook. In that date there was a hidden meaning he had discovered and wished he had the courage to share it with others. He feared they would mistakenly ridicule his understanding of it. Besides, he didn't need reassuring proof about its importance. The proof had already been revealed years ago in the *Zohar*. The trouble was not many people understood the wisdom in those scholarly volumes. They were full of revelations about the Creator, His universe, His relationship to man, and of course the messiah. He believed that many rabbis claiming to have reached distinction were among the ignorants about the *Zohar*. Sabetay considered these books the key to holiness and to comprehending God's magnificent kingdom.

His anniversary day, the 9th of Av, of the Hebrew year corresponded exactly to the day prophesied in the *Zohar* and other biblical literature to be the blessed day when the messiah would be born to mankind. This prophecy had been carefully studied by cabalistic scholars. It was unequivocally resolved that it corresponded also to the anniversary of the destruction of King Solomon's Temple in Jerusalem by Nabuchadnezzar in 586 B.C.E. Subsequently, Jews rebuilt the temple, but, it was destroyed again by Romans on the very same day of the month in the year 70 C.E. The prophecy fixed the arrival of the messiah to that day, but the exact year was secretly coded in the *Zohar*. There were many such coded examples on how to decipher this blessed year. If one learned the code, then one would discover the blessed year to be the 408th year of the sixth Hebrew[6] millennium or the Hebrew year 5408. In the Gregorian calendar it corresponds to the year 1648, just four years away.

Cabalists learned to believe that ancient biblical writers were in the habit of coding secret messages in their writings. The code they used was a form of a rabbinical arithmetic called *gematria*. In Hebrew there are no special characters for numbers, letters of the alphabet are used for numerical values. Thus, all words made up of letters of the alphabet also have numerical values equal to the sum of the values of its letters. Sabetay had recorded in his notebook a few codified examples from the *Zohar* pertaining to the year of the messiah. One such example hiding the blessed year was in the biblical statement: *they that lie in the dust will arise*. Anyone familiar with biblical prophecies knew that one of the duties of the messiah was to resurrect the dead, called the sons of Heth. If one added up the letter of this paraphrased biblical statement the sum adds up to 408. His conclusion was that the 408th year of the sixth millennium, or 5408 (1648) had to be the date.

Countless of times he had performed these calculations. His conviction wasn't exclusively based on the word of the *Zohar*. He had his own findings from the Bible. One such discovery was a sentence in the Book of Leviticus: *"this year of Jubilee ye shall return every man to his possession."* The first word[7] in that sentence 'this',

---

6. The Hebrew New Year falls around the autumnal equinox. Most of the year it precedes the Gregorian year by 3760 years. The Hebrew month of Av falls around August. The days of the year in the two calendars don't always coincide because the Gregorian calendar runs strictly according to the solar cycle while the Hebrew calendar follows a complicated arrangement of lunar and solar cycles. The Hebrew calendar is said to begin with creation, six millennia earlier.

7. J. Kastein.

in Hebrew, had the numerical value of 408 too. This was more revealing to him than the preceding example because the year of Jubilee was known to be the year of redemption and unification in the Holy Land. Moreover, man's only real possession being his soul, the year 408 of the current Hebrew millennium, men had to return to their Creator with just their souls. Each time he read this passage blood rushed to his head from the excitement. Amazing! he said to himself, how clear the meaning and message in that sentence was! A little further in his notebook he discovered an entry of three of the most frequently occurring words in the Scriptures: prayer, penitence, and charity, all being paramount attributes for the fulfillment of redemption; all had the numerical value of 408.[8] Satisfied, he turned to other pages with many such examples, pointing to the same date! He leaned back on his pillow and let his thoughts flow freely. How could anyone in his right mind dispute these facts as coincidences? One had to be totally blind at heart to deny that truth. The current Gregorian year was 1645 and this meant only three short years remained to 'the year of Jubilee.' He had known of this for some time. The paramount reason why he insisted on his swift ordainment was obvious. In those remaining years when God decided to contact an earthly man, He would look for a man of God, most assuredly a man who knew His laws, a rabbi like him. He shivered and felt a sense of urgency that the world had much to do in preparation for the event.

The Christian date of 1666 mentioned in the Book of Revelation and in Evelyn's article was not derived from direct Hebrew sources nor did it have the same significance. For Christians it was the date prophesied for the *Second Coming* of Christ to establish a messianic kingdom on earth. That date was revealed by early Christian mystics from *gematria*, too. But the logic of that numerology was found to be faulty by Sabetay. He had recorded the steps of that computation somewhere in his notebook. Just

---

8. See Scholem p. 93.

as he was about to search for it the candle had consumed itself. Feeling very tired and now in the dark he folded the notebook and placed it on his table. He slipped entirely under the covers and, before falling asleep, tried to visualize how this elected messenger of God would know who he is and how he would reveal himself. He attempted to imagine the process, but out of reverence for his Creator he stopped and rationalized that it was not up to him to meddle in God's business. God had his ways, incomprehensible as they were to men. He smiled and murmured the words: "Incomprehensible indeed!" remembering that he had just experienced a miracle: his ordainment at the age of eighteen.

He closed his eyes but couldn't fall asleep. The thoughts of the evening had stirred him profoundly. He couldn't shake the anxiety and apprehension from wanting to know who would be the fortunate one to be summoned for the divine task. Would it be he? Would the spirit of God be revealed to him as clearly as it had to prophets in the Bible? He yearned deeply for the unique privilege of making a covenant with his Creator. He was ready to receive authority and guidance to lead his people to redemption and ultimately reunification in the Holy Land. Concerned about the awesomeness of his desire, he questioned if he was sufficiently pure and holy to be so presumptuous. There had to be other men in the world seeking the same glorious assignment. Did he really lack the personal attributes to win that trust, as Escapha reprimanded him? His teacher had referred only to qualities for a parish rabbi. So be it! He accepted that! All these years of intensive learning just to be a parish rabbi! It made no sense to him. He could never be satisfied with such a mundane preoccupation. Without further nourishment, the knowledge acquired at the yeshiva would most certainly go stale! His earnest desire was to enter the secret realms of spirituality unraveling the realm of the soul which decides between reason and feeling, between fortitude and intuition, between knowledge and emotion, and ultimately, between belief and faith! Old patriarchs succeeded at that, and for that reason they became harvesters of the human soul. Convinced of the path he had chosen for himself, he closed his eyes and fell into a sound sleep.

ॐ

Monday morning, before going to work, Mordehay woke Sabetay out of a sound sleep. "Sabetay, I am sorry to do this to you but it is time for me to go to work. I want to know your thoughts on the papers I gave you to read. I didn't press you last night but today it will be the first thing Rycaut will ask me when he comes to work. If he doesn't come this morning, for sure he will ask me tonight as I am invited for supper at his house to discuss business. I have a hunch we will not be talking business. He will drill me mercilessly about the Jewish viewpoint on the contents of the papers. I need you to give me some ideas on what to say. I will look terribly uninformed and embarrassed otherwise. I know this because he has to write back to England about the Sephardi point of view on the messiah."

Sabetay stumbled out of bed rubbing his eyes and moistened his lips with his tongue. "Father, let me wash my face and I will meet you downstairs." A few minutes later he came down in his house robe. His face was washed and his hair under his scull cap was brushed. His short beard was also brushed around his chin. Sabetay still had no idea what Rycaut wanted to know. He was ready to brief his father in general terms about his views on the two articles. Beyond that, he had to be asked explicitly what else they wanted to know. The topic of the messiah was voluminous in Judaism. He sat in the living room facing his father. Clara brought a tray of hot tea and a few pastries with the intent and hope her son would forget about fasting and eat.

"Yes, I read the two articles. Since I have no idea what you want to know, here is my general assessment. The German article is totally void of credibility and it is downright crude and sacrilegious. The author's description of the messiah is wild and raw to say the least. Since God created man in his own image why in heaven's name is the messiah portrayed as a monster I will never know. That writing is trash and should be discarded entirely. Besides, proof of the unworthiness of the German article is in the fact that there is no town in Asia Minor named Ossa. I consulted the atlas and I conclude that this birth place of the messiah is a total fabrication, like the rest of the paper. The English article makes a lot of sense for Christians and even some sense for Jews. I have to review the writings of St. John in the New Testament to confirm what is my current understanding of the date suggested in the Book of Revelation. You may say all this to Señor Rycaut if you like."

Actually he knew the wording of that prophecy and the process by which the date 1666 was arrived at. The New Testament was not exactly reading material for aspiring rabbis, but in Escapha's classes they had discussed the prophecy about the coming of the Christian messiah. Escapha wanted his students to compare and analyze the wording in the New Testament with the literal wording in the Book of Daniel. The assignment had intrigued Sabetay who made a point to dwell on the subject very deeply, so much so that Escapha congratulated him for his fine analysis. He stopped waiting for his father's reaction. Surprised by the superficial account his son gave him, Mordehay said in astonishment: "That's it? Is that all you have to tell me? Rycaut probably knows this much or more. Really Son, I will be going empty handed. He will be asking me the Hebrew interpretation of many messianic concepts, including our prophesied date of the messiah. What is the official Judaic position on this? You have to give me more, Sabetay! You have to tell me much more. You can't let me go like this!"

Sabetay didn't care to dwell further in what was an irreconcilable debate between Christians and Jews. He answered: "There is no official Judaic position, Father. In fact the old conservative rabbis, who claim to be the final authority on Judaism, don't read anything beyond the daily prayer book. They are too busy enforcing old policies. Not only do they remain silent and insensitive about messianic questions, they forbid the lay people to read enlightening books on the subject like the *Zohar*."

"For heavens sakes, Son, then tell me what the *Zohar* says!"

He realized his father wouldn't be satisfied as easily as he had hoped. "You are suddenly interested in the *Zohar* and you never

asked me these questions before. You have to be specific," said
Sabetay.

"I have a good reason to ask now. I told you, my *patron* (boss)
wants to know. I owe him a lot. If it weren't for him I would have
remained a poulterer all my life. We would have been living in
misery in that small and dilapidated house. You seem to have
forgotten this! You should feel indebted to him as well. He doesn't
ask much of me and I feel I want to live up to any favor he asks of
me. Señor Rycaut is not Jewish. I think I told you this. He is of
the Puritan faith and his correligionists are the ones spreading
prophesies in England about the messiah being expected in 1666.
I asked him what kind of religion the Puritan faith was. He said it
was a new faith that emerged in England following the Reformation. I don't know what that means, but he surprised me when he
said they accept our Bible as well as the New Testament." He
paused for a moment thinking he had answered one important
question: "Come to think of it, if they read our Scriptures why is
it they can't find out for themselves what the Jews believe about
the messiah?"

Sabetay laughed at his father's simplistic reasoning, and responded: "Father, the Old or New Testaments write nothing about
a clearly legible date. No matter how progressive the Puritans may
be, I suspect they don't read cabalistic writings. That's where the
full and precise logic concerning the prophecy and its date can
be found."

Mordehay understood and said: "Then, begin by telling me what
the *Zohar* says: concept, logic of the prophecy, date, etc. For
Heaven's sake, Rycaut will ask me all this."

"First, you must explain how it is that Hebrew scholars rely in
the prophecies of the *Zohar*. The prophecy about a date is not
written as you and I would write it. It must be deciphered from
hidden meanings of the patriarchal writings. The year of Jubilee
for us is not 1666; it is 1648." Mordehay's eyes opened wide as
his son continued: "To be exact it is the 408th year of the sixth
millennium which is our current millennium. The chiliastic concept of an ultimate salvation of man is not utopian in the sense of

a dream as some Christian scholars would like you to believe, nor is it an invention of the Christians. . . ."

He was interrupted: "Sabetay stop using these fancy words! I don't know what they mean."

"You see Father, the subject of divinity is not simple as you like me to make it. Some scholars believe the dates I gave you are of the messiah's birth date, others like me read deeper into hidden meanings in the *Zohar* and discover they represent the dates he will reveal himself. Considering that messianic prophecies were made a millennium or two before, bickering on the exactness of the date for a difference of eighteen years seems to me to be senseless. You may tell Señor Rycaut that I find myself disagreeing with the Christian concept not necessarily because of the date but because of the purpose and mission they have chosen for the messiah. I will explain this shortly. But now I want you to take with you and read a short exposé on the Jewish concept of the personality of the messiah."

He rushed upstairs to his room, facing his shelves he pulled out a reprint of a book in Hebrew entitled *Moreh Nebukim Dalalat al-Hairin* (Guide to the Perplexed) by the twelfth century Sephardi scholar Rabbi Moses Maimonides. The binding was in pretty bad shape, revealing frequent usage of the reference. He straightened out the few loose pages and, before going downstairs, he thought of a second book that was relevant to the question. This was a book about Isaac Luria Esquenazi, in his opinion the greatest of all cabalists from Safed, written by his student in early 1600 and printed for the first time in 1629. He pulled it out and went downstairs. Before handing the Maimonides' book he said: "This is easy reading and short. Read chapters eleven and twelve and you will find that Maimonides' description of the messiah is very low key. He says he would come as a man like any other man, even to a point that he may go unnoticed by many. Maimonides warns us with a sentence which has remained printed in my memory." He was going to open the book and read it but after what he just said, he handed the book to his father and recited it from memory:

And do not think that in the days of the messiah there will be any departure from the normal course of things or any change in the cosmic order.

"You see what I mean, Father? Now, this second book gives more details and substance to his personality. Remember, Father, one has to read a lot to get true meanings because modern cabalists contend that all notions depend on each other, and no concept can be explained without probing into their related notions. I am just going to quote what the book says about the messiah." There was a bookmark already at that page which he opened.

> . . . a righteous man, born of a man and woman, and he will grow in righteousness until the end of days. . . . On the day appointed as the end, the soul light which was preserved in Paradise will be given to him and he will become the Redeemer. . . . He will awake with an infusion of prophetic powers and arise from his sleep . . . and he will recognize himself as the messiah. . . . As Moses ascended to heaven in body and soul and remained there for forty days, so this messiah will remain unknown to others . . . until the day he will reveal himself fully and all Israel will recognize him and gather around him.[9]

"You see, Father, the Jewish image of the Redeemer is more human and compassionate. His appearance will not be as bombastic, flamboyant, or as garish as the Nuremberg paper described. I forgot to mention that the reference to the Ten Tribes of Israel in the English paper were descendants of the twelve sons of Jacob. They had been led into captivity by Shalmaneser the king of Assyria in 850 B.C.E. and have not been found to this day. The fate of these tribes has obsessed Jewry ever since, so much so that their discovery is intrinsically tied to that of the coming of the messiah. They have become for us as important as the messiah himself. Why? How could this sizable population of ancestors, whose destiny was declared to be eternal, disappear without leaving a trace? Off and on

---

9. R. L. Weiss & C. Butterworth, eds. *Ethical Writings of Maimonides* (Dover, New York, 1975).

in our history there has been unsubstantiated reports that some-one has been in touch with one of the tribes or the other.

"There is one major point I have deferred mentioning. I waited to speak about it last. It is a major point of disagreement between Jews and Christians. For them the appearance of the Redeemer will be *the Second Coming*. For us it is the first. They believe Yeshua (Jesus) was a messiah whose advent became his *First Coming*. As you know he died as a martyr in the hands of evil forces and without being able to save mankind from sin and corruption. This is an important concept for them. Inspired by the prophe-cies of Daniel claiming a second coming, they await Jesus a sec-ond time; this time as a victor over evil. Jews have not recognized Jesus as having been divinely anointed for a messianic mission."

After answering a few more questions Sabetay ended by saying:

"You may keep Maimonides' book for a while. Read and quote as I did. The other book is too profound and I am not sure Rycaut would be interested in such exclusively cabalistic points of view. That is all you need to satisfy his interest and curiosity."

Now Mordehay felt gratified. He had something substantive to report. He thanked his son and bid him a good day. Sabetay went up to his room, put on his phylacteries and prayer shawl and began his morning prayers.

5

ر

$\mathcal{M}$ordehay left his house happy and ready to fulfill his promise to Rycaut. Most Sephardis didn't like their families socializing outside their clan. This general reluctance was also shared by Mohammedans; not on account of religious bigotry but because of their cultural disparities. In the Turkish culture the female was never allowed to display her face outside her own family. Europeans accepted the custom but failed to understand why Sephardis, who in many respects acted in western traditions, chose not to socialize outside their own group. Accordingly Rycaut never invited to his house the Sevi family when Mordehay came to discuss business. But unlike the Ottoman Turks, Sephardis were well informed about current events in Europe even though the empire was culturally isolated from the rest of Europe. Sephardis considered themselves Europeans.

But the details of the enormous religious reforms in Europe brought by the Reformation in the past one hundred years was not well known to most Jews. Those who were informed considered the schism in Christianity to have little or no importance to Judaism. They believed that Christianity by a different name remained just as antagonistic to their faith. However, the Puritans in England, searching for a new morality and spirituality found themselves driven towards a devotion rooted in personal betterment in the eyes of the Lord. They were drawn away from the autocratic rule of the Popes and towards the Old Testament, even though the latter remained unauthorized or of little significance to Catholicism. The bible became for the Puritans the moral code of conduct as it had been for Jews all through the ages. Every act and facet of life was found to have a divine meaning in the Good Books, so much so that they regarded themselves as personalities in the Book of Judges; as such they dedicated themselves to save the oppressed. For centuries England had been unkind to Jews and mistrustful of them. The Puritans changed all that. They advocated openly the use of the Torah as their code of law. In fact, their leader, Oliver Cromwell, was urged to make the Puritan point of view known to the British Parliament. In one of his speeches to Parliament Cromwell said[1]:

> When they tell us, not that we are to regulate the law, but that the law is to be abrogated and subverted and perhaps wish to bring in Judaical law instead of our known laws settled among us, this is worthy of every magistrate's consideration.

This new shift in religiosity became the reason Englishmen, including Rycaut, were so much interested in the Jewish concept of religious ideals. Rycaut was not the only foreign correspondent in Asia Minor reporting on Judaism to European readers. The Dutch and the French had taken similar interest, but Rycaut felt privileged to have the Sevis as friends and as a direct source of information. The Dutchman Thomas Coenen and the French Chevalier de la Croix had to search hard to find willing sources for Jewish news, and often reported dubious findings from uninformed Sephardis.

Mordehay was at Rycaut's doorstep for dinner on Monday evening. The reason he had accepted the dinner invitation to a non-Jewish home was that the entire dinner would be prepared and cooked by a Jewish caterer, delivered and served in kosher plates. His host waited for him with great anticipation for he was to bring from his son important clarifications on the subject of

---

1. *The Messiah of Ismir*, Joseph Kastein p. 32, (see Acknowledgment).

the messiah. "Mr. Sevi welcome! I am happy to see you. Come in and make yourself at home. How is the family?" he asked with a smile, pulling Mordehay by the hand he kept shaking.

"Fine. Very fine. Thank you," answered Mordehay, overwhelmed by the friendliness.

The butler waited by the door. Mordehay handed him his white rain caftan, and after removing his overcoat, gave it to the butler.

"Perhaps you wish to remove your turban," said Rycaut.

Mordehay always wore a scull cap under a headdress foreigners mistook for a turban.[2] Sephardis were uncomfortable when anyone referred to their headdress as a turban. In the local language to wear a turban meant literally conversion to Islam. Rycaut wasn't familiar with that subtle metaphor, and Mordehay didn't take time to explain. He removed his headdress and they walked to the ornate drawing room decorated with superb Turkish furnishings. The canapes and chairs were designed low to the ground. A long hammered copper with leather top table sat in front of the oriental couch. Brass oil lamps and chandeliers hung all around the room, and mother of pearl inlaid end tables and knickknacks blended perfectly with the artistic beauty of a magnificent Sparta carpet on the marble floor. Rooms in a Turkish mansion did not have doors. They were parts of the house separated by open arches and half-walls. This gave a sense of depth and intimacy from every area in the house. Rycaut's family liked this oriental concept very much, except for the bedrooms. They had doors installed in them to feel as private as they would in England. Mordehay peaked into the adjoining dining room. The maid, her face covered with a veil, was putting the finishing touches on the dinner table. The

---

2. There was a definite distinction between the turban Moslems wore and a headdress worn by non-Moslem residents, even if it might have looked the same to Europeans. Both were shaped around the head from a scarf-like material. The nonsectarian headdress came in different colors and almost always was performed in the shape of a doughnut. The Moslem turban was always white signifying purity and was wrapped a special way to form nearly an inverted 'V' that sat low on the forehead.

two men sat in the luxurious living room and a few minutes later
the butler brought two glasses of scotch. He went back to the
kitchen and returned with a freshly prepared *nargileh* (water pipe)
and placed it next to Mordehay. Then, Rycaut lit his long and
arched western meerschaum pipe and picked up his whiskey glass
at the same time. Mordechay didn't pick up his glass.

"To your health Señor Sevi."

Mordehay responded likewise: *"Lehayim."*

It didn't take long for the incidental conversation to turn to
matters Mordehay expected. Rycaut was the first to ask: "Did you
have a chance to read the articles I gave you? Perhaps you spoke
to your son about them. I heard from an associate how wise and
scholarly your son must be for him to be ordained at eighteen.
You must be very proud of him. Who wouldn't be?"

Very flattered with Rycaut's compliment, Mordehay took a puff
of smoke from the gurgling water pipe and answered with a con-
tented smile on his face: "Indeed, I am very proud of him. Yes, I
spoke to him about the articles."

Anxious, Rycaut expected Mordehay to say more. He took a sip
of his scotch and pressed again: "As we enjoy our scotch and smok-
ing before dinner, would you care to appraise me on what he said?"

Mordehay felt confident that he was prepared to answer any
questions. While he held the flexible nozzle of the water pipe on
one hand, he had pulled out of his pocket his own mouth-piece
and fitted it at the end of the water pipe. He brought the mouth-
piece of the water pipe to his mouth, sucked a puff and exhaled,
producing a gurgling sound of water in the glass bowl of the water pipe. He detected the fine taste of the Persian tobacco burning slowly under the charcoal braises. He had practiced earlier
what he would say to his host:

"You see Señor Rycaut, from the beginning of time, my people
have depended on divine guidance through the intermediary of
prophets to whom God had revealed Himself. Most of these revelations seemed to occur during times of severe oppressions. From
the time Romans exiled Jews from the Holy Land, there have been
about two dozen men who, moved by a fervent faith in The Lord,

pronounced themselves messiahs. This was a promise our God in Heaven had made to us in the Scriptures. Unfortunately, they all became martyrs in trying to reunite my brethren dispersed in the Diasporas. In spite of their high qualities of piousness, devotion, and leadership they have not merited sufficient public confidence to be accepted as true messiahs. As a result, they were born mortals and they died as mortals."

Suddenly Mordehay felt the kind of feeling teachers must experience instructing their impressionable students. He sucked another puff, and in that interim of time Rycaut took the opportunity to question him on the last two sentences.

"Forgive me for interrupting. I am curious Señor Sevi. Are you including Jesus among the two dozen men you mentioned? If you are, then I understand why Christians remain skeptical of Jews ever accepting a Redeemer in the image of man. I don't mean this disrespectfully but it has been suggested that Jews are likely to mistrust God Himself if He came down in the body of a man. I beg you not to take my bluntness as an insult to your people, but this perception appears to be at the root of our religious differences. This is one of the few key issues my readers want to clarify. You said Jews have rejected every messianic candidate that came along, endowed with great wisdom and vision. In your opinion, Señor Sevi, would Jews ever accept a messiah? What special indicators and qualifications do you expect of him before he is accepted? Are there guidelines in Judaism to that effect? I am asking these delicate questions because my people want to know why your people have been stubborn at accepting our Lord Jesus Christ. There must be a defensible reason."

Mordehay didn't expect a jump so soon into a difficult question for which he had no answer. He was not a cultured man. Most of his life he had been a poor bread earner with little time to read beyond his prayer book and weekly newspaper. Oh, how he wished Sabetay was in the room to help him. He knew he couldn't satisfy Rycaut on that question about Jesus. He figured he should be honest about it and thus avoid mistaken opinions and generalizations that may open the door to other such questions. His ego somewhat deflated, he resolved to confine his statements to what Sabetay told him to say. He answered: "I don't know how to respond to that . . . !"

Restless, Rycaut pressed on: "What I meant to say was that during the past three centuries England had Wycliffe, Cranmer and Naylor as reformers, France had Lefèvre, Bohemia had Huss, Germany trusted Luther, Switzerland believed in Zwingli and Calvin, and Scotland in Knox. Each revealed himself a prophet or a messiah if you like. Each succeeded in leaving a lasting legacy in our Christian faith. I don't know of any such reformists in Jewish history. I think I am familiar with the men you had in mind, but what is astonishing to us Christians, is that none have been able to make an impression on Judaism. Beginning with Bar Kohba in 132 C.E. who lead a war against the Romans, then David Alroy in the twelfth century rising against the Persians, to Moses Botarel in Spain, to David Reubeni in Portugal one hundred years ago, and the latest, Solomon Molho in Greece, all have been proclaimed false messiahs in spite of their spiritual wisdom, profound faith, devotion to Judaism. Am I correct in this assessment Señor Sevi? I want to be sure and explain all this correctly to my readership."

Mordehay sensed he had inadvertently opened the door to an area of knowledge not familiar to him. He wanted to get back on track to what his son had briefed him. "I am not privileged to know all the answers relative to the history of messiahs. But my son told me that we weren't the only ones rejecting messianic candidates. Mr. Rycaut, early Christianity also had its rejected messiahs. Among them weren't Aldebert and Eons in France rejected?" He repeated once again: "We weren't the only ones," trying to figure out how he could stir the conversation to what he knew. "All I know is that our great sages[3] of the *Cabala* and the *Zohar* devoted

---

3. The study of mysticism in Judaism goes back to antiquity. Progressively these studies developed and evolved into collective works we now call: *The Book of Formation*, the *Cabala*, and most recently the *Zohar*. They are all said by A. E. Waite to be: *Studies of the secret tradition in Israel unfolded by Sons of the Doctrine for the benefit and consolation of the elect dispersed through the lands and ages of the greater exile.*

their lives studying this subject. They revealed many messages with hidden meanings in our Holy Books. These writings were able to specify a date for the year of salvation. My son tells me there are many such messages in the Holy Books pointing to a messianic year. Contrary to what you told me at the office, for us the date is not 1666. It is the year 5408 of the Hebrew calendar corresponding to the Gregorian year 1648, just four years from now . . ."

Rycaut's eyes opened wide as he heard, for the first time, the mention of a Jewish messianic date. He interrupted and inquired hurriedly: "Señor Sevi, is the year actually written down in the Holy Scriptures? Which book might this be? This is one of the many important questions my readers want to know. Which Holy Book gives that date? Please tell me!"

Confident for having led his host to where he wanted him in the conversation, he sipped his drink, took another deep puff and said: "I am glad you asked this. My son has discovered many such references in the Scriptures. But I should add quickly that these references are in a coded form and need to be deciphered by a cabalist. Sabetay is exceptionally good in *gematria*. . . ."

"What is that?" quickly interrupted Rycaut.

"It is a kind of rabbinical arithmetic. My son explained that the word is borrowed from the Greeks. They called it *Heometria*. For them it was a kind of mathematics used to calculate the Earth's dimensions. My forefathers borrowed just the word; not the method for which it was designed. For early theologians, Jewish and Christians, *gematria* became the field of cryptographic arithmetic or numerology giving special meanings to words. . . ."

Rycaut's interest flared. He didn't allow Mordehay to finish. "That is interesting but how does it work?"

"I was coming to that. You know that Hebrews use characters of the alphabet for their numbering system. Each letter has a value and therefore a word, besides its linguistic meaning, has a quantitative value made up of the sum of values of each of its letters. Sabetay says that the old rabbis and prophets used to hide meanings of words within their numerical value, for future scholars to decipher. He gave me a few examples to show you how it works. The most significant of these hidden meanings is at the root of the Hebrew concept of Creation. You and I know that our sages have always pondered if anything existed before Creation. I don't mean to question you, Señor Rycaut, but do you know what existed before Creation?" With a smile on his face Mordehay searched to see if Rycaut was as surprised as he was when he learned of the answer the day before. Rycaut shook his head to mean: No. Satisfied Mordehay went on: "Our *Zohar* solved this question through *gematria*. . . ."

Marveled, Rycaut wouldn't let him finish. He reached for the notebook in his vest pocket, pulled the tiny pencil lodged inside the cover, and said: "Really? Incredible! You said before Creation, didn't you? What could have possibly existed before Creation? All I can think of is void, nothing!"

"I knew you would say that! No! It wasn't void. The answer had always been buried, as one would expect, in the very first Hebrew word in Genesis: *Beresheet* (In the beginning). If one adds the values of each Hebrew letter in that word, one comes up with the number 913." Rycaut was writing furiously what Mordehay was saying. "This in itself does not appear to be significant; does it?" Rycaut shook his head and pressed his lips to signify that he had no idea. Mordehay continued, knowing he had captured his undivided attention. "When the old rabbis looked at the value of another Biblical phrase: *'in the law it was made . . . ,'* they discovered that it had the same value 913. Hence our illustrious rabbis deduced that they had discovered the hidden answer. God's . . . Law . . . existed . . . in . . . the . . . beginning . . . before . . . Creation." He said this, pausing after each word for added emphasis. "Only one thing can be concluded from that: that Creation was a result of His Laws! In other words, God's Law preceded the physical world." Mordehay observed how fascinated his host was, writing everything down as quickly as he could. Proudly he questioned him: "Do you see the importance of *gematria*, Señor Rycaut? It is the key that unlocks divine mysteries!"

Though captivated by that example, Rycaut thought it was taking them away from his principal interest: the messiah. He declared: "Oh, how interesting! As you can see, I've written this example in my notes. But my initial question was more focused on how *gematria* explains the Year of Redemption or any other fact relating to the messiah? Did your son explain this to you? I will be interested to know."

Mordehay took on a rabbinical haughtiness and carefully mimicked what Sabetay had told him: "Many words like salvation, prayer, penitence, charity in our Bible are frequently used in the context of redemption. They, too, give the clue to the date I mentioned. . . ."

"Is that so? But you must tell me!" exclaimed Rycaut.

Mordehay went on to explain that all these words in Hebrew add up to a magic number of 408. He quoted other passages from the Bible hinting a messianic date his son had listed for him with the same numerical value of 408.

The butler interrupted the conversation when he announced that dinner was ready to be served. Rycaut regretted the interruption. He feared the diversion might take the conversation away to other subjects. They moved to the dining room and sat at the ends of a long table beautifully dressed with an embroidered table cloth, expensive kosher china and silverware, and two huge candelabra each with six large candles placed at the center of the table. Waiting to be served, Rycaut, driven by the astounding magical powers of *gematria*, was yet unconvinced by its ability to reveal everything Mordehay said it could. Before questioning him further he asked himself: wasn't Mordehay's argument similar in many ways to the way the Christian date of 1666 was revealed? Was there a difference? Jews had their *Zohar* and Christians had their *Revelation*. Bible reader Rycaut was familiar with the Christian logic fixing the second arrival of the messiah to the year 1666. In early times the Second Coming (*the parousia, adventus*) was proclaimed as a certainty. This was epitomized in the writings of Daniel (7:13–14):

Behold one like the Son of man came with the clouds of heaven. . . .
And there was given him dominion, and glory, and a kingdom that
all people, nations, and languages, should serve him: his dominion
is an everlasting dominion which shall not pass away, and his kingdom that which shall not be destroyed.

St. John had reworked this utopian concept into The Revelation, the last book of the New Testament. The book conceived at
the time of the persecutions of Christians by the Roman emperor
Domitian (81–96 C.E.) tried to encourage believers of the new faith
and uphold the glory of the Christian martyrs. In doing so it gave
Daniel's prophecy a Christian aspect of the messiah. St. John's
vision of a messiah referred to a messianic year of 666 in their
millennium mystically identified as the 'number of the beast' that
would be subdued when the dominion of the holy people, saved
by the Son of man, would be established. Combining the concept of a millennium and 666, readers of the last book of the New
Testament had arrived at 1666.

"True!" admitted Rycaut. On what grounds could he criticize
Mordehay about the rabbis' arithmetic. Tired of waiting for
dreamful Rycaut to take the first spoonful of the lentil soup,
Mordehay dipped his in the bowl and began to eat. Rycaut remembered a paper written by one of his colleagues that the millennium concept existed in the Hebrew Scriptures long before
Christ. The two mythical characters *Gog* and *Magog* represented
in Ezekiel's prophecy were the image of evil, becoming for Christians the Antichrist who had to be defeated by the angels of God
and cast into hell before ultimate salvation. In Revelation 20:4 it
was prophesied that:

. . . and I saw the souls of them that were beheaded for the witness of Jesus, and for the word of God, and which had not wor-
shipped the beast, neither his image . . . and they lived and reigned
with Christ a thousand years (millennium).

The millennium was specific enough from this quotation. Staring at Mordehay enjoying his soup, Rycaut lost interest in eating.
Entrenched in Sabetay's suggestion that many messages relating

to the messiah were encrypted in both bibles, he remembered the rest of the citation from the Book of Revelation 13:18 about the 666 beasts that had to be slain:

> Here is wisdom. Let him that hath understanding count the number of the beast; for it is the number of a man; and his number is six hundred three score and six.

No sooner did he recollect these words did an account by a Dutch holy man come to mind, a man who, using the Hebrew *gematria*, had revealed the name of the evil man, the Antichrist, that had to be slain. His discovery came after adding up the numerical value of the phrase 'count the number of the beast' in the above quotation and having the same numerical value as Nero Caesar, the blasphemous beast of the times, the symbol of Rome, the anti-Christian power. Yes! the Hebrew spelling of Nero Caesar had the value of 666. It seemed to Rycaut that Sabetay, through the lips of his father, was giving him the clue to making these mysteries fit together. Sabetay's deciphering power was beginning to make sense to him. As to the disparity in years between the Christian and Hebrew dates, he argued, like Sabetay, that the difference of eighteen years in a millennium and a half was indeed minute. He concluded that this in itself should speak in favor of the reliability in the two prophecies.

Rycaut was not entirely naive as to overlook the fact that in both religions there had been a fair amount of reliance on collages of phrases, sentences, and paragraphs. He had to be forthright in his article for the English readership. His mood changed and a smile of satisfaction appeared on his face. "What a wonderful idea!" he thought. He was about to dip his spoon in the soup when a crucial question surfaced which he thought was relevant to his paper. Since Jews and Christians expected salvation about the same time, would it not have to be the same messiah saving both? His readers would be asking this for sure. But, then how would Christians and Jews decide to reunite in the same Holy Land? This was not a trivial question. There were great and irreconcilable differences between the two faiths. How would they fare side by side in the Holy Land? Searching for a rational answer, he arrived at an excellent explanation. He would give his readers the answer Justinus Flavius, a Christian father in the first century, gave a Jew who asked him the same question. The Jew had asked: "Do you Christians believe that Jerusalem will be built up again, and also do you believe that your people will assemble under Christ, and together with the patriarchs and the prophets?"

Justinus is said to have replied: "While not all Christians believe in this, I, like many others, are united in the belief that the Saints will indeed live a thousand years in a rebuilt and enlarged Jerusalem to accommodate all of us. Jews and Christians."

Great! Rycaut decided. The feeling of reunification must have existed from the first century of Christianity. Now he was totally clear how he would write the article.

The butler brought the second course. Rycaut hadn't touched a drop of his soup. Mordehay had benefited from his host's silence and preoccupation to finish eating his delicious first course without interruption. Rycaut ordered the butler to take his soup bowl away. Happy about the way his thoughts began to organize for his paper, and seeing Mordehay hesitant to dig into the chicken course, he assured him it was absolutely kosher. It came from his old store across the synagogue. Mordehay shook his head in approval and said: "*Buen provecho.*"

Rycaut didn't understand *espagnol*. He asked what it meant. Mordehay couldn't find its equivalent in English, he did his best to explain: "It wishes you a good appetite."

"Oh, thank you," replied Rycaut. "I wish you likewise."

They ate while the butler filled the glasses with a wine. Before taking a sip, Mordehay asked.

"What kind is it?"

"It is a kosher Rumanian wine with a Turkish label: *Murfatlar*. It comes from the shores of the Danube occupied by the Turks."

Mordehay looked for the kosher seal on the bottle and approvingly said:

"Good! Very good!," chewing a piece of the roasted chicken.

Rycaut wasn't sure if he was referring to the chicken or the wine. For a moment they ate in silence. Rycaut's mind was still on the makings of his paper while Mordehay was totally preoccupied with the meal. There were still a few loose ends to tie together in the story he was to write about the messiah.

"Señor Sevi, what is the Jewish understanding of the origins and personality of the messiah? Is there a general agreement on this? What I want to know is what your people think of his roots and his personal appearance. The German publication I lent to you seems to suggest a creature not like you and me. In fact it depicts a supernatural being with incredible attributes and abilities. It is hard for me to conceive such a description. Jesus came in the image of man, why in heaven's name should he look like a monster in his second coming? In my way of thinking the German author allowed his imagination to be carried away with fantasy. I believe the messiah must come as a man just like any other man. But, ultimately something, some attribute, must distinguish him from an ordinary man. Wouldn't that be necessarily so? Did you have a chance to discuss this with your son?"

Mordehay wasn't surprised by the question. Sabetay had already covered that very well. He had the answer in his pocket and waited to pull it out at an opportune moment. He put his fork down and said:

"You are right. I spoke to Sabetay about it. It appears that our rabbis are not all in agreement on this. Most think that the messiah has to be a Son of David, meaning a descendant from the House of David. Others say he has to be the first Son of God, Adam, the primordial man, or *Adam Quadmon* as we call him. There are yet others who believe he should be the son of Joseph. Our ancestral Sephardi rabbi, Rabbi Maimonides doesn't dwell on such glorious sounding personifications. Though he was a great scholar, his writing style is simple and down to earth so that ordinary people can understand him. His description of the messiah is the most credible in my point of view."

He tried to reach the inside pocket of his cassock but his long beard stood on his way. With one hand he pulled his beard aside and with the other he removed a small sheet of paper. He handed it to the butler standing on the side of the dining room, waiting for them to finish their second course. The time it took the butler to walk the length of the table and hand it over to his master, Mordehay added:

"My son gave me a book by Maimonides in Hebrew in which these passages are found. I have translated them for you, knowing you might be asking me this question."

Rycaut unfolded the paper and read silently:

> No one is in a position to know the details of and similar matters until they have come to pass.
>
> He will be a righteous man, born of a man and woman, and he will grow in righteousness until the end of days. . . . On the day appointed as the end, the soul light which was preserved in Paradise will be given to him and he will become the Redeemer. . . . He will awake with an infusion of prophetic powers and arise from his sleep . . . and he will recognize himself as the messiah. . . . As Moses ascended to heaven in body and soul and remained there for forty days, so this messiah will remain unknown to others . . . until the day he will reveal himself fully and all Israel will recognize him and gather around him.[4]

Rycaut found this description most credible and interesting. The whole concept was condensed in these short sentences. When he finished reading he said: "Beautiful! May I keep this?"

"Of course," answered Mordehay chewing his last piece of chicken.

Rycaut looked happy and fully rewarded with the outcome of the productive evening. He was sure he had all he needed to write about the Hebrew position, one which evolved not only from the bible but also from cabalistic writings. Many learned Christian scholars respected the teachings of the *Zohar* and the *Cabala* for in those books on Jewish mysticism they had discovered proof of the truth of Christianity. Early scholars stressed the analogies

---

4. R. L. Weiss & C. Butterworth, eds. (Ethical Writings of Maimonides, 1975).

between some teachings of the *Zohar* and many of the Christian dogmas. *The Book of Formation*, and later the *Cabala* suggested the concept of Trinity before the birth of Christianity. Also, during the Spanish Inquisition, when the Church tried to convert Jews, debating Christian scholars used arguments in the *Zohar* as proof of the truth of Christianity and concluded from it the irrelevance of Judaism. Yes, he should make reference to passages in the *Zohar* affirming the concept of Trinity if he could find them. If not, he will ask Sabetay for help. The more he thought about it the more he became convinced of his arguments likely to have a great appeal among his readers.

Supper ended with a glass of brandy imported from England. Rycaut thanked his guest for his unsparing help. As soon as Mordehay left, he rushed to his study and began writing his much awaited treatise from the Orient.

6

In the months that followed, potent social and political forces were
at work fermenting Sabetay's spiritual life to greater depths. The
preoccupation by the public and the newspapers with the messiah
seemed endless. They searched for news and fresh claims of messianic sitings. For the poor, the oppressed Christian or Jew, this
preoccupation was not the sporting exercise the gentry of England
amused themselves with gambling, it was their only hope of salvation from the misery they were unable to shed. Asking themselves:
"How does one prepare for such a blessed event?" the wise and the
pious pointed to the wisdom of the Bible, the only manual explaining how to rise to that momentous occasion: *Shed all material pos-
sessions and turn to prayers and meditations begging for atonement of
your sins.* Many had already done so. As an exemplary act of devotion they paraded the streets wearing sack clothes waiting for the
messianic order to repatriate to the land of their ancestors. English
newspapers began to report that a group of wealthy Jews had un-
dertaken their migration to the saintly city of Jerusalem that already
had too many poor and whose livelihood depended on alms from
the Diaspora. The spirit of the expectant mood was intense and in
everyone's mind, including the leaders of Christian churches who
kept a close eye on any surge of manifestation of a supernal event.

It had been the belief of Jews throughout their long history in
exile that God will send to Earth his messiah, but accepting a

divine messenger in the image of a man was not an easy matter. That same perplexed feeling occurred during the time of Jesus, and even more dramatically soon after the patriarch Moses saved his people from Egyptian bondage. In spite of their astonishing miracles the bible says these exceptional leaders performed, Jews still remained unconvinced that they possessed the attributes of a messiah depicted by ancient sages. Three millennia after the extraordinary accomplishments of the patriarch Moses, his descendants were still forbidden by the precepts of Judaism to perceive him as a Son of God. Moses is portrayed as a great leader but a sinner nonetheless.

In his paper Rycaut accused Jews of vacillating, and acting inconsistently with regard to whether or not they believed in the words of their Scriptures heralding the truth in a promised messiah. For that reason he wrote, he failed to see the purpose of Jews rekindling the messianic utopia when in the past they had rejected many worthy candidates. He explained the Jewish paradox as follows: The underlying purpose of Jews to maintain the messianic hope was intrinsically an emotional matter within their soul. For them, living in a Diaspora and bearing the longing of their ancestral motherland and the misery in exile, they need to covet that hope of salvation even though, deep in their souls, they don't believe it will happen. Rycaut's reporting included many of the Jewish concepts Sabetay had given him through the intermediary of his father. It was published in many English papers and it had an enormous success. European readers demanded more such reportings, preferably on a more intimate level with local spiritual leaders. Thus, his mission as a correspondent was assured as long as the messianic preoccupation prevailed.

Mordehay's business was better than ever. He and his two sons were now wealthy in their own rights. They were accepted as important members of their community. This fame and opulence meant nothing to Sabetay. The only material things he needed were a private room and meals when he broke fast. Poor Clara, yet unconvinced of his happiness, and having misunderstood the root of his disdain in his first marriage, arranged a second one.

She had searched thoroughly in her community for the character and temperament of an eligible young girl that matched those of Sabetay. Convinced to have found her, she arranged the wedding. To honor his parents, as Judaism demanded, he yielded once again. The wedding took place, and the short-lived union went the way of the first. Unbeknownst to Clara the girl happened to be one of the damsels who danced with Alegra and teased him in his dreams. The disappointed parents were given the same excuse that the *Ruach Hakodesh* (The Holy Presence) appeared to him and ordered him to divorce her for she was not the bride destined to go to Heaven with him. Noble as the justification sounded, it did not impress his disillusioned parents. Malicious rumors resurfaced again about his inability to make love to women as the Lord demanded of every man. He was charged of many ugly things, none of which were complimentary to someone who aspired to become a very special spiritual leader. He prayed daily and paid no attention to the gossips.

The state of fermenting religious aspirations in Europe finally boiled over. The spiritual consciousness of the people flared to a point that affected the politics of the continent. The fate of Jews and New Christians in England hung in the balance of power between state and religion. Civil war originated in England in 1640 on account of governing issues known as The Bishop's War. The public challenged the power of episcopacy, the right of bishops to run the government. Then came the wars of the Roundheads, the Puritans against the monarchy of Charles I, demanding religious reforms and surrender of the armed forces. In the end, when Charles was executed, religious tolerance of New Christians emerged, and with it came a sudden consciousness in the immediate expectancy of the messiah.

The intolerance towards the Jews in the vast British Empire remained, but was nothing compared to the massacres of their brethren in Poland and the Ukraine. For years, the Polish Crown and nobility used the educated Jews as agents and stewards to manage and exploit their immense estates in Poland and in most of the Ukraine. Initially East European Jews enjoyed this limited freedom and became wealthy and important. They were admired by the landlords in spite of the protest by the Church and the Jesuits of Poland. The serfs and peasants hated them for their role as tax collectors. In that region hatred was not limited to Jews. Poles hated the Russians. Catholics hated the Russian Orthodox, and the peasants hated the nobility and the Jews. To complicate political matters further, Tartars, nomadic tribes from the east, constantly pilfered and plundered the cultivated fertile lands of the peasants on the banks of the Dnieper River. To defend themselves against these barbaric invaders, a half military and a half peasant militia named Cossacks was organized. In this volatile mix of hatreds, Jews found themselves caught inextricably in these convoluted detestations. It didn't matter that Jews were merely agents of the nobility; in the eyes of the peasants they were part of the tyrannical power that subjugated them.

In time, reports emerged from Poland of intense cruelty, bondage, and murders unleashed at Jews. Sephardis who remained safe in the Ottoman Empire waited with anxiety to learn the ultimate fate of their brethren in Eastern Europe. When the Polish wars ended in 1648, the year designated by the *Zohar* as *the year of Jubilee*, the last count of Jewish casualties amounted to three hundred thousand. World Jewry couldn't comprehend how such a holocaust could take place during what was supposed to be a year of salvation. What had gone wrong with the prophecy? A Rabbi of Cracow painted this sad picture in his sermon:

> "In the year 1648, to which we all looked forward as a garden of heavenly glory, the year in which the Children of Israel would return to their home, my blood was shed in torrents."

Similar cries came from a Rabbi of Posen:

> "In the very year 1648, when I hoped to recover my freedom once more, the evil-doers gathered to wipe out Thy people."[1]

---

1. J. Kastein, *The Messiah of Ismir* (John Lane, 1931).

In the three years after his ordainment, Sabetay heard these cries and bewilderment from his northern coreligionists. People began to say that God had slumbered all through the slaughter. He wasn't listening to prayers and supplications. He had abandoned His people. How else would He have allowed such atrocities against his chosen people at a time when the messiah was expected? Sabetay went to the streets in God's defense. He preached at the synagogue and at public places to stop the raging blasphemy. He warned them it was time for Jews around the world to stand up and be counted as loyal to their faith and trustful of the Creator's intentions, no matter how difficult it was to understand His ways. He demanded immediate repentance and atonement.

At the same time, he wished in his heart he had been given the divine authority to rally His people to seek Him more intensely with prayers. But then, if he assumed that responsibility on his own, without His authority, he feared he wouldn't be taken seriously by his community. His unyielding demands for an early ordainment, his steadfast refusal to accept the assignment of a parish rabbi, his divorcing twice, and his inability to make friends, all stood in his way. How could he make his people understand that he had done all these things only to please and serve the Lord better. He had to wait; wait until the voice of God or the voice of one of His angels summoned him as patriarchs were summoned in biblical times. He needed more time to prove himself.

The year 1648 was about to close. It was difficult to admit that he, and other Jewish men of the cloth had been wrong in their cabalistic assessment that it would be the year of the messiah. The miscalculation disturbed him, especially when it turned out to be the disastrous year of a holocaust. He took this disappointment very hard. He blamed himself for failing to comprehend the written words in the *Zohar*. Shaken by the misjudgment he went into seclusion. He increased the frequency of penitence and imposed on himself a schedule of fasting from one Sabbath to the next. He ate three meals on that day and one at dusk after reciting the special blessings of *havdalah*. The fourth meal was ritualistically called *the banquet of David*, or the banquet of the messianic king. He plunged his body on a regular basis in the cold waters of the Gulf of Smyrna during early morning hours. He slept many nights in the dark dungeons of an old Grecian fortress on top of a hill Turks called *Kadife Kale* (Velvet Fortress). Like the old patriarchs, he meditated in the dark.

One Friday evening Clara became hysterical when Sabetay didn't return home in time for services at the synagogue and, more importantly, to break his weekly fast the morning after. Gradually she had become used to the idea of him not coming home for two, or at most, three nights. Sabetay had reassured her not to worry for he liked to sleep in the dungeons, an experience he said was similar to sleeping in biblical caves. It made him feel the holiness of the ancient patriarchs in the Holy Land when they secluded themselves in caves for meditation. But not coming home for five days spelled death for Clara. What she didn't know was that Sabetay expected to hear divine voices in the dungeon, certain that God was in the process of searching for a pious and pure servant to carry out His mission. He was making himself available.

Clara begged Mordehay and her older son Eliyah to go look for him. Every precious hour was crucial for his survival. Mordehay attempted to calm her: "Clara dear, you have to stop imagining the worse. Sabetay is not a child. He is a grown man. He is accustomed to fasting and he knows the countryside well. You know it is not the first time he has slept outdoors. I am sure he is all right. Don't worry. Besides, we can't do anything in the dark. We can't see anything. Please calm down."

Eliyah added: "I will go looking for him as soon as the first rays of sunlight brighten the sky."

These words failed to give her comfort, fearing that a terrible fate had fallen on her son. She sobbed continually and wiped her tears with the edge of her apron. She had just finished preparing his weekly meal. "How can I be calm when I know something has happened to him? Deep in my heart I feel it! I know his schedule and he shouldn't be where he is for this long a time. Something awful must have happened to him. We must go look for him," she begged again and again.

"Father is right. We can't see anything in the dark. I will go looking for him very early in the morning. Now calm down please," beseeched Eliyah with a heavy heart. "I love him too, you know. Besides, I feel somewhat guilty about all this. Since his ordainment I have been the one encouraging him to devote himself to saintliness and pursue a life of total devotion to the faith. Now, of course, I question if I shouldn't have advised moderation! I know it is too late for me to say this."

Mordehay try to comfort his son: "Oh! Eliyah don't blame yourself. I don't think anyone tried to talk him into being what he is. In fact I don't think anyone could have dissuaded him from the path he has taken. He was like this the day he was born. Ask your mother how many times I tried to steer him into what I call a normal life: get married, have children, buy a house, and enjoy life. God knows I tried my best." Mordehay felt a choking feeling in his throat. "Your brother has only one thing in his mind: to be with His God. He is the only person I know who has taken God as his only friend, wife, family, and everything dear to the heart and possession of a man during his lifetime." He paused, realizing he wasn't making things easier to cope with. He changed the subject and asked: "Where do you think he might be?"

Eliyah looked puzzled, for he had no idea. He raised his shoulders slightly to indicate that. He didn't wish to alarm his mother by advancing a guess. But Clara knew how to find him. Sabetay always confided in her many of his personal feelings because she never laughed or ridiculed him. Responding to the question her husband asked, she said:

"Moses Pinheiro must know where to find him. He is his closest friend and I know they go meditating together in the countryside. I am sure he knows where to look for him. You must go to him first and ask him to help find your brother. He will be just as upset when he learns he has been missing" She cried again and said: "Oh, My Lord I won't be able to sleep tonight! . . . Who knows where he is lying down . . . frail, tired, sick . . . May the Lord protect him . . . He is such a pure soul!"

She wiped her eyes again. Mordehay took her in his arms and the two walked upstairs to their bedroom. There was no Sabbath celebration that night and no one slept in the Sevi family. Clara imagined the worst. She saw her son emaciated down to the bones and rotting in a dungeon. It was the first time she ever felt regret for agreeing to send him to the yeshiva to become a rabbi. Why couldn't he have grown like her other two boys? She remembered her own mother saying: "Too much studying is bad for the brain." Her mother had been absolutely right.

At the crack of dawn, Eliyah rushed to Moses' house. He found no one awake at the Pinheiros' home. The maid, still in her nightgown, opened the door, surprised to see Eliyah at this early hour. He said he wanted to talk to Moses. It was very urgent. A few minutes later Moses came to the door yawning and scratching his head.

"Hello Moses. I need your help urgently. Sabetay is missing," he said this fast. "He didn't come home last night. It was his night to break fast. He hasn't been home since last Sunday! God All Mighty! Where do you think he might be? My mother thinks you might know. Will you help me find him?"

"Missing? What do you mean?" asked a startled Moses.

"I told you. He didn't come home last night. He has never missed a Sabbath eve before. I beg you to come with me before it is too late!"

Moses frowned as Eliyah spoke. Without asking another question he said: "Sure, as soon as I get dressed." He turned around and headed upstairs to get dressed. Half way up he stopped to remind Eliyah: "Come to think of it, I haven't seen him all week. I was going to come to visit him, to see if he was sick or something. Now I am worried too. I will skip services this morning. This is much too important."

He disappeared, rushing to his room. There was another reason why Moses wanted to visit Sabetay that week. He had completed his seminary work successfully and had been ordained. He was going to invite him to a celebration arranged by his parents. His medical studies had delayed his ordainment by a year.[2]

Next to Clara, Eliyah was most devoted to Sabetay. Being the oldest son, he hadn't been pampered or spoiled like his other two brothers. From a very young age he was taught to be aware of the importance and responsibilities of an elder brother. That morning, duty-bound to find Sabetay, was a perfect example of his devotion. His brother Joseph and his father conveniently passed on to Eliyah the responsibility of finding Sabetay. Mordehay had a good excuse due to the worsening gout condition which did not allow him to wander in the hilly countryside.

Moses came down quickly. He was still wrapping his sash around his midriff. They went out the door in a hurry. Eliyah followed his steps. The route they took was one of the narrow and rocky trails leading to the old Grecian military fields and ruins at the top of a hill overlooking the city and the waters of the gulf. At the beginning of the climb they didn't say anything to each other. Partly up the hill, panting and perspiring, Moses thought he should tell frightened Eliyah where he was taking him: "It is just a hunch, Eliyah. I don't really know where he is. I have gone with Sabetay a number of times to the country and more often to the top of this hill. Your brother picked up the idea of meditating in natural surroundings from the writings of a veteran cabalist who claimed to have been inspired by nature and felt there the presence of God. Sometimes Sabetay took these short excursions with young Talmudic students who I know respect him for his limitless knowledge of Judaic literature."

Eliyah had only one thing in mind: to find Sabetay. He wanted to know how sure Moses was where he was taking him: "Do you really believe we will find him here? What would he be doing? In my way of thinking, it doesn't take nearly a week to be inspired. I hope he is . . . ."

Moses guessed what Eliyah was about to say. To distract him away from that sinister thought he interrupted him. "Your brother

---

2. All through the Middle Ages to the eighteenth century many rabbis were also physicians.

has a remarkable mind. Unlike most of us he is able to memorize and retain everything he reads. Everybody at the yeshiva, including me, has a great admiration for his command of talmudic and cabalistic knowledge. But this isn't the only reason why I like to be with him. He is the most pious person I have ever known. This means a lot to me for I come from a family of rabbis and none match the purity and devotion to the Lord as your brother does. Yet I feel a great sorrow and concern on days when he suffers from those chronic and terrible headaches rendering him incapable of uttering a single word. I should know the misery that incapacitates him because I have studied medicine. I wish there were a cure for that mysterious yet common affliction. There isn't one known to man. No one is sure if the ailment is physical or in the realm of his soul. I have recommended that he go see an exorcist. Medicine doesn't hide the fact that science is not always able to solve all the ailments of man. Unfortunately, the soul remains totally outside the domain of medicine. You must have noticed that when his sickness strikes, he behaves like a different person. On his normal days he is brilliant and illuminating, and during his affliction he acts like a thoughtless child. Because of these ups and downs, misguided friends and colleagues regard him as an eccentric and few go as far as . . ." He wasn't going to complete his sentence, but the end of it had to be obvious to Eliyah. He had to finish his sentence: "labeling him a lunatic. I know for a fact they are wrong. They should ask God for forgiveness for accusing him of such an ignoble characterization."

Moses stopped only for a short time to catch his breath. He didn't intend to lose precious time. They were walking too fast on that steep road. Eliyah welcomed the temporary halt. He was very concerned that a week without eating was injurious for anyone, including Sabetay who was accustomed to such deprivation. A minute later they resumed the climb and Moses continued briefing Eliyah:

"Your brother is also blessed with a special and complex soul. He has been endowed with a rare and ancient holiness found only in the souls of ancient patriarchs. Remember, Eliyah, many great men were initially judged to be mad, insane, or fools just because they possessed attributes not found in ordinary men."

Moses heard a slight murmur come from behind him. He turned around and looked at Eliyah. He hadn't realized Eliyah had been sobbing as he spoke. He was sobbing because Moses was expressing feelings about his brother Eliyah thought were known only to him. Thankful for the kind words he said to Moses: "God bless you Moses. I see that you love my brother very much. . . ." He looked around to see how far they had walked and asked: "Do we have much longer to go? You seem sure of where we will find him. I pray the Lord he is alive." Moses didn't answer and didn't stop. It was Eliyah's turn to express his feelings: "Moses I, too, feel frustrated about his fate. I want to help him but I don't know how. He asks nothing of us except food and security, and he doesn't complain about anything. He seems totally content living the life of a recluse either in his tiny room in my parents' house and now in the fields with his God. At least when he was at the yeshiva he had some contact with others, like you, and he inter-acted with people. The truth is my family expected he would want to serve our expanding community, get married and have a fam-ily, mingle with people, participate in the daily life of others. I remember my father lecturing him about this so many times. We were wrong, Moses. He has shown no desire for that sort of life without deprecating it for the rest of us. I don't know what to do, and I know I am speaking for my father and mother as well."

He stopped. He sobbed again. Moses let him cry. There was no one except them on this stony and dusty road leading to the fortress.

"Let's resume walking," demanded Moses. "My advice to you is to take your brother as he is and love him as he is. Do you un-derstand that? He is resolved to a life dedicated to comprehend our Lord as best he can. He awaits for the Creator to recognize his devotion and in return to be allowed to become His servant ready to do His will. Do you understand what I mean, Eliyah?"

Eliyah nodded, still sobbing, and couldn't speak. But Moses knew he didn't fully understand what he tried to say. "Eliyah, what we are talking about is rare but not new. From the age of six, when I first met him he already knew he was different from the rest of us. He wanted nothing else but to be different. He couldn't wait to get his hands on scholarly books and begin to understand the mysteries behind the stories in the bible. He has done that to his satisfaction. Now, as an adult, he strives to acquire the magic key his idol cabalist Rabbi Isaac Luria Esquenazi seem to have found to understand the complex mysteries of creation. He became fascinated by Luria's life, his writings, and his accomplishments. Luria was one of the greatest rabbis we've ever known. He founded the important center of Jewish mystic studies in Safed, Galilee. Because of his greatness Safed grew from 300 to 2000 families in a short time after the Sephardi exile from Spain and Portugal. He was born in 1534 of an Ashkenazi father and a Sephardi mother." At this point Moses thought of injecting his opinion of Sabetay's admiration of Luria. "I suppose Sabetay was quick at drawing a parallel from that union to that of your father who, if I am not mistaken, was a descendant of an Ashkenazi[3] family and your mother a Sephardi Jewess. Anyway, Rabbi Luria became the supreme scholar and protagonist of all mystics. None was able to match his depth of knowledge and extent of reach into the mysteries of Creation and the Deity. He was known in cabalistic literature as *ari* (lion in Hebrew), a name formed from the initials of *Alohi Rabbi Isaac* (the saintly Rabbi Isaac). His doctrinal writ-

---

3. The two different appellations of the names Ashkenazi and Esquenazi in this reference need an explanation. The first designates the denomination of Jews from East European lands. The second, derived from the first, is paradoxically a common family name of the Spanish Sephardis. In Sephardi tradition, beginning as early as the fifteenth century, they adopted the Spanish custom of using a family name instead of the biblical practice of 'son of.' The family name Esquenazi originated in cases when an Ashkenazi or Romaniote Jew married a Sephardi girl, swearing to uphold the Sephardi tradition. The spelling is a Spanish interpretation. What is paradoxical is that the Esquenazi name became one of many almost exclusive Sephardi family names.

ings demanded a level of intelligence and vision only few brilliant minds possess. In many respects his writings became the ultimate test of intelligence to divinity scholars. His doctrine was the primer, the textbook, that taught about the mysteries of the universe, the very special relationship of God and man, and of the Creator. He was also well-respected for his methodical approach to analyze, comprehend, and cure the ailing of the human soul, much the way physicians comprehend and cure the human body. With his intellectual and spiritual superiority, he was able to acquire a unique clairvoyance to be able to read on the face of a living person the nature of his soul, and better still the identity of the previous deceased owner of that soul which had transmigrated[4] into the living body of the man he faced. That is how good he was. In the same manner, he was able to read secret sins encapsulated in a soul and prescribe the proper redemptional medicine in the form of a variety of penances. He was the supreme harvester of the human soul. For that reason many thought of him as the messiah. His work was so profound and convoluted with mystical theories that those who tried to comprehend him were ultimately forced to abandon the efforts before they lost their mind. I am one of those. Not your brother!"

Moses had chosen the shortest but steepest trail to the top. He was trying to inform Eliyah why his brother had become the way he was. He had more to say about Sabetay's love affair with Luria: "Like Luria, in order to serve God fully, your brother chose that most difficult path our Midrash tells us. To arrive at the knowledge of our Creator one must become like one of the **four** characters in our entire biblical history. Eliyah, I want you to know that your brother set for himself this formidable goal."

---

4. The mystical concept of transmigration was common in a number of ancient religions, and was defined as the process by which the soul is thought to transfer from a deceased person into the body of a living one. This assumes that God has a limited number of souls at His disposal and that the released soul of a deceased person was immediately given to a new born.

Curious Eliyah asked: "Who were these people?"

"No less than Abraham, Hezekiah, Job . . ." Moses stopped suddenly. Eliyah waited impatiently to learn the name of the fourth person. He was sure he heard him say four, not three.

"Moses I agree these are extraordinary credentials to match. You didn't tell me who the fourth person was."

The road began to level off and the two could see the top of the ancient fortress stand proudly as if to remind people below not to forget they were just temporary dwellers in this land of eternal history. Instead of answering, Moses exclaimed: "Ah! Here we are. It shouldn't take us very long to start looking for your brother."

Eliyah still waited for Moses to stop ignoring his question and waited to hear the name of the fourth sage who claimed to have understood the attributes of God. He pressed: "Moses, please don't leave me in suspense. I know you are avoiding answering me. Who was the fourth person?"

Moses regretted to have initiated that conversation. Mentioning the first three names didn't bother him for they had become historic legends. The fourth candidate hadn't announced himself yet. He was not really a person like the others. He was like supreme royalty with a sacred title not awarded to any man. He wished he hadn't brought up this matter for he didn't want to shock Eliyah who didn't want to forget it. "Yes Eliyah you are right. I said there were four who arrived at the knowledge of the Creator. I gave you the names of the three, the fourth is not a person like the others, or you and me. He is a special messenger of God. He is a spirit of the Lord in human form. He is . . . the *mashiah* . . ."

Moses' voice trembled as he mentioned that name. If he had said this to anyone else he would have been angry and swear at him maliciously for having dared to equate Sabetay to the messiah. He tried not to leave a false impression. "Your brother knows perfectly well what I have been telling you. He has not mentioned this to me, or anyone else, to my knowledge. But from the frequent discussions we have had, it became obvious that he believes in what I said. Please don't ask more questions. I feel very uncomfortable as it is, for having confessed this much. Besides, there is also the possibility that I understood him wrong. I will say no more." In his state of mind Eliyah had not yet fully comprehended why Moses was so concerned at this perilous time about his brother's aspirations. His mind was totally fixed at finding his brother.

They arrived at the ruins and Moses suggested they split and search in two directions. He headed for the underground dungeons and Eliyah searched at ground level around and behind marble columns and strewn remnants of past architectural relics. After half an hour Eliyah discovered a handkerchief he thought belonged to his brother. He called Moses to show it to him: "What do we do now?" he asked looking very apprehensive. "I am reasonably sure this is his handkerchief. He must be somewhere around here, but where could he be? We searched every part of these ruins. Moses! we're so close we can't abandon our efforts now!"

"No, you are right. I have no intentions of doing that. We will look in one more place. The Jewish cemetery on the east side of this mountain. He always loved this old and abandoned burial ground. He enjoyed reading the headstones of Sephardi ancestry. Come follow me."

They descended the hill from the east, a much gentler slope. The cemetery was located approximately a thousand feet away. Perspiring and exhausted under a brilliant hot sun, they entered the ornate front gate that showed signs of neglect. This cemetery had been abandoned a few decades earlier. The weight of the crawling wild grape vines on the ornate iron gate had forced it out of its rusty hinges and made it to lean towards the ground. They walked with difficulty, pushing wild brush and thistle out of the way. Eliyah, walking behind Moses, at the top of his voice called: "Sabetay!, Sabetay!" but received no reply. The echo of his voice could be heard far away. Moses walked as if he knew where he was heading. He kept signaling Eliyah to stay close to him. They advanced in the direction of a cluster of black marble mausoleums at the far end of the cemetery. The narrow path seemed to have been trampled recently by footsteps, but they couldn't be sure whose they were. Once, Sabetay had brought Moses to this site to pray and meditate. He remembered him saying how much he loved this peaceful corner.

The black mausoleums belonged to members of the illustrious family of Solomon Molho who was burnt at the stake by order of the Holy Roman Emperor Charles V in 1534 at the commune of Mantua in Lombardi, Italy. His family escaped the inquisitors of the Emperor and the Church and they found refuge in Smyrna. According to legend the family swore that Molho's soul mysteriously ascended to Heaven before he was burned to death leaving his body ashes on the ground. The family received permission to collect his ashes, sealed inside an urn, and after shipping the remains to Smyrna they buried them in one of the massive black marble mausoleums.

Moses knew why this man's grave was so important to Sabetay. He was the most recent messianic pretender. He was born in Portugal and converted to Catholicism during the relentless drives by the Church to convert Sephardi Jews before leaving their land. A brilliant student at the prestigious university of Coimbra, the same university Moses' great grandfather had attended, he accepted baptism and changed his name to Diego Perez. The Portuguese began persecuting the new converts they called *Christâos Novos* (New Christians). Solomon escaped with many others and settled in Bologna, Italy. Once free of persecution, he returned to Judaism. He became a rabbi and one of the great cabalist of his time. He, too, was a master at *gematria*. He practiced the business of reading other people's souls and told them of their future. They came to him from many distant lands to have this great diviner and visionary read their fortune. He was so well-known that he wrote a book about his most famous forecasts and prophecies. He forecast that Israel will be liberated as soon as sinful Rome was sacked and decimated in his century. It so happened that in 1527 Rome was sacked by the imperial troops of Charles V, and Pope Clement VII was imprisoned in Castel Sant Angelo. Jewish eyes instantly focused on Molho as a prophet for having predicted the event. Euphoria swelled in Bologna were he was arrested and

ordered to be burnt by the Holy Tribunal of the Inquisition for
having proselytized. Sabetay was one of a few who were convinced
that Molho ascended to Heaven before his body was burned. He
told Moses that his spirit took to Heaven the invaluable key he
had been seeking: that which opened the door to the knowledge
of God. By visiting his ashes frequently, sealed in the mausoleum,
he hoped through intense meditation, Molho's spirit would ultimately permeate into his own soul.

When they reached the area of the mausoleum Eliyah saw a
man, half naked, laying down on the cold black marble above the
grave. He raised his voice and said:

"Moses! Come! Come this way! There is someone here. Oh,
Dios de los cielos (God in Heaven) please hurry."

Moses turned around and walked in Eliyah direction. They both
recognized the parched and half naked body of Sabetay stretched
with his face down on top of Molho's grave. The way his body
laid suggested as if he was kissing the marble top of the grave and
wanted to get inside. Sabetay's once plump and healthy flesh
looked dried like a lifeless grayish sack of skin and bones.

"*Sabetay, Oh mi querido hermano Sabetay,* (Oh my dear brother
Sabetay,)" cried Eliyah at the top of his voice lifting his brother's
cold body and pressing it against his. "Oh! my God what are we
going to do? Moses, I don't know if he is still alive."

Moses placed the two trembling fingers of his right hand around
Sabetay's throat and felt a weak pulse. "He is still alive! Thank
God!" he exclaimed. "We must carry him home at once."

Eliyah was a big and robust person. He had the bony structure
of his father but was much taller. Until recently he had worked
in heavy construction projects before his father's good fortune.
Moses helped lift Sabetay's body and placed it on his brother's
back. They removed their sashes around their waist and tied them
into a longer belt to secure Sabetay on Eliyah's body. Moses took
off his overcoat and covered emaciated Sabetay. They began the
slow and careful descent on the same rocky and dusty road. From
time to time Eliyah stopped and rested. There was no conversation until they reached the house. Clara turned hysterical and

totally incoherent when she saw Eliyah carrying Sabetay's parched body. She screamed, grabbing her son's hanging bare arm while Eliyah tried to carry the body upstairs to the bedroom. There wasn't sufficient room on the stairway to allow him, Sabetay, and his restraining mother. Nearly exhausted, Eliyah yelled to Moses:

"Get her down! Pull her away from my brother! I can't climb the stairs with her hanging on my brother's arm!"

Moses did as he was told. He grabbed Clara from her waist and pried her hands open to release her grip. He pulled her down the stairs apologizing: "I am sorry Señora. I am very sorry for doing this to you."

Eliyah took the body to Sabetay's room. By this time Moses had released Clara and rushed to help Eliyah. Gently he untied Sabetay's body from Eliyah's back and the two men put him in bed. Moses requested they leave Sabetay as he was, with his loin cloth and shoes. In his unconscious state they forced some water into his mouth. Clara, somewhat calmer now, was instructed by Moses to keep him warm under the covers. He assured her that in time he would wake up starving. He checked his pulse again and placed his ear on Sabetay's chest to verify the regularity of his heart beat. Before leaving he said with a smile: "He will be fine. I will be back the day after tomorrow to check him."

"God bless you, Moses," said Clara wiping her tears with the end of her apron.

Eliyah stayed awhile to catch his breath and his wits, then he left to reassure his wife. Clara sat by Sabetay's bed hoping to be present when he woke up. This was the first time she realized that her son was beyond normal piousness and perhaps beyond the realm of earthly men. She wished she knew how to alter his life, but she didn't. She finally agreed with her husband that it was perhaps too late to change him. All these years, in silence and solitude, he had carved into his body and soul the spirit and conviction of an ascetic recluse wanting nothing from earth; he lived just to feel the presence of God.

When Mordehay returned from morning services he called for his wife, still sitting by Sabetay's bed. Clara rushed downstairs and fell into his arms crying. She said with a face full of tears: "We have a saint in our family. No mortal man would go to such extremes to prove his worthiness to the Lord." Mordehay told her he had met Eliyah in the street who had already briefed him.

Sabetay remained unconscious the rest of that day and night. Frustrated, Mordehay went to work Sunday morning. Assured by Moses that he would be fine, Clara took every measure Moses recommended to restore Sabetay's health. Worried, Mordehay couldn't remain at work. His mind was so preoccupied with his son's dilemma he couldn't concentrate on his bookkeeping. He returned home. Sabetay woke up for a short time that afternoon. He was barely able to speak. When he saw his mother sitting at his bedside, he smiled like a drunkard, slowly realizing what must have happened to him. In a faint voice he said to her: "Suddenly . . . I felt exalted laying on the grave. . . ."

Clara, delighted to hear his voice, begged: "Don't speak yet, Son. You must have some broth before you talk. Moses wants you to rest." She called her husband upstairs to share her relief from her anxiety. Sabetay wanted to express all what he felt inside him, in spite of the fact he encountered difficulties expressing himself.

He lifted his hand a few inches above his colorful quilt as if to say to her: Let me talk. She smiled and he spoke faintly: "Earlier . . . I had a vision . . . ordering me to go to the mount," he smiled with his eyes focused past her. He wetted his scorched lips with his tongue and continued with a trembling voice: ". . . . An angel came to meet me . . . and took me above the clouds . . . ," frowning and squinting as if he was trying to recall, he added: "There, . . . I heard mysterious voices, among them that of . . . Solomon Molho speaking to me . . . ordering me to save Israel from further harm. But I didn't know how! . . . Mamaritta, I didn't know how! I was troubled . . . I was very much troubled because I didn't know how! . . . I waited for him to tell me. . . ." He moved his head sideways back and forth, then, as if he had found relief from pain, he smiled again and his eyes looked far far away. "Then, . . . the prophet Isaiah appeared and spoke to me. . . ."

He paused and kept swallowing as if he tried to push down what was choking him. With the help of Mordehay, who lifted his head, Clara managed to give him a few sips of broth. She spilled half of the broth on a napkin, unable to see clearly with her eyes full of tears. As he swallowed he continued relating his marvelous experience: "Now I remember vividly . . . the prophet pronouncing his famous verse to me. . . ." He wet his lips with the broth still in his mouth. He made a deliberate effort to articulate clearly every word: "*For the day of vengeance is in mine heart, and the year of my redeemed has come* . . . Mamaritta, . . . it was so beautiful up there . . . It was then that . . . I heard the voice of the Lord saying to me: *Thou art destined to be the savior of Israel* . . . , *the messiah* . . . , *the son of David* . . . , *the anointed of the God of Jacob* . . . , *and thou art destined to redeem Israel* . . . , *to gather my people from the four corners of the earth to Jerusalem* . . . I don't know how . . . to describe that voice. It was like . . . many harmonious voices in one. I was so thrilled . . . and exhilarated but I wasn't afraid . . . yet I trembled. I waited all my life . . . to hear Him . . . speak to me. It was beautiful. Then, . . . I saw a lightning bolt flash the heavens . . . and I came down the cloud . . . just as Isaiah described to us the *mashiah* would do . . . and suddenly all voices abated. . . . In that awful silence I saw myself back on Molho's grave . . . I don't remember how I got here."

The expression on Sabetay's face changed again. Now, he looked solemn and unafraid. He had exhausted all the strength within him. He saw his mother looking at him lovingly, confused and crying. To cheer her up he put on an angelic smile and began to sing faintly her special Castilian love ballad:

> To the mountain I ascended
> To the river I descended
> My Mamaritta I met there, . . .

He tried but couldn't finish the rest of the ballad. He closed his eyes and fell asleep. With tears in her eyes Clara finished the rest of the song:

The king's daughter bright and fair.
There I saw the shining lass
As she came up from the bath.
Her arched brow dark as the night
Her face a gleaming sword of light
Her lips like coral red and bright
Her flesh as milk so fair and white.

After hearing all this, nervous Mordehay couldn't bear to stay home while Sabetay slept. He went to work once again and, as before, he couldn't concentrate more than an hour. He had to talk to someone. He needed guidance and advice. What was he to do? No one in his Jewish community would lend him an ear if they knew his son had meddled in God's affairs. They would shun him like the plague. He thought perhaps Rycaut would be compassionate and understanding. He walked to his consular office still unsure if he was doing the right thing.

Upon learning of the incident Rycaut canceled all his appointments and insisted on visiting Sabetay personally. He wanted to witness Sabetay's demeanor in the wake of his extraordinary vision. His reporting the news before anyone else was sure to draw international attention on him. In particular, a short interview with the saintly young rabbi would certainly bring him fame. Clara had never met Rycaut although her husband spoke constantly about him. Rycaut drove Mordehay in his carriage. When they entered the house, Clara ran into Mordehay's arms sobbing.

"What is it, dear? Is Sabetay not feeling well?" Mordehay asked without introducing Rycaut.

"No, it is not that," she replied wiping her tears on his overcoat. "After you left he woke up again. It was only for a few minutes. He repeated his account of meeting with God and Isaiah by His side telling him he was to become the *mashiah*. Our son is to become the *mashiah*? I am confused! I don't know what to think! I am scared Mordehay!"

She burst into new tears. He, too, became totally shaken while Rycaut, not knowing *espagnol*, wanted to know why Clara appeared so crushed. He kept asking Mordehay: "What happened, please tell me what happened."

Mordehay translated Clara's account to Rycaut. He was more concerned about his wife than what Sabetay said. He turned to anxious Rycaut: "Before I came to see you I heard my son speak about Solomon Molho, Isaiah, and being anointed by Isaiah. Now my wife says that he woke up again and told her . . . ." He hesitated but he had to say it: "God asked him to be His messiah."

Rycaut immediately fell to his knees, brought his hands together and murmured a few repetitive words Mordehay couldn't understand Rycaut's ritualistic performance. Rycaut stood up and asked:

"What else did he say? Did he tell you how he met God! Tell me! Please tell me!" Mordehay didn't answer Rycaut. He patted his wife on the back trying to calm her down while Rycaut repeated his question in an emotional state. Mordehay asked Clara to go upstairs to Sabetay, he said he would follow shortly. He asked impatient Rycaut to sit down. He went over everything about Sabetay's confession to his mother and about Solomon Molho's grave. Rycaut was totally exhilarated. One question after another passed through his inquisitive mind. Was this the event Europe waited for? Was this the first signal of the manifestation of the messiah? It had to be. Otherwise how would Sabetay speak to angels, Isaiah, Molho, and hearing God's voice? Yes, it had to be so! He asked Mordehay if they could go upstairs. He wanted to have a look at Sabetay. Rycaut was hoping Sabetay would be awake and say a few words in his presence, words similar to those heard by Clara. Unfortunately Sabetay was still asleep. Upstairs, in the presence of Clara, Mordehay saw Rycaut puzzled looking around the room as if he had sensed something unusual. "What do I smell?" Rycaut asked sniffing all around.

"What are you saying?" asked Mordehay.

"I smell something strange but pleasant."

Mordehay sniffed a few times and then turned around towards his son's bed. "Now, so do I," he replied. He asked his wife in *espagnol* if she had done anything in the room that would cause the strange smell. She replied that the smell had been in the room ever since they brought Sabetay from the mountain. Mordehay moved closer to the bed. The smell was coming from there. He lifted the quilt and the two men looked at each other in astonishment. The pungent sweet smell had its source in Sabetay's body. They suspected first he had been washed or changed. That wasn't it. He still wore his dirty shoes in bed just the way Eliyah and Moses put him there. Bewildered, Rycaut said to Mordehay:

"I can't place the type of this odor. It is like the fragrance of a flower I never smelled before. Mordehay, I don't know what you are thinking, but I am beginning to suspect a mark of divine intervention, here. After what you told me, and now this pungent odor, I have no other explanation except that your son has been touched by the Holy Spirit." He kneeled once again in front of Sabetay's bed and murmured the same incomprehensible words in a form of prayer. Trembling and in a state of excitement he said: "I must leave immediately for my office and send a special courier to London."

Rycaut left the room precipitously repeating the same words which now Mordehay could hear distinctly: "*Hosanna, hosanna,* Mary Mother of God, Blessed be The Lord!" Mordehay didn't know what they meant. When Rycaut arrived at the office he wrote a short report categorically attesting that the city of Smyrna, not Ossa as the Nuremberg report claimed, nor Scotland as Evelyn had written, was the site God revealed his messenger. He gave a few details of the human attributes of Sabetay and how he had been privileged to know this saint personally since he was eighteen. He knew his father with whom he was associated in the export business. Then he wrote the exact words Sabetay spoke to his parents when he woke momentarily after he was brought unconscious from the Jewish cemetery on a mountain top. His report reached England in a record of nineteen days. In the meantime details of the extraordinary event spread quickly by word of mouth in Smyrna and nearby communities. The enormity of the news left many dumbfounded and terrified at the same time. Had Sabetay been touched by the divine spirit or was the incident one of his eccentric behaviors? The reaction was mixed. When Rycaut's report arrived in London it caused a sensation and the English press quickly dispatched the news to all the major cities of Europe. Instantly European eyes focused on the Orient. Cautiously they waited for the purported messiah's next move. They held their judgment until new evidence of a miracle or instructions from the messiah surfaced. In Smyrna the poor, the pious, and the suffering gathered at Sabetay's doorstep begging for salvation from their misery. The rich Jews and the clergy who saw their dominions threatened, became incensed at Sabetay for daring to provoke his brethren with such fantastic exaltations.

Moses was expected to visit Sabetay and check on his progress. Before leaving his house, fearful of being drawn by Sabetay into a messianic debate, he walked to his bookshelves and pulled out one of Maimonides' volumes entitled *Laws of Kings and their wars*. He opened it to chapter eleven to read once again and reassure himself of its meaning before he faced Sabetay. The relevant passages had been underlined:

> The messianic king will arise in the future and restore the kingdom of David as it was of old in the first dominion. He will rebuild the sanctuary, gather the dispersed of Israel, and restore all the laws in his days as they were before. . . . Anyone who does not believe in him or does not await his coming repudiates not only the other prophets, but Moses our Master and the Torah as well. . . . Balaam prophesied about both messiahs: the first messiah, David, who saved Israel from the hand of their enemies, and the final messiah, who will arise from his descendants and save Israel from the hand of the sons of Esau. . . . Do not suppose that the messianic king needs to give signs, perform miracles, and make new things happen in the world, or resurrect the dead and do similar things. It is not so. . . .
>
> If a king arises from the house of David who mediates on the Torah and performs the commandments . . . compels all Israel to follow and to repair breaches; and who fights the wars of the Lord— he is considered to be the messiah. If he succeeds in what he does and he rebuilds the sanctuary on its site and gathers the dispersed of Israel, he is certainly the messiah. He will prepare the whole world to serve the Lord together. If he does not succeed to this extent or is killed, it is certain he is not the one whom the Torah promised. . . .

Daniel long ago prophesied about Jesus of Nazareth, who imagined he was the messiah and was killed by a court of law. . . . All the prophets declared that the messiah will redeem Israel, save them, gather their dispersed, and strengthen their [obedience to] the commandments. But he caused Israel to perish by the sword and to have their remnant scattered and degraded. He replaced the Torah and led astray most of the world to serve a god besides the Lord. . . .[5]

He put on his overcoat, picked up his white umbrella and went out. Walking to Sabetay's house he recalled many of the messianic arguments they had before. On a number of occasions Sabetay hinted he had proof of his descendency from King David. Moses warned him to be cautious about such claim for he will be challenged and pressed by skeptics to show a difficult proof of that lineage. Sabetay's special qualifications of saintliness: arch piousness, superior knowledge of the Sacred Books, and extreme devotion to the Lord, all qualifications not even mentioned in Maimonides' list of attributes. He had to find a way to convince Sabetay about the awesomeness and dangers of his aspirations. Moses had not yet been informed about the vision Sabetay had over Molho's grave.

Near Sabetay's house, he saw hordes of poor people squatted in the street and around the house. He managed to reach the door, stepping past sitting bodies, and knocked at the door. Clara answered. She looked very happy and relieved to see him.

"Good morning, Señora Sevi. How is Sabetay today? I have come to see him."

"Of course, come in. I was expecting you."

She shut the door quickly to keep strangers from forcing themselves inside. "He woke up only for a few minutes at a time. He stayed awake long enough to tell me he loved me. I followed your advice and forced liquids into his mouth for as long as I could. I remained at his bedside all through the night and saw with my own eyes how restless he was with bad dreams. If he is awake

---

5. *Laws of Kings and Their Wars*, Moses Maimonides, translated by Weiss and Butterworth, Dover Publication, 1975.

and knows you are here he would want to talk to you and perhaps have another bowl of broth. I just finished preparing it. It will do him good. . . . My poor angel lost so much weight . . . ."

She cried. Moses reassured that her son was in no danger. Pleased to hear the encouraging words of a physician, she went to the kitchen and he went upstairs. Sabetay was still asleep. He sat by his bedside and waited. He looked around the room and saw for the first time that books occupied most of the space. A notebook on his night table, fully opened to a page entitled *Chilias*, caught his attention. He knew the meaning of the Greek word and wondered what Sabetay had written about the millennium. To pass the time away he picked it up, flipped a few pages, and discovered that it was Sabetay's personal work book and diary. He thought first to put it away but he couldn't. He felt a great desire to learn more about the perilous course his friend had embarked on. He surmised the book contained details of his true inner self. Concerned that he would be found reading his private secrets, he read as fast as he could. The more he read the more alarmed he became. Every page in the notebook pointed to one thought: the messiah. The book was divided into multiple sections, each beginning with a title page in Greek or Latin for no other purpose but to elude curiosity. The text in each section was written in Hebrew characters but in *espagnol*. A section entitled *Annus mirabilis* (wonderful year) caught his attention. He read the first paragraph and understood it was a collection of thoughts based on facts about his life. The first entry was on the significance of his birthday, 9th of Av, and its coincidence with the anniversary of the destruction of the Temple in Jerusalem. That date had been prophesied by the *Zohar* to be that of the messianic salvation. Sabetay had attached paramount importance to this coincidence of his birthday with the presumed date of the blessed event. There were other notes about his life suggesting through *gematria* a sequence of proofs showing that he possessed some of the attributes of the messiah. It seemed to Moses that in Sabetay's style of writing he made a concerted effort not to be definite and positive about his affirmations, yet to a learned person like him Sabetay left no doubt about his conviction of whom he thought he was portraying in the text. In the list of attributes matching those of the messiah he had quotations from various prophets referring to the permanent state of illness of the Savior. One was underlined and read: *"He will be a man of pains and acquainted with disease . . . he will always be suffering . . . from a specific disease."* Moses couldn't readily identify the source of most of these quotations. Next he had written a paragraph on his thoughts about the mole on his left arm and its significance of being located in the same spot as that of King David's mole. For Moses, who had hopes of questioning Sabetay how he would prove his lineage, now there appeared no doubt that Sabetay already had the answers.

He didn't have time to read everything. He flipped pages to another section entitled *Annus mundi* (world year). This was a hodge-podge of arithmetical calculations of Hebrew calendric years and prose, showing also correspondences of Hebrew and Christian calendric dates. One such calculation caught his attention. It was about the year 5408, explaining how it had to be the year of the messiah. This section was so disorganized Moses abandoned it. He flipped pages to nearly the end of the notebook. The last section was entitled *Dominus illuminatiomea* (The Lord my enlightening). It seemed to contain the spiritual experiences during Sabetay's recent meditations spending days in the dungeons of the Velvet Fortress. Moses wanted to read this part carefully. Perhaps in it he could find the sequence of events that led Sabetay to near death on top of Molho's grave. The first paragraph began with a disquietude wondering about a strange smell he had noticed emanating from his body. The smell seemed to remain unabated even after a thorough bath. Just as he started reading this curious sentence he was struck by the same smell Rycaut and Mordehay noticed when they visited earlier. Puzzled, he stood up and lifted the quilt. Sabetay rested the way he and Eliyah had put him to bed with his shoes on. He had not been washed or cleaned and the odor originated from his body. He checked his left arm and saw a good size mole on the inner side. All this began to trouble him. He covered him up and before he resumed reading in search of more answers, Sabetay woke up. Moses smiled at him and quickly placed the notebook on the night table.

"Good morning Sabetay. How are you feeling?" he asked. He was sure Sabetay had not seen him with the notebook in his hand.

He strained his eyes focussing at the person standing by his bedside and asked with a faint voice: "Is that you Moses?"

"Yes, it is me. I came to see how you are recovering. Don't try to speak. Your mother is bringing a bowl of soup. You need to rest and eat well. Eliyah and I found you exhausted and unconscious. I see that you have come out well, thanks to your mother's vigil over you. If you listen to her and eat what she brings you, you will get up in no time feeling your old self again. I will come back in a few days and we can talk longer."

He was examining him when Clara walked in with the bowl of soup. Moses was very disturbed by what he had read. He waited until Clara finished feeding her son, after which they both went downstairs. Clara informed him of Sabetay's description of his vision over Molho's grave. Moses was incredulous, listening to how far his childhood friend had pressed his convictions. It was too late to save him now. He excused himself assuring Clara that her son was on his way to recovery. That last word made him think: recovery from what? Indeed on his way home he walked very saddened. His friend had already embarked on a very perilous mission, one which had been tried many times before and each time ended in great societal turmoil, false hopes for the poor and sufferings, and martyrdom for him in the end. He also questioned if he weren't too quick at judging the outcome. Shouldn't he draw him into a debate before jumping into conclusions?

While recovering in bed, meetings were called by the city fathers to decide what official position they should take regarding the wave of unrest generated in the community on account of Sabetay's revelations. They had remained silent for a few days but that encouraged believers to parade in the streets, causing fights between them and others with opposing views. Even the local government whose policy was not to interfere with Jewish problems, demanded the rabbinical council to put an end to the dem-

onstrations. At these meetings some members insisted on excom-
municating Sabetay on the grounds that he had tempered in God's
affairs and was suggesting he was the messiah, had already spoken to saints, prophets, and even God. Liberal members disagreed.
They recommended ignoring the whole affair as it never happened.
As long as Sabetay did not openly declare himself in public they
had no grounds for issuing a punishment.

Most furious among the skeptics was Rabbi Escapha, Sabetay's
teacher and once his mentor. He felt betrayed, for he had staunchly
defended him prior to his ordainment. Heated discussions went
on for days until it was resolved that no action needed to be taken.
The Rabbis asked the community to ignore what they had heard.
This was all fine, but that decision didn't change anything. The fire
that had ignited in the minds and hearts of the people was not as
easily abated as the liberal rabbis surmised.

7

$\mathcal{S}$abetay recovered fully in two weeks' time. Being conscious of the number of poor and sick people squatting around his house, and the frequency of visiting elders warning him about the consequences of any intentions he might have to arouse the community, he decided it was best to remain cloistered at home until the excitement about his vision abated.

It was late Fall of 1648. Fresh gruesome reports on the war in Poland poured in at an alarming rate. Messages about the horrible fate of Polish and Ukrainian Jews were sent by carrier pigeons to European and Middle Eastern Jewries. Ukrainians, Cossacks and Tartars whose lands were owned by Polish nobility, revolted under the leadership of Bogdan Chmielnicki, nicknamed by Jews as Chmi'l. The dissatisfaction against the landlords was so deep and widespread that Chmi'l was able to unite these three different groups in spite of the hatred they felt for each other. They united under the common battle cry: "Down with the Polish landlords and the Jews." As the Polish army retreated, Jews fled from the plains to the fortified cities hoping the royal army would protect them. Instead, Poles surrendered them to the advancing insurgent revolutionaries hoping to save their necks. The towns of Nemirow, Tulczyn, Bar, Ostrog, Zaslavl, Dubno, and Constantinov fell to the advancing enemy and residing Jews were slaughtered by tens of thousands. The war spread to Lithuania and White

Russia. Similar massacres took place in Pinsk, Chernigov, Homel, Lublin, etc. The carnage turned into one of the worst holocausts in recorded history. The persecution of Ashkenazi Jews surpassed the savagery of the Spanish Inquisition.

Of these horrible accounts, one in particular stood in Sabetay's mind as a shining example that God had not slumbered. A noted Ashkenazi Rabbi and cabalist, named Nathan Hannover, wrote in a European newspaper that he had found proof of the coming of salvation in spite of the savagery that prevailed. In his article entitled: "The Deepest Abyss" he brought to light a Hebrew phrase of past sages: "*Cheble moshiah iabo leolam,*" which translated into "the labor pains of the world bear the messiah, initials of which corresponded to Chmi'l."[1] Being a staunch cabalist, he discovered that the name itself held the secret of the eminence of the messianic prophecy. This is how he explained it: the name of the butcher *Chmi'l* heralded the Hebrew phrase clearly and loudly. "Wait," he wrote further, "that is not all. From *gematria* the number corresponding to Chmi'l suggests the year 1648, the year of grace." As a scientist feels triumphant upon the discovery of a new phenomenon, he clamored that the phrase not only predicted Chmi'l's genocide, it prophesied the year of the arrival of the messiah.

"Brilliant!" exclaimed Sabetay when he read Hannover's article. "How much more proof do people expect before they have absolute faith in the prophecy of Ezekiel who also warned of wars and sufferings before the year of Israel's redemption?"

Exhilarated by this fresh hope, and tired of being confined in the house, early one morning he decided to go to the yeshiva. He was fired by a desire to surprise his trusted friend Moses with Rabbi Hannover's revelation. He put on the long overcoat his mother had sewn with a dozen little pockets hanging below the waist. The pockets had a very important significance in the fulfillment of a special commandment on charity. According to Maimonides "*there are eight degrees of charity*." The least deserving was: "*to give with re-*

---

1. J. Kastein, p. 49.

luctance or regret . . ." At the other end of the scale: *"the eighth and most meritorious is giving in such a way as to prevent poverty in general."* But this last one was a difficult task for a whole community to live up to, let alone a lowly individual. The seventh degree, though not particularly easy to live by, became an achievable goal for an individual. The overcoat with pockets was the perfect instrument with which to practice that charity: *"to bestow charity in such a way that the benefactor may not know the comforted person."* This was accomplished by filling the pockets with piasters (Turkish coins) while anonymous beggars followed behind and dug into the pockets while the benefactor made a conscientious effort not to look back while his pockets were being gradually emptied.

At the yeshiva, Sabetay was not happy to notice that students and teachers made an effort not to acknowledge his presence. Some thought of him adversely, and turned their faces away in disdain. Others avoided him, not knowing how to address a person who had been anointed by the prophet Isaiah. Unconcerned, he went looking for Moses, who had been appointed instructor soon after his graduation. He searched from one classroom to another. Finally he found him standing in a corridor with Isaac Silveira. Moses was giving Isaac comfort before he was called in to his final examination.

"Sabetay!" exclaimed Moses when he saw him marching towards him with his unbuttoned overcoat flying behind. Isaac didn't say anything. He wasn't happy to see Sabetay at this crucial moment. If there was one thing he didn't want at this stage was controversy for associating with Sabetay. He excused himself and went in the direction of the principal's office. "What are you doing here? Are you all right?"

"Moses, I feel fine, believe me. I need to talk to you."

Sensing the urgency in Sabetay's voice, and guessing that his friend wanted to discuss some aspect of his strange aspiration, he replied: "Sure. Isaac just went in for his final examination. I'd like to be here when he comes out. Do you mind if we go to the courtyard and sit on a bench? It is cold but a beautiful sunny day."

They sat under a huge fig tree which must have been planted nearly a century ago. Moses waited for his friend to open the subject.

"Moses, you are the only true friend I have and I must talk to you before I burst from the enormous anxiety I feel within me."

To inject a bit of joviality, Moses teased: "By all means, Sabetay I don't want to see you splattered all over the courtyard." The joke went totally unnoticed.

"Do you trust me, Moses? Do you trust my piety? Do you trust my devotion and love for my faith and my God? Do you think I am schooled and proficient in the words of our Torah, our Talmud, our Midrash, our Cabala, our Prophets and all that is holy? Do you think I am capable of usurping all these divine values for personal gains?"

Moses didn't answer because he had a good idea where the questions would lead. Sabetay didn't wait for his answer either. "I came to tell you of my impressions about a fantastic article I read . . . ." He was interrupted by Isaac returning with a pale and disappointed look on his face.

"What is the matter Isaac?" asked Moses. "You are supposed to be in the examination room. Why aren't you there?"

"One of the examiners didn't show up. They postponed it for tomorrow. I can't stand this anguish any longer," he complained.

Moses smiled compassionately. He knew the agony Isaac was going through. Sabetay didn't share that feeling. He looked irritated about his interruption. "You better go home and rest," blurted Sabetay.

"I am going home all right, but not to rest. I have to brush up on a few concepts that seemed to have slipped my memory this morning."

He said goodbye and left. Before Sabetay resumed, Moses had an idea. It was his assignment as an instructor to take three rabbinical students to the countryside twice a week to introduce them to the practice of meditation and debate. He suggested: "How would you like to go walking to the countryside, the way we used to do when we were students?"

"Splendid idea! I love it!" he answered assuming Moses meant the two of them.

"Do you mind if I took three young students with us? I am entrusted with that responsibility."

Sabetay felt imposed and trapped into someone else's obligation. It sounded to him as if he had been asked to chaperon three immature and silly teenagers. He couldn't very well refuse; he had already agreed. Well he resolved, he could still debate Moses while the students played their silly games.

Moses took a few moments searching for the students. When he found them he introduced them to Sabetay and they began their walk towards the same stony and dusty road leading to the Velvet Fortress. By this time every one in the city had heard of Sabetay's bizarre advent and notoriety. As soon as they cleared the last dwelling on the road, reciting the morning prayers the group walked up the hill. After the final 'Amen' the students waited eagerly to be addressed by the new celebrity in town. They knew of him as the genius who memorized all the holy books, the man who was visited by angels, who had risen above clouds, who spoke to the prophet Ezekiel, and who was told by God he was destined to be His *mashiah*. Impressionable as they were, they didn't pay much attention to the negative characterizations of him. From the corner of his eye Sabetay spied on the three young men whispering and turning their heads frequently to peek at him. He became attracted by their childish game. He thought he would enjoy provoking them the way he provoked Isaac in the past:

"What does AMIRAH stand for?" he asked them abruptly. He walked ahead. The young students, caught by surprise, stopped to consult each other. They felt embarrassed for not knowing the answer. They looked at Moses, hoping to get a clue from their teacher. Preoccupied with the meaning of that difficult question one of the students fell on the stony road. His prayer shawl was too long and in the excitement he stepped on the end of it, stumbling and falling to the ground. The other two rushed to help him. He wasn't hurt. They walked fast to catch up with the two senior men. Sabetay had shaken their inflated confidence. Not realizing why he asked the question, Moses gave them a hint: "It is an acronym for one of the most frequently used praises to the Lord and it is found in the prayer book."

That hint was sufficient for the student who had fallen and was dusting his clothes. "Oh, I know," he said running towards his teacher. "They are the first letters of the Hebrew praise: Our Lord and King, His Majesty be exalted."

He was correct but Sabetay didn't acknowledge it. Instead, he asked: "What is your name?" Panting the student replied: "Joseph Calmari." Sabetay followed: "Joseph, many past sages struggled in vain to comprehend the Mystery of the Godhead which encompasses the Deity, the divine essence of the Creator, and His cosmos. They died in great disappointment and frustration. Only a handful of wise rabbis in our history have acquired that knowledge. I am one of them!" He said this proudly pointing to his chest: "The *Cabala* says: *He who shall know the Mysteries of the Gates of Understanding in the Cabala shall know also the Mystery of the Great Jubilee.*[2] What rank would you give a rare man for having acquired that knowledge?"

Sabetay waited for an answer. The students were overwhelmed by the supreme and difficult question. Without realizing, Joseph Calmari had already answered the question. They had a superficial knowledge of the *Cabala* and they had heard of the Mystery of the Godhead mentioned. They couldn't imagine that any man, including the contributors to the *Cabala*, understood the metaphysical notion it represented. All three shook their heads and answered in unison: "We don't know!"

Sabetay looked pleased for having baffled them. Smiling, he turned to Moses to show his enjoyment. Instead of explaining, he surprised the young students with another revelation about himself. "I have reached this highest level because I understood

---

2. This quote represented for Sabetay his whole purpose in life, his doctrine and the roots of his faith. He understood the Great Jubilee to mean the messiah.

the distinction between the Emanator, the hidden God called *En-sof* (the boundless), inaccessible and hidden in the mystery of his secret recesses, and the *emanation* the sphere of the ten divine attributes. This emanation that emerged from the Godhead, created the higher and nether worlds and transformed the hidden God into our accessible God. Of course you wouldn't know that! Did you know there are ten distinct attributes in this process of emanation?" He asked again, knowing they wouldn't have the slightest idea. "Did you know that seven of them form the structure of Creation and are manifested to the visible universe, each of which is symbolized by one day of creation; each revealing a different aspect of the creative power of God?"

Ironically, these were concepts he had discovered only recently. His purpose for boasting was that he boiled with anticipation to delight Moses and hoped to gain a greater degree of reverence from him. The presence of the students was an excuse to ventilate his pride in front of his friend. But to the students he sounded like an angel fallen from the sky, speaking to them in *espagnol*, using an abstract vocabulary from the heavens. Never had they been in the company of a person who knew the hidden recesses of the Creator. They walked close to him, worried that they will miss important information. Moses trailed behind knowing the source of this wisdom: The *Zohar*, the encyclopedia of the mystics.

"Now that I have acquainted you with the scheme making up the attributes of God, what is one of the most important of these attributes of *En-sof*, the boundless?" They shook their heads, again. His reason for asking the question and his decision to answer it had an ulterior motive. He wanted to implant, only suggestively, the important connection that existed between him and God, hoping they, in turn, would spread it in the community.

"It is symbolized in *The Holy One Blessed Be He*, and in the name of the Godhead, the Tetragrammaton: YHVH or Yahveh. Remember I said 'symbolized' because the mystery is that God who revealed Himself to Israel in His Torah **was not** the inaccessible *En-Sof*, but the aspect of His power manifested to our people. The Tetragrammaton is our God, superior to the entire emanation. He is also signified by the letter 'V' in YHVW and is called the husband of the tenth attribute, the Kingdom. That in turn has emanated from the ninth attribute we call the *Shehinah*. This attribute contains the salvation of man from evil and sin. In it is locked the secret spelling the time and place for the appearance of our redeeming messiah which will have the key to all these secrets . . ."

But as soon as he mentioned the word messiah, one student interrupted and asked hurriedly:

"*Rabbino*, since you seem to know the dominion that embodies the essence of the messiah, you must be the one who has found the key releasing that essence. You must have the secret, and it follows that you must know when the *mashiah* is to arrive. Won't you tell us?"

Sabetay laughed, happy to have steered curiosity in the young lad the way he wanted. "To some extent, yes," he replied.

"When? When? Please tell us!" asked Calmari.

"I will tell you this much. Only when there is a sincere desire on the part of our people to return to the Torah, and only then this ninth attribute will rise from the dust, it will lift up and become exalted and it will send us the messiah. We can all help lift the *Shehinah* from the dust. Lately, it seems man has felt this awareness and is beginning to strive to create that redeeming environment. All three of you can be very helpful in this respect."

Moses hadn't said a word. He listened with concern while walking behind them. He had a feeling Sabetay was speaking to him and not to the students. The last statements said it all. He understood from his words that Sabetay wanted to spread his candidacy for the messiah without declaring himself, waiting for the right moment to proclaim himself. What he had read in the notebook, and now this suggestive confession all fit together. What Moses didn't know was how he planned to convince the Jewries in the world.

They arrived at the top of the hill from where they could see the old fortress dominating the city. The cold breeze from the sea blew over their faces, watering their eyes and refreshing their faces. Puffy clouds were swept by the sea breeze while the sunlight gave them a pinkish brightness. Intoxicated with excitement, Calmari asked a question Moses had in mind: "How would one person arouse the hearts of hundreds of thousands of Jews dispersed across many lands on earth? Each of these lands is ruled by a powerful monarch. The Holy Land, where the children of Israel are to be reunited, belongs to the most powerful monarchs of all: Our Sultan. How . . . ."

Sabetay didn't let him finish. It was a question he had wrestled with and for which he hadn't found an answer. "That, my dear young man, is another key God holds and will deliver in the hands of the servant He chooses for the mission. The messiah will know that answer when God gives him the authority. The whole process consists in harvesting all the living souls and making them follow him. Harvesting two or three souls or one hundred is not a major problem, but harvesting the whole nation of Israel requires the hand of the Lord. Without Him it can't be done! When the time comes, He will instruct His messenger how to do it. A voice from behind a bush or behind a rock will tell the messiah what he needs to do. God's power will be on his side and no potentate on earth can defeat it."

Moses concluded from this answer that Sabetay expected to hear from the Lord. It was Calmari again who was asking the question. Childishly he said: "*Muy honorable Rabbino*, from what you have been telling us I can see how saintly you are. I hope you don't mind me asking if you ever rose above the clouds as some people in our community say you did? Will you do it again for us? I'll be so grateful to you forever!"

Pleased with the young man, Sabetay answered: "Only after you answer my question that remains unanswered."

"What question was that?" asked Calmari.

"What rank would you give a man who has understood the mystery of the Godhead?"

All three pondered for a moment, but only Calmari had the courage to say it: "AMIRAH!" he screamed with excitement. "I thought I had already answered that!"

Sabetay was happy beyond himself when he heard this young man say what he wanted to hear. In fact he liked the response so much that in the days that followed he related this incident to everyone he met. As a result the nickname AMIRAH stuck to him.

It seemed that Sabetay forgot what he had promised the young student, who restated his question: "*Rabbino*, did you ever rise above the clouds? Will you do it again for us for us?"

Sabetay smiled and asked him: "What did you say your name was?"

"Joseph Calmari," the young student replied.

"I, too, have a brother named Joseph. You seem more interested in divinity than your two friends. Because I like you, Joseph, and since you have demonstrated an unusual alertness to all my questions, I will do it again for you." He pointed to the sky and said: "But you must keep your eyes on that cloud up there until I tell you to look down."

All three students raised their heads instantly to look at the passing cloud. They squinted and waited in great excitement. A few seconds later they heard him exclaim: "You may look down. Well did you see me? Did you see me go up and down. It is simply beautiful up there."

From the look on Sabetay's face and the fire in his eyes, they had no doubt he had climbed up to the clouds and came down swiftly. They had a feeling the whole performance was too fast to have made an impression on them, except for their fast pounding hearts. Not wanting to disappoint Sabetay, Calmari said: "I think I saw a shadow over my head. I couldn't make out what it was; it happened so fast. But I smelled a strange odor at that very moment; an distinct odor that wasn't there earlier. I don't know how to describe it. It was a very pleasant odor."[3]

"So did I!" said the other two.

Moses knew what they were talking about. The ebullient and inquisitive Calmari asked: "What is that smell AMIRAH?"

---

3. G. Scholem, p. 139. Also J. Kastein p. 21.

"It is the smell of the Garden of Eden, young man. Nowhere else would you be able to smell it. . . ."

Moses, who had been observing these charades, smiled and decided to put an end to the excursion. Sabetay was disappointed. He was having such fun. He told Moses he wasn't going back with them. It was such a nice day he was opting to remain by the Grecian ruins to pray and meditate the rest of the day. Moses advised him not to wander too long; his mother will be more concerned this time. He and the students came down the hill fully rewarded by the experience. Calmari asked about the significance of the odor: "Rabbi Pinheiro, I will not be able to rest until you explain the source of that heavenly odor. Was AMIRAH joking when he said it was a smell from the Garden of Eden?"

Moses was unsure of what to say. A few days earlier he had been puzzled discovering the same odor when he visited Sabetay. He had no idea about the source of the odor or why Sabetay was the only person carrying it. He dismissed its importance, saying to the students: "Rabbi Sevi does not lie. All the years I have known him he hasn't lied to me or anyone else. To the best of my knowledge the odor may be from an herb Rabbi Sevi puts on his garment to expunge his natural body odor. This practice is frequent, especially among persons who perspire heavily." To inject humor he reiterated a popular misconception about French women: "That is how the famous perfume industry was created. French women are not known to be fond of daily baths. Sprinkling themselves with perfume is nearly effortless and the result considerably more effective in attracting men."

The students laughed and Moses was satisfied he had changed the subject away from a difficult impasse. But had he? When the exhilarated students returned to the yeshiva they had many wondrous experiences to pass on to friends and relatives. The heavenly odor was at the top of the list. They did a superb job publicizing the episodes with AMIRAH. Naturally, what seemed to have drawn most attention was the "odor." It became a mystery confounding and frustrating the Jews of Smyrna. It seemed that the more this subject was discussed the more questions surfaced. What kind of an odor was it? How did it differ from other body odors? Garden of Eden? How does Sabetay know how the Garden of Eden smells? Such secrets belonged to saints. As expected, most had a difficult time dismissing the idea. Explanations abounded from the ridiculous and comical to the lofty and the sublime. And what about this new title of AMIRAH? What was its significance, anyway? The entire congregation found itself divided either with indignation or with deep humility. Arguments led to fierce fights in the streets. The Turkish authorities had to interfere once again. The disputes were so disruptive and damaging to the community that city fathers met once again to seek a resolution concerning Sabetay's new disclosures. Although furious at his antics, most elder rabbis found no grounds for punishment. He hadn't done anything to breach Judaic laws. But this was the kind of news Europeans expected from a presumed messiah. Rycaut didn't fail to report the boiling controversy in the cities of the Ottoman Empire.

The preoccupation with the special odor didn't go away. It lingered and infected the curiosity and imagination of the Sephardis. Those who wanted Sabetay to be admonished insisted on a thorough examination by their best physician in Smyrna. He had to prove, once and for all, if this odor was from an ingredient that would wash away or, as many believed to be, indelible from the Garden of Eden.

Sabetay, upon learning the commission of rabbis was to take up the matter of a mandatory physical examination, shocked the community further, announcing he was submitting himself voluntarily to the highly respected physician Dr. Baruch. The news of his bold act was so valiant and bombastic that it temporarily overshadowed the news of the defeat of the Ottoman fleet by the Venetians. Sabetay's challenge became the number-one preoccupation of the Jews of Smyrna. Rycaut remained close to the Sevis, waiting for the outcome of the "holy test," a provocative expression he used in his reports. The commission of rabbis was taken by surprise. It had not yet voted if it would ask Sabetay to submit to the examination, much less what course of final action would be required after the doctor's decision. They asked Sabetay to postpone his medical visit for a month. He agreed. This delay gave bookies in the empire and in Europe time to fix gambling odds and accept bids. As the day approached, crowds gathered around Dr. Baruch's clinic, anxious to be present when the verdict was announced.

On the appointed day, Sabetay marched down to Dr. Baruch's clinic with a crowd of supporters behind him. The scene in the street looked like the retinue of a prize fighter walking to the rink and making all sorts of gestures to intimidate the skeptics who shouted insults. He entered the physician's office alone. The council had posted guards at the entrance of the clinic and were under orders to let no one in except Sabetay. Everyone waited silently and impatiently.

Dr. Baruch asked Sabetay to strip naked and take a hot bath prepared especially for him. He did as he was told. Two aids scrubbed him thoroughly from head to toe and ushered him to the office where the doctor waited to examine him. Not a single word was exchanged during the examination. Dr. Baruch, knowing the world waited to hear his expert opinion, examined him meticulously. He probed with a magnifying glass the surface of his skin, his under arms, his genitals, and all parts known to have odorous glands. He repeated the same clinical steps a number of times, just to be sure. In the end he asked Sabetay to get dressed while he stepped out to analyze his findings. When the doctor returned Sabetay said: "Well?"

Dr. Baruch was in a somber mood. He asked him to walk to the window. It was the first time he had spoken to him since he entered the clinic. They both looked at the mob outside moving around impatiently. Sabetay didn't know what to make of the doctor's request. He waited and the doctor spoke. He appeared very shaken: "What you see outside my window is just a small group of people waiting for my decision. You must realize that I have an awesome responsibility towards them. What I say will affect many lives, especially those poor pious souls waiting for deliverance from poverty, pain, sickness, bondage, and oppression . . . ."

Like the rest of the world, Sabetay waited to hear the result of the examination, not a lecture on responsibilities. He interrupted: "You haven't told me your decision, Doctor."

It was no use stalling. He had to say what he had found. "Yes, I smelled an unusual odor that seems unwashable and that I can't explain. This is highly unusual, especially after my assistants scrubbed you thoroughly and effectively. Now I ask you to be truthful to me. I am a doctor and have sworn the Hippocratic oath that I would uphold the high ethical and moral standards of my profession. Like you, I am a kind of rabbi that cures the body while you cure the soul. Let me ask you. To what do you attribute the odor? Did you have it all your life as far as you can remember? I caution you to be truthful to me," he warned.

Sabetay failed to understand why the doctor pressed him to be truthful. He, more than anyone, would be conscious of truthfulness and a responsibility towards the public. He answered resentfully, for he didn't need to be lectured about honesty. "Doctor, I have taken an oath infinitely more severe than yours in the presence of our Creator, holding the Torah in my arms. I find no petty comfort in succumbing to deception, especially with such a simple matter as an odor. I like to remind you that I came here on my own accord, knowing well what people out there would do to me if they knew I lied. The punishment would be stoning in the community square until I die. Since you asked me the source of the odor I will tell you. Not long ago, as you might have heard, I had a vision in the old Jewish cemetery. The patriarch Isaiah anointed my body with a special indelible oil and commanded me not to reveal the mystery to anyone until such time as it became absolutely life threatening. I believe that moment is here now and I have divulged that mystery to you. As you said, the whole community awaits the truth. I will turn your question around and ask of you what you asked of me: Can you be truthful to your oath?"

Dr. Baruch was confronted with his own question. Instead of answering, he wanted credible proof about the odor. He asked, "Did you have other visions regarding the odor?"

"Yes."

"What was the nature of the subsequent visions?"

"Again, I must warn you of dire consequences that will come upon you if you should reveal any of part of these revelations. Your only responsibility to the public is telling what you found or did not find in your medical examination. The rest must be kept in confidence. Are you able to do that, Doctor?" warned Sabetay.

"Yes," was the reply.

"Very well. After I was found unconscious on Solomon Molho's grave and the prophet Isaiah had anointed me, three nights in a row, I heard warnings in my sleep saying: 'Do not touch my anointed Sabetay Sevi.' The third night the same voice alerted me that I would be revisited by another patriarch who would anoint me, once again, on the twenty-first of the month of Sivan."[4]

He stopped but the doctor begged to know more. "Is it proper for me to ask who anointed you the second time?"

"I will answer you so long as you take upon yourself the responsibility of the oath you made to me. Do you?" asked Sabetay.

The doctor thought for a moment. Was he getting too involved in this mysterious affair? He concluded it was too late to ask that question. He had already become involved. He answered hurriedly: "Yes, I am ready to assume the responsibility."

"Very well, then. It was the prophet Elijah in person."

Sabetay wanted to put an end to this matter once and for all. He asked the doctor firmly: "Now I'd like to know what you are going to tell the euphoric public and the commission of rabbis who await the results of your examination."

Perplexed, afraid, and void of any answer Dr. Baruch asked: "What should I tell them? Your odor is definitely not of human origin. Never in my long career of examining thousands of bodies have I experienced such a sweet and fragrant odor on a human or from a plant. I repeat: What should I say without breaching my oath?"

Angry at the doctor for not having the courage to tell the truth, Sabetay replied: "It is up to you," and on that note, left the clinic.

When people outside saw him walk away briskly, they pulled out of his path. They demanded to know what the final decision

---

4. This is the ninth month of an ordinary Hebrew year.

was. He didn't answer them. A group of belligerent opponents surrounded him, trying to force him to admit he had lied. When his supporters saw them bully their man, they came to his rescue with sticks and stones. A fight broke out and Sabetay was extricated from the malevolent group. He was escorted to his home unharmed. Upon the urging of one zealot, the crowd forced itself into the clinic demanding to know what the final result was. Overwhelmed, the doctor said he had to abide by the promise he made to the city fathers that he would only reveal the result to them. He would send the report swiftly. It was up to the Rabbinate to make the decision public.

This only made the suspense more acute. The news that the examination had been completed traveled fast. Rycaut, who had written the accounts leading to the examination, now waited to communicate the result of the "holy test" to his English readers. Proof from the doctor's report was especially important to Rycaut and his English Christians. He had already informed them about Sabetay's vision, the saintly odor, the requirement of a holy test. If that test proved to be positive, they wouldn't have to wait until 1666. The flame of excitement had already been lit, and the English bookies had began to shift the odds in favor of the Hebrew date of 1648.

A day after the medical examination, the Rabbinate received Dr. Baruch's report. Now they deliberated frantically about what to do next. Rabbis in the council always seemed to take a long time to agree on anything. A week went by without a public announcement. Mobs stormed the office of the Rabbinate and demanded to know the final result. Fearing the angry crowd, Rabbi Escapha came out on the balcony of the office with the medical report in his hand. He announced in an innocuous fashion:

"Dr. Baruch has qualified the findings of the examination as follows: He could find no medical or physical reason for the persistent odor on Rabbi Sevi's body . . ." The crowd roared but Escapha lifted his free hand demanding silence. "I am not finished . . . I am not finished. The doctor states he could not identify the odor belonging to anything he had ever smelled before. The only explanation he gave is that he believes it is a miracle." This time the crowd went wild. The mob had heard what they came to hear. From that point on they didn't care what else was in the report. Above the loud cheers Escapha's voice could not be heard, but he was not finished. He wanted to make public the council's decision, but the crowd turned wild and unruly. Fist fights broke out again, and Escapha knew he wouldn't be able to subdue the melee. He said quickly what he had to say, knowing no one in the noisy crowd heard him: "Take it for what it is worth. We, as your city fathers, have not yet decided at an implication of this event. We have agreed on one thing only. Because Sabetay has not in reality taken any action to stir a public disorder, no charges are to be leveled against him. Good day and I urge you to stop fighting and attend to your daily business." He turned around and shut the balcony door behind him. The report and the council's decision were made public in the Sephardi weekly.

People expected from the council an admonition or a recognition of Sabetay's holy status. As long as there was no judgment they took it upon themselves to assume what they wanted. Now the world and the people of Smyrna waited for further revelations from the man of God.

$$\backsim$$

The war in Poland was coming to an end. The cardinal of Gniezno, Jan Kassimir, was elected king of Poland. He opened negotiations with Chmielnicki and the massacres ended. All was quiet in Eastern Europe. In the meantime a group of refugees from Palestine came to Smyrna and rose to proclaim Sabetay as their savior. The messiah had been promised in 1648 and, since no one else besides Sabetay rose to qualify or claim that authority, they proclaimed him openly the *mashiah* without his approbation. These refugees invaded the synagogues in Smyrna attempting to round up more devotees. More violent disturbances broke out in the streets.

Sabetay watched gleefully without getting involved. He remained in his house meditating on what to do next. It was not easy to subdue his burning temptation to declare himself. His vision over

Molho's grave, then the miraculous impact of his body odor, and now the ever-growing support of his people, intensified his desire to offer himself as the redeemer of Israel. As a truly pious man well-read on the tragic outcome of past messianic movements that rebelled against the establishment, he decided the time was not yet ripe. He would wait for the Lord to judge his worthiness. But he questioned, hadn't he been summoned by the Lord over Molho's grave? Not to his satisfaction. God had not said he had been chosen. The words of the Lord were clear. He said: *"Thou art **destined** to redeem Israel . . ."* He would have liked to hear: *"Thou art the redeemer of Israel."* But, he thought, in any case the Lord had begun to prepare the hearts of the multitudes to be receptive to him. In the meantime the date of the prophecy had to be postponed. The year 1648 was ending. One question about his life concerned him very much, and wouldn't leave his mind: his mysterious disease. Was it a curse or a blessing? He was more inclined to view it as an important attribute of the messiah as Isaac Luria defined:

> . . . . When the Holy Ancient One[5] wishes the health of the world, He afflicts a just man with pain and sickness and heals the rest of the world through him.

He wanted very much to believe in these wise words for they fitted him perfectly.

ڴ

Sabetay was in the habit of praying alone. A year had passed since the mayhem over his vision and the ensuing discovery of

---

5. God has many names in Judaism. Some names are permitted to be spoken while others are forbidden. This spoken name is attributed to the Absolute God. In the cabalistic system dealing with Deity, the existence of the Absolute, *Ain Soph*, God, Unapproachable and Unconditioned, is established. Then, the manner in which this withdrawn nature manifests itself to the living consists of ten divine attributes, namely: The Supreme Crown, Wisdom, Intelligence, Mercy, Severity and Judgment, Beauty, Victory, Glory, the Foundation, and ultimately the Kingdom.

the heavenly odor. On the eve of Hanukah 1649, he decided to attend services at the synagogue Neveh Shalom with a very specific objective in mind. During services he waited with apprehension until the traditional silent prayer was invoked and the entire assembly bowed their heads in silent meditation for a few minutes. Total silence reigned in the sanctuary. Unnoticed, he stood up and walked to the *alememar* (bimah), the dais from which the Torah is read. With a loud and clear voice he broke the silence by pronouncing loudly one of the forbidden and unspoken names of God (*Shem ha-mephorash*). Heads covered with prayer shawls, the faithful raised their heads instantly. He repeated the word again defiantly. To the unsuspecting faithful, deeply absorbed in private prayers, it was as if a canon shell had fallen from the sky. Did Sabetay really say what they heard him say? If so, he should know that since Jews went into exile from Palestine, more than a millennium and a half ago, that word had never been uttered. A moment of fear enveloped the synagogue. Many had studied the Talmud and they knew only three people were permitted to pronounce any one of the Ineffable Names[6] of God: the High Priest in Jerusalem, the martyr just before he died and turned his soul to his Maker, and the messiah. Since Sabetay was neither of the first two, he had to be hinting messiahship. In that case Judaic laws would have to subject him to a severe punishment of forty lashes. Everyone knew Sabetay had to be familiar with the punish-

---

6. In other religions, too, God has many names: Creator, Lord, All Merciful, The Maker, etc. These are not proper names like God or Allah, they simply infer God's powers. The name YAHWEH or YAHVEH is only an acronym of one unspeakable name. In Jewish liturgy these letters are not read Yahveh they are read *Adonay*, no direct relation to these letters. The *Zohar* explains that God requested this. No one is supposed to know the reason. Knowing man's curiosity, in his unrelenting search of knowledge of the divine, few cabalists claim to have unraveled the mystery of God's real names. Supposedly there is one with twelve letters, one of forty-two letters, and so on. The Ineffable Name Sabetay spoke, was of seventy-two letters.

ment before he breached this Talmudic law. In the few seconds it took the congregation to realize what had happened, Sabetay waited, erect and determined, to witness the reaction.

Suddenly came one thundering voice shouting: *"Mashiah! Mashiah!"*

Requited, Sabetay looked to see who had the courage to recognize his claim by implication. Heads turned towards the lonely voice heralding the saintly name. It was young Rabbi Isaac Silveira. Of all the people in the synagogue Sabetay would have never suspected him. In the past he had argued and quarreled with him, and now, defiantly, he was coming to his support. This was no small feat. Isaac had already passed his examinations and had become rabbi in his own right. While all eyes were still upon Isaac, two more voices thundered the name of the messiah. This time it was Moses Pinheiro and Joseph Calmari, the young student who had impressed Sabetay the day he went for a walk with the three students. The rest of the congregation remained baffled. Was this a conspiracy arranged by Sabetay? Everyone respected Moses Pinheiro as a serious and level-headed teacher at the yeshiva. His brother-in-law was the distinguished Italian Rabbi Joseph Ergas. Why would he stand in support of Sabetay? As the heads of the congregants turned back and forth trying to assess the meaning of this unforgivable interruption in their morning service, a group of refugees from Palestine stood up and moved next to Isaac and Moses in a show of solidarity. Terribly shaken, the chief rabbi signaled the officiating rabbi to speed up the service and bring it to a close.

Sabetay's behavior was such a breech of talmudic law that city fathers had to meet immediately. Once again the debate was plagued with the same legal technicalities as when they assembled to decide what to do about the odor. One thing was certain. Sabetay had pronounced the Ineffable Name of God, which in itself was punishable with forty lashes, but others claimed it was more than that: he declared himself the messiah! He did it by implication! They demanded excommunication. But when the voting took place there wasn't a majority to impose a sentence.

Rabbi Escapha turned angry and furious at the indecision of his colleagues. He had supported Sabetay so staunchly at the time of his ordainment. He felt totally betrayed by the incident of the odor and now by this provocation. Sabetay was no longer the insignificant nuisance he thought he had become. His latest public act was a resolute and flagrant provocation of the establishment and religious laws.

Sabetay, in the meantime, was enjoying a period of great success in winning an increasing number of supporters. His headaches and depression had vanished. He rejoiced that he had launched a challenge to the establishment and had won the allegiance of his friends Silveira and Pinheiro. He went to the streets speaking against the establishment and the archaic laws they defended. Isaac Silveira became his devoted advisor. Sabetay began to indoctrinate Isaac with many of the ideas he had recorded in his private notebook. Accordingly Isaac took a more aggressive stand and began to leak words that Sabetay held visible proof of descendency from King David: the mole on his left arm, in the same spot as that of the venerable king of the Jews. Moses Pinheiro, however, remained aloof from the small organized movement that had formed.

That whole year, until mid-1650, Isaac Silveira projected himself as the disciple of the future messiah. Sabetay warned his overzealous friend that under no circumstance would he allow him to say that he was the messiah. Only Sabetay was to determine when and how he would declare himself. He waited for definite confirmation from the Lord. With sermons and speeches in the streets Isaac and Calmari were able to gather nearly one thousand followers in support of Sabetay's movement, preaching people to pray and seek repentance for their sins, a prelude to the arrival of the blessed event. They organized public meetings in the courtyards of the synagogues, which wouldn't allow them inside, preaching sermons expounding the truth about the prophesied messianic era, and their one and only candidate who had been called to duty by God and had been anointed by the prophet Isaiah. With fiery speeches Isaac warned the crowds to pray for their Lord, repent their sins, and join the movement, for this was the last opportunity to heed the messianic prophecy. If it was ignored, as the city fathers wanted them to do, God was likely to abandon Israel in the Diasporas forever.

On August 1650, Isaac made a very unusual announcement. Sabetay's birthday was on the 9th of that month, the same day as the anniversary of the destruction of the Temple in Jerusalem, and that day was to be celebrated at noon at the top of the mountain by the Velvet Fortress. Sabetay was to perform a miracle to convince the remaining skeptics of his endowed divine powers. He was to stop the sun for one hour on its heavenly orbit! One can imagine the level of anxiety and fear the announcement generated. What courage! What confidence! What a challenge! These were the reactions of followers as well as skeptics, Jews and non-Jews, yearning to be present and observe the miracle of the century. The holy books spoke of miracles during messianic times and this had to be one of them.

On the announced day and before noon, the top of the mountain filled with people from the city and its surrounding communities.[7] All foreign correspondents were present to record and herald the event around the world. They came with folding chairs, spy glasses, sun shades, and rain covers. Following a short religious service officiated by Isaac, Sabetay appeared on a dais, brilliant and illuminated. The crowd went into a frenzy shouting: *Mashiah, Mashiah*. Isaac Silveira stood by him as his disciple, arms raised, asking the crowd to be calm, for it was a few seconds before noon. All at once total silence and choking fear reigned. As the clouds rolled by, the only sound heard was that of the wind sweeping over the mountain. Sabetay, with his eyes closed, lifted his arms towards the firmament murmuring inaudible words. At that very instant a huge dark cloud moved in and obstructed the sun light. Progressively it got darker until the light falling on the ground was so dim that the terrified crowd feared that Sabetay not only stopped the sun but had extinguished it. Screams of horror and panic propa-

---

7. Poet Emanuel Frances of Leghorn, 1667, quoted by Scholem p. 148.

gated quickly from the summit to the city below. Women and children fell to their knees praying for forgiveness of sins. The cloud suddenly burst into a turbulent hail and the entire hill became covered with ice crystals the size of marbles. Instantly umbrellas unfolded to seek protection from what the crowd conceived was punishment from heaven. "*Basta! basta!* (Enough! enough!) *Bendije sea el nombre de Dios* (Blessed be the name of God)," begged the crowd. The massive cloud past over the mountain and the sun lit the area again. The audience was not alone in being alarmingly surprised. Astonished, Sabetay blessed the crowd speedily and disappeared from the stage. Unsuspecting the magnitude of the miracle, shaken Isaac told the assembly that the messiah's objective had been met. He ordered everyone to go home to reassess the sincerity of their faith in the light of what they had seen.

After this incident the outpouring of support and love for Sabetay became so widespread that this time the senior rabbis vowed to take positive measures. Outraged by the recent spectacle, Rabbi Escapha volunteered to become the prosecutor in a case against Sabetay. He was no longer in the mood to mollify the growing hawkish attitude of the city fathers, who demanded the death sentence or, at the very least, excommunication.[8] Shortly after the episode on the mountain, Escapha compiled sufficient evidence to convict Sabetay. After a fiery speech delivered to the members of the commission he pronounced:

> "Whoever strikes him down first, deserves well, for he will lead Israel into sin and succeed in making a new religion. He who pronounces the Name [of our Lord] with its proper letters, has no share in the world to come."

An older rabbi stood up and proclaimed: "This is reminiscent of the times of Jesus. We must not allow it to happen in our beloved city."

---

8. Though excommunication was appropriate in this case, unlike its frequent use in Christianity, Jews refrained from using this penalty even under more dire circumstances.

When it came time to decide on a sentence for Sabetay, Escapha, pointing to a section of the Mishnah, angrily demanded banishment from their city. This, he said, was the least punishment Sabetay deserved. The commission voted unanimously to pronounce the *cherem* (ban) against him, forbidding him to remain in the city of his birth forever. They summoned him to hear the verdict and for him to plea in his defense. Sabetay refused to appear at the court. A written copy of the verdict was sent to him.

> "By command of the angels, passed on to us as the judgment of the Lord, we, the rabbis of this city, banish, cast out, curse and condemn Sabetay Sevi, in accordance with the holy Torah and the six hundred and thirteen rules set down therein. . . . Cursed be he by day and night, cursed be he when he lieth down, cursed when he riseth up, cursed when he goeth out, and cursed when he cometh in. . . . His name shall be blotted out from Heaven and his memory shall die out from the host of Israel. No man shall have anything to do with him; none shall speak or write to him. None shall render him a favor or give him refuge beneath his roof. None shall stand within four arm's length of his presence, and none shall read anything written by his hand."[9]

His exile from the city was ordered to take place no later than January, 1651. Defiant and audacious, Sabetay returned with the courier who brought him the verdict a written message to Escapha: *"My little finger is bigger than your loins."*[10]

One could imagine the shock and consternation this sentence created in the Sevi family, who huddled around him trying to figure out what was to become of him alone and in exile. He was unable to provide for himself the simplest needs to stay alive. With his strict fasting schedule, if Clara didn't keep track and cook accordingly, he would most certainly die. She viewed the punishment not as a ban but as a death sentence. She requested an audience with Rabbi Escapha. Her request was denied. Rycaut,

---

9. See Kastein p. 64.

10. See Scholem p. 149. A quotation by Sabetay from Kings 12:10.

who had reported all these miraculous happenings to his readers, came to the Sevi's house offering to appeal on Sabetay's behalf to the Turkish authorities. Eliyah clarified that Turkish laws had no similarities to English law. The Turkish courts supported any rabbinical decision unless the case concerned a Moslem. Besides, the Turkish authorities were fed up with the frequent demonstrations and violent confrontations in the streets.

Sabetay had not foreseen the likelihood of the harsh sentence. He anticipated, at worst, flogging, in which case he planned to use the onus of that punishment as psychological warfare against the establishment. Deeply concerned about his misjudgment and the grief he had caused his mother, he locked himself in his room with an excruciating manic attack.

Mordehay and Eliyah decided Sabetay should go to their relatives in Patras, Greece, the birth place of his parents. There he could count on the help of his relatives. Eliyah promised to support him financially wherever he went. In the meantime he would retain the best Talmudic lawyers to overturn the recent court's decision.

Word about the banishment spread in all parts of the empire and in Europe. Letters from well-wishers began to pour in from major Turkish cities and as far as England. One pious Englishman wrote that suffering in exile was prophesied as a prerequisite in the coming of the Lord's kingdom. Suffering was the manifestation of revilement and persecution, a necessary misery to give credence to the cause.

Not knowing what awaited him on the other side of the Aegean Sea, every winter morning before his departure he atoned by plunging his body in the cold waters of the sea. In his meditations Sabetay begged the Lord to tell him what was to become of him.

CHAPTER

8

The shores where Sabetay swam were on the southern part of the Gulf of Smyrna. The frequent north-eastern wind brought waves crushing onto these rocky shores and often spilling on the cobblestone pavement of the main thoroughfare. Absorbed by the restless events of the week he failed one day to pay attention to the severe windy conditions and the swelling of the sea. He walked to his favorite bathhouse that belonged to the Pinheiros.

Shore bath houses were simple wooden cabins built on wooden piles driven into the sea bed and connected permanently to shore by a long and narrow wooden pier. The cabin sat at the far end of the pier where the water was deep enough to dive. The only function of the cabin was to provide privacy for changing clothes. It had a trap-like door on its floor with a permanent wooden ladder extending slightly below the surface of the water. This mode of entry into the sea was for older people who didn't dive nor wanted to be seen in their bathing suit. The most wealthy Sephardis in the community lived in that district. Almost every home along the shore had a cabin, nearly identical in design and color of paint. Owners strived for uniformity and painted their cabins bluish gray to blend with the color of the sea. Sabetay had been given permission, since childhood, to use the cabin anytime he wished. He didn't need to ask permission every time he took his habitual bath.

In his younger days he discovered one of the piles closer to shore spurted fresh spring water through its rotted hollow core. Apparently that pile had been driven deep enough into the soil to reach an artesian well. Unaware of the geological fact, Sabetay declared a miracle this oddity of a fresh water spring in the salt water of the sea. It became a ritual for him to drink a few swallows of fresh cool water and recite a special blessing.

The day before his departure into exile, absorbed by the uncertainties of the days ahead, after changing his clothes he stepped down the ladder and released himself into the rough sea. He was not a good swimmer. Swimming near so many cabins required only the ability to float and paddle from one cabin to the next. It didn't take long for him to discover that the storm had created a large whirlpool under the cabin, pushing his body towards the open sea. Terrified of losing control of his movements, he exerted all his strength to escape the strong current. With a few arm strokes he managed to grab the cabin ladder. Before he was able to climb up, a huge regressing wave snapped the ladder away from the structure with him hanging on it. Still holding the ladder, the angry sea churned him like a piece of driftwood. That was when he realized the extent of his danger. As the crest of the next incoming wave pushed him towards the rocks he thought he would be crushed against the boulders, breaking his body into thousands pieces. Fortunately, the path of the wave carrying him to shore was towards one of the firmly anchored wooden piles. Afraid and shaken he was able to grab a pile with all the strength he could muster. The freed ladder went crashing on shore and smashed into pieces. To his astonishment and joy the pile he had grabbed happened to be the one spurting fresh water and the one he had blessed so many times. He remained hugging the pile tightly as his body bobbed up and down each time a wave swept ashore and returned back to the open sea. He prayed furiously for his life. In the middle of one prayer an idea occurred to him. He thought he could swim a short distance from one pile to the next in the direction of shore soon after a wave was heading for shore. This miraculous idea saved his life. Once safe on shore he attributed his rescue to divine intervention. Since ablution was considered an act of purification, he presumed the Lord intervened to save his life because he was pure.

Out of the water, he walked the length of the pier to the cabin, put his clothes on, and rushed to a final meeting he had planned with leaders of his new movement. He arrived late and emotionally elevated. In his excitement, before greeting anyone he related the miracle of the rising whirlpool and his mysterious rescue by the fresh water pile, with which many present were familiar. Sabetay's first request was to propose that day to be marked on the calendar[1] as a new holiday proclaiming: *"the rising of the messiah's soul from the depth of the abyss."* Tampering with the Hebrew calendar was a sin and punishable with forty lashes. He pulled out his notebook and noted it down while his disciples prostrated with humility and reverence—all except for Moses Pinheiro. Moses had stayed uninvolved since he stood up in support of Sabetay the day of Hanukah at the synagogue. He decided to come to this last meeting. Moses' single-mindedness didn't escape Sabetay eyes. A recent supporter and leader Rabbi Abraham Barzelay, reminded the group that the miracle had a precedence in history. He quoted loudly a passage he said was from the *Cabala*: *"He rose from the abyss and beheld the crooked serpent. He is our Redeemer,"* then added: "We shall mark this day as the day when our Lord rose from the sea, and we will make it the most important holiday in our Hebrew calendar."

Sabetay knew the source of Barzelay's quotation. It was not from the *Cabala* as he claimed; he was paraphrasing the New Testament, referring to an analogous incident that occurred to Jesus. Consciously, yet without saying it, Barzelay made an analogy of Sabetay's event to Jesus' fight with the serpent in the waters of the Jordan River. He could not very well give the source of his quotation, for Jesus was not an heroic patriarch in the eyes of Jews. Regardless, Sabetay found the quotation very appropriate. To show

---

1. See Scholem p. 145.

his pleasure at Barzelay, he nodded and smiled at him, hoping to communicate to him silently that he was pleased.

They spent the rest of the morning discussing plans for the movement during his exile. He designated Rabbi Isaac Silveira as his disciple and spokesman and Rabbi Moses Pinheiro as the local leader. When they completed the structuring of an organization in Smyrna, in an emotional farewell Sabetay said: *"The city which has driven me out would one day welcome me back as King of Israel."*

This was a spirited message he had formulated earlier as a reminder of the courage and determination he wanted to leave behind. All stood up and cheered: *"Mashiah!, Mashiah! The whole world awaits to be redeemed!"*

He asked to meet privately with Moses and Isaac. One by one as the group left the room they wished him well and kissed his hand, hoping to welcome him soon as their victorious messiah. Except for him and his two trusted friends, the room emptied. With a smile on his face he said he had two questions, one for Isaac and one for Moses. He spoke to Isaac first. "I am leaving tomorrow and I think this is an appropriate time to confess our feelings about each other. I was always anxious to know the answer to one question that puzzled me since that day before Hanukah at the synagogue. How is it that after so many years of antagonism between you and me, you decide to be the first to stand up for me when I spoke the Ineffable Name of God?"

Isaac smiled and answered him: "AMIRAH! Perhaps it was because I could not measure up to you, no matter how I tried. This shortcoming turned me envious and repugnant at times. However, I want you to know that deep in my heart I knew the Lord had favored and blessed you with divine attributes. Forgive me if I deceived you all this time." He kneeled and kissed Sabetay's hand. Now Isaac waited to hear how Sabetay felt about him. There was no reciprocal response. This kind of intimacy was not in Sabetay's personality. He never cared to share with anyone even a minute part of the love he had reserved for God. Nevertheless, he thought of reserving a special honorific reward for Isaac when the time came to establish the Kingdom of Israel.

He explained why he wished to speak to them in private: "All my life I thought of this great moment when I would be launching myself into God's services. I did everything my body and soul could endure to appeal to Him. Now I know His hand has touched me many times, leaving me with distinct hints of his love for me. I know He will call me to duty when He deems the time to be right. I beg you not to believe, as the elders of this congregation want you to believe, that my banishment will disperse my followers and my ideals as the wind disperses sand particles in the desert. Nothing can be further from the truth. On the contrary, it will make me stronger and my followers more united. I am repeating what I said earlier. The city that has driven me out will one day welcome me back as the King of Israel. You will be here to attest to this prophecy. Now, I would like to speak to both of you about certain changes in our Talmudic laws and of holidays I find paramount and wish to place in action when I announce the new order. I will . . . ."

Moses had made two unheeded attempts to interrupt him while he spoke. He finally got Sabetay's attention. "What is it Moses? I was about to mention your responsibilities during my absence from Smyrna. Can't you wait?"

Moses wanted to know what question Sabetay had reserved for him. "What was the question you had reserved for me? You didn't ask me yet."

Sabetay smiled, assuming Moses knew what he would say. "I have not seen you since the day you and Isaac stood up for me at the synagogue. I was wondering what changed your mind and made you come to this meeting? Could it be because you think it is the last? In spite of it you heard me appoint you the leader of the movement in Smyrna."

"No AMIRAH, I came to confess and open my heart to you. Contrary to what you are presuming, I will not be here when you come back . . . ."

Sabetay frowned. "What do you mean?"

"Sabetay, I know this will come to you as a shock. No longer can I hide a feeling of involuntary deception I might have created the day you spoke up at the synagogue. I want you to know that as much as I love you and respect you as a great Hebrew scholar, in good conscience I cannot accept the awesome possibility that God, Blessed be His name, ever intended to make you his messiah, because . . . ."

"What are you saying!" interrupted Isaac shocked by the statement.

Sabetay, too, was shocked and stunned but didn't react. He knew Moses from childhood to be a person of great compassion and integrity. He would not disappoint anyone unless it was a matter to be in conflict with his conscience. Sabetay had always admired him and envied how Moses was able to live in perfect harmony with his personal attributes in peace and tranquility.

"I am sorry to disappoint you, Sabetay, but what I told you is what I perceive as my truth. I know what is in your mind as I face you. You want to know why I stood up at the synagogue to support you? The truth of the matter is that my action was meant to protest what I felt was a malicious and mistrustful congregation. Perhaps I acted inappropriately. I didn't think then it would be interpreted as an unqualified support for your cause. I simply felt a deep compassion towards you, personally. I am truly sorry to deceive you. I admit that you possess saintly qualities and attributes, more than any man I know. But when it comes to the messiah it is not up to the people or me to make that decision. It must be the Lord's. He needs no help from us. His chosen one, holding His hand, will be at work immediately. I have no doubt you felt this way all along. I have no doubt also that in truth and sincerity you are convinced He will choose you for the divine task. I am also convinced that before this happens you will succeed in moving world Jewry to renew itself spirituality. I have no doubt about all this. What is missing in your movement is the ultimate gift from the Lord: A divine spirit . . . ."

Isaac became outraged and tried to interrupt him again: "I don't believe what you are saying . . . ."

"I am not finished, Isaac!" objected Moses. "Please give me the opportunity to say what I came to say." He paused for he was out of breath. "Now I have a personal confession to make to Sabetay. If you don't mind, Isaac, I must do this in privacy. It is not a matter that concerns you."

Sabetay remained quiet. Isaac looked at Sabetay waiting to be told to stay. Sabetay hadn't blinked an eye. He stood looking at Moses stoically. Finally, Isaac opened the door and went outside.

"AMIRAH, this is possibly the worst day of my life for I know I am hurting your feelings. I, too, hurt inside for harboring such secrets from you. Two days after you fell sick on Molho's grave, I visited you while you laid unconscious in your bed. Waiting for you to wake up, I found on your night table a notebook which seemed at first an insignificant document. I keep such a book myself where I write extracts and quotations from what I read. I became curious and wanted to know what kind of material you were reading then. I am ashamed to admit that I have read much of it even after I had discovered that your notes were of a very different nature. I should have stopped the moment I found that out. I didn't. Before I leave, I would like to ask for your forgiveness for that awful sin. I swear to you that what I read will be locked in my mind forever, so help me God."

Moses waited to be forgiven as the Bible demanded after a confession. Sabetay appeared to be in a trance, as if he hadn't heard a word he said. His eyes were focused far far away. Had he been listening? Moses repeated in a louder voice: "Sabetay, will you forgive me? I cannot live without your forgiveness."

Sabetay rocked his head back and forth as if he was coming out of the trance and answered this time: "Yes. Sure. I forgive you. You still haven't told me why you said you will not be in Smyrna when I come back?" He phrased his last words as if he didn't care about Moses' earlier confession.

"It has nothing to do with you. My brother-in-law Joseph Ergas has invited me to Livorno (Leghorn) in Italy. In his new post as director of the great Cabalistic School he wrote about the availability of a vacant position. I don't have to tell you that I feel greatly honored. I accepted it."

Sabetay looked shaken once again. Why had Moses chosen to show disapproval of his messianic aspirations when all he had to say was he was leaving town? That would have been sufficient. He couldn't understand the purpose of his earlier confession. Now his most trusted friend was removing himself from his life at a time when he needed him most. The mention of Rabbi Joseph Ergas also bothered him. This man had written a number of inflammatory papers decrying Sabetay and his movement as a band of impostors. Was that really why Moses had turned against him, to please his brother-in-law? Without making a comment, he yelled at the top of his voice and called Isaac, who waited outside. Ignoring Moses' presence he said: "You know Isaac, I have always found our Hebrew calendar inadequate and lacking realism."

Moses understood Sabetay didn't care to speak to him anymore. He said: "Good bye and God Bless you Sabetay," and left the room feeling torn apart. He knew he would never see Sabetay again.

"Now, Isaac I have a very definite agenda for the future of Israel. There are too many laws and holidays that don't make sense anymore. You must help me clear the mess. We must replace them with holidays celebrating our current and up-to-date history, especially those commemorating the rise of our movement. We should stop preoccupying ourselves with events that happened thousands of years ago! We must change also the cumbersome structure of our calendar. It is clumsy, it has no basis in scientific logic. It is a patchwork of arithmetical manipulations designed by old rabbis to fit a ridiculous set of holiday arrangements. It is so complicated and cumbersome that the public cannot figure out which commemorative occasions fall on what date. What is the sense of having a calendric system that the ordinary public cannot tell when holidays or birthdays will fall during the year? It is absolutely and positively ridiculous."

He unbuttoned the front of his vestment, reached into his inside pocket and pulled a few sheets of folded paper. He began to read and explain what he had written.

Sabetay took more than an hour to give Isaac minute details about the history and the arithmetical makings of the Hebrew calendar. He explained in the greatest details the dietary concerns of the original framers of the calendars. The Hebrew day begins at sundown. Since Jews are forbidden to cook meals on Sabbaths, paramount in their concern was not allowing the day after the eve of a holiday to begin on Friday or Sunday. If they had allowed the first day of the New Year and Yom Kippur to fall on Friday, cooking would have to be done on Thursday for Friday (the holiday) and Saturday (the Sabbath), both non-cooking days. With the same logic if the first daytime was allowed to fall on Sunday, cooking would have to be done on Friday. In each case it was not healthy to preserve food for more than two days. Thus, the traditional Hebrew calendar took this into account and the eve of such holidays were postponed a day or two if necessary. Thus, the New Year can only occur on Monday, Tuesday, Thursday and Saturday. Since the fifth century C.E. there developed a desire to follow the solar cycle in addition to the lunar cycle upon which the Hebrew calendar is based. All these special requirements had placed severe arithmetical conditions on the design of the Hebrew calendar. To abide by all these requirements the calendar had to have six different lengths of years, leap months, and variable number of days (29 to 30) in the lunar months.

When he was finished, Sabetay said to Isaac: "Now, go home and put it all together. I remember you being strong in mathematics at the yeshiva. Don't forget to check your calculations when you compare your results with the calendar you have home and those of previous years. But whatever you do, don't mention to anyone any of my plans to simplify this mess eventually. Not yet. I warn you. You may wind up exiled like me."

"AMIRAH! You are very smart. I have always said there is none like you. How in heavens name were you ever motivated to put all this together? It looks like the work of the *Mashiah*."

They both laughed at the pleasing and flattering joke.

"Isaac, I must remind you seriously that I have never claimed to have merited that title yet. A distinction must be made between *Mashiah the candidate* specified in my visions, and *Mashiah the designate* when the Creator finally orders me to take that assignment. It is the same distinction as a Crown Prince and the King. I have yet to receive the order and the powers to overcome the evil forces of world kings and emperors. That time is not far. However, only when I announce it, it will be known worldwide. Please remember that."

"Blessed be the day," responded Isaac, seeing that Sabetay was readying himself to leave. He had a final question to ask: "Come to think of it, AMIRAH, how would you design a brand new Hebrew calendar?"

Sabetay smiled and then placed his index finger over his lips in a sign conveying "silence of a secret." Removing his finger he said: "We shall leave the assignment for when I return to Smyrna; I will proclaim my findings then. Now there are many serpents standing on the way of divine redemption. Good bye, my friend. I will keep in touch and you certainly will hear the day when the Lord will crown me the Son of David. All that remains to be said at this moment are Isaiah's words." Lifting his right hand and shaking his forefinger as a warning gesture to those who oppose him, he spoke like a patriarch: "*Cast ye up, cast ye up, clear the way, take up the stumbling block out of the way of my people . . . .*"

Sabetay wasn't sure if he would ever see Isaac again, not because he doubted of ever returning, but because he was so engrossed with the size and dimension of his worldly mission that an individual like Isaac could eventually get lost among overwhelming accomplishments.

9

$\mathcal{A}$ midst a mixed crowd of well-wishers and gleeful opponents, Sabetay boarded a Dutch ship that was to take him to Patras. It was a drizzling and gloomy day in January 1651. From the deck of the ship he looked at the pier with sadness, uncertain of what had been written in the Book of Life about his future. He felt torn and removed on this foreign vessel with a foreign crew while his family waved white handkerchiefs, hats, uttering words of greetings he could not discern from the noise of the crowd surrounding them. The family, too, shared his grief and wasn't sure if this was the last time they laid eyes on him. On land, those opposed to his mission stood silent and spiteful hoping his misguided idealism would whither away in the solitude of his exile.

One person standing on the pier was utterly delighted to see him leave. He was his former teacher, Rabbi Escapha, who ended up loathing him and couldn't wait to witness the ship disappear in the horizon. At sentencing he told his colleagues he was making it his duty to be at the pier to witness the scoundrel leave the city. Moses Pinheiro also stood on the pier waving from time to time a red handkerchief hoping to be singled out from all the others. He loved him as a brother he didn't have. He regretted to have been embroiled into a serious dogmatic set of events which were contrary to his beliefs. Fate had made him read the contents of Sabetay's notebook and on that day he began to understand how

much different Sabetay was spiritually than him and the others
around him. Like him, people yearned to meet God after death,
but Sabetay insisted on meeting Him during his lifetime.

On deck Sabetay fixed with his eyes on his family, clustered
together waiving, while his dear mother wiped her tears constantly. He whispered silently telling her he will miss her the
most during his exile. She had been for him his total life support and the provider of unconditional and unselfish love and
understanding. He knew he would never be able to replace that
assurance of love and security wherever his fate was taking him,
in spite of the fact that Eliyah pledged to send him all the funds
he needed to live comfortably however long it took him to achieve
his noble goal. Comforting as that was, he would gladly trade
his brother's generous offer for the privilege of remaining at his
mother's home. He looked for Isaac among the well-wishers but
could not find him. He worried if Isaac, the only man who had
pledged his life to him, would remain as faithful to his cause
after his departure.

The Dutch captain yelled at the top of his voice ordering
sailors to prepare for sailing. Two tugging tenders with six row-
ing sailors in each pulled the vessel away from its berth. When
they cleared the calm waters of the sheltered port, new orders
were issued to drop the sails. The gentle morning wind filled
the main sail instantly and the ship submitted to the power of
nature. Sabetay remained on deck looking at his beloved city,
the only residence he has ever known. Waiving sadly as the ship
moved out to sea, one thought weighed heavily in his mind. The
Zohar had been wrong in prophesying the year of Redemption.
The year 1648 was now three years behind and there had been
no sign of a divine phenomenon. It was most difficult to accept
that the great wisdom in these sublime books had been wrong.
All through his studies, these mystical writings had become more
supportive of his faith and a great source book of wisdom than
the bible relating mostly to the historical accounts of his people.
The only justification he could find was that there had to be a
divine reason for the postponement of the redemption date.

Whatever the reason, he expected as in the days of antiquity, God to speak to a chosen patriarch revealing the timing and scope of his divine mission. He will spell out the logistics of herding millions of Jews in the scattered Diasporas and leading them to the Holy Land.

Alone on deck, he saw the outline of his native city disappear gradually. The ship moved west towards the exit of the gulf. He felt totally abandoned. He remained on deck, drenched, his face sprayed with rain droplets swept by the misty wind. In a meditating mood he looked up at the sky and then to the waves breaking on the hull of the ship and asked in an audible voice what was to become of him, all alone without his parents or a single follower. His lips quivered as he spoke. No sooner did he utter his last word, he thought he heard the sound of a voice saying something to him. Totally surprised, he hadn't paid much attention to the words that were spoken except perhaps he had heard his favorite nickname AMIRAH. He fixed his eyes more pointedly on the waves in the direction of which he had been murmuring. To his surprise, the message repeated itself: "AMIRAH, don't think you are alone. I am with you, and I shall always be with you."

Yes, this was exactly what he thought he had heard. But the voice didn't come from the direction of the waves below. Startled, he searched with his eyes trying to locate the source of the voice that had answered his plea. Was he experiencing another miracle? His mood changed to one of great excitement. He fell on his knees and asked meekly: "Who speaks there?"

This time a laughter came from behind his shoulders. He turned around quickly to catch a glimpse at the voice. There, against the gray light of the misty sky stood what looked like an angel covered up to his head with a black cloak. He was unable to see a face. The cloak was dripping with rain. For a moment he was certain it had to be an angel of God. Waiting to be addressed again, he kept quiet. A male voice inside the cloak said to him: "I didn't mean to startle you, AMIRAH. It is me, Isaac, Isaac Silveira. You thought perhaps I abandoned you. I couldn't let you go alone. Who would care for you? Who would love and support you?"

Momentarily, Sabetay's face showed a great disappointment. The voice inside the cloak was that of his friend and not from the divine messenger he had hoped to be. Isaac said: "Don't look at me so frightened. Aren't you happy to see me?" He uncovered his head, walked towards Sabetay, and kissed his wet startled face. Sabetay smiled thinking of his premature anticipation of the Lord's angel, but nonetheless Isaac's surprise presence on board had to be conceived as one of a providential design. What Sabetay didn't know was that bachelor Isaac had been approached by Eliyah and promised travel and living expenses provided he cared for his younger brother.

Sabetay slept well on board that night, reassured that his seemingly uncertain future would be easier to bear now that Isaac was with him. In early morning he went up on deck and saw that the rain had stopped and the easterly wind blew briskly in a favorable direction. He was told that by sunrise the eastern coast of Greece would be visible. Patras, however, was on the western end of the Morean Peninsula connected to the mainland by a narrow strip of land. The ship had to sail two hundred miles south at the bottom end of the peninsula and north again to reach Patras. With the persistent favorable wind the ship had no trouble reaching that small town, the birthplace of his parents.

As it turned out, Sabetay and Isaac found Patras much too small and considerably less enlightened than Smyrna. They decided this was no place to launch a universal movement. Two weeks later they decided to leave for Salonica. Although a pilgrimage to Jerusalem was in their eventual agenda, they knew they had to gain substantial recognition in the more liberal cities of the Turkish empire before venturing into that arch-conservative biblical capital. They had no illusions that winning the support of large cities without winning the Holy City wouldn't accomplish much. The final conquest of Jerusalem had to wait for after they were able to rally considerable support in Salonica, Constantinople, Smyrna, and to some extent in Eastern Europe.

Sabetay wrote to Eliyah explaining why he had to move to Salonica, a city that boasted 22,000 Jews and only 10,000 Turks, and 4,000 Greeks. It had thirty-three *Cals* (Sephardi communities) with the same diversity of synagogue denominations as in the much larger city of Constantinople. Because the majority of the population was Jewish, the city was nicknamed "Mother of Israel." This was not the first time in history a city outside the Holy Land was nicknamed as a Jewish city. Granada in Spain, during the Moorish occupation, was nicknamed by the Moors as Gharnatât-al-Yahûd (Granada of the Jews). After the expulsion of Sephardis and converts from Spain, and the migration of East European Jews fleeing the Polish wars, many of these Jews settled in Amsterdam. There were so many Jews in that city, it was nicknamed "Dutch Jerusalem."

Salonica[1] was known for its important rabbinic and cabalistic centers. Within a few years after Iberian Jews arrived in the Ottoman Empire it became the largest Sephardi center in Europe. In his letter to Eliyah, Sabetay explained all this. He also included a special message to his mother, whom he missed the most. On one page he had a calligrapher write decoratively the Castilian love poem he sang to her frequently. He wrote a note at the bottom of the page: "As you read my loving words, dear Mamaritta, my song will ring in your ears. The art of the calligrapher and my music have similar purposes: the calligraphy will please your eyes and the music of my song will please your ears. Together they will tell you how much I love you." It didn't take long for Sabetay to receive Eliyah's approval to move to Salonica.

---

1. The original name of the city founded in 386 B.C.E. was Thessaloniki. During the Crusades, in early thirteenth century, it was an important staging point for Christian troops arriving from Europe before they went to battle in Palestine. During that period the city was governed by French speaking Crusade commanders and it was renamed Salonique. In early fifteenth century, the Turks occupy the city and call it Selanik. A century later when Sephardis arrive in large numbers from the Iberian Peninsula carrying with them the Spanish alphabet without the letter 'k', they renamed it Salonica. In modern days, under Greek occupation, the name reverted back to the original Thessaloniki, meaning, victory of the Thessalians who lived in Northeast Greece in the area called today Macedonia.

They took the ferry to Loutrakion on the mainland and by coach Sabetay and Isaac went to Athens to transfer into another coach bound for Salonica, an ancient Macedonian seaport saved physically and culturally from the ravages of war during the Turkish conquest. Since 1492 many Sephardis escaping the Iberian onslaught resettled in that historic city by the sea. For them, it offered the security of a seaport, the existence of a high culture, and more importantly, a great degree of tolerance by the Turks who allowed them religious freedom. The city was not considered strategically of military importance to the Turks, and for that reason they didn't object to being outnumbered by the new foreign immigrants.

When Sabetay arrived they moved into an inn at the heart of the city. Equipped with a list of Sephardi names, Isaac Silveira went scouting around the city in search of a friendly district in which to live permanently. The list was a compilation of names of business associates and leaders sent to them by Eliyah. Isaac, who cared for Sabetay's daily needs and made all the social arrangements, had no idea how friendly these people would be when they learned of Sabetay and his banishment from Smyrna. He did not discard the possibility that Rabbi Escapha had also sent letters to many Grecian cities warning his colleagues about Sabetay. An additional problematic question for Isaac was that the city Jewry had not forgotten the turmoil of a previous messianic contender, Solomon Molho, who lived among them not long ago. The memory of that devastating experience remained fresh in their minds.

One day, after his daily search of friendly contacts, Isaac rushed to the inn to report the good news. "AMIRAH, I hate to interrupt your prayers! You must listen to my discovery! Please stop praying for a few minutes!" Sabetay starred castigatingly at Isaac for he didn't like to be disturbed at prayer time. Isaac pressed again: "I have just met a wonderful and friendly person. His name is Rabbi Joseph Florentin, a noted cabalist and a very influential city father." Noticing that he had failed to draw Sabetay's attention, he raised his voice this time and demanded: "Are you listening?

This is urgent. Not a single day since we arrived in Salonica have I had such a success!" Sabetay turned his head and nodded without making a comment. "Rabbi Joseph Florentin is not just an ordinary acquaintance. He is the help from Heaven we have been waiting for. I met him at the conclusion of this morning's service. He welcomed me as a new member of his synagogue. All I had to do was mention that I live with you, and before I knew it he invited me to his home for breakfast. He is very pious, kind, and above all very courageous . . ."

Sabetay interrupted him: "How were you able to find all this at one breakfast session with a man you didn't know before?"

"Wouldn't you call a person courageous if he was not afraid to say openly that he had heard of you and was acquainted with the reason that forced you to leave Smyrna? He was much interested in your hopes and your profound knowledge of the Talmud and especially of the *Cabala*. Listen to this! I haven't told you the most important part of that news. He is opening his house to us, AMIRAH! Do you know what this means?" He paused, knowing he wouldn't get a response. Then he continued: "I will tell you what it means. He is offering us an open door to his city! We don't have to start from the lowly man in the street," Isaac answered his own question proudly.

Failing to notice the slightest sign of delight on Sabetay's face, he became annoyed and complained: "I don't see you excited the way I am! I repeat, he is a very important man, AMIRAH! He can give us the support and exposure we need to the people of this great city. Living in his house and meeting his friends and associates should be very important for us. He said he has a very large house and we can move in anytime we want. What do you think of that?"

"It is very nice of him. I had every confidence in the Lord that He would be kind to us, more sooner than later," answered Sabetay casually.

"Is that all you have to say?" shouted his friend. "This was not just a coincidence, you know. I spent days trying to find such an important contact. I couldn't believe him extolling your greatness,

your saintly visions, your knowledge of the *Zohar*, and your claim
to have understood God and His Creation. I was greatly surprised
that he knew all this! He didn't exactly seek us, you know. It took
a lot of effort on my part to convince him that meeting and studying with you would greatly enhance his scholarship." He paused
again, and feeling unappreciated he said: "You never acknowledge
what I do for you."

Isaac had exaggerated his power of persuasion over Florentin,
who was a well-known scholar and had heard of Sabetay's profound knowledge of the modern concepts of Lurianic *Cabala*.
Florentin was well versed in the traditional cabalistic writings[2] of
past centuries that were considerably easier to digest than the
more modern writings of Luria. He wanted very much to learn
Sabetay's understanding of the *Zohar* and his interpretations of
the modern mystics. Though he didn't mention it to Isaac, he was
less interested in the personality of Sabetay and his messianic
aspirations. Isaac waited for a compliment, however small from
Sabetay. When he didn't get it he said pleadingly: "Oh, AMIRAH
I wish sometime you would give me the recognition I deserve. I
don't care what you say! I am making plans to move into his house!"

---

2. Mystical thoughts are known to have existed in Judaism since the
days of Abraham. Before written records were kept these theosophical
theories and arguments pertaining to God and His Creation were past
on by word of mouth. The first known organized compilation of such
writings outside the tenets of Judaism were found in *The Book of Formation* (*Sepher Yetzirah*) attributed to a number of different authors, among
them: Abraham, Moses, Rabbi Akiba ben Joseph in the first century C.E.,
Shimon ben Yohay in the second century C.E., etc. Many tracts were
added to these occult discourses known as the *Cabala* up to the thirteenth
century C.E. when a Spanish Rabbi named Moses Shem Tob de León
came up with a new and revolutionary book on mysticism we now call
the *Zohar*. Since then and up to the period of Sabetay Sevi many cabalistic schools in Europe and in the Holy Land extended these writings to
supreme levels of questions and answers about the attributes of God, His
creation and even before creation.

Suddenly he remembered that he had been advised by Florentin about something important to tell Sabetay. He stopped complaining and said: "Incidentally, I must also tell you that Florentin suggested caution in our initial conduct and the claims we make in the community, at least in the beginning until they get to know us better."

Sabetay didn't respond. He didn't care much about the advice coming from a stranger who had never met him. Like it or not he had no choice. How else would he be able to do God's work outside the city's important circle of influential people without the help of this respected scholar?

They moved into Rabbi Joseph Florentin's comfortable mansion without wasting time. As Isaac thought, in a short time, Florentin and his associates became very impressed with Sabetay's ascetic life and his profound knowledge of divinity. What pleased them most was his willingness to debate, support or reject, defend or criticize in great details the mystical philosophies of the cabalistic schools of the past and modern days. Eventually, he was sought by the few Talmudic centers in the city on a regular basis.

৵

During the five years he resided in Salonica, Sabetay developed a feeling of having found a second home in friendly Florentin's lovely house. He never felt obligated to his host for his generosity, because he knew he gave back his knowledge in return. It was a perfectly equitable arrangement. The only thing he missed and could not replace was the presence and love of his mother. In Salonica he discovered among the Andalusian Jews a new Castilian poem[3] which instantly had a great appeal to him. He had never heard it before in his city of birth. He like it so much that he composed a tune for it and sung it often to remember it by heart. He intended to make it a gift to his mother for when he was to meet her again. But alas! the news from home did not speak

---

3. Author unknown.

well about the health of both parents, or his brother's appeals to
the rabbinical court of Smyrna to repeal Sabetay's sentence of
banishment. Concerned that he might miss the opportunity to see
his mother again, he mailed the written words of the poem describing the best he could the tune he had composed for it.

Venga mi señora madre	Come my dear mother
Que me bese y que me abrase.	Kiss me and hug me.
Presto que no se detarde,	Quick do not delay,
Que no quede sin contentarse.	Leaving us without satisfaction.
Sacrificios allegaremos	We will offer sacrifices
Día cada día.	Day every day.
Al Mashiah lo veremos,	Hoping to see the Messiah,
Asentado en su silla.	Installed in his throne.

The five years in Salonica had lapsed without controversies. He
gained the respect of many religious elders and was a frequent
speaker in Talmudic and Cabalistic sessions. While his life regained
tranquillity and comfort, he struggled inwardly. But peace and tranquillity was not the reason that had brought him to Salonica. He
could have given up his lofty ideals and stayed in Smyrna for that.
He hated to see his ambition slowly wither away, especially when
his awful dreams had returned urging him to recommit himself to
the divine cause, even though the punishment he had received in
Smyrna had been traumatic and much alive in his mind.

A number of times, at gatherings with his colleagues, he made
sincere efforts to ignore the many proddings about his past and
his aspirations. It was not easy to resist the temptation to open
that subject. However, during one of his Talmudic sessions in
1657, a young rabbi, wanting to test him or perhaps embarrass
him, prepared a question thought to be profound, convoluted, and
philosophically full of dangerous pitfalls. He asked his question
at a moment when Sabetay was tired of mollifying the group. He
said: "Rabbi Sevi," with a sneer on his lips, "I would like to hear
you explain in the simplest terms, as I have heard you treat many
difficult subjects, a concept appearing to most of us as obvious

yet too profound to be fully understood. The question is repeated many times in the liturgy of our Yom Kippur holiday: '*What is Man that Thou are so mindful of him?*' I was asked the same question by my students and each time I try to answer it I find myself stumbling, groping for a deserving answer. Could you clarify it for us?"

One could see on the faces of the attendants how happy they appeared waiting to hear the answer from the great Talmudist. Isaac, who was in the habit of accompanying Sabetay everywhere he went, recognized the likelihood of a direct challenge to Sabetay to open his heart and finally divulge all that was within it. Philosophical discussions on the essence of man had been the subject of many disputes among scholars, some ending in violent arguments and others sending renowned scholars into disgrace and disrepute. Just when Sabetay was gaining recognition among the city rabbis, it appeared to Isaac that it was no time for Sabetay to shock, anger, or offend colleagues who had been friendly to him. But proud Sabetay wasn't about to be daunted and intimidated by a young novice. He saw the sting, perhaps suggested by an older rabbi, and he figured it must have been intentionally planted to embarrass him. He had been challenged and he wasn't backing away. He closed his eyes in deep concentration to recall the words of the *Zohar* about "Man." A high degree of memory retention having been one of his attributes, when he opened his eyes, he looked inspired and illumined. He lectured:

"Young man, I pray that you possess the intellectual maturity to understand the wisdom in our *Zohar* concerning your question." He paused and took on an authoritative stance they hadn't seen before. "The cardinal doctrines of these writings embrace the nature of the Deity, the Divine emanations, the cosmogony, the creation of angels and of man. To make his existence known and comprehensible for his role in Creation, God had to become active and creative. As he created the whole universe the finishing stroke was man who is the acme of his creation. That was the reason for which he was formed the sixth day. Man is both the import and the highest degree of creation. When man was created everything was complete, including the upper and nether worlds, for everything is comprised in man, God's microcosm. Man unites in himself all forms and processes which shaped creation. Just as we see in the firmament above, covering all things, the stars and the planets, which contain secret things and profound mysteries studied by those who are wise and expert in astronomy, so are the mysteries of the skin of man which is the cover of the body, and which is like the sky that covers all things below." He paused again but for a different reason. He wanted to give his lecturing a different direction, a more self-serving direction, a direction he felt more comfortable in. "Did you stop to think that the human form is shaped after the four letters which constitute the Tetragrammaton 'YHVH'?" All eyes and ears were opened wide as his listeners felt he was about to link man to God. Looking sharply in the eyes of his interrogator he continued: "The letter Yod (Y) in Hebrew[4] has the shape of man's head, the letter Heh (H) is in the shape of his arms and shoulders, Vav (V) has the shape of the chest, and Heh (H), again, the shape of his two legs. The entire universe proceeds from this holy Name." He used his fingers to describe the shape of the letters with man's body parts. He took a deep breath and continued. "But man is not just body. It needs a soul to function. The souls of the whole human race are stored in the World of Emanations, and each is destined eventually to inhabit a human body. Every human soul consists of a trinity of attributes. The Spirit, the highest of attributes, is the source of the Intellectual World. Then comes the Soul as ordinary people understand it, is the seat of the moral qualities. And finally the Cruder Soul, immediately connected with the body, is the cause of its lower instincts, the Material World." He spoke at length about each of the attributes of the parts of the soul and as they are related to God. When he finished, Sabetay saw an opening to plead his cause, the cause of the messiah. The ground work

---

4. The letter "Y" in Hebrew approximates an apostrophe with a bold head. The letter "H" resembles an upside down "U," the arms and shoulder. The letter "V" is a long vertical stroke defining the body, and the letter "H" is again depicted by the two legs.

of his reasoning having been established, he had to conclude what he thought logically derived from it. He justified the decision to work his way into the messianic advent because he thought the subject had been forced upon him. Pointing his right forefinger at young rabbi, he continued: "Ultimately there has to be an end to this process of transmigration of souls from the dead to the living. When all the existing souls in the World of Emanations have descended and occupied human bodies and have passed their period of probation and have returned purified to the bosom of the Infinite Source, then the soul of the messiah will descend and the great Jubilee will commence. You didn't ask me to speak about the messiah, but I must because it is an integral part of the creation of man and the ultimate salvation God has reserved for him. I believe fervently that the time is near, very near for that stage in Creation. I sense it in my bones and my soul." In an authoritarian tone of voice he exclaimed: "I should know, for that is the reason they called me AMIRAH!"

Up until the last sentence they stood captivated by his imagery in placing man in perspective to the whole of Creation. Bringing in the subject of the messiah and emphasizing the timing of his eminent appearance was not what they expected. They stood still, stymied and bewildered at what they thought was another prophecy and not a follow up to the innocent question the young rabbi asked. Had Sabetay been born in Salonica and had he grown among those men they would have taken him for granted. Their knowledge about his past and the mere newness of his approach, backed by such authoritative command of biblical knowledge, gave the assembly mixed sentiments: enlightenment, and at the same time great fear. Many of his colleagues, including Rabbi Florentin, were very impressed and felt rewarded for having adopted Sabetay in their city. The happiest was Isaac who originally feared controversy.

After that episode word spread in the city about Sabetay's unparallel saintliness and wisdom, seldom found in a man in his thirties. Five years of docility in Salonica was more than enough for Sabetay. He worried he was losing the sensitivity he had developed so diligently in Smyrna, a sensitivity that made him feel saintly and close to God. The service he had been rendering in this new city had nothing to do with his divine cause. Feeling rewarded by the positive reception of his discourse by the Salonican colleagues for a subject he had imprisoned in his heart during the past five years, Sabetay burst alive again. The severe headaches returned as well as the dreams he found himself at times in the midst of biblical characters urging him to missionize, and at other times in the presence of satanic monsters attempting to destroy his faith.

In that period of depression he resolved that the time had come to resume his one and only agenda: the yearning to proceed with his probing, testing, and harvesting of new souls in the ministration of his messianic objective. The year 1648 having expired without divine intervention, now there was no question that the second prophesied date of 1666 had to be the viable date. There was much to do in the nine years remaining. The little success he had accomplished in Smyrna had been misguidedly interrupted by the old establishment, but not wiped out. His disciple Barzelay kept him abreast by mail the slow progress his movement had been making at winning converts. If he could only succeed in winning the trust of the Salonican rabbis, then a pilgrimage to Constantinople, Aleppo, Cairo, Jerusalem, and even Smyrna had to yield similar approvals. Encouraged by the recent round of success, he decided to apply himself diligently to the search of a single symbolic and yet innocuous act or performance that would test his colleagues' perception of him as a saintly person and hopefully deserving of the trust reserved to the messiah. But he had to be very careful. The test had to be strictly of a suggestive nature and not offensive and shocking as he had been in Smyrna. A straight and bold assertion of any kind was likely to send him, once again, into disgrace. If the idea was properly conceived and liked, he would rekindle his messianic ministry in Salonica.

Secretly and hard at work, he searched for ideas to present at his following Talmudic session. One idea suggested itself to be effective and totally appropriate from readings in the Talmud and the Book of Proverbs. The saintly books described symbolically the Torah, the epitome of truth, as the wife of all who love truth. The concept was implicated in the passage: "*That those who seek truth from the Torah must feel like the bridegroom coming out of his chamber.*" As a playwright conceives his play upon an idea or an event, Sabetay conceived an enactment of a perfect symbolic skit. Without Isaac's knowledge, he arranged a short yet creative skit in which he would be the only actor. Instead of meeting his colleagues at the regular Talmudic sessions, he asked Isaac to invite them to a sumptuous banquet in Florentin's mansion offered in his name. The guests were told the banquet was in appreciation for the kindness they had shown him. In one corner of the large dining hall he erected a small stage in which he placed a white bridal canopy with a Torah scroll in it. He decorated the stage with white flower arrangements and drew a silk white curtain to keep it hidden from his guests.

The invitation cards announced an enactment of a mystical surprise after the meal. The guests arrived with great anticipation. After the sumptuous meal and the joviality the good wine created, everyone waited to know what the great surprise was. Sabetay announced they were to attend an important wedding ceremony officiated by him. The idea of participating in a wedding ceremony to end the festivities was a novel one. They applauded their host's ingenuity. Proudly, he walked towards the stage all eyes turned to him. He climbed the stage, pulled open the white silk curtain and revealed a decorated bridal canopy. The guests' first reaction was to search for the bride and groom. Instead, they saw a Torah dressed in white, propped on top of a white chair. What elevated their expectations was knowing that Sabetay in his inexhaustible knowledge of lores and customs and of mysticism was most likely to amuse them with a very unusual and symbolic wedding. They were almost right about that. He remained standing on stage waiting to see if anyone had yet discovered the true meaning of what he was about to portray. They suspected nothing except a traditional wedding with a bride and groom missing on stage. "Was that all?" they murmured to one another. When they realized there wouldn't be a bride and groom, they surmised all sorts of possible enactments except the one Sabetay had in mind.

"My dear friends," he said to break the bleak silence. "Should I proceed further?" The attendance nodded in a sign of approval. He entered the canopy, picked up the Torah and came forward on stage with a glowing face, clasping the scroll tightly to his side as if it were his bride. He began to perform the wedding ceremony as each of them had performed many times during their rabbinical career. "Wait a minute!" one exclaimed. "Where are the bride and groom?" They couldn't understand the significance or implication of a wedding ceremony without the couple. Left with an intense puzzlement they questioned each other without a satisfying answer. They waited to be told about the logic of this seemingly curious performance. Something appeared to be terribly wrong. They asked him to stop the priestly words for a wedding. Isaac was the first to panic when he saw outrage on the guests' faces. Sabetay stopped in the middle of his ritualistic prayers but remained quiet, expecting someone to recognize the symbolism of his skit.[5]

Suddenly from the end of the dining room an old rabbi stood up and shouted loudly: "This is a travesty! This goes beyond a simple cabalistic symbolism! May God have mercy on us witnessing this sacrilege!" Only Sabetay surmised the angry rabbi's consternation. All faces turned towards the interrupting rabbi, hoping to have a clue at what was going on. Sabetay stood pale knowing he had not accomplished his goal. But why? Why weren't they accepting his right to claim the symbolic essence of what he had performed?

The rest of the guests were completely confused. They demanded to know the meaning of the symbolism which apparently turned one old rabbi so indignant. They shouted: "Explain yourself!" Sabetay, not totally sure of what the old rabbi understood by his act, let him explain. According to well documented prophetic writings the symbolic act meant that as a groom to the

---

5. da la Croix, *Mémoire*, Paris, 1684 as quoted by Scholem p. 159.

Torah Sabetay was heralding himself the messiah. "What? How dare! This is sacrilegious!" Such shouts were heard while all faces turned grim and outraged. The guests were so shocked by the mad suggestion that they stood up ready to leave, angry for having been duped into a bizarre and sacrilegious scheme.

Sabetay begged them to wait only a few moments to hear what he had to say. He remembered his previous mistake in Smyrna for not bothering to explain why he allowed himself the right to exceed Talmudic laws. They remained standing while he explained:

"My dear friends, I know you wish to hear from me why I chose to enact that scene." he began. "I can't understand why scholars like you want to deny the wisdom of our prophets? I have done exactly what they tell us in the Book of Proverbs." Explanation after explanation he tried to calm them down while they remained standing: "Didn't the prophets declare that the Holy Torah is the epitome of truth? Didn't they specifically say that the Torah is like the bride of those who love truth? Didn't you in past sessions admire and acknowledge my saintly wisdom? Why not give me that right? Why turn against me now? I am wedding the Law, the daughter of the Heavens. What my old colleague said is true. Why won't you give me the right that I possess the saintliness of the Redeemer?" As he made that last plea, he saw heads nod in disagreement. To hold them back from leaving, he continued: "That was all I meant when I performed the marriage ceremony. Many of you had told me, time and time again, that I had reached the epitome of understanding of the Scriptures. Not one of you claimed to have grasped the truth as I have. Are you denying me now that entitlement and privilege? Is there anyone here who thinks he can challenge my supreme understanding of all our sacred books?" He paused momentarily to see if he had calmed them down. The expression on their faces hadn't changed, for they feared most was being in the presence of someone insulting the tenets of the Talmud. But Sabetay wouldn't stop pleading: "I will be happier if you sit down and discuss with me what I just said. I will prove, as I have done before, that I am endowed with divine wisdom and deserve to perform this beautiful ceremony. I beg you to sit down!"

He waited. Faces turned left and right looking at each other's perplexed expressions. In the few moments it took to decide what they should do, one of the oldest of the rabbis pronounced what appeared to be the general consensus:

"Rabbi Sevi, there is no disagreement among us on your eminence in the words of the Lord. We are ready to grant you that. But that is all. To go beyond and bestow upon you divine attributes the kind of which were synonymous with those of Moses, King David, and other biblical patriarchs is totally insane. Never would I permit myself to do what you ask! Never! To admit such a preposterous claim would lead me to heresy and misguided martyrdom, neither of which I desire to be part of. Good day!"

Just as that speaker was about to leave, a young rabbi named Isaac Levi, ironically a relative of Rabbi Escapha, felt spiritually moved by Sabetay's performance. He tried to speak on Sabetay's behalf but his pleas went unheeded. His voice was immediately smothered with boos and more boos! The guests demanded their overcoats. They left Florentin's house full of disappointment and anger, not yet sure of the punitive action required for the insult leveled at Judaism. Isaac Silveira could see the handwriting on the wall: a repeat of the repudiation they were given in Smyrna. But then he understood Sabetay's position. How does a man who deeply feels was born the messiah convince his people of being endowed with that divine mission? How? Sabetay had to do it in either of two ways: Rise above the ordinary people and prove himself worthy or wait till God handed him magical powers as he had done in biblical times generating extraordinary miracles. Then, out of fear of God, Israelites united behind patriarchs.

Within hours of the banquet, all but Rabbi Isaac Levi gathered to press charges of heresy against Sabetay. They elected a commission to serve as judges. Rabbi Florentin, who hadn't said a word until then, went to court to defend his guest. He pleaded tersely but vigorously that mistakenly the witnesses had overestimated the implications of what had transpired at the banquet. He began:

"Esteemed colleagues and judges. There is no denying that Rabbi Sevi has surprised all of us with a symbolism drawn out of the Holy Books. Unfortunately, and I emphasize the word 'unfortunately' we hastily presumed that by his act he permitted himself to believe he was acting as a prophet, and yes as the messiah. Why? I ask you. Why couldn't any man use rightly or wrongly this symbolism to demonstrate what the Good Books implied by it? Why couldn't any man, rightly or wrongly, claim sainthood on the basis of his perceived abilities, devotion to our Creator, and eminence in spirituality. I say it is wrong for us to assume he has broken any laws. It's my judgment he has done nothing injurious to our faith or transgressed our tenets. Nowhere in the Talmud can you find the hint of a law specifically forbidding his amusing and informative skit much less our right to inflict a punishment because of it. The most one can say is that the choice of his example was very unusual and perhaps not pleasing to some of you. Let me ask you, then: is this a crime?" Florentin was delivering his speech with great emotion. His angered face was covered with perspiration. He wiped his forehead and lips with a large handkerchief almost the size of a napkin, and went on: "Before you rush into a decision, I would like to leave you with another serious and far reaching thought. If, in fact, you find him guilty of openly revealing himself as the messiah, then how would you, or you, or you recognize a messiah?" He pointed individually to three silent judges as he repeated the word "you." Then to bring drama to his concluding remarks he pointed to the many witnesses: "Can you? Can you? Can you?" No one answered. Wiping his perspiration again, he continued: "I don't know how I would recognize him either because our books do not give a physical description of him. We have all read many news accounts that he had already been born and is living in some part of the world, awaiting for the Divine Order before he assumes his mission. If we believe in these accounts, then it stands to reason people in that part of the world have already seen him, talked to him, and so far have not been able to identify him for what he is. I come back to the question: How does one recognize a messiah, living among us and prior to his mission? Oh! But you will say I will know when he begins to perform miracles. Then I would too! In the meantime how do we

really know? Our great Rabbi Maimonides warned us not to expect a heavenly angel to announce his arrival or for him to astound
us with miracles like a magician overwhelms his audience. Our
history is filled with claimants of divine inspiration and yet we
have rejected them all, including the one considered most holy
by Christians, the Jew of Nazareth. . . ."

In his anger and passionate desire to save his friend, Florentin
realized he shouldn't have made that last statement, but it was
too late to retract it. Objections and shouts filled the courtroom,
but Florentin raised his voice above them: "We rejected him from
Judaism in spite of miracles he is said to have performed . . ." The
listeners cried louder: "Stop that blasphemy! Don't mention him
in our presence! Enough said!" But fiery Florentin wouldn't yield.
He raised his voice even louder: "Our ancestral brethren who
believed in him were forced to create a new religion. Does it have
to come to that, I ask you? I am not alone in having great doubts
if we Jews will ever accept the Lord himself if He entered our
lives and concealed Himself in the body of a simple man . . ." This
time the judges felt insulted. They wanted to hear no more. The
head rabbi signaled Florentin and the witnesses to stop. It took a
while for quiet to reign in the court room. They waited to hear
the head rabbi's directives. In a calm voice he said: "Let me remind the audience that every man charged with a crime is entitled to a defense. I will not tolerate any more interruptions of
Rabbi Florentin's defense of the accused." Then he turned to
Florentin and said: "Now, let me remind you that we are ready
for your summation. Please proceed."

Florentin knew he faced a court that had already made up its
mind. He decided to heed the advice of the head rabbi and give
his summation: "Dear colleagues, before you make up your minds,
think of the awesome responsibility of judging a holy man . . . "
Even that sentence appeared objectionable. The sounds of protest filled the courtroom once again. Florentin had a difficult time
being heard: "Let me finish, please. Let me finish," he begged. "I
plead with you, if it is his wisdom you don't wish to condone, then
fine. But please let us not damn this great spiritual leader because

of an insignificant issue over a performance enacted in a friendly way and attempting to please you! If, on the other hand, you believe he wanted to prove his divine qualities to us, let him do so! Aren't we sufficiently mature intellectuals to know if we wish to accept or reject his claim? I find nothing damaging to our faith in that! Gentlemen and distinguished rabbis I end my plea by begging you to show your noble character when making your final decision of not guilty in the unjust charge of heresy."

Isaac had a feeling it was too late for such a stirring plea. Sabetay had already shaken their faith and had scared them the way he had the conservatives of Smyrna. They weren't afraid of what Sabetay had said or done, they feared that a calamity from Heavens would fall upon the city if they harbored such a contemptuous rabbi. In spite of Florentin's lofty appeal, the prosecutor demanded condemnation and a list of penalties ranging from public flogging to banishment.

Sabetay did not appear at any of these deliberations including the final sentencing. As it had been in Smyrna the conservatives in Salonica got their way. The council served Sabetay with an order to leave the city immediately. The order made it clear that failure to comply would result in a sterner punishment of perpetual banishment. Feeling no regret, Sabetay viewed the sentence as a necessary suffering. He remained firm in his belief of the Judaic tenet to uphold the coming of the messiah even if martyrdom was the only way to gain the hearts of his people. Without bitterness he instructed Isaac to prepare to leave. But where?

The incident divided the Jews of Salonica into two fronts: those who believed in Sabetay and those who opposed him. The two sides waged battles in the streets without mercy. The normally peaceful Jewish quarter became a battle ground.

After writing to his brother and receiving approval, Sabetay and Isaac embarked for the largest city in the empire: Constantinople. The city was the seat and capital of rabbinical authority in the Ottoman Empire. This great and old capital of the vanquished Byzantium Empire was also the seat of the Caliph. Ever since the establishment of the Ottoman Empire two centuries before, the

Caliphate, which had been almost always in Arab Baghdad, was transferred to Constantinople by virtue of occupation of Arab lands by the forces of the Sultan. It so happened that the city was also the seat of the authority of the Eastern Orthodox Church. It had been that way since the realm of Constantine, the first Roman Emperor to convert to Christianity in the fourth century C.E.

Though Sabetay failed to win the Jewish masses of Smyrna and Salonica, in each of these two cities he left behind large groups of supporters. What these groups lacked in numbers, they made up in zeal and determination to keep his movement alive. It was always difficult to estimate the number of backers at any one time during his life. Those numbers varied from tens of thousands to nearly a hundred thousand depending on the kind of sensational news his ministry generated. His mission required universal acceptance. In spite of his exile from Salonica, the misery of world events indicated that an earnest anticipation of a messiah was decidedly in his favor. In Europe the messianic euphoria had reached climactic dimensions. An Englishman named Jacob Naylor, a Quaker, while plowing his field, heard a voice speaking to him in a similar manner God spoke to Abraham. The divine voice said to him: "*Get thee out of thy country, and from thy kindred, and from thy father's house.*" Naylor left his plow at the site where God spoke, declaring he had been appointed messiah to save his people from corrupted traditional Christianity. He arrived in Bristol, England, escorted by a band of disciples. Two women led his horse singing Isaiah's words: "*Holy, holy, holy, Lord God of Israel.*" The people in that city asked him: "*Art thou the King of the Jews?*" to which Naylor responded: "*My kingdom is not of this world but of my Father.*" Then they asked: "*Art thou the Lamb of God in whom lieth the hope of Israel?*" His response was this time: "*Were I not the Lamb of God I should not have sought you that ye might devour me. And the hope of Israel lieth in the justice of the Father, though it may be found by whomsoever chooseth to find it.*"[6]

---

6. J. Kastein p. 83.

This was the kind of news Sabetay searched for, news that would turn his people to recognize him as their long awaited messiah. These were powerful statements and dangerous assertions Sabetay wished would happen to him and his people. A few years earlier, when he was banished from his native city, another Englishman named George Fox considered himself a patriarch and founded the Quaker religion to which Naylor belonged. Sporadic news from abroad kept pointing to the eminence of a divine redemption. Why weren't Jews inspired by them? What Sabetay felt in his soul was also being felt by others in Europe. He figured God must have been testing a few candidates, as pious and as pure as he was. A feeling of urgent curiosity overwhelmed him about what the ultimate choice in this divine contest would be. This thought alone gave him added encouragement to speed the pace of his movement.

10

～ず〜

Sabetay turned thirty-two years of age when he and Isaac arrived
in Constantinople[1] in the year 1658. Isaac rented a comfortably
furnished small house with two bedrooms, a small kitchen and a
narrow and long reception room they planned to use as a living
room. His lack of success in Salonica was not what he expected,
but he was not totally dissatisfied. He had met many important
people who, if he did well in the future, may join his movement.
He left a nucleus of believers under the leadership of the young
rabbi Isaac Levi, the invited young rabbi at the banquet who refused to take part in his condemnation.

Eliyah became exceedingly wealthy in the naval trade. He advised Sabetay to spend less time with the pious and religious leaders and concentrate more on the wealthy of Constantinople. He
stressed that the lessons they learned from Smyrna and Salonica
had proven that the wealthy were the ones who wielded the power
of persuasion. The pious and the poor, having nothing to lose, were

---

1. Effectively, the official capital of the Ottoman Empire was Edirne
(Adrianople), an insignificant city located inland on the European side of
the Bosphorus and northwest of Constantinople. Sultan Mehmet II preferred to stay at the palace in this tranquil town. However, the rest of the
world considered Constantinople the real and effective capital, the way it
had been for centuries as a political and cultural center of Europe.

already on his side for they didn't need much encouragement. They were already convinced by the words of the Bible that the meek shall inherit the earth. The opinion of the rich was different. They demanded firm assurances that the rising new order would not diminish their social and economic power. Isaac took sides with Eliyah:

"I agree with your brother," he said to Sabetay. "Historically, great conquests were made by one of the following three forces: the power of the sword, the power of wealth, or the power of persuasive speech. The poor don't figure in this. I will go as far as saying that of the three forces the power of the wealthy is the most important. Don't you agree?"

From the beginning Sabetay had been indignant of the rich and often verbally abusive towards them and the intellectuals who dared question his wisdom and judgment on holy matters. Angry, he retorted: "You are wrong. That is not the way of God! On the contrary, I must intensify my efforts as an impartial servant of Lord. He would not want me to ignore any man, rich or poor. As He commands me, I intend to extol my wisdom and knowledge to all the people. I will continue to impress them with acts of biblical significance in order to raise their consciousness towards Him! Do you hear me? I don't need advice on this matter! Also, I will not relent in my criticism of faulty and irrelevant traditional Talmudic laws and customs! I will continue to speak loudly against the antiquated conservative establishment for that is what my Creator wants me to do. I don't want to hear another word about the rich and the poor. Is that understood?"

During the first days in the new city, feeling defeated, Sabetay locked himself in his room sulking and woeful. He went into long sessions of meditation attempting to communicate with God to seek His advice in light of what his brother wrote. After a few days of self-inquiry and meditation, he emerged happy once again convinced to have heard Him repeat to him: "Thou art destined to become the messiah of all my people." That was all the assurance he needed.

꒜

Nearly half the population of Constantinople were non-Moslems. The largest minority was Greek Orthodox because it had been the capital of Orthodox Byzantium until a century before. Then came the Armenian Orthodox minority, and then the Jews. The Jewish community maintained forty-four synagogues, each belonging to small Sephardi groups and modeled after the social system they had in the Iberian Peninsula before the exile. It was common to find Castilian, Aragonese, or Portuguese synagogues, and even very localized urban synagogues as they existed in Córdoba, Toledo, Barcelona, and Lisbon. Initially when Sephardis came to the Orient they were obligated to live in a designated part of the city, but after a hundred years these restrictions were lifted by the Ottoman authorities. But, since Sephardis didn't know any other form of community living, they preferred to keep themselves segregated on their own free will. There were many advantages in that decision. They could speak *espagnol* at home, in business, and in the streets without molestation from the imposing nationalistic Turks. They kept their own schools, they built homes and stores fitting their special needs, etc.

When Sabetay arrived in Constantinople, nearly every adult in the Jewries of Europe and the Middle East had heard of him by word of mouth or from newspapers. Jews fervently believed in the messiah as foretold in the Holy Scriptures, but most were puzzled and confused about Sabetay's candidacy. For nearly a decade, they have been reading the news he engendered. Since he didn't declare himself publicly, they didn't know how to think of him or his candidacy. At times they were troubled and at other times elated and moved by his frequent actions. At times he acted like a saint, and a few days later he was capable of a foolish thing. Some claimed he was the Son of God, but others questioned why he hesitated to assert himself. True, he had been in trouble with the communities of Smyrna and Salonica but only for indirectly implying he was the messiah. They said he had been anointed by the prophet Isaiah, and that God had spoken to him. They say he had proven his saintliness by performing miracles. Wouldn't that mean he is the messiah? Why doesn't he say so? Why does he allow conservative rabbis in the cities to treat him in an ungodly way? His efforts had done nothing to reach the hearts of the common faithful. He refuses to confront the establishment and each time he gave the appearance of having lost the battle.

Not all, however, harbored these questions and doubts. If Sabetay gave the signal, many were ready to march with him to the Holy Land and reestablish God's Kingdom on Earth. Those who were ready to follow him were not just Levantine Jews, they were East and North European Jews, and some New Christians of the Reformation waiting impatiently for someone to declare himself. Sabetay was much aware of this segmentized support. He had agonized over everyone of these concerns. He wished he could explain his cautious and reluctant attitude to all those who doubted his resolve. He was not a fool. To begin with, without overwhelming public support he would be charged of heresy by the conservative establishment. The punishment for that would be stoning to death by Jews in the Ottoman lands, or burning at the stake if he ventured into Christian lands. But, this was not what he feared most. An infinitely more cruel sentence awaited him if he challenged the Turkish Sultan and claimed the Holy Land under his empire as the messiah had to do. For that bold and courageous act, most assuredly, he needed God's personal approval and protection. Revolutionaries in the Ottoman Empire saw their tongue cut and hung on their neck like a necklace, paraded the city on a donkey sitting backwards. Then, the body would be cut in four pieces and allow to rot in a public square. A few days later, hungry wild dogs will be brought in the square to regale themselves devouring parts of the body.

As it was, in spite of his disagreement with his brother's advice, Sabetay found himself drawn into educated circles of the rich where he expounded and discussed Hebrew mysticism, a very fashionable topic in those days. The first impressions he made in this new city were very positive as they had been in Salonica. This complacent rich society was delighted that he had brought a new and fresh point of view on an old and uncompromising religion. Tired of following old tenets permitting no room for debate, the intellectuals discovered in this controversial man a new spirit they had been looking for. Among the many who sought him on a personal basis was Rabbi Abraham Yachini, recognized in the city as a great scholar, cabalist, and a mighty preacher *"equal to none."* When they met for the first time it was like an electrifying encounter; each took the position that it had to be written they would meet some day. They discovered much in common. Yachini was so amazed with Sabetay's unusual interpretations of cabalistic concepts that he couldn't wait to introduce him to others with the same interest, and especially to a man known in the city to be the greatest authority on mysticism.

"You must meet Eliyah, Eliyah Carcassoni. He is an old recluse and meets only a few who devote themselves to care for him, like myself and other select patients. He is a rebel among the city rabbis who have threatened him with excommunication if he didn't change his ways and adhere to traditional Judaism. They are upset about his practice of cabalistic exorcism. He is very good at it, and I know he cures many troubled souls who otherwise can't find peace of mind. The ruling rabbis don't seem to understand that the practice of exorcism is not entirely new in Judaism. I suspect the way he practices it is in direct competition with the medical profession, to which many of the complaining rabbis belong. Rightfully, he thinks of himself as a physician of the soul; and why not? His use of exorcism is definitely beyond the domain of medical science that treats the body. One of his major successes has been in the practice of transmigration. In difficult cases, when he cannot cure a severely damaged soul, he replaces it with one that used to belong to a deceased person known to have been happy and admired in his lifetime. So many patients want to see him that he accepts only a few, enough to provide his livelihood." Yachini injected a jibe at this point. "No wonder physicians are jealous! He is capable of replacing a new soul in an old body, whereas they are unable to reverse the order and give a new body to an old soul.

Carcassoni's accomplishments make them very envious." He laughed but Sabetay's mind was locked into what Yachini said earlier. Yachini continued: "While physicians complain constantly to the Commission of Rabbis that he should not be permitted to practice sorcery, as they call it, his patients swear they are totally cured and happy with his treatments when physicians have told them their ailment is incurable. He is a fascinating person. Would you like to meet him? I can arrange that."

The time it took for Yachini to describe the master exorcist, Sabetay was thinking about a cure for himself, his excruciating headaches, his bad dreams, his spells of acting incoherently at times, his depression and sudden changes of mood not always appreciated by his admirers. He had always been an advocate of practical Cabala. When he heard Yachini's offer to introduce him to Carcassoni, an apparent master of the trade, he accepted without divulging the reason. The wise man might be the healer he had been seeking for his mysterious illness. But he had to proceed with caution. An able cabalist who can read the troubled parts of a soul could very well read other secrets it sheltered. He had to know the man well enough before he submitted his soul to scrutiny. He said to Yachini: "Would I like to meet him? I insist on it. How soon can you arrange a meeting?"

Yachini arranged to meet Carcassoni the next day. It so happened that the master exorcist had an important visitor from Jerusalem named Rabbi David Habillo, a collector of charities for the Holy City. As this encounter turned out, Sabetay became more interested in Habillo than the exorcist. He learned that this visitor was also a noted Lurianic Cabalist who had written many tracts in that field. During the visit each, in a different way and yet equally interested in each other's knowledge of mysticism, became very fond of each other. However, Sabetay failed to develop a warm personal attachment to Carcassoni, and consequently decided against seeking his help. He never saw Carcassoni again.

Yachini, Habillo, and Sabetay became good friends. The subject that seemed to attract Sabetay into friendship was dreams and their personal interpretations in mystical terms. They each claimed to have had dreams with some transcendental significance. They met many times, but at one meeting Yachini and Habillo rushed to tell their experiences. It appeared that Yachini dreamt the most. He was in his forties, older than Sabetay but younger than Habillo. He was tall and impressive, a stature so indispensable to an effective orator. His voice had a reverberating quality and he wore a happy face when he spoke. He was a well-adjusted person. He had a special notebook in which he recorded all his dreams. He read a favorite sample to Sabetay and Habillo:

"Once I dreamt that a camel was pursuing me from one room in my house to the other. I must tell you that I live in a very large house which I can well afford from generous revenues I derive outside my rabbinical career. I am also a poet and a celebrated *sopher* (scribe) calligrapher known in Europe for my superb penmanship. I copy foreign texts for collectors and scholars throughout the continent, especially for dealers in Amsterdam." He paused to apologize for having digressed from his intended story. "Anyway, I was telling you that I dreamt of this camel stubbornly pursuing me throughout the house. As I ran away from it from room to room determined to keep the camel away from me, I locked my doors with intricate locks that I seemed to have in my possession. The camel opened every lock without any difficulty and pursued me. From one room to another I ran until I found myself in the last room facing this most determined camel. Trapped, and standing still, I realized it did not have an evil purpose. As I faced the animal I saw it transform into a naked maiden. I was overwhelmed by her beauty. She approached me slowly, asking me not to be afraid. Would you believe it? Just the contrary happened. I began to tremble and I suppose I must have looked like an adolescent virgin about to be seduced." He stopped to laugh, and then added: "Of course I am not a virgin as I have been happily married all these years. Anyway, as I trembled she moved ever closer, embraced me, and kissed me. She ordered me to marry her queen who was kept forcefully hidden behind the moon. This queen wanted to be set free and the key to unlock the force that kept her captive was sealed in my agreement to make love to this gorgeous maiden who stood undressed before me." At this point, Yachini appeared to be living the scene. He scratched his black beard and after a blissful laugh he continued: "As I sit here telling you this story, and as I remember the beauty of this maiden, it should have been a pleasure to accommodate her wishes. Wouldn't you say?" He chuckled nervously this time. "But somehow for a reason I fail to comprehend I remember being in an intense state of fear. I shall never forget that feeling. I trembled and she enjoyed seeing me suffer . . . . "

Yachini was taking a long time describing the way he felt and not what he finally did. Habillo couldn't wait to know the final outcome. Impatiently he demanded: "Well did you or didn't you? Don't tease me any longer. Stop rambling about how you felt!"

This warning brought Yachini back to his story. " . . . . Oh, of course. What else could I have done? I fell obligated to save her queen." He laughed nervously. "I made love to her but for some reason it was entirely joyless. All I remember is thereupon the appearance of another maiden who, with the stroke of her hand, lifted the sun and the moon and I saw my destined queen, shining as the sun. At that very same moment, still shaking from fear, I awoke."

Habillo looked at him with disdain, while Sabetay sat unimpressed. In Habillo's opinion Yachini had built his story to a climax and then deflated it to nothing. "Are you sure you told us everything?" he questioned disappointingly.

"By the truth of the Torah I swear that I have not withheld anything." Yachini thought for a moment and then added: "Except that when I awoke I discovered I had ejaculated."

Habillo laughed in such a manner as to embarrass Yachini for having failed to do a man's job. Sabetay found the episodes amusing but without ethereal significance. While Yachini was speaking about his naked maiden, he had been thinking about his own dreams with naked maidens, guarded by a watchful flame that wouldn't let him near them. He chose not to reveal his dreams, especially after Habillo ridiculed Yachini's performance.

Yachini wanted to read another of his dreams, but Habillo turned to Sabetay asking him to tell one from his samples of dreams. Sabetay had already dismissed the idea of sharing his experience with the young damsels. Instead he related his most recent dream: "Since my arrival to your city," he began, "I had a new vision in which Job, the Biblical symbol of suffering, appeared to me and uttered the following sentence: '*You have issued out of the womb.*' Job did not elaborate what he meant by his enigmatic statement. Coming from a saintly man who had spoken to God, I knew it had to be a sentence packed with mystical symbolism and power. Job waited to see if I had understood the essence of his sentence. Searching in my mind how I would reply, I felt as if I was being tested by a messenger of God for my candidacy of the messiah." Though his words were sincere, Sabetay felt embarrassed for opening his heart inadvertently; so unlike him. He showed a nervous smile and proceeded: "After a few minutes of contemplative pondering I am happy to say that for a reason yet unknown to me I came up with a meaning that satisfied Job as he expected me to do. As vividly as I remember, I looked at him and answered that his sentence could have meant only one thing: that I had began to study the holy Torah in my mother's womb. Exceedingly pleased with my ability to comprehend mystical symbolism, Job asked me to construct a second meaning from his statement. I answered timidly that it suggested the date of the current year. He asked me how so? I said, from *gematria* the numerical value of his statement was 5418 (1658). Utterly satisfied, Job confessed he had known of me enunciating the Ineffable Name of the Lord, and no saintly man except me had wedded the Torah as I had in Salonica. He complimented my cabalistic sensitivity and intuition. Before leaving my dream, he advised me not to be concerned with the misguided attitudes of the rabbis of Smyrna and Salonica who failed to understand the importance of my actions."

Yachini and Habillo were so impressed with Sabetay's confession that they immediately kneeled to him as if in reality they faced the messiah. Nobody could have had such a dream unless he was the incarnation of a divine being. Surprised, Sabetay saw them pledge their devotion to his cause committing themselves as apostles who would spread his cause blessed by the Creator. Yachini was the religious leader of one of the largest congregations in Constantinople, and Habillo traveled through the Middle East raising funds for the Hebrew institutions of Jerusalem, and visited many congregations in Turkey, Syria, Iraq, and Egypt. Together, they had important contacts with large segments of the Jewish population in the entire Middle East, and could provide for Sabetay the widespread influence and acknowledgment he needed.

David Habillo was a wealthy man in his own right. He became so impressed with Sabetay's dream, his holiness, spirituality, and his rich use of mystical symbolism that days later he had a special gold ring made for him. He had asked the jeweler to carve an artistic design on the face of the ring concealing a cabalistic symbol. His intent for giving Sabetay the ring was beyond the implication of a gift. He wanted Sabetay to decipher the intricate meaning of the symbol the goldsmith had carved onto it. It was like submitting Sabetay to an ultimate test of holiness. The design in the carving consisted of a modified Hebrew letter 'shin' (Hebrew 'sh'). This letter has the shape of three nearly vertical brush strokes joined at the bottom by a heavier horizontal stroke. The three vertical strokes are each capped with a decorative apostrophe. But what made this ring different was that the modified carved letter had four vertical strokes instead of three,[2] and as such was no longer a letter in the Hebrew alphabet; it was Habillo's intended puzzle. He and Yachini presented the gold ring. Yachini hadn't been told about the significance of the design, but he was very anxious to find out if Habillo was able to surpass Sabetay's knowledge of cabalistic mysteries. When Sabetay opened the gift box and saw the ring his eyes lit up with excitement and spontaneously burst into joy, saying:

---

2. The phylactery worn on the forehead has both letters impressed upon it.

"Oh, I am overwhelmed my dear friend." He pressed the ring on his chest near his heart expressing great pleasure. "I can't find adequate enough words to tell you how immensely grateful I am for this divine gift. Your confidence in me overwhelms me. I shall wear it all my life for it fits me very well and hopefully it will speed the onset of my ministry."

He said this deeply moved. Habillo was very happy to have pleased his friend, but he was yet unsure how Sabetay interpreted the symbol.[3] Yachini, on the other hand, stood puzzled not having understood the spellbinding attribute of the gift. He asked quickly: "I must admit I can't see how anyone could be so intoxicated with happiness over a variation of the letter *shin*. But I am not that blind to see that you two share a secret which I beg you to divulge. Else, I will die of anxiety."

Habillo and Sabetay laughed at Yachini's puzzlement and theatrics, but most of all Habillo was immensely pleased that Sabetay had at least recognized a very special significance in the ring, even if it wasn't his intended one. Curious and maintaining his broad smile he said to Sabetay: "I know what I had in mind when I ordered the gold ring. Now, I'd like to hear, in your own words, what you see in my gift."

"Oh, but this is the most precious gift ever given to me not only by a friend but by a seer into my future." Habillo smiled and nodded in approval. Sabetay continued: "There can be only one meaning to this heavenly symbol of a four arm '*shin*', a letter which at a first glance divulges the initial of one of many God's names: *Shadday*. But, as Yachini has observed, this is no longer a letter in our alphabet. Most importantly the four arms of the symbol can only designate the Tetragrammaton, the four consonants of the ancient Hebrew name of The Creator: YHVH (YaHVeH) . . . ."

Instantly, as soon as Habillo heard Sabetay unlock his hidden secret, he fell to the floor grabbed his hand wearing the ring and kissed it in total reverence. Yachini did the same. Sabetay begged them to rise and sit by his side. He didn't let go of Habillo's hand

---

3. Scholem p. 173.

and continued to explain more precisely and in greater details than Habillo ever realized what else was implicated in his symbol.

"The alphabet letter *shin* with three heads represents the Trinity in the *Cabala*. I quote:

> The Ancient of Days has three heads. He reveals Himself in three archetypes, all three forming but one. . . . They are revealed in one another. These are: the secret hidden 'Wisdom'; above it the Holy Ancient One; and above Him the unknowable One. None knows what He contains; He is above all conception. He is therefore known to man as 'Non-Existing.'

The *Zohar* also attributes the three-times repetition of the word 'holy' in Isaiah's extolling to the Holy Father, the Holy Son, and the third time to the Holy Ghost. Early Christian scholars who were amazed by the similarity of the teachings of the *Zohar* to Christian precepts deemed it their duty to promote the wisdom of this great book of mystics and used its contents selectively to convince Jews to convert to the new and true faith of Catholicism. Two hundred years ago, the Catholic scholar and great cabalist Pico de Mirandola convinced Pope Sixtus of the paramount importance of the *Cabala* as an auxiliary to Christian dogma. He said to him: *'No science yields greater proof of the divinity of Christ than the magic of the Cabala.'* He also convinced the Pope that the modern writings in the *Zohar* contained the concepts of the doctrine of the Holy Trinity, the Fall of the Angels, the original sin, the necessity of redemption, and the incarnation of the Divine Word. Following de Mirandola's advice, the Pope became acquainted with all these relevant passages in the *Zohar*, and was so impressed by them that he ordered their translation into Latin . . ." Sabetay realized he had drifted away from Habillo's simple question. He stopped, and somewhat embarrassed for bringing Christianity into his explanations, he said: "I apologize for the digression. I couldn't help explaining the deep and far reaching implications of this beautiful ring . . ." He paused again and collected his thoughts. "It occurs to me that I haven't yet explained the significance of the fourth stroke in this symbol. The fourth stroke adds to the Divine's holiness Satan's holiness, for satanic actions aren't always considered evil or infernal in the *Zohar*. It is precisely for this completeness that I am so very pleased. As it is said: *'The letters of the name of evil demon who is the prince of this world are the same as those of the name of God: Tetragrammaton. He who knows how to transpose them correctly can extract one from the other.'*

"The fourth stroke widens the realm of holiness because it includes actions thought at first to be evil, which turns out in the end beneficial to mankind and blessed by our Creator. This is the message I tried to convey many times to conservative rabbis. Objecting to and criticizing canonical laws are not always evil or sinful. It is a fundamental human right and a commandment. This right is inferred in all aspects of freedom given to man. When I do strange and daring things they should not be interpreted as being contrary to Judaic laws. Not so! What may appear to be inspired by Satan is not always evil. To affect changes in a faith that had become dormant and stale through the ages, may appear to be breaks in tradition; but in reality they are the only means to bring new life into our faith. In fact we must break the will of those who resist change." With a broad smile on his face he turned to Habillo and added: "Believe me, my dear friend, as I said to you earlier that I will wear this ring until the end of my days; I meant it. I know that those who meet me in the future will become as inspired by it as I am. Thank you my dear friend. I shall think of you when God orders me to make appointments for the new leaders of His Kingdom on Earth."

Yachini and Habillo were astounded at the depth of knowledge Sabetay was able to convey from a simple gift. Now they were totally convinced this man, who had been exiled from Smyrna and Salonica, possessed all the qualities of the messiah.

In the Middle East, the use of symbolism wrapped into the making of a gift or conveying a warm feeling was considered fashionable and smart. Among mystics in particular the gift was an effective tool for packing many feelings into one gesture. Such gifts were given to demonstrate the latitude and depth of appreciation of the donor. It so happened that Sabetay was so moved by his friend's gift that a few days later he decided to create one of his own symbols to test the receptiveness of the colleagues he had been meeting on a regular basis. His intention had an usual and much deeper purpose. With Yachini and Habillo at his side, he felt very secure if he was to promote his one and only agenda. In early February, 1659, he invited to dinner many rabbis and wealthy men who had shown much admiration of his knowledge. He thought it was time to marvel his guests over a mystical creation he had dreamt and was anxious to unveil. His living quarters were much too small for such a gathering. Isaac, who had been his faithful companion and servant, arranged the gathering in the social hall of the community center. He sent invitation cards with a special note printed on them: "Come prepared to celebrate the celestial sign of the season."

Moved by the curiosity provoked in his note, they came with great expectations. When they arrived, they were informed to wait until the end of the feast for the unveiling of the surprise. If this seems to resemble a repeat of the banquet in Salonica, it was. Had Sabetay been as effective an orator as his new friend Yachini, he would have been assured in convincing these invited souls simply with the power of his speech. His oratory skills not being one of his best attributes, the only avenue he had to convince the elite about deserving to be the messiah was by impressing them of his indisputable superiority in holiness and saintliness.

Excitement grew during the meal. His guests were much aware of the breadth of cabalistic knowledge Sabetay possessed in creating the intended surprise. As soon as the meal concluded he asked the guests to adjourn to another room in the community center where he had made arrangements for a special event. Sabetay went to a closet and pulled out what appeared to be a baby cradle. He pushed the cradle to the middle of the room for everyone to see what was inside of it. They hovered around and saw it held a very large fish dressed in baby clothes. He prayed through the week that this group of rich and educated guests would, unlike the group he had gathered in Salonica, appreciate the message implicated in his symbolic skit and approve of it. After everyone had a chance to examine what was in the crib, he asked them to sit down. He began by relating Habillo's present of the ring to him and what it symbolized. In return, he said, he wanted Habillo to explain the meaning of the crib and the fish. Somewhat taken by surprise, Habillo stood puzzled looking at the crib and betraying an embarrassment for not having the slightest clue. He looked at the other guests who carried the same puzzled expression. Finally, he admitted he didn't know.

Sabetay gave him a hint: "A simple knowledge of Hebrew astrology is required and you should remember the wording of the message I had written in the invitation."

All at once everyone dug into their pockets to recollect what was in the message on the invitation card. It said: 'Come prepared to celebrate the celestial sign of the season.' Smiling and amused, Habillo and the guests still remained puzzled. He couldn't stand any longer the agony that gnawed him. He demanded to know.

Sabetay was thoroughly pleased to have stumped his guests. Salonica still in his mind, cautiously he revealed the secret: "Our early ancestry, observing the heavens above the horizon, were able to recognize clusters of stars that resembled specific images of creatures on earth. What was most intriguing to astronomers was that within a belt of the firmament approximately 16° wide fell the paths of the moon and the planets, and in the middle of the belt our sun's ecliptic path. Furthermore when they divided the belt into twelve parts, each part revealed a characteristic outline made up of clusters of stars. Each cluster, approximating the outline of creatures or mythical characters, was given a name and for years astrologers predicted important historical events on the basis of the attitude of these stars . . . ."

That was all he had to say for the guests to show relief and satisfaction. Sabetay had described the signs of the Zodiac and the fish in astrology was one of those signs. But what was the connection of the fish to the cradle? There had to be more implied in Sabetay's symbolism. Sabetay was purposely taking his time, concerned that a wrong turn of his explanation might precipitate ill feelings. He resumed his explanation:

"One of these signs called *Dagim* (Pisces) is in the shape of a fish. The time in the year when it is in full view in our firmament is during the Hebrew month of Adar (approximately correspond-ing to the end of February). Need I remind you that this is only a few days away?" He waited again to see if anyone had unlocked the remaining part of his symbolism. Habillo was dying of curios-ity. He couldn't wait any longer. Full of anxiety and at the end of his patience, he pressured Sabetay:

"What is the mystical symbolism in this imagery? Fine, I un-derstand now that the fish hints the time of the year. But surely you don't mean just that! Please tell us!"

"I am coming to that," responded Sabetay. "I thought by this time somebody would have guessed the full meaning of the cradle. The idea is taken from an early Jewish credo asserting that the redemption of Israel would take place during the sign of Pisces. This means of course that the messiah would be born and ready to make himself known to the world. The cradle signifies his birth during the sign of Pisces . . . " He paused to detect any reaction so far. As he glanced around the room, faces looked as expres-sionless as they had been earlier, and no one said a word. He continued: "At the end of each day and during my vesper prayers I come out with the feeling that salvation is ever closer." He paused again before delivering slowly his final message: "What you should have guessed is that the symbolism heralded the birth and arrival of the messiah as the old Jewish credo tells us. As every Jew in the world prays for this arrival, I am praying that this day be the day of his birth. Amen." He stopped, his heart beating faster than usual, and cautiously he said: "This is my prayer and prophecy."

He was hoping to catch an enthusiastic reaction. Instead, he saw the same horrified looks he remembered seeing in Salonica when he performed another symbolic act with the same intent. Except for Habillo and Yachini who had already acknowledged him as their Savior, no one besides them kneeled and prayed. Knowing Sabetay's past intentions and his confrontations with the rabbinical establishments in two other cities, the fear–stricken guests left in a hurry without saying a word. Sabetay, in his great disappointment went into a severe depression. He was distraught about his new failure, and worse yet for having deceived God in his new attempt to convince and rally the faithful.

As it had been in the past, news of the incident spread into the city at an alarming rate. The elders fearing Sabetay was tampering with Hebrew laws and harvesting souls away from traditional Judaism, they dreaded a religious upheaval in their city. He had already attracted much interest for his outspoken views on religion and had amassed a fair size of admirers and followers among the lay population. To make things worse for the establishment, Rabbis Habillo and Yachini had taken themselves to preach in the streets on behalf of Sabetay. Fearing a schism in Judaism in their great city, the elders decided to punish Sabetay before matters went too far. They dispatched a rabbinic officer to his home with orders to administer him with thirty nine lashes[4] and to instruct him that he was forbidden to speak to any Jew in the city subject to a penalty of excommunication. Sabetay submitted to the whipping willingly. The punishment left him nearly paralyzed with a severely bleeding back.

His friends Yachini and Habillo were angry and shaken by the unfair punishment imposed by the old establishment on such a godly and pious man. They tried to win back supporters with speeches stressing that the punishment had been more a reflection of fear of the old establishment than of breaking a Judaic law. While Sabetay was locked in solitude in his room, Habillo and Yachini did everything they could to convince their coreligionists that Sabetay was, in their true faith, the messiah they awaited,

---

4. The number thirty-nine had a very important significance in talmudic laws. The official punishment for the crime required forty lashes not thirty-nine. But the law also emphatically stressed that it is a heinous sin and crime to make a faulty count and deliver forty-one lashes, one lash more than required. To be on the safe side of the talmudic law, the count was always stopped at thirty-nine. Author owes this explanation to Prof. Lou H. Silberman, University of Arizona.

and nothing stood between Sabetay and his people. Habillo couldn't understand why most rabbis like him were so adamant at accepting him. Yachini had the answer. He explained to Habillo with another question: "Why is Sabetay our Lord so adamant to declare himself publicly as the messiah when he and others know he has been touched so many times by God, and many of us are ready to accept him? What more proof does Our Lord need?"

"You are right." said Habillo. "I think this has been the problem all along," He says he is waiting for the Lord to tell him when the time has come. Those who believe in him don't know that. They are satisfied that he is the only saintly man around who could rally them to the Holy Land. I think you and I can be of great assistance to him in this respect. I, for myself, will do all I can to launch a campaign declaring him as our one and only Savior. I know it is not going to be easy to reverse what has already taken place. But I feel obligated to put my name forward and be counted as his servant in the service of God."

"I will do more than that. You can be sure of that," retorted Yachini.

"What do you plan to do?" asked Habillo.

"I don't know yet, but I will find a way to restore hope in his growing movement."

Nothing else was said about it. Two days later Yachini rushed to see Sabetay to comfort him. He carried with him a very important document in his hands. Suffering Sabetay had instructed Isaac he didn't want to see anyone. Inside the reception room Yachini insisted to Isaac that he had uncovered divine proof of Sabetay's foretold messiahship. Isaac wouldn't let him in, but Sabetay overheard the claim. He yelled through his open door to let him in. Yachini entered the room with a rolled up document tied with a blue ribbon. Sabetay was sitting up on his bed with his back uncovered, showing bright red laceration lines crisscrossing from his neck to his pelvis. Isaac had just finished applying a glazy ointment on his back. He warned Yachini that he couldn't stay more than a few minutes. Sabetay hadn't slept in two days because he couldn't lie down on account of the pain.

Yachini said he had incontrovertible proof in his hand that Sabetay was indeed the awaited messiah. The moment Isaac heard the word "proof," trying to avert another false encouragement and more punishment he shouted angrily: "What proof? My Lord had more than enough punishment from the people of your city. Now, if you don't mind Rabbi Yachini, please leave us alone."

Yachini ignored Isaac's demand. Sabetay hadn't moved from his still posture. Anxious to prove his point Yachini untied the ribbon around the old parchment. Indignant, Isaac grabbed it away from him. Yachini explained that the hand-written pages appeared to be the first two pages of a very ancient document he had bought from a collector who didn't know its significance nor where the rest of the manuscript was. "Regardless," he said "the first page is revealing enough. Read it loudly!" he ordered Isaac.

The first page, bleached with age, had only a title on it. Isaac read: "The Great Wisdom of Solomon." He turned his head to look at Yachini as if to question what this title had anything to do with Sabetay. Yachini ordered again: "Read what is on the next!"

Isaac did as he was told but read silently to himself. He stopped, looked astounded, and turned his head towards Yachini. He asked sternly: "Is this real?"

Yachini didn't answer yes or no. Instead he insisted again: "Read it loudly so that our Lord can hear you! From my knowledge of parchments, as I deal with them all the time, this one is centuries old. Read it loudly!"

Sabetay still remained frozen sitting on his bed. Perplexed and yet anxious to discover what was in Yachini's document, he shouted at Isaac to read it loudly:

"I, Abraham Asher, cloistered in a cave for forty years, in distress because the mighty monster that dwelled in Egypt still sat upon his throne. I tried to solve the mystery why the Age of miracles would not come. But then I heard the voice of God saying: In the year 5385 [1626] shall be born a son to Mordehay Sevi by the name of Sabetay. He shall overthrow the mighty dragon and kill the serpent. He shall be My Anointed and shall sit upon My Throne. His kingdom shall last forever, and no other but he shall be the savior of My People Israel . . . ."[5]

He read slowly to the bottom of the page which ended abruptly in the middle of the sentence, suggesting there had to be more to this prophecy. When he stopped reading Isaac thought this was too self-serving at a time when Sabetay was charged of being an impostor. Could this be some kind of a joke? He respected Yachini too much to think that as a fine calligrapher, he wouldn't have faked the document to restore Sabetay's lost credibility. No, he wouldn't do that, he concluded. Besides, faking the text is relatively simple. Faking a parchment bleached by time was impossible. In the short time it took Isaac to realize all this, he fell on his knees in front of Sabetay begging him to be his servant forever. Yachini did the same. Sabetay, who up to this point hadn't moved from his sitting position, without showing any emotions lifted his right hand and blessed them both. The prophecy in the document came as no surprise to him; he had heard the same words from the Creator.

Isaac and Yachini were quick at spreading the news of the ancient parchment hoping it would solidify public support in Constantinople and mollify the harsh stand of the ruling rabbis. While many lay Jews joined his movement, the ruling rabbis weren't impressed. In desperation they claimed the parchment was a fabrication by Yachini to foment more conundrums among the city Jewry. As a result, Sabetay was ordered to leave Constantinople. On the advice of Yachini, Sabetay went to the streets with the ancient parchment in his hands and showed it in public squares. Though moved by the evidence, public support failed to be decisive enough to force the overturn of the sentence. Nevertheless, many in that great city felt touched, and as he had done in Smyrna and Salonica, Sabetay left behind a sizable following with Yachini as their leader.

Eight months after his arrival in Constantinople fiercely angry, as the Patriarch Moses had been when his people went back

---

5. See Kastein p. 77.

to idolizing the sacred cow, he cursed the city publicly, imprecating disaster to fall upon it if his opponents didn't mend their evil ways and modified their stand with respect to the words of the prophecy spelled out in the parchment. A cloud of fear enveloped the Jewish communities of Constantinople, worried that perhaps Sabetay's curse would materialize.

Eliyah had kept abreast of the political climate in Smyrna. In his opinion the feelings that prevailed in that city at the time of Sabetay's banishment no longer existed. Moreover from the bits of news the population of Smyrna had been receiving from Barzelay, his apostle, concerning Sabetay's spreading influence in other cities, he began to draw the hearts of the Jewish population towards their native son. In the eight years that had lapsed since he was banished from Smyrna, the number of followers in that city had grown considerably in size. Opponents and city elders did not have sufficient support to carry out the punishment of death if he returned. There was another important consideration in Eliyah's encouragement. Rabbi Escapha, his teacher, now a chief rabbi and still his ardent adversary, was much too sick and old to fight his return.

CHAPTER
11

⨎

$\mathcal{E}$ight long years passed since Sabetay had seen his aging parents and his beloved city. Many events of considerable importance had taken place in the meantime, but none had changed his ideals and his ascetic spiritual life. The hardships he had suffered had hardened him in his personal relationships with other men. He had learned to become cautious before trusting anyone eager to benefit from his wisdom. Angered by the staunch rigidity of the conservatives, he stiffened his determination to fight them with an equal amount of zeal. In spite of many urgings from his advisors to declare himself, he continued to remain reluctant. He knew that Luria, during his short life of thirty eight years, died reluctant to declare himself, even though he had acquired all the messianic attributes. Instead he had said that he had abhorred the unworthiness of his generation. Sabetay, who followed closely in his footsteps, was beginning to feel the same way. But unlike Luria, he was determined to change people's ways. Expelled from Constantinople, he was accompanied by Isaac and Habillo who commanded considerable respect in world Jewry. He came along to lend his support in the event Sabetay encountered hostilities in Smyrna.

Not long after his arrival, the front page of the community newspaper heralded in big letters: SABETAY'S CURSE COMES TRUE! The news referred to the curse he had put on the city of

Constantinople. The Jewish Quarters of that city went aflame. It was the biggest fire recorded in its history. The Jews of that big city suffered immensely. When Isaac Silveira brought the news of the tragedy, Sabetay appeared happy and vindicated.

"Good! I warned them didn't I?" he said in a manner which appeared to Isaac he was happy to hear the news.

"Forgive me, AMIRAH, I had no idea I was bringing good news," said Isaac. "Why would you feel pleasure in such a calamity, even as I know you were wrongly treated by them?"

Unimpressed by Isaac's reproach he lectured: "Isaac, I see that you are angry with me. Believe me, the satisfaction on my face is not because of the loss of lives and property caused by the fire. No, not for that! It is just that you and I are differently stirred by the news. You react the way people must with tears and sorrow, incapable of comprehending neither the reason nor the source of the calamity. I am not vindictive. But I see in the event the finger of the Creator calling his people to repentance. I assure you there will be a lot more wrath descending upon the earth before the kingdom of our Savior is established. You ought to know that the Scriptures call upon us to accept such apocalyptic cataclysms in order to induce people to atone their sins and mend their evil ways before redemption can begin. There are many such signals coming through to me every day! I feel them all the time! For example, as we are speaking of this fire and the Jewish quarter is burning into smoke, did you stop to think what the *gematria* equivalence of the word smoke (*ashan*) is?"

Isaac stood perplexed at Sabetay's attitude and more so at what seemed to him an irrelevant question about the numerology of smoke. He shrugged his shoulders and said: "No! But . . . ."

Sabetay exasperated him further by saying: "I have. From *gematria* the word *ashan* has the value of 420."

"So? What do I care? We are talking about lives perished in the fire. Those are the numbers that matter to me, not the number 420 whatever it means!" responded Isaac annoyed.

"Don't say that Isaac. Can't you see the word itself gives you the prophesied date of this fire. It gives our Hebrew year 5420

(1660) in our current millennium. I can't understand why you fail to see the hand of the Creator in this fire! He is leaving an imprint of his divine will on the city that ridiculed Him through me. He ordered the fire so that they heed his message and atone their sins, else there will be more catastrophes next year and the year after, and the year after!" Isaac left the room unimpressed by the justification of an undeserved cruel punishment. He went to his room to pray for the souls caught in the fire.

The news of the fire put people on alert, assuming that Sabetay's curse was the reason for the calamity. For many of his followers it became the first divine warning Sabetay had been telling them all this time. Euphoric feelings sprung in many cities of Europe about the significance of the disaster, and more importantly about Sabetay's powers. Posters, paintings, and etchings of him appeared in books and newspapers by artists who had never laid eyes on him. Some renditions depicted him sitting on a royal throne and under a celestial crown held by angels while he conducted his royal duties amidst and surrounded by patriarchs and the leaders of the Ten Lost Tribes. Other portraits were less complimentary. They showed him in multiple scenes of being arrested, executed, and dismembered, according to the mode of punishment of the Turks. European Protestant and Jews thought it was time to heed the message of God. Sabetay was only a recent comer on the scene. Not long ago, the frenzy of the millennium had been rekindled by the apostate Solomon Molho, the Marrano,[1] who proclaimed himself Christ. Jacob Melstinski in 1550 declared himself Christ in Poland and had chosen twelve apostles.[2] Six years later David Jorries appeared in Delft as Christ. Three years after Jorries'death, his body was exhumed by the Catholic Church and his remains were burnt at the stake by the executioners of the Inquisition. In 1614 Ezekiel Meth named himself Grand Duke of God's Kingdom and portrayed himself as the Archangel Michael. A year later

---

1. A. Marrano is a Spanish Jew converted into Catholicism.
2. J. Kastein pp. 84–91.

Isaiah Stieffel came out shouting: "*I am Christ, I am the living word of God.*" As the memory of these willful patriarchs faded because of the public's uncertainties, new ones appeared. In 1624 Philippus Ziegler, the secretary of the Palatinate State of the Holy Roman Empire in Bavaria prophesied that a messiah of the line of David would be born in Holland. And in the year 1648, the Jewish messianic date, Hans Keyl declared that an angel of the Lord appeared to him warning that the State of Württemberg would be invaded by the Turks, the plague, and pestilence. The same year the English Parliament received a published book by the Puritan Edward Nicholas entitled *Apology for the Honourable Nation of the Jews*. In this book the author damned the Papists and proclaimed that the "*weal and woe*" of the nations of the world depended on the treatment they gave the Jews, for God had made them survive since the beginning of history. Six years later Jacob Naylor, the Quaker, was told by Abraham that he was the messiah. The Scandinavian Oliger Pauli saw a vision of God proclaiming him King of the Jews. In France too, appeared the book of Isaac de Peyrère, a Huguenot who prophesied that the Diasporas around the world were at an end. The Jews would return to the Holy Land any time soon. A Silesian nobleman von Frankenberg, then a Tyrolese nobleman Johannes Mochinger, then the Dutchman Heinrich Jesse, and the Bohemian mystic Paulus Felgenhauer, all prophesied the same message that God was about to send His messiah on Earth.

Nowhere in the Christian world of the seventeenth century was this passion more buoyant than in England and Holland. A noted Dutch rabbi by the name of Menasseh ben Israel ha-Levi wrote a book in the year 1650 entitled *Miqveh Yisrael* (The Hope of Israel) which stirred incredible interest and emotions among Christian and Jewish scholars. The book was to be the ultimate proof that the day of salvation for Israel was at hand. He warned Christian states not to be unkind to Jews in their territories for the stay of the Israelites in their land would not be long. Those states which persisted on mistreating his brethren would soon suffer severe retributions from God.

Sabetay's curse and Menasseh's argument in his book seemed to converge in a timely fashion to provide the unquestionable proof that God wasn't going to order His Messiah, already born, to begin His mission until people mended their ways. Menasseh based his arguments on an eyewitness account from a Marrano named Antonio de Montezinos who swore under oath having seen and met the Ten Tribes of Israel, sent into exile in biblical times by the Assyrian King Shalmaneser. These tribes had been lost trying to find their way to Israel. The mystery behind the sudden and total disappearance of these tribes puzzled Christian and Jewish scholars for generations. How could so many people be lost without a trace? But legends affirmed that their eventual discovery will coincide with the coming of the messiah. Therefore, Montezinos' discovery was not just an anthropological find, it implicated more importantly the coming of the messiah. He said he found the biblical people in Ecuador, South America. He learned from a leader of one Lost Tribe that after the Assyrians set them free, they were lost in the desert of Arabia. It took three millennia for succeeding generations of these tribes, in search of Israel, to wander from Africa, to Tartary, to China and to South America even before the Indians arrived in the continent. Montezinos returned to Amsterdam deathly ill from a tropical disease and told his discovery to Rabbi Menasseh. On his death bed he swore solemnly of having told the truth.

Rabbi Menasseh sent a copy of his book to Oliver Cromwell, head of the English Commonwealth, to warn him of unjust English laws restricting Jews in his land. The book was personally endorsed by Menasseh, who affixed on the first page of his book the hand written message: "*Let me remind you Your Highness that prior to the advent of the messiah the prophecy in Deuteronomy 28:64 has to be fulfilled*:

"And the Lord shall scatter thee among all people, from the one end of the earth even unto the other; . . ."

He wrote this quotation in Hebrew making sure to underline the words "the end of the earth" (*qtseh haaretz*). He explained further that the literal translation of that Hebrew word was "Angle Terre," French for England. The book made a commanding impression on Cromwell and members of the English Parliament. New Christians and conservative Catholics who believed in the millennium regarded Menasseh's warning as an affirmation of the return of the Jews to the Holy Land, establishing the Fourth Monarchy.

The messianic candidates of the past centuries had come and gone, and seeing how Europe was lit with anticipation, Sabetay considered himself the only living, viable, and chosen servant of God. He wished his own people would heed these warnings and develop the same enthusiasm as that of the European Christians. There was hardly any time to reflect; the structure of the world was about to change forever.

On his birthday in August 1661, he was summoned urgently to Rabbi David Habillo's quarters in Smyrna. His faithful friend and mentor was dying of a stroke resulting from the shock he suffered upon learning of a lawsuit brought against him by the fathers of the city of Jerusalem. He and his son were accused of embezzling funds from the charities they collected. Habillo wanted Sabetay to give him the last rites. As Sabetay stepped out of the door, squatters around his house nearly tore his clothes apart pulling him to listen to their individual misfortunes. They grabbed his garments digging for coins in the pockets of his overcoat. They threw themselves at his feet, trying to slow him down asking to be blessed. The struggle to extricate himself from that mob took so long, that Habillo died before he could get to his house. Before his death, Habillo had made arrangements for Sabetay to replace him in his function of collector of alms. The fathers of the holy city welcomed the idea only because of Sabetay's popularity, even though they secretly disapproved of his messianic claims. Unbeknownst to Sabetay, Habillo's intention for recommending him was to exhort Sabetay to go to the Holy Land and impress the holy men there the way he had impressed him.

When Sabetay was informed about his new role, he accepted the assignment thinking it was time to move on with his ministry.

The only regret he felt was leaving his parents who were ill. He ordered Isaac to make plans for his trip south. "AMIRAH, I have looked into it already. I knew sooner or later you would follow the advice of Habillo, God bless his soul. I, too, think it is time to move on and to test the mood of our brethren in the South. Knowing you would want to know, I have looked into the travel arrangements. Going by land on horseback from Smyrna to Jerusalem is too risky without an armed escort, and it is very arduous. Besides, we don't have friends along the way. Not yet, anyway. Habillo, God Bless his soul, was in the habit of traveling by sea. Before he died, he told me he had received many requests for you to visit important congregations in the South. They have heard so much about you. Oh, AMIRAH, one look at you will suffice to convince them that you are the one, the real one. There is no one besides you!"

"Which congregations are you talking about?" interrupted Sabetay, annoyed that Isaac had perhaps mapped a trip without his knowledge. He figured he and Habillo must have been working behind his back.

"I have arranged for us to sail south to the beautiful Island of Rhodes. The ship has to sail by that island anyway. There you can rest, pray, meditate, and swim the beautiful blue waters of the southern sea while we stay as guests of chief Rabbi Solomon ben Moses de Bossal. In a letter written to Habillo de Bossal had expressed a desire to study the *Zohar* with you. He heard how totally proficient you are in modern cabalistic literature. He is looking forward to study under your guidance."

"How is it I wasn't told about this?"

"You were too busy with keeping up with correspondence, the business of the movement in Smyrna, and caring for your parents. I anticipate one month stay in Rhodes will make our host measurably happy and produce innumerable followers. Habillo also advised we sail from Rhodes to the Syrian port of Tripoli where there is another important Jewish community, and from there to Alexandria, Egypt. Before you enter the Holy Land we must make every effort possible to raise as many legions of Jews as we can,

giving you the true image of a King of Israel. Then you can face
those acrimonious rabbis who think they own God and His glorious Kingdom. To command respect and power, a king must have
his knights and his nobility at his side. A king never travels alone,
AMIRAH. I am particularly thinking of one such knight you must
have at your side."

The only support Sabetay counted on was that of the Lord. He
couldn't understand all this gibberish from Isaac about knights
and legions. To show his irritation at dependence on human authority, he retorted: "I always have Him on my side! What knight
are you referring to? Who is the man you have in mind?"

"Sorry AMIRAH. Forgive me. I didn't intend to put anyone else
above our Lord. When I spoke of a knight I was referring to a rich
and noble man with considerable political power. I want you to
know he is also an ardent cabalist most anxious to meet you . . . ."

"Who are you talking about? Will you tell me who is this man
of nobility and power you think will make a difference?"

"He is the one and only Rabbi Raphaël Joseph, the Egyptian
viceroy's *Saraf Bashi* (treasurer). They don't call him *Tchelebi* for
nothing. He has just been appointed to the position and title of
Master of the Mint. He lives in Cairo yet his ecclesiastic influence
and dominion extends to the rich seaport of Alexandria and to
Jerusalem. He is said to be the richest and most generous man on
earth. Because of this, the rabbis of Jerusalem lure him for advice
in soliciting financial help. What is most surprising is that with all
his wealth he is the most self-denying man of God. All during the
day he fasts, like you AMIRAH, and at night when his family sits
down to eat sumptuous meals, he eats nothing but *pulse* (a pottage
made of pods from beans, lentils, beans, etc.) He wakes up at midnight to study the Law in holiness and purity. In the silence of night
he turns to the Lord with all his heart and soul. He immerses in
ritual baths, like you, and he flogs himself frequently. In spite of
all the fortune he possesses, he wears sackcloth on his body during
his mortification periods. His whole congregation and those of other
cities in Egypt are obedient to him. How could you not want to
meet such a man of God and influence?"

Sabetay had seen the name and fame of this man in a list of generous donors, but not in the personal terms Isaac described. Impatiently he asked again: "I began by asking you about our trip to Jerusalem. Instead you speak of these people and places and nothing about what I want to hear. You haven't said anything about the Holy City! When do I go to Jerusalem?"

Isaac was so wrapped up in the extended trip he planned, he could focus only on one detail at a time. He did not answer Sabetay's question; not yet. "He heard so much about you. He has written to ask if you would do him the honor to live in his mansion, and this way he could study with you. In return for the benefit of your knowledge he will sponsor your trip to the Holy Land. I think he said he may even accompany you. He is a man of great insight, power, and means. What a great opportunity this would be for you! Don't you agree? True, it may delay your trip to the Holy Land for a while, but think of what your mission will gain when you capture the hearts of these two great men as I know you will, AMIRAH. This is what I meant when I said earlier that you will go to Jerusalem like the King of Israel."

Sabetay wasn't sure about the benefits of stopping in the Island of Rhodes, but the part about his stay in Cairo began to interest him. It had been the city of residence of Maimonides, the world renown ethicist and philosopher. He ordered Isaac to make arrangements for the trip as soon as possible. He regretted the separation away from his ill parents but it was Spring, 1662, four years to the Christian date of the prophecy.

In the beginning of summer of that year they set out to sea following the itinerary Isaac had arranged. By coincidence, the day of departure fell on the day Escapha died. The first time Sabetay left his native city Escapha rejoiced his departure. This time it was Sabetay's turn to rejoice. His one time mentor who had turned enemy had departed from the scene. He had no doubt the hand of God had smote this man who stood on his way.

The Island of Rhodes, the largest of twelve islands in the Dodecanese Archipelago, is located off the south-western shores of Asia Minor. Sailing south from Smyrna on the Aegean Sea was like living through the heroic legends of antiquity. These waters were traveled heavily from the time of the Minoan-Mycenaean Grecian civilization, a millennium and a half B.C.E., to 1500 C.E. when the Ottoman Turks occupied them. After the collapse of that early civilization in 1400 B.C.E., the 550 square mile island became a powerful independent kingdom. Its historic harbor alone was unique and known to be the oldest in existence in the Mediterranean Sea. During the Crusades in the eleventh to thirteenth centuries it became a staging area for Christian armies attempting to invade the Holy Land. After eight such military attempts the Christian armies abandoned the hope of capturing the Holy Land from the hands of Islam. What remained of those armies was a religious-military order called the Knights of St. John of Jerusalem who first entrenched itself in the Island of Cyprus and then was forced to move to the Island of Rhodes vowing to fight the Turks as long as it took. They converted Rhodes into an almost impregnable fortress but in 1523, after two centuries of defying the Turks, the religious order was defeated. It transferred its forces to the Island of Malta, further west in the Mediterranean Sea. After the Sephardi exile from Spain in 1492 some Spanish Jews sought refuge from one island in the Mediterranean to the other. But most island authorities would not accept them for they feared repercussions from the powerful Spanish Kingdom which controlled the sea.

The two hundred Sephardi families who lived in the island received Sabetay and Isaac with great pomp as their ship moored in the ancient seaport five days after it left Smyrna. Sabetay was received as the most saintly man of the century, destined to become the Savior of Israel, the *Mashiah* who would extricate the Holy Land from the hands of the Moslem Turks and gather all the children of Israel in that Promised Land. His short stay in Rhodes was triumphant thanks to Rabbi de Bossal, who became exceedingly impressed with Sabetay's knowledge of the divine. His sojourn was the most satisfying and rewarding since the beginning of his ministry. All through Europe, as in Rhodes, the most pressing question was: Why was it taking Sabetay longer than the prophesied date in the *Zohar* to declare himself? To reassure a Rhodesian congregation who asked the question prior to his departure from the island, he explained in the following way. He used a Talmudic passage written centuries ago by Rabbi Shimon ben Yohay and asked the congregation to pay attention to the special coincidence between his name in Hebrew, Tzvi, meaning deer, and the creature in the Talmudic passage. "Strangely enough," he said, "the very unusual condition of a species of a red deer called the *hind* that ben Yohay used in his allegoric story answers your question about the timing of Israel's redemption. The womb of the *hind* is so narrow that she cannot, in a natural way, give birth to her young. She needs assistance. When she crouches for delivery God sends a remedy in the form of a serpent to bite her at the opening of the womb, enlarging it and thus giving birth to her young." He paused to give time to his audience to ponder about the connection between the womb of the deer and the day of redemption. "Now the *Zohar* in its great wisdom compares the deer, in need of the serpent, to my mission in need of a universal atonement. When the Creator will hear me say that Israel is ready to repent, then He will send the messiah. To help unleash the *Shehinah*, the messianic powers, I intend to spend a year in solitude in the Holy Land in the cave of Shimon ben Yohay, the visionary of this revelation. I intend to call for the serpent when I am convinced that Israel is ready to repent."

Sabetay's answer had an miraculous impact on the small community of Rhodes. His moving answer to a frustrating question was printed in every major newspaper in Europe and the Middle East. It was the stuff believers wanted to hear. He impressed the people of Rhodes so much that they declared him their Savior and wished him equal success in the Holy Land.

Before boarding the sail ship, the people of Rhodes roared with excitement and chanted like a legion of soldiers readying themselves to launch an offensive on the enemy: "Sabetay Sevi, our *Mashiah!* The one and only messenger of God to bring redemption to Israel!"

On the gangplank Rabbi de Bossal kneeled to Sabetay's feet proclaiming his total devotion to his cause. Nearly five hundred adults and children surrounded the dockyard to experience the devotion of their leader and to wish Sabetay well. If the short stay in Rhodes was successful, that in Tripoli was equally so. Yet these gratifying experiences were small accomplishments compared to the magnitude of the total following Sabetay needed to claim the universal recognition he aspired.

The port city of Alexandria is located at the western edge of the Nile delta as the river spills into the Mediterranean Sea. It was Egypt's major seaport. When Alexander the Great, King of Macedonia, conquered Egypt in 332 B.C.E. he gave his name to that city and made it the capital of Egypt. Since then Alexandria had been a center of Hellenic scholarship and science. From antiquity, the city gave refuge to many different cultures, Egyptian, Coptic, Greek, Jewish, Roman, and Islamic. With the rise of Islam, Egypt fell to the Arab invasion in the middle of the seventh century and in 1517 to the Ottoman Turks who governed it from Constantinople. For Sephardi Jews the city had a special significance for it had been the home of the twelfth century Talmudist, philosopher and writer Rabbi Moses Maimonides who fled to Egypt from religious persecutions launched in Córdoba, Spain by the Moorish chieftain.

The arrival in Alexandria was even more triumphant than in Rhodes and Tripoli. To Sabetay it seemed that the places he had been visiting lately were competing in being the most friendly and gracious to him. Tchelebi Raphaël Joseph, Master of the Mint, welcomed him and made sure the reception was the greatest Sabetay had ever seen. Sabetay stepped out of the ship in a magnificent attire and headdress both made of raw silk embroidered with white and blue intricate Star-of-David designs. He had the attire tailored in Smyrna for momentous occasions such as this. Isaac had insisted he should look imperial, and he did. The style and richness of his clothing reflected opulence and nobility worthy of the Kings of Israel. Raphaël was the first to greet him with a warm embrace. As an official of the city of Alexandria he pronounced the welcoming speech. Shouts rose in the air calling: "AMIRAH, Our Lord and King, His Majesty Be Exalted, open the gates to the messiah!"

Sabetay was touched by the magnitude and reverence of the reception. His host, too, was dressed in keeping with his lofty position. Since both men were accustomed to an ascetic life, all this display of pageantry was meant for the public. The crowd loved it and waived banners displaying colors of biblical kings of Judah. Sabetay was to discover later that his host wore under his stately garment underwear made of sackcloth and a shirt made of animal hair, the garb of the penitent.

They traveled south to Cairo in a gilded carriage. Sabetay and Isaac were given luxurious quarters at Raphaël's mansion. Sabetay was to spend two months in Egypt before going to Jerusalem and remit the funds he had collected in Smyrna, Rhodes, Tripoli, Cairo, and Alexandria. During this period he learned of Raphaël's immense generosity, hospitality, and obsession in helping his congregation, especially the pious, the needy, and the starving scholars of the Talmud. Once a week he invited at his table fifty or more needy Jews to have a sumptuous dinner while he sat at their table fasting. He did all this unselfishly not because he wished to atone his sins or win special favors in the eyes of God, but because it was his way of saving the race in a world hostile to Jews. Raphaël became aware of Sabetay's boundless knowledge of the deity and of the *Zohar*, his fortitude, and his heroic qualities; attributes which he lacked and wished to acquire. There was an instant attraction between the two men. Younger Raphaël treated him in his mansion with an unusual child-like submission to this authority in the knowledge of the divine.

Sabetay's presence in the land of Pharaohs became the focal point of interest of Jews everywhere. Analogies began to surface that perhaps a repeat in Jewish history was about to take place. Like Moses, they waited for him to be ordered by God to take his people out of Egyptian bondage and into the Holy Land. The suggestion pleased him very much. But this time it wasn't the Red Sea or the Pharaohs that stood in the way of the Israelites; it was the immense geographical extent of the Diasporas spread around Europe, the acrimonious rabbis of Jerusalem, and most importantly, the mighty military powers of the Ottoman Empire. He had no idea how he would surmount these towering difficulties. He didn't care to think about it for fear of an eventual disappointment and for fear of meddling in God's affairs. His only hope was that, when the time came, God would show him the way by addressing him from behind a bush or a rock as he had done to Abraham and Moses.

Late that summer of 1662 Sabetay, accompanied by Isaac, left for the Holy City in a well-equipped caravan, uncertain about the reception that awaited him. If one thing lifted his spirits it was that he was no longer the insignificant religious trouble maker the conservative rabbis of Smyrna and Constantinople portrayed him as being earlier. He was arriving from Cairo with the much-appreciated funds he had collected, and escorted by Raphaël's agents ready to vouch for him and assist him in any way he deemed necessary. He saw the occasion as an opportunity to impress the city fathers in Jerusalem not only with his ability to raise moneys for them, but with his unmatched spirituality deserving the respect of a holy man.

The Jewish community in Jerusalem numbered about two hundred families, mostly poor and pious Sephardis. Jewries all over Europe supported these desperate people for they had no means to sustain themselves. Since the time of the Romans when they were expelled from the Holy Land and were forbidden to return, the fear of loosing their biblical rights to their ancient homeland had become an undying obsession. By giving generously, Diaspora Jews made every effort to maintain a permanent Jewish occupancy for the sole reason that when the time came for all Israel to reunite, under messianic leadership, their foothold on the land would be assured. The Jewishness of the Holy City had to be maintained at all cost. A rich Livornese family had financed a small but reputable academy in the city from which many scholars graduated. A plague epidemic had devastated the city in mid-sixteenth century, and a good many Palestinian Jews had fled from the black sickness to neighboring countries. Sabetay's arrival with a purse was indeed very timely. There existed a superstitious conviction in the Jewish Quarter of Jerusalem restricting building of new homes. According to a legend, a great fire was expected to descend from heaven and burn the city and its surroundings to cleanse the area from the abomination of the Romans, Christians and Moslems before the messiah and the Jews of the Diaspora came to reclaim it. This discouraged many well-to-do Jews in the Diasporas from moving to Jerusalem.

To compound the misery in the city, the Turkish governor demanded excessive extortion moneys from the alms collected abroad. Given all these hardships, why anyone would want to live in Jerusalem was a question often asked. There had to be a redeeming answer for the Diaspora Jewries to keep supporting the concept of the city's inextricable link to the Jewish people. Indeed there was. The answer was rooted in another self-serving conviction that, as residents of the Holy Land, they belonged to a privileged group favored by God. This privilege had been assured in the good books.

Sabetay met the city elders to account for the charities he had received. That encounter was cold and strictly business-like. Every attempt by Isaac and Raphaël's emissaries to open a dialogue about Sabetay's movement failed. The elders feared that the slightest form of friendliness towards him would ignite demonstrations. Disappointed, Sabetay became very distraught and ill with intense headaches. It was the worst attack since his disappointment in Constantinople. This affliction alternated from a state of uncontrollable emotions and excitement to severe depression, and then back to hallucination, delusions and violent derangement. Isaac couldn't do anything for him. He had to wait until the spell ran its course. The condition became worse at night time. They triggered such awful dreams that Isaac, who sat by his bedside, saw him fighting and struggling with creatures, perhaps serpents, demons, Satan, whores and the like.

Isaac fell asleep sitting next to his bed. Startled by a loud call, he opened his eyes and saw the room flooded with sunshine. The call was repeated:

"Isaac wake up. Why aren't you sleeping in your bed? I want to get up, get dressed, and go out. You have to move away from my bed. Where is Moses?"

Aghast, Isaac looked at him to see if he was feeling as good as he appeared to be. "Which Moses do you speak off?" he questioned.

"What is the matter with you this morning? Why do you ask which Moses? Moses Pinheiro of course! Did you think I would be asking for Moses of the bible?"

Isaac understood that Sabetay wasn't totally free of the affliction that ensnared him. They hadn't seen Moses Pinheiro since they went into exile from Smyrna more than a decade ago. Sabetay's eyes appeared glassy and without color or focus. Isaac deduced he was hallucinating. Before he could say anything, Sabetay jumped out of bed and proceeded to dress himself. "AMIRAH you must stay in bed and rest. You can't go out yet," he begged.

Sabetay laughed and mumbled a few obscure words. Isaac tried to hold him back but Sabetay became violent. He pushed him hard against the wall and Isaac fell to the ground momentarily unconscious. When he regained consciousness Sabetay was gone. Isaac had no idea where to look for him in this unfamiliar city. Four hours later he was back.

"Where have you been, AMIRAH? You know you should not go out in your condition . . . ."

This time Sabetay looked happy and normal. He answered casually: "I feel a lot better. My headache is gone. I met a lot of people in the street and I had a great time. I think I will break fast now and have something to eat."

Isaac was delighted. He ran to the kitchen to ask the maid to bring lunch. Sabetay hadn't eaten in five days. As he gulped the food while Isaac watched him with contentment, the door bell rang. The maid came to the dining room and said that a man from the Chief Rabbi's Office was at the door asking for Rabbi Sevi. Isaac rushed to the door and asked the stranger who he was and the purpose of his visit. The man said he was the flogger from the Chief Rabbi's Office and he had been ordered to flog Sabetay with forty lashes. Horrified, Isaac asked to know the charges. The muscular man explained that Sabetay had transgressed a Talmudic law. He had preached in the streets of Jerusalem a few hours ago, drawing large crowds and insisting that certain Jewish holidays had to be abolished. His act against the Talmud was a punishable sin. He asked again for Rabbi Sevi or he would search the house until he found him. Sabetay heard the arguments from the dining room. He came out and told the flogger he was ready for the punishment if the flogger was ready to receive his from the Lord. The man didn't understand what Sabetay meant. He removed his clothes and submitted without protest.

While he was recovering from the lacerations of the savage whipping, a leader of the community of Jerusalem, Rabbi Moses Hagiz came to his house to see him with an urgent request. When Isaac learned who he was, he told Hagiz that Rabbi Sevi wasn't seeing anyone. Sabetay heard the conversation from his bedroom and yelled at Isaac to let him in. Sabetay knew of him by name for he was the director of the Talmudic Institution in the Holy City. He had no idea why the great scholar wanted to see him. He had never met him before and he didn't discount the possibility that he was coming on behalf of the elders who ordered the flogging.

Rabbi Hagiz was ushered into the bedroom where Sabetay suffered from the wounds. Confronted with that familiar but horrible look of Sabetay's back, Hagiz spoke first: "I am sorry. I am terribly sorry. I swear on our bible that I wasn't aware they had done this to you. Forgive me for intruding . . . ."

Isaac became furious. "Why did you come, then? Now you know what his back looks like. You can go and report to your clan the atrociousness of what you have seen."

"I am very sorry. I didn't come for that. Believe me. I wasn't aware of it. You must believe me." He turned around and was about to leave when Sabetay repeated Isaac's question: "Why did you come, then?"

Rabbi Hagiz was old and meek. He suffered terribly from the curvature of the spine. Bent severely to a point where his long beard reached his waist, he raised his head with considerable effort to look into Sabetay's eyes. "You must believe me that I had no idea such a sentence was inflicted upon you. From a letter sent to me by Rabbi Raphaël Joseph I learned that you are a pious and noble scholar. I simply came to ask a favor. From the state I see you are in, I am not sure you want to hear what I came to ask."

"Try me," answered Sabetay who by this time figured Hagiz had nothing to do with the punishment.

"I came to beg you to go back to Alexandria and raise more funds for the impoverished community and especially our school . . . ."

Incredulous Sabetay interrupted with anger: "I have just come back from Alexandria with a generous sum of money for exactly the purpose you speak of. I have delivered it to the Rabbinical Council. I suggest you go back and take your claim to them. Good day."

Isaac was ready to escort the old man to the front door. Rabbi Hagiz lifted his head again and with a motion of his right hand signaled Isaac to wait. He said: "I am aware of this Rabbi Sevi. I know you have served us well already . . . ."

"Then what is the problem?" retorted Sabetay.

"The problem is that word leaked to the Turkish Governor about the purse you brought. He sent a detachment of *Janizaries* to seize the whole purse of funds. We don't know who betrayed that confidence. The fact of the matter is that we are now in a more dire state than before. We have to wait months for new moneys. Permit me to say to you, though I am sure you need no reminder, there is no divine fulfillment more urgent and worthy as the one of the charity to the great city of King David."

"We are aware of that Rabbi Hagiz. You need not remind us of it!" answered Isaac. "We have already done our share. It is not our fault if you lost the funds."

Sabetay became curious how far was Hagiz ready to go in return for the favor he was asking. He interjected:

"Rabbi, you must realize that going back to Cairo and returning with more money is not as simple as you make it sound. The trip on horse back is arduous and dangerous. Besides, those who have contributed will be angry when they learn what happened to their donations. If it was difficult to raise the money in the first place, it will be exceedingly more difficult to confront them a second time in such a short period. What kind of sacrifice are you prepared to offer?"

For some reason the old rabbi expected the question. He suspected Sabetay wouldn't be interested in his proposition unless there was a comparable offer behind it. His dedication to the Talmudic school was so profound that he came prepared to convince him at any cost. "If it means anything to you," Hagiz began, "the existence of my school entails so much to me and to the world of Jewry that I am ready to become your servant and follower in return for a promise to do what I beg of you." He said this without hesitancy. The words coming from this cripple and dedicated old man took Isaac by surprise. Clever Sabetay was not surprised but he was touched nonetheless. He agreed to the old man's request knowing that he will have an important ally in the great city in the days to come.

"Very well then," answered Sabetay.

Barely able to kneel down, Hagiz lowered his head and kissed Sabetay's feet. Isaac had to help him stand up. Hagiz blessed them both and left fully satisfied.

When his wounds were healed, to keep his promise to the people of Rhodes, on his return to Alexandria instead of taking the sea route, he decided to return by way of Hebron south of Jerusalem. The saintly town was known as the patriarch Abraham's burial site.

"Why are we going out of our way into isolated areas of the desert?" asked Isaac, worried that Sabetay might suddenly have another attack of his illness, this time in the wilderness.

"My dear Isaac, traveling all this way from Smyrna without becoming imbued with the spirit of the old biblical prophets would be a gross travesty. Hebron being the resting place of the father of Judaism, Abraham, it is also the site of the caves of Machpelah where biblical patriarchs came to be in seclusion with Abraham and the Creator. I have always wanted to come here. Besides you heard me make the promise to the people of Rhodes. I am looking for a special cave where Shimon ben Yohay, the father of our Holy Cabala is buried. I want to be alone in the cave for a few days while you will set a tent outside and wait for me. I don't know how long I will stay inside."

Realizing this diversion would take some time, Isaac dismissed the two agents Raphaël provided. They were instructed to report back to their employer about the unforeseen delay. In Hebron, Sabetay stopped long enough to say a prayer over Abraham's grave and went searching with a guide for the cave he had in mind. Isaac and the remaining servants set up a tent outside and Sabetay covered his body with sack cloth, put on his phylacteries and prayer shawl and took up residence in the cave. Before entering it he ordered not to be disturbed for any reason. They were to wait until he came out on his own accord.

Isaac nearly went insane worrying about him, cloistered in the small and smelly cave. The second day he ordered a servant to go in and place food at Sabetay's feet. When he returned he reported that his master looked past him without seeing him. He even waved his hand in front of his eyes without detecting a blink. The servant swore his master had gone blind. Now worried even more, Isaac ordered the servant to remain in the cave making sure his master didn't see him. He was to observe secretly from behind a rock and report immediately any sign of concern or trouble.

Two weeks passed and Sabetay was still in the cave. He hadn't moved from his original posture sitting on the ground with his legs crossed. All the servant could hear was murmurs varying in intensity and accompanied by strange body gestures, twitches, and on occasions Sabetay's eyes would fill with tears. One day the servant saw Sabetay stand up and walk faintly towards the entrance, he rushed to hold his arm, sure he had gone blind. Sabetay pushed him aside insisting he didn't need help. As he came out, the light was so blinding he covered his eyes with his prayer shawl. Only then he reached for the hand of the servant and they walked to the tent. While Sabetay sat alone in the tent the servant went to alert Isaac, occupied with chores by the fire pit. Emotionally overtaken, the servant said to him: "Rabbi Sevi is out! I brought him to the tent!"

"How is he?"

The servant replied: "My master shed tears last night and murmured prayers endlessly. At nights he recited psalms with a mighty voice, the voice of joy and the voice of gladness until the light of dawn, at which time he began the morning service. His demeanor was awe-inspiring, different from that of any other man I have seen or heard. I could not stop looking at him because it was a mysterious sight. He radiated a healthy face the like of which I had never seen. I didn't see him eat or drink, yet his face showed no pain or suffering." He stopped only to catch his breath. "What was a true miracle was when he came out of the cave his blindness had gone away. He could see again!"

Sabetay had an abundant meal and slept the whole day. The day after, they resumed their travel to Alexandria. Sabetay didn't feel like talking during the long trek back. Isaac figured he was still living the many dreams he had in the cave in company of biblical characters. When they arrived in Alexandria, Sabetay was given a letter from his brother which had arrived a few days after he left for Jerusalem. He opened it only to find that his father and mother died in an interval of two months. His brother wrote to say he buried them side by side and gave them the best funeral permitted by Judaic law. At the end of the letter there was a special paragraph:

"Before Mother died she asked to hear, for the last time, the Castilian poem you sang to her. I sang it myself the best way I could. I was unable to sing it with joy the way it was meant to be sung. My tears and my choking throat impeded me from doing justice to your song. I am sorry about that, but mother died with a smile on her face as soon as I finished singing."

Totally shaken Sabetay went to his room and fell into tears. He was filled with regret he hadn't been near his parents when they needed him. His first move was to tear his garment as a sign of mourning, he sat on the floor, and after closing his eyes he sang his mother's song loud enough for her to hear it in heaven. Everyone in Raphaël's mansion heard it. Sabetay refused to come out of his room for over a month. Terribly worried Isaac urged his host to intervene. Raphaël knocked at his door and entered without waiting for a reply he knew he wouldn't get. Sabetay looked awful. He hadn't shaven in a month. His beard, hair and eyebrows covered practically his entire face. He wore a black cassock purposely torn in the front. He sat on the floor over his bent knees praying furiously. Raphaël interrupted his prayers:

"My dearest AMIRAH. You see, I got into the habit of addressing you by this saintly title." He paused to see if there was a reaction. There was none. He continued: "I came to remind you that you have been cloistered in your quarters for much too long a time to pray and shed grief in the misery of the loss of your parents. Though I am younger than you are, I do not presume to preach you. But our Talmud specifically orders the faithful to come out of mourning at the end of thirty days and resume the life God has given him. The commandment, I believe, is for the simple reason that in a divine gift of life one has important obligations and duties to perform in the world He created."

Sabetay listened but did not move from his position. Raphaël walked closer and sat on the floor next to him. He continued: "You have come back from Jerusalem with the specific task of raising additional funds for the Talmudic school. These much-needed monies are to compensate for the thievery of the *Vali* (Governor) in Damascus. Tragedy and famine can strike the Jewish population of our Holy City to such a degree that they may never recover from it. Not long ago, the plague had decimated a significant portion of the population. We cannot let our brethren down nor can we lose our hold on our Holy City which is the hope and aspiration of Israel. It seems to me the future of Israel, as prophesied in our books, now depends on you, and you alone. I don't need to remind you that as the Scriptures say, the dead, including your dear father and mother are waiting to be resurrected and march triumphantly to the land of our ancestors. Without the Holy Land we are nothing, just wandering people without a destination. I would not want to be the one responsible for undoing the promise of our Torah. I would certainly prefer death than betray this holy covenant. Come, we have much to do to secure the flow of life blood to our ancestral city."

This plea seemed to touch Sabetay's heart. He raised his eyes to look at his host. To cheer him up Raphaël reached into his pocket and pulled out a letter addressed to him from a Moroccan Sephardi friend named Yacob Saportas now living in Amsterdam. He said before handing him the letter: "I have a letter I want you to read. It is from a fine rabbi I have known since the time he and his family lived in Tlemcen, Morocco. He is one of the finest Talmudists I have ever met. He ran into an ideological conflict with the local chieftain in Morocco and he was forced to flee to Amsterdam. The letter has nothing to do with religion or his exile. It deals with an amazing account of a young woman who had raised incredible controversies in Europe by her actions and by her insistence that she will marry no one except the messiah when he finally declares himself. Her stories have been in the press of many nations with a variety of different characterizations. So far, the attitude of most people towards her has been one of ridicule. I am not sure this is a fair impression of her. Here, take the letter and read it for yourself. It may amuse you or you may feel compassionate and sorry for this woman as I do."

He placed the letter in Sabetay's hand, without telling him that Saportas was not an admirer of Sabetay. It was not clear to Raphaël if Saportas' letter had a sinister motive behind it: hoping perhaps that he would eventually pass the letter to Sabetay. Raphaël said before leaving: "Don't forget! Israel waits for you!"

When Raphaël left the room Isaac entered to see if Sabetay wanted to talk. Lifted by his host's words of comfort, Sabetay stood up from the floor, walked to the chair by the window, and sat in it. It felt very good to his body after so many days on the floor. He looked at the letter clinched between his fingers and opened it. He had no desire to read someone else's concerns. He stared at it for a while and then decided to have a look at it. It began with complaints by Saportas that he hadn't been able to find a rabbinic appointment in Amsterdam; there were too many rabbis in that small country and Ashkenazi congregations wouldn't hire a Sephardi rabbi if he was the last rabbi in the world.

He glanced quickly to see if Isaac was still there. Satisfied, he continued reading the part about a young woman called Sarah. The rest of the letter seemed to be about her. "You will never believe the incredible story circulating in this city about a young woman named Sarah who pretends to be of the Jewish faith and swears that she has constant dreams telling her that she is destined to marry the messiah, whoever he will turn out to be." That first sentence drew a resonant chord and his interest sharpened. "This of course implies, as many people here seem to believe, that the messiah is about to announce himself. Personally, I'll believe it when I see it! It appears that her dreams have convinced her she is destined to be crowned Queen of Israel. Mind you, I am not in the habit of writing gossip or trivial events, but I find it interesting because she has been able to raise considerable attention and excitement in Holland, in Germany and in Poland. At this very moment when I write this letter, there are dozens of versions of her testimonies circulating in the press from people who claim to have close relationship, and even sexual intercourse, with her. In the minds of most men, excluding myself, the latter relationship seems to have sparked that extra measure of attention."

Sabetay would have dropped the letter at this point knowing the rest of it was about a promiscuous woman he didn't know. However, his eyes remained fixed at the introductory phrase "She has constant dreams telling her she is destined to marry the messiah." Dreams and messiah had been an integral part of his life. He was pleased someone besides him shared that experience. He read on: "Sarah is said to be a native of Poland. Nobody has come out yet claiming to know her parents. From her personal accounts, her parents died when she was six years of age. As an orphan the State put her in a convent. She says her early childhood memories were stormy and frantic but she remembers being a Jewess. If she is telling the truth, the trauma this must have caused her living in a convent as a Jewess is understandable. For ten years, she lived among images of saints, church candles, burning incense, hymns and prayers either in the seclusion of her cell or among nuns praying for a Christian God.

"One day when the Jews in town were burying one of their own, they discovered behind a grave a beautiful blonde girl in a thin white nightgown. Astounded by the site, they asked her who she was and were she came from. Sarah told them her life story as she knew it. She said to the surprised Polish Jews that two nights ago her father's ghost appeared to her and complained that he could find no peace in his grave knowing that she was in a convent and raised a Catholic. She asked her father's ghost what she should do. The ghost told her to go to the Jewish cemetery, for Jews would be burying a dead man and they would help her. She agreed and the ghost helped her float down from the top floor of the convent. He held her up so tightly that the marks of the ghost's nails were still on her delicate white skin which she showed the men in the cemetery. When they saw the marks, they became convinced of her incredible story and they hid her in one of their homes.

"A few days later she was found missing in the convent. The authorities searched from house to house and found her. She was brought to the commissioner of police who was a Polish nobleman of the Catholic faith. When Sarah complained that she didn't want to be in a convent, he adopted her. A few months later, her stepbrother fell in love with Sarah and wanted to marry her with the delight of her step-father. The night before the wedding her father's ghost appeared to her again and told her she could not marry a Christian. He ordered her to return to the faith of her ancestors. When she complained that there was little time to change her mind, the ghost offered to take her to Persia where the father was buried, having fled from Poland during the Chmielnicki massacres of 1648. Sarah agreed and the spirit transported her through the air to Persia with nothing on but a thin nightgown. If you think this story sounds like a fairy tale," wrote Saportas, "wait until you read the rest of it. Once in Persia she was taken to her father's grave where an angel clothed her in a coat of skin inscribed with divine names. She was told the coat belonged to Adam the progenitor of the human race. Before leaving, the angel revealed to Sarah that, having obeyed her father's spirit she was destined to become a queen by marrying the messiah who was due to be born during her youth."

Sabetay, reading Saportas' letter, decided he didn't like his style of constantly ridiculing her. He, on the other hand, was drawn by Sarah's fascinating life story. Before reading the remainder of the letter, he went to reread, carefully this time, from the beginning. All the accounts appeared explainable in mystical terms. He raised his eyes and looked at Isaac still in the room and managed to smile faintly at him. Isaac had no idea what was in the letter drawing his companion's interest. Sabetay returned to read where he had stopped.

"There are many skeptics here who don't believe her story. But a reporter in Amsterdam swears Sarah invited him to sleep with her in order to prove that she carried on her body the permanent marks of fingernails from her father's ghost. The reporter swears he saw the marks with his own eyes, and he was shown the skin coat with many names of saints Eve had embroidered for Adam.

"Now I leave it up to you to believe what you want. In Amsterdam she lives with her older brother who remembers fleeing with his father to Persia. He also swears his sister was taken away by soldiers during the Polish wars and she appeared one day in Persia exactly as she had sworn in her testimony. Apparently the two found their way to Amsterdam, having been told of the boundless tolerance of the Dutch people towards Jews. It became her desire to live among Jews if she was to find her prophesied groom, the messiah. Her brother is now a tobacco sorter in Amsterdam, a low-paying job, and Sarah supplements their income by fortune telling. I say, if the other accusations about her of being solicitous are correct, she does more than fortune telling with her clients."

Saportas' letter ended with a suggestion that someday he would like to write a book about her for there was much to write, especially her rumored harlotries and adulteries which he chose not to include in the letter.

This seemingly strange story fired Sabetay's interest. Was she the one in his dreams destined to be his wife? Contrary to what Saportas and others thought of her, he liked Sarah's spirit, imagination, and daring personality. She wasn't afraid of saying or doing what wasn't exactly traditional. Sabetay looked out the window, dreaming and searching for his true feelings. He looked at the sandy desert outside seeking inspiration. Then he turned to Isaac and handed him the letter. Sabetay tried to imagine what Sarah looked like. How interesting it was that a moment ago he was preoccupied with thoughts about the loss of his parents; now, unexpectedly he found himself drawn by Sarah's story. He wished he could have a glance at this spiritually attractive woman. He had never felt this way before about any woman, much less a woman he had never seen or known. "Was it strange to feel that way?" he asked himself. "Why not?" he decided. Didn't the prophet Hosea say: *"take onto thee a wife of whoredoms?"* Maybe that saying meant to be a clue for him. Strange that Sarah had meaningful dreams like his, and interestingly enough dreams telling her to marry the messiah. The mysticism surrounding the life of this woman interested him intensely. He regretted there was no time to establish contact with this enchantress. He had a commitment to raise money and leave for the Holy Land soon.

ᘺ

In the spring of 1665, as Sabetay was preparing to return to Jerusalem with the new funds he raised, Isaac rushed to speak to him completely out of breath. He held in his hand a Hebrew newspaper published in the city of Cairo. He found Sabetay deeply engrossed reading a book by Samuel Gandoor he had picked from Raphaël's extensive library of cabalistic books. Isaac knew not to interrupt him unless it was urgent or important. In this case it was very important. Terribly excited he said: "Sorry AMIRAH, you must take a moment to read this. The news is all over the country and I wouldn't be surprised if it hasn't reached all corners of the world."

Sabetay ignored him. To draw his attention Isaac threw the newspaper on the table and slammed the door behind him in a dramatic move. Sabetay realized Isaac must have brought news of great importance. He put his book away and walked to the table

where the newspaper waited. He didn't have to search for the news
Isaac mentioned. In large Hebrew letters the headlines read:
"NATHAN OF GAZA DECLARES HIMSELF PROPHET."
Caught by intense curiosity he began to read the details.

"A man of God named Abraham Nathan ben Elisha Hayyim
Esquenazi, popularly known as Nathan of Gaza, or Gazati, at
twenty years of age revealed himself publicly as a visionary prophet
in the town of Gaza. He is the son of Rabbi Elisha Hayyim ben
Jacob, born in northern Europe. He came to live in Jerusalem
among the large Sephardi community. The father is an emissary
of the Jerusalem community raising funds in Poland, Germany,
Italy and Morocco. Nathan was born in Jerusalem in 1644 and
while his father traveled all over Europe he attended the yeshiva
directed by the noted Rabbi Moses Hagiz . . ."

Sabetay stopped reading to reflect on the name of the rabbi
who headed the yeshiva in Jerusalem. This was the same person
who had committed himself to his cause and had charged him
with the obligation of collecting the emergency funds. What a
mysterious coincidence he thought, and continued reading.

"Nathan showed to be an extremely gifted student and a brilliant intellect capable of profound thinking and writing ability.
Until a few months ago, he had been an accomplished student,
and recently he was ordained at the early age of nineteen. What
is most interesting is that at his early age, he became fascinated
with the mystic writings of the cabalists and in particular and most
importantly the writings of the great Isaac Luria." Another mysterious coincidence, Sabetay thought. "He accomplished most of
his learning of the *Cabala* by studying alone and from time to time
he says with angels who taught him the most difficult parts. Most
of the time, he was able to form his very own understanding of
these most difficult concepts. As a consequence, he developed
his own personal key to unlock the mysteries of that intricate
subject few people can understand. What is even more unusual
is that he submitted himself to an ascetic life of the cabalists at
that early age. When he was eighteen, a wealthy Sephardi Jew
originally from Damascus, and now in Gaza, asked Rabbi Hagiz

to propose a groom for his daughter who was said to be perfect in beauty except for a defect in one eye. Hagiz picked his best student Nathan for the groom. At the wedding Nathan agreed to adopt the Sephardi customs, dropping the biblical appellation of 'ben Elisha Hayyim'; he was given the family name of Esquenazi."

Fascinated by the newspaper account of this young prophet, the article ended promising more news about him in the days to come. A feeling of envy enveloped Sabetay. Unlike Nathan he had never had the courage to reveal himself. Barely twenty years of age and having nearly the same kind of formative training, this young man from Gaza came out claiming to be a prophet without hesitation. A sad feeling of uncertainty about himself came over him. Yet, he rationalized, there was a great risk and responsibility in that kind of boldness. Declaring one's self was easy. Delivering the task expected was something else. That agonizing question had always been with him. What he feared most was deceiving his Maker and his people, not the ridicule he might suffer, the ruination of his public image, excommunication, flogging, or even a death sentence for heresy. Nevertheless this didn't stop this young man, nearly half his age, to demonstrate a courageous conviction. One thing was certain. Declaring to be a prophet was less risky. A prophet is still a mortal who is especially gifted with visionary powers and wisdom. A messiah is a being in human form but belonging to God's realm.

The news he held in his hand demanded serious investigation. Sabetay rushed to see his host Raphaël and convinced him the newspaper announcement needed to be substantiated. The news was much too important for world Jewry and certainly paramount for the future of his movement. Raphaël agreed and dispatched the revered Rabbi Samuel Gandoor, a member of the rabbinic school in Cairo, to head a mission to Gaza to investigate the case.

When the team returned three weeks later, Rabbi Gandoor, many years Nathan's senior, could not find sufficient epithets and praises to describe the eminence of this young man of God. He emphasized that he and his commission had examined him thoroughly and for many days about Talmudic concepts, his life history, and the basis for his claim calling himself a prophet. According to Gandoor, all of the answers he gave were found perfect and illuminating. He read to Raphaël and Sabetay a particularly impressive comment Nathan had made to him:

> "Those who know me can truthfully testify that from my childhood until this day the slightest fault or sin could not be found with me. I observe the Law in poverty and meditate on it day and night. I never pursued the lusts of the flesh, instead I have always sought new forms of mortifications and penance with all my strength. I never derived worldly benefits from my message."[3]

This report, including the thought of Sarah, tormented Sabetay each in a different way. Gandoor's praises of Nathan left him unconvinced that Nathan deserved the saintly title. He pressed Gandoor: "How did Nathan come to believe he is a prophet?" he asked.

"I asked him that same question," he replied. "Nathan claims he was visited by blessed souls from Heaven who initiated him into the secrets of the *Cabala*. He said he studied the difficult writings with angelic tutelage and without the help of a mortal master. He described these visitations as a sight like onto a pillar of fire that spoke to him. At times the sight looked like a human face. He said he identified the spirits that spoke to him, but he would not reveal their names under any circumstances. I observed him practice the art of practical mysticism very carefully. Witnesses I interviewed told me he was able to read from a patient's eyes the nature of sins he had committed. He is very successful in prescribing effective penance to a sinner in order to cleanse his soul."

These last words appeared to convince Sabetay, and moreover he felt a sudden attraction to meet Nathan. If Nathan was as successful with exorcism as Gandoor said, this prophet might cure his affliction. Sabetay was both impressed and covetous although

---

3. Amarillo A., Sabatian Documents (from the collection of Saul Amarillo, quoted by Scholem p. 204).

he wouldn't admit to the latter for it was a sin. He resolved that he and Nathan were very much alike, yet Nathan's forthright determination appealed most to him.

The money raising campaign was more successful than the first. What made it so was the use of the argument Raphaël gave to Sabetay when he convinced him to come out of mourning. The sum of two thousand gold ducats[4] was raised, and would assure the Talmudic school in Jerusalem, and many of the poor in the Holy City another year of sustenance. Now anxious to meet Nathan, Sabetay readied himself to leave for the Holy Land. The anxiety over what to do with Sarah remained churning inside him, but the prospect of meeting Nathan had first priority. He traveled on horseback. During the long and boring hours in the desert, accompanied by Isaac and two armed guards, he tried to imagine what Nathan was like. Had he been endowed with more elevated spiritual and mystical presence than he? If it was true, perhaps Nathan was God's choice for the divine mission. In that case he would abandon his efforts and kneel to him. All through the journey he tried to imagine the outcome of this great encounter.

---

4. One hundred thousand dollars in western currency. When distributed equally among the 250 families living in the Holy Land at that time, it amounted to four hundred dollars per household, a comfortable purse for a year.

12

Nathan had been thoroughly advised of Sabetay's past: the banishment from Smyrna, the orders to leave Salonica and Constantinople, and the floggings in Constantinople and Jerusalem a few months earlier. In his assessment of him, he sympathized with the courage he showed fighting alone the arrogant and despotic authority of the ruling rabbis in the Ottoman Empire, while the European rabbis, though much interested in the advent of the messiah, only watched and listened from a distance. Learning from Sabetay's lessons, if he was to be universally accepted as a prophet, he, too, had to convince that bastion of opposition and indifference that the words he spoke were the words of God. As Sabetay did, he, too, harbored a deep-rooted conviction that God had entered his soul and that He spoke to Israel through his lips. They were willing agents of God. The man they called messiah had already a sizable following and a mature organization. But any movement, past or present, directed at marshaling the will of hundreds of thousands of people, wouldn't succeed without the skills of politics. Any leader, whose ideals and mission are being promulgated, cannot personally and by himself harvest so many souls. It takes an efficient organization of convinced and dedicated followers to spread the word and be willing to die for the cause, if necessary. Christianity took a couple of centuries to mature from a cult to a well-organized religion, when it decided to distance itself from Judaism. Sabetay and Nathan had no desire of becoming martyrs as in the case of Jesus, letting the course of centuries to solidify their ideals and create a new form of Judaism. They both thought that perhaps working together they could accomplish their goals during their lifetime.

As soon as Sabetay was ushered into Nathan's living room, in a surprising move and before taking a good look at Nathan, Sabetay kneeled to him and begged for forgiveness for not having paid homage to him during his previous visit to the Holy Land. Embarrassed that a wise man, nearly twice his age and of considerable reputation for his holiness, would kneel to him, Nathan kneeled too, only to help Sabetay get up on his feet. The two embraced and Nathan led him by the hand to sit on chairs arranged to face each other. Nathan asked the retinues on both sides to leave the room. They had many personal feelings and views to share and discuss. Once alone, they were hesitant on where to begin their much anticipated exchange of ideals. Before they spoke, they smiled and they simply looked at each other with curiosity, pleasure, and reverence, all mixed into one feeling.

In physical appearance Nathan was much different than Sabetay. He was constitutionally thinner and taller. His skin was darker and bonier, not like Sabetay's baby-like complexion. His massive nose and cheek bones protruded noticeably forward under a special cowl he wore most of the time in lieu of a prayer shawl. This loose hood made of the same material as his rabbinical robe reached down to his shoulders. His robe extended down to his black polished shoes and appeared to be tailor fitted tightly on his slim body. A long line of closely spaced buttons secured his robe from his neck down to his feet. If the robe differed from the oriental design and looked like the garment of a western bishop, it was because of the influence of his father, born in Europe and still traveling in those countries, who exerted a western influence on his son. His personality was much like Sabetay's but he was considerably more outspoken and cunning. Like Sabetay he had no formal schooling in the field of *Cabala*. He had to search and find for himself answers to complex concepts. He, like Sabetay, learned to trust his judgment, convinced that the source of his comprehension descended from the wisdom of the Lord.

The meeting was long, spiritual, and sentient. It was as if two brothers, separated at birth, met for the first time. There were many questions to ask and many emotions to pass on. Sabetay felt a very strong kinship towards Nathan, one that permitted him to trust and respect him, a sentiment he had not experienced since Moses Pinheiro faded away from his life.

As soon as Sabetay felt at ease, he told Nathan he desired one favor of him: his treatment of cabalistic exorcism to pardon his sins and cure his chronic affliction. Totally surprised by such a request coming from a man of God, Nathan agreed and asked what troubled his soul. Sabetay opened his heart to all aspects of his illness and the circumstances associated with his demonic dreams. He began with the dreams of the dancing damsels, the flame threatening his indulgence in sex, the many visions of the past with biblical prophets, the saintly voices assuring him he was the messiah, his anointment, his encounter with the spirit of Solomon Molho, the miracle of the sea, Yachini's discovery of the parchment prophesying him as the messiah, his prophecy of the fire of Constantinople, and so on.

Nathan did not look surprised or alarmed by this confession. His primary interest in Sabetay ran in a different direction. He wanted to know more about his path to holiness, the outer and unexplored realm of understanding of God and his universe, the phases of creation, God, and man, His ultimate achievement. He wanted to know how much further Sabetay had gone in the science of the Deity and the human soul. He questioned him intensively on these matters. Distracted by Nathan's questions, Sabetay returned to his plea for a cure of his affliction. He hadn't realized that all the while he was being analyzed and examined. Finally Nathan gave his surprising diagnosis:

"I assure you Your Eminency that I find your soul pure, sin-free, and totally impeccable the like of which I have never seen. You need no prescription for penance and you should stop blaming your affliction as a sign of lack of grace in the eyes of our Lord.

Just the contrary, as it is said in the good books, the affliction is an integral part of your messianic character." Then, Nathan impressed Sabetay using the following cabalistic passage:

> "When the Holy Ancient One, Blessed Be He wishes the health of the world, He afflicts a just man with pain and sickness and heals the rest of the world through him. When such a man is strong like Jacob; it is said: This righteous man, chosen by the Holy One, bears the most cruel afflictions willingly for the redemption of his generation; as a result he is held as their savior, and the Holy Blessed One appoints him shepherd over all the flock, to feed them in this world and to rule over them in the world to come."[1]

Sabetay recognized the quotation was from the *Zohar*. Nathan concluded by saying: "I have no doubt you possess the undisputable attributes of the *Mashiah*."

Unquestionably delighted while listening to Nathan's praises, Sabetay answered:

"Besides my Creator you are the first holy man who has been able to recognize everything which is written in my heart and soul. You are a true prophet of the Lord. I came to Gaza to be saved by the prophet and instead I find myself affirmed to the sublime role of the messiah, a role I knew since my childhood that the Creator had saved for me. I have never revealed myself as you have because I wasn't totally convinced that my Creator wanted me to do it just yet. I had sought His approval for so long and so profoundly. Now you, a wise man of the All Merciful, a declared prophet, have read my soul and recognized me. This gives me the assurance I have been waiting for. From now on, I will find the proper moment to reveal myself loudly and clearly for all the world to know."

They arranged to spend a few weeks together in total solitude and intimacy, sharing their inspirations, knowledge, and future of what appeared to be a shared objective and a joint mission. On

---

1. A shorter version of this homily appeared in Chapter 7. It was a quote from Luria's cabalistic interpretation of the messiah's suffering.

Sabetay's urging Nathan went with him to Jerusalem to submit the alms he brought from Egypt. There was an important purpose in Sabetay's request for the joint appearance. Nathan was highly respected among rabbis in the Holy City, even after he revealed himself prophet. When they met the city fathers they were shown gratefulness for the alms, but no reaction whatsoever about their association. It wasn't what Sabetay expected. Annoyed, he had not forgotten that Rabbi Moses Hagiz, present at the meeting, had made a commitment to him during his last visit. In an angry and unexpected move, he approached the old rabbi and extended his hand to him. Unafraid and resolute, Hagiz stood up and in the presence of his associates and Nathan kissed Sabetay's gold ring Habillo had given him. Openly in front of his conservative colleagues he pledged his support for Sabetay's cause now blessed by Nathan. Angry yet reserved, the Jerusalem rabbis didn't say a word.

~⟲~

It was the day before the Jewish Pentecost, the fiftieth day after Passover, 1665. Sabeaty and Nathan returned from Jerusalem to Gaza. Nathan decided to give a banquet at his home in honor of Sabetay, with a very special yet secret goal in mind. He invited scholars from Jerusalem and Safed including his former teacher Rabbi Moses Hagiz. Sabetay had already Nathan's support but to convince the world's Jewry, he needed the unequivocal support of the arch-conservative Jerusalem rabbis. Once that was accomplished, the rest of the world would follow, and most importantly the Sultan will have to react kindly given the magnitude of the expected religious re-affirmations and the upheavals prophesied in the bible. Nathan's banquet was expected to be the crucial turning point for the movement. He had much to gain from the success of the banquet. He was due to become the prophet to a universal movement. If the attempt failed, he would be implicated only indirectly. But Sabetay could be risking his life.

At one end of the long banquet table Nathan's servants installed a raised decorative chair resembling a royal throne. Its imposing

structure didn't escape the attention of the guests. When everyone was seated, no one occupied the throne. The food and the
wine generated high and happy spirits. When the feast ended and
the atmosphere in the dining hall became very friendly, Nathan
stood up at the end of the table opposite the throne, raised his
silver goblet and waited to be noticed. Slowly the boisterous voices
calmly abated, and putting on a solemn look he lowered his eyes
and recited loudly:

> "Blessed is he who cometh in the name of the Lord. May the mer-
> ciful God bless our King, Sabetay Sevi!"

While the suspecting guests tried to figure out what the eu-
logy for Sabetay meant, the old and half bent body of Rabbi Hagiz
struggling to stand up, caused further consternation. His colleagues on either side of him helped him stand up. He raised his
silver goblet above his head loudly said: "Amen."

It was obvious that Nathan had arranged with Hagiz for this
approbation. Because of the respect he and Hagiz commanded
he expected the enthusiasm to carry over to the others. Knowing
Sabetay's persistent reluctance to declare himself, he had not
discussed any of this plan with him. Nathan expected everyone
to raise their goblet, and then he would ask Sabetay to occupy
the vacant throne at the head of the table. It was a clever move
but Sabetay, caught forcefully into that most important decisive
moment, wished Nathan had informed him about it. All faces
turned to Sabetay waiting for his reaction. Nathan and Hagiz
smiled, convinced they had finally sealed the ultimate approval
locked all these years in Sabetay's lips. In this critical moment of
decision, a moment familiar to Sabetay from two earlier attempts
to be recognized in the same setting, he sprung to his feet and
shouted angrily in *espagnol*:

> "*Callasen*! (Be quiet!)"

Sabetay didn't care to explain his rebuff. He left the dining room
in a hurry. Nathan lowered his goblet and stood as confused as
the guests. He declared the end of the banquet, and the dumbfounded colleagues dispersed silently in an atmosphere completely

opposite to the fanfarish mood in which it began. When they were alone, Nathan demanded an explanation from Sabetay. Tormented by the ineptness of his ungratefulness he explained awkwardly:

"I cannot make myself shake the uncertainty of my worthiness, even though you told me differently." He paused, placed his hands on his face moving them up and down as if he tried to soothe the pain of an invading headache. Knowing he had not satisfied Nathan by his weak excuse, precipitously he added: "It is not I who desires it; you yourselves call me and force upon me this awesome office. The responsibility lies with you, not with me." He turned around and walked away. Nathan attributed this seemingly ungrateful behavior to his affliction.

It was the eve of the Pentecost holiday. Sabetay was unable to attend services on account of a severe headache, vision impairment, and hallucinations. He remained in his room. Nathan,deeply concerned about Sabetay, surrounded by a crowd of faithful at the synagogue, he went into a trance. With his eyes closed and his body shaking he was driven to repeat loudly the words spoken to him by the spirit in his vision: *"Hear Nathan my beloved and do according to his word. Rabbi Hamnuna the Ancient said that Sabetay like Moses was very meek."*

The first time he said those words went nearly unnoticed. He repeated it three times. Finally they understood he was pronouncing a prophecy. Many congregants did not fully understand the meaning of the reference to himself and to Sabetay. What exactly was the holy man's message? What was the meaning of interrupting the service and making reference to Sabetay as Moses? They stopped praying and when Nathan recovered from his spell they asked him: "What was the true meaning of what you said?" Perspired, pale, trembling, and with an emaciated look on his face he said the prophecy was from the angel[2] Haniel that spoke

---

2. Angels in the *Cabala* are spiritual beings outside humanity having different classifications according to their designated roles in their divine hierarchy. There are many such classifications expressed by various cabalists. Haniel is the angel delivering the Grace of God.

through him: "The angel wanted me to announce publicly that Sabetay, like Moses, is meek and humble. Moses, too, resisted intensely being called *Mashiah*. Consequently, he never revealed himself. I am telling all of you that in body and soul Sabetay is worthy of being King of Israel. Then Haniel concluded: *Thus saith the Lord, behold your savior cometh, Sabetay Sevi is his name.*" As soon as he finished explaining, two congregants fell in a trance to the ground, speaking unconsciously, and announcing the arrival of the messiah. It became obvious to the congregation that they had been visited by a divine spirit for the purpose of convincing them that Sabetay was indeed the messiah.

The news spread like fire. It didn't take long for the Holy City and the world to learn about the visionary event in Gaza. Sabetay recovered from his illness. When Nathan saw him feeling better he told him what had happened at the night vigil of Pentecost.

> "In the middle of the service a vision appeared to me. It seemed to have lasted twenty-four hours. The vision was in the form of a supernal light the like of which I had not seen. It had to be that during the primordial light of the seven days of Creation. The light displayed an engraving of your image just as that of Jacob was said to be engraved according to legend. Your image announced: 'Thus said the Lord, behold your savior Sabetay Sevi cometh.' These words were repeated loudly through my mouth a number of times until the faithful understood their meaning. They too went into a trance and said they saw the same light as I have . . . . What more proof do you require that you and only you can be the messenger of God we await so anxiously?"

Nathan hoped that with these words Sabetay would be convinced of his worthiness and reveal himself once and for all. He was right. It so happened that after this convincing story Sabetay felt it was time he heeded Nathan's advice. Thus, on May 28, 1665, finally, he went to the synagogue in Gaza and announced himself to be "*the anointed of the God of Jacob.*" Everyone understood that in biblical terms Sabetay declared himself the messiah. He proclaimed the date to be remembered as "*the day on which the AMIRAH's kingdom began to grow.*" Europe waited for this glorious moment. News releases covered every newspaper in the Ottoman Empire and in Christian Europe. No one however, expected Sabetay to move fast and in a derelict fashion. Drunk with enthusiasm, he requested twelve men, symbolically representing the twelve tribes of Israel, to accompany him to Jerusalem to sacrifice a lamb on the site of the destroyed Temple. This had been a tradition in biblical days for celebrating an event of divine significance. Isaac and Nathan were horrified by his plan. They advised him against it, explaining that the Temple grounds were also Islamic holy grounds. The idea of him conducting such a sacrifice on the grounds of the holy mosque would most certainly precipitate severe retributions from the Turkish authorities. Sabetay agreed to put his plan temporarily in a list of future endeavors. His notebook was full of such projects inspired by ancient biblical traditions. If he, the designated *Mashiah* and the future King of Israel couldn't push for reforms, abrogate laws and demand new ones, who else would?

As a revolutionary he wanted to be remembered by the reforms he initiated. He said to Nathan: "You are a wise man and from this day on I decided to call you The Holy Light and I will insist that everyone address you by this holy name. The honorific title belonged to one of our wisest ancestors, Shimon ben Yohay, in whose cave I spent many weeks and I came out inspired by his spirit. In all your wisdom, can you tell me where in our holy literature the right to change and abrogate Judaic laws is discussed?"

Without hesitating a single moment Nathan answered his question: "You will find the reference in Jeremiah." Assuming he had convinced Sabetay to be more cautious and forget the idea about the sacrifice, he turned to a different subject: "I am burning with excitement. I want to tell you about a dream I had last night. Listen to this! Last night the prophet Elijah appeared in my dream and commanded me to go to the cave of the prophet Samuel in the hills surrounding Jerusalem and search for a spot in that cave containing the remains of an old pious rabbi who desired to be buried there four centuries ago. I was instructed in the dream that near that rabbi's casket I will find an earthen vessel containing proof of your messiahship. I want you to come with me. This is considerably more important than the sacrificial ceremony you had in mind."

Bubbling with new excitement Sabetay forgot about the matter of abrogating Judaic laws. They went to town looking for a group of religious men to accompany them as witnesses. They rode to the entrance of the cave, entered it, and identified Samuel's sepulcher. They began to search for the site of another grave, the one Elijah mentioned in Nathan's dream. They were exhausted digging in so many places to find the earthen vessel. Just when they were ready to abandon the effort, they heard a voice commanding them to dig ten feet away from where they stood. They resumed digging and found the urn. Now not one of the accompanying rabbis dared to doubt the authenticity of Nathan's dream. They removed the vessel gently. They carried it to the entrance of the cave, and opened it. It contained a document, stained by water which had seeped into the cave. They unfolded the parchment and saw a short note pinned to it. The note read:

> "The messiah of Israel.
> The author of this prophecy is a pious rabbi who had been a total recluse for forty years, eating and drinking in total purity. On every new moon he came to town blindfolded to attend services at the synagogue with a curtain drawn between him and the other members of the congregation. This way he saw no one and no one saw him."

When they finished reading the note, everyone except Sabetay, looked puzzled and surprised. The note was written on a different quality parchment than the document to which it was pinned. It wasn't signed so they didn't know who wrote it. Whoever he was had to find the casket before them. They quickly removed the note and began to read the first lines in the document:

> "He will subdue the dragon and take away the strength of the crooked serpent, and he will be the true messiah."

The reader stopped. Surprised, they looked at each other in consternation. This sentence, which appeared to be a prophecy, didn't make sense by itself. There had to be at least one other page which must have been removed. Without that page, it was impossible to know whose prophecy it was and who was the messiah referred to? Only Sabetay knew the answer to their puzzlement. He was standing away from the group, and now after the sentence they had read, he connected this document to the partial document Rabbi Abraham Yachini in Constantinople had given to him. He always carried that incomplete document inside of his habit and near his heart. He reached over his garment and pulled the folded parchment page. He walked to where the others stood and placed his page on top of the newly discovered document. They asked to know if it was the missing page. How was it he had it in his possession? He explained. The reader began to read aloud the page Sabetay provided:

> "I, Abraham Asher, shut cloistered in a cave for forty years, in distress because the mighty monster that dwelled in Egypt still sat upon his throne. I tried to solve the mystery why the Age of miracles would not come. But then I heard the voice of God saying: 'In the year 5385 [1626] shall be born a son to Mordehay Sevi by the name of Sabetay. He shall overthrow the mighty dragon and kill the serpent. He shall be My Anointed and shall sit upon My Throne. His kingdom shall last forever and no other but he shall be the savior of My People Israel . . . .'"

They turned to look at Sabetay, partly bewildered and partly in awe. How could a man who lived four centuries before have known about Sabetay? But then, one never questions the mysterious ways of the Lord. Quickly the reader turned to the unearthed page and read and continued reading:

> ". . . . He will subdue the dragon, and take away the strength of the crooked serpent, and he will be the true messiah. He will fight in wars without weapons. He will establish a kingdom that will last forever and there will be no redeemer besides him . . . . Do not

grieve over the fall of the messiah for thou shall wait and see the power of this man . . . He will perform wondrous, awesome, and strange things, and he will submit himself to martyrdom to abide by the will of his Creator . . . ."[3]

Now, the unearthed pages made sense. Nathan's vision and Sabetay's miracle page had a divinely inspired continuity. The impact the complete document had on the religious men who had come to witness a miracle was indescribable. In fear they fell to the ground and kissed the messiah's shoes. Sabetay was totally exalted. It was the first time he heard the entire account of the prophecy. Nathan took the parchment and instructed the witnesses to spread the truth as they saw it. The news of the discovery moved quickly from ear to ear. The resolute Jerusalem rabbis, accustomed to hear news of fraudulent evidences, still remained unimpressed. The public reaction was just the opposite. High levels of exaltation rose in the Holy Land and abroad. Public demands were heard everywhere for the people of Israel to submit to the messiah and his prophet. Worried conservative rabbis warned abomination from the Lord if the faithful allowed himself to be duped and blinded by such stories. Counter pressures mounted on the Hebrew clergy, thus creating rebellious groups against the establishment. A commission of five rabbis was called in to investigate the authenticity of the messianic claim. As a result, many severe doctrinal and theological tests were designed to unravel the truth about the messiah and his prophet once and for all.

During all of these tribulations Nathan volunteered to subject himself to the inquests. Sabetay developed another long and painful seizure of his illness and did not take part at the inquest. To test Nathan's supernal powers, one of the tests consisted of the following: Two names were written in total secrecy on a piece of paper, one of a new born child and the other of a recently deceased person. Nathan's assignment was to divine the names and the personal characters of the two individuals listed in the folded

---

3. Original text in A. Saportas, a variant form translated in G. Scholem.

paper. He was not given any hint whatsoever. Nathan closed his eyes and went into deep concentration. When he opened them, without hesitation he reached for a pen and paper and wrote two names down. Along side their names he wrote the status of each individual. For the dead man he wrote: "*death had redeemed him.*" and after the baby's name he wrote: "*He is free from sin.*"[4]

What an incredible feat this was! One would think that this performance would have sufficed to prove Nathan's exceptional powers. It was not so. They subjected him to a second and more rigorous test. The following day another rabbi was sent from Jerusalem to Gaza to experience a fresh prophetic feat. He demanded to observe and evaluate a newer prophecy by the prophet Nathan. Nathan told the rabbi to go to the town cemetery and look for an old man with just an animal skin around his loins carrying a vessel in his hand. "When you find him," he said, "take the vessel and pour the water in it on his hands while you say: 'Forgive the children of Israel!'"

The examiner did as he was asked. He went to the cemetery but found no one. He returned to Nathan ridiculing him that his prophecy had failed and so had the test. Angry Nathan accused him of being blind and failing to look diligently. He ordered him to return with wide open eyes. Sure of having proved Nathan a fraud, the examiner went back expecting to come back with the same story. This time, when he arrived at the gate of the cemetery he saw the man answering to the description he was given. He took the vessel from his hand, poured the water on the hands of the strange man and said as he was instructed by Nathan: "*Forgive the children of Israel!*"

The old man replied: "*Let my blood forgive thee!*"

Running and trembling, and not having understood the meaning of what the old man said, the examiner returned to Nathan asking first who that strange man was. Nathan said it was the prophet Zechariah whom the Jews had killed and his blood washed

---

4. See J. Kastein p. 103. In Judaism a new born is free of sin.

away. Fearing Nathan's wrath the examiner ran out of the house and returned to the Holy City. He reported to the city fathers exactly what had happened, swearing to the truth over a bible, concluding that Sabetay's prophet had the power to perform not only a new prophecy but an astounding miracle.

৵

This remarkable incident spread as fast as the others since Sabetay met Nathan. The hearts and souls of most Jews in the Ottoman Empire were inflamed with awe and hopes. Taking advantage of this enormous success, and now that the messiah and his prophet had declared themselves, Nathan suggested to Sabetay that it was time to win all the hearts of the Jewries in the Diasporas of Asia and Europe, and carry their glorious victory to all corners of the world. Sabetay agreed, but he had one important item in his agenda to fulfill. He had not forgotten the young lady named Sarah. While in Gaza he wrote to his friend and mentor, Tchelebi Raphaël, saying that the thought of Sarah wouldn't leave his mind and that he was sure she had to be the woman predestined to marry him. He was coming back to Cairo soon, and would he contact Sarah and ask her to be there to meet her future husband.

Raphaël sent a messenger to Rabbi Yacob Saportas in Holland asking him to find Sarah and submit Sabetay's proposition. The messenger searched every town and district where Jews lived in Holland. Disappointingly the messenger discovered that she no longer lived there. From people who knew her, Saportas found that she had moved to Livorno, Italy, a town known for its renown cabalistic scholars, assuming that either the messiah would emerge from that cluster of divinity scholars, or that they would be the first to know when he appeared. A messenger was sent to Livorno to find Sarah and ask her to come to Cairo to meet the messiah. The richest man in Egypt, Tchelebi Raphaël Joseph, was providing her travel and living expenses.

Sarah agreed to come to Cairo but warned that she needed concrete assurances of Sabetay's worthiness before accepting to marry him. Accompanied by the messenger, she boarded a ship and arrived in Alexandria. By carriage she was taken to Cairo where Sabetay expected to arrive any day. She was given separate quarters with a maid and a fine wardrobe. When Raphaël met Sarah he assured her that Sabetay was indeed the future King of Israel and would be coming soon from the Holy Land where he had gone to meet his prophet.

"Not so!" said Sarah taking Raphaël by surprise.

"What do you mean?" he asked somewhat annoyed by the daring reply.

Sarah looked tired from the sea voyage. In a troubled voice she said: "I have reasons to believe what I just said. You see, I didn't sleep well last night. Just as I had dozed, a vision appeared to me. I saw the man you want me to marry to be in great peril of his life on the high seas. Then my father's spirit appeared again telling me that he was pleased with my choice of husband and that he would try to help overcome that danger. At that point I woke up and couldn't sleep the rest of the night. I didn't find out if he was saved or not."

Raphaël laughed and responded: "Pardon me, but I couldn't accept what your vision told you as the truth. It is my sincere opinion that you have been misinformed. You see, Sabetay Sevi, Our Lord, left on horseback from Egypt and is coming back on horseback. His plans did not include travel on the high sea. I suggest you put yourself at ease and rest the remainder of the day. Good day." Raphaël left her quarters concerned if the man in Sarah's vision was really Sabetay or one of the many admirers she was gossiped to have had in her life.

Two days later Sabetay arrived. After tersely greeting Raphaël he said he had an eventful, rewarding, and revealing trip. He asked anxiously: "Is Sarah here?"

"Yes, she is here awaiting to meet you."

"Thank The Lord! I changed travel plans in order to speed up my return. I decided to board a ship destined for Alexandria and come from there to Cairo on horseback. As it was, I didn't gain any time at all. We were delayed by pirates pursuing our ship and the captain had to veer many times in the dark to elude the pursuers. In answer to my prayers the Creator confused the pirates and made them get lost in the sea. Would you believe that?"

"Now I would," replied Raphaël, without mentioning a word about Sarah's vision.

Sabetay went to his room bathed, shaved, and put on fresh clothes before he came down and entered the drawing room where Sarah waited to meet him. She exclaimed:

"This wise man is my husband!"

Sabetay replied: "This maiden is my bride!"

Two weeks later wealthy Raphaël prepared the most opulent Sephardi wedding ever given in Cairo. At the reception, feeling like the father of the bride he kept repeating: "After all, it is a royal wedding. When was the last time Cairo had seen a royal wedding such as this? It has to go back a few centuries before Alexander the Great conquered the last dynasty of the Pharoahs."

The wedding in Cairo was far from being a union between two people in love. It was more like a royal spectacle performed by the King of Israel and his Queen. Under those circumstances a honeymoon, a period of solitude for the two lovers had no significance. Two days after the wedding Sabetay, Sarah, and Isaac returned to Gaza where Nathan waited for the inauguration of a pilgrimage to other cities in the Ottoman Empire and Europe, where thousands of Jews and many Christians awaited to see them in person, touch them, and follow them into a destiny which had been prophesied so many times by so many sages, Christians and Jews.

The trip was also to take them to Smyrna, symbolizing a grandiose pilgrimage to the city of birth of the messiah. To Sabetay it meant more. It was to be the realization of a prophecy he had made fourteen years ago. He never forgot for a moment the words he had uttered angrily before embarking for Patras: *The city which has driven me out would one day welcome me as the King of Israel!*" Nathan's father, who traveled extensively in Europe, was designated as the agent to spread the word and foment surges of support in Smyrna, Constantinople, Salonica, the island of Rhodes, Venice, Livorno, Amsterdam, Hamburg, Frankfort, Paris, London, Posen, Lemberg, and many other cities of Europe. If younger and less experienced, Nathan saw in this wave of euphoria the spark of victory, Sabetay remained cautious and concerned for he knew well the harsh and cruel power of the opposition. This power was partly in the hands of the orthodox ruling rabbis, and mostly in the hands of the imperial monarchs who occupied Israel and many of the lands of the Diasporas.

Isaac and Sarah became close friends making the arrangements for the long journey north. In the beginning, the euphoria of a royal pilgrimage was so intoxicating that Nathan hardly had time to think of the political implications of the drive that was about to begin. He spent many hours privately weighing the benefits of accompanying Sabetay. Unlike Sabetay, he was a pragmatic man. He couldn't see how he would be an asset to the movement, trailing behind Sabetay whose personality was complex, domineering, and certainly unpredictable. There was only room for one leader during this long journey. He had not forgotten Sabetay's rebuke when he tried to help him at the banquet. To the surprise of everyone he announced he was staying behind, and use his epistolary talents to send supportive letters and public announcements to chief rabbis in the cities Sabetay was to visit. His written word was well known to be effective and was appreciated by many.

A few days before the departure Nathan wrote to religious leaders asking them to prepare their communities for a spiritual climax for when the messiah entered their city:

> "Hear my words, Brethren of Israel: the messiah has come to life in the city of Smyrna and his name is Sabetay Sevi. Before long he will establish his kingdom and will take the royal crown from the head of the Sultan and place it on his own head. The King of the Turks, like a Canaan slave, shall walk behind him[5]. . . . The messiah shall not conquer his enemies with ordinary weapons made

---

5. Turks were traditionally very bellicose and protective about insults leveled at their leaders and more so at their religion. A statement such as this would have cost Nathan and Sabetay their life if it ever reached the attention of the Sultan.

by men. No indeed, with the breadth of his nostril he shall rout them, and by his word alone he shall utterly destroy them. . . . On that day shall the dead rise from their graves. I hasten to tell you these tidings."[6]

Sarah began to feel the way of Sabetay's previous two wives. Her husband hadn't asked her into bed since they were married. Before becoming his wife, she was able to seek male companionship when and where she wanted. Now, a queen, she had to behave and learn the discipline of virtue. Still lustful and in her late thirties, what was she to do without the physical love in the arms of a man? She became despondent realizing that her marriage, though initially symbolic, would remain that way the rest of her life. She wasn't sure she could cope with it. Whatever her feelings were, she didn't intend to solve her problem by divorcing Sabetay. She had to find another way; a discreet one, close and within reach.

Isaac's relationship with Sabetay had also changed. Preparing for the long journey, Sabetay was less available to both Sarah and Isaac. Sabetay trustingly left them alone to discuss various aspects of the trip. As it turned out, the two discovered a personal attraction for each other and their companionship seemed to fill their individual loneliness. Ultimately this fondness led them secretly into bed in each other's arms. For Sarah this turned out to be not only accommodating but decidedly satisfying when she discovered that bachelor Isaac was capable of being the kind of lover suiting her intense sexual desires. Isaac enjoyed the pleasure Sarah gave him, but invariably became filled with remorse even as Sarah assured him that Sabetay never laid a hand on her. Therefore, she concluded that in the eyes of the Lord she wasn't his wife. Isaac failed to find solace in that assurance, and eventually became consumed with guilt.

The starting date for the trip north was set to July 20, 1665. Before leaving, Sarah insisted she and her husband needed to look

---

6. See J. Kastein p. 123.

as dignified as a royal couple. From the flow of donations of her brother-in-law Eliyah, the wealthy Egyptian friend Raphaël, and others who sought his blessings, she ordered new and expensive wardrobes sewn for her and Sabetay. Aroused by Sarah's urge to look apostolic, Sabetay ordered from the best jeweler in Gaza two special gold rings. He had already one symbolic ring given to him by David Habillo. In one of the rings he asked the inscription of one of God's names: *Shadday*. In addition to the cabalistic meaning of the divine name,[7] from *gematria* the numerical value of that name was 814, the same as Sabetay. The other ring was to be engraved with a crooked serpent. When the ring-maker looked horrified by the request, Sabetay explained: "The holy serpent and demons are part of Creation even if it has an unpopular role in the relationship between Adam and Eve. In fact demons existed prior to Creation. They were authorized by Our Maker to go about the world and ravage therein. But, I have my own personal reason for making that choice. You see, the numerical value of the *holy serpent* is the same as *Mashiah*. I intend to sign and seal all my official correspondence with that ring. Now that I have enlightened you, you can remove that disgusted expression from your face."

Unbeknownst to anyone else, Sabetay had one last act he had sworn to perform before starting his pilgrimage north. From biblical accounts he had drawn the conclusion that a sacrificial ceremony had to be performed on the site of the destroyed ancient Temple to commemorate the coming of the messiah. He ignored early warnings of Nathan and Isaac that such a move would violate Islamic laws and put him in confrontation with the Turkish authorities. An old Sephardi proverb gave him courage to pursue this ideal regardless of the consequences: *It is the traveler that makes the path he travels on; not the other way around.* The site of the old Temple in Jerusalem was also the holy Moslem sanctuary

---

7. According to the *Zohar* there are three Supernal Degrees of Divine Essence. In one of them God revealed himself by the name of *Shadday*.

Haram esh-Sharif, the so-called Mosque of Omar, captor of Jerusalem soon after Mohammed and his religion of Islam rose from the sands of Arabia. Sabetay appointed Rabbi Najara of Gaza as high priest and representative of the tribe of Reuben and ordered him to carry out the sacrificial ceremony.

It didn't take long for the intended plan to fall on the ears of the Jerusalem rabbis. The city fathers became terrified that Sabetay planned to enter the Moslem sanctuary. This act would most certainly insult the Turkish authorities, who would respond with savage measures against all Jewries in their empire. They sent the following message to Sabetay hoping he would change his mind: "*Why would you want the death of Israel, and why would you want to destroy the Lord's inheritance?*" A rabbi from Jerusalem named Samuel Primo, who had become a staunch supporter of Sabetay, sought him quickly in Gaza and managed to convince him finally to abandon his daring plan. Unhappy Sabetay answered him: "*Woe! I came so near, and now it has been postponed far off.*" Yet he refused to be entirely defeated by the opposition. In a substitute defiance he marched on the streets of the Holy City with an entourage of forty men. The group included three eminent rabbinic scholars from Jerusalem by the names of Samuel Primo, Moses Galanté and Daniel Pinto. All three had vowed to follow him to final victory.

The angry city fathers saw an eminent threat from a new order, and decided to get rid of Sabetay by **any means possible**. They circulated rumors that Sabetay had not been forthright with the monies he collected in Egypt. They charged him with embezzlement. They also denounced him as a rebel to the Turkish authorities, producing as evidence the letter Nathan wrote to the communities of the Empire in which he specifically admitted that Sabetay will force the Turkish Sultan to yield his royal crown and walk behind him as a slave. Sabetay was summoned to a Turkish court. While the city fathers rejoiced for having delivered him a mortal blow, to their great disappointment the Turkish *cadi* (magistrate) acquitted him of all charges. How was it possible? Rebellious treason had always been punishable by death. As true as this was, so was the importance of a fat bribe in the hands of the *cadi* by none other than the Master of the Mint Tchelebi Raphaël of Cairo. The bribe was so generous that the *cadi* not only acquitted Sabetay, he gave him permission to ride a horse around the city seven times wearing a green mantle. Preposterous! the rabbis exclaimed. Jews were not allowed, in the first place to ride a horse in the city, much less to wear a green mantle, the sign of high holiness for the Moslems. Just when the conservative rabbis thought they had damned Sabetay in the eyes of the authorities, he was given the right of religious sovereignty in Jerusalem.

Finding himself exonerated, he retaliated against the inveterate rabbis who had accused him. He shocked them vindictively by issuing an order to ten of his followers to eat the fat of the kidney which was forbidden by Hebrew dietary laws. As if this mockery wasn't enough, to add salt to injury he recited the following benediction as they ate the forbidden food: "*Blessed art Thou, O Lord, Who permittest that which is forbidden.*"

That was all the old rabbis could take. They wrote letters, ahead of Sabetay accusing him with the recent breach of the talmudic laws:

> "We, the rabbis of the holiest city, find this man who spreads these innovations to be a heretic. Whoever kills him will be considered to be as one who has saved many souls, and that blessed hand that strikes him down will be blessed in the eyes of God and man."[8]

The impact of this message had little effect on the euphoria that had already begun to boil in world Jewry. On the 20th of July 1665, the day before his birthday, Sabetay and his entourage consisting of the twelve apostles, his wife and Isaac, the three rabbis from Jerusalem Samuel Primo, Moses Galanaté and Daniel Pinto, and the ten slaves caring for the needs of the caravan were ready to leave for Aleppo, Syria. He had been awaited with great anticipation by their chief Rabbi Solomon Laniado. There was a slight change in the management team. Samuel Primo, one of the three

---

8. A slightly different version appears in G. Scholem p. 249.

rabbis from Jerusalem who had impressed Sabetay so much with his astute political flair, was appointed his personal secretary. Primo took over everything that had to do with the movement: travel arrangements, correspondence, personal consultations, and Sabetay's public appearances. He was more than a secretary, he became his trusted press agent. This assignment took away from Isaac and Sarah whatever small contact and responsibility they had with Sabetay. The appointment offended Isaac so much that he saw himself being pushed further into the arms of lustful Sarah.

13

᠊ᢌᢀ

The first stop in the ambitious pilgrimage was Damascus, then Aleppo in Syria, territories occupied by the Ottoman Turks. The reception in Damascus was friendly but the one in Aleppo was tumultuously ecstatic. The Jews of that city felt totally taken by Sabetay's holiness and unanimously submitted to him as a large congregation. The impression he made in Aleppo was so deeply emotional that the city produced twenty prophets and four prophetesses experiencing visions varying in details but always involving the personality of Sabetay who had harvested their souls. These agitations didn't sit well with the Turkish authorities. After what happened in Jerusalem they issued orders to watch the movement carefully for excesses in rights resembling anarchy. But as long as the euphoria remained confined to benign spiritualism, the authorities were instructed to do nothing to stop any of these outburst of public elation.

Relying on the formidable success in Aleppo, Sabetay and his group hastened to reach Smyrna. He became driven by a desire to make that city, which had witnessed his first admonishment, the scene of his great success. In the fifteen years since leaving Smyrna, the emotional and political views of the Jewry towards him had improved considerably. His older brother and his disciples had cultivated and harvested the spiritual field to the fullest by keeping supporters, as well as the opposition, abreast of

Sabetay's victories abroad. Sabetay was enjoying one of the most successful periods of his mission. It was his sense that God had finally approved of him, and nothing could stop further conquests until the day of Jubilee. If Sabetay appeared in a hurry to leave Aleppo it was because he wanted to spend the Day of Atonement in Smyrna. His surreptitious reason was to attend services at the main synagogue of Neveh Shalom where he had once shocked the conservative clergy banishing him for pronouncing an Ineffable Name of God. He intended to arouse stronger feelings of consciousness now that he had power behind him.

Six weeks before the Day of Atonement, on August 12, 1665, Sabetay and his pilgrims left Aleppo for his native city of Smyrna. An Italian correspondent wrote on the occasion of Sabetay's departure:

> ". . . . The messiah lived among them, and they depended no longer on Nathan's supportive letters, for they saw with their own eyes and heard with their own ears. . . . They begged him at Aleppo to stay with them for at least two months, but he refused. He was in a hurry to reach Smyrna before a time he had scheduled for his return. . . . The city of Aleppo felt the abundance of his grace. On the [Yom Kippur] holiday, at the sound of the shofar, the congregation fell to the ground and remained lying there, cold and motionless. A heavenly message in Hebrew was articulated through their mouths they did not understand. In the end they understood the message to mean: 'Sabetay Sevi our redeemer and holy one.'"[1]

Two of the apostles, Moses Galanté and Daniel Primo, stayed behind to nourish the fervent spirit the Jews of Aleppo developed during Sabetay's stay. The Jews of Smyrna, in a euphoria similar to that in Aleppo, were reported to have observed, night after night, unusual displays of comets in the skies. They flocked to the streets to observe the rejoicing of the heavens in anticipation of the arrival of the messiah. Vesper services normally conducted Satur-

---

1. From C. De la Croix, Memoire, Vol II, 1684, quoted and translated in G. Scholem p. 258.

day evenings were performed every evening outdoors in the streets while the faithful watched in the darkening skies the propitious celestial displays that seemed to accompany their prayers.

As the time of Sabetay's arrival drew closer, they waited at the eastern gate of the city for his triumphal entry on horseback. For weeks they had prepared and rehearsed songs, dances, and many other forms of jubilation. Portrait artists visited Sabetay's brother to get a physical description of the saintly man. Many renditions of these drawings and large engravings were made especially for this occasion. Some of these artistic conceptions were very elaborate. One depicted Sabetay wearing a royal crown and surrounded by his royal court. Another showed him sitting at the head of a long table instructing his twelve apostles. One in particular, which seemed to catch most of the attention, showed Sabetay on a magnificent Arabian horse, dressed royally, leading an army of believers against the sinners of the world. It appeared that the artist of this militaristic scene was inspired by a similar painting of the Holy Roman Emperor Charles V leading his army in the conquest of Europe. The Turkish authorities did not allow the display of any flags known to be the national symbol of another nation. Jubilant Jews paraded the streets with the biblical King David's flag bearing the emblem of the six-pointed star. They were quickly confiscated. Multicolor banners without a symbolic significance were allowed and to no one's surprised they turned out to be in white and blue the colors of the Kingdoms of Israel. Of special importance during these preparations was the expectation of seeing the beautiful Queen of Israel, dressed royally and waiving at her Smyrna subjects for the first time.

One morning in early September, 1665, a man ran breathlessly through the city gate heralding the sighting of the messiah's party. He yelled in a frenzy: "The *Mashiah* is coming! The *Mashiah* is coming!" People flocked to the eastern city gate to meet their king and queen. As they ran they shouted: *"Mashiah!, Mashiah!"* The narrow gate was soon blocked by the joyful demonstrators. The traveling party was forced to come to a halt at the gate. Sabetay drove his horse on top of an embankment and raised his arms triumphantly. People in the crowd demanded silence for their messiah was about to speak. Smiles and tears in their faces they waited to hear his first words of approval of their tumultuous welcome. Instead, angry Sabetay shouted:

"You must stop calling me *Mashiah*. Instead, you should pray and repent your sins. You must prepare yourselves for the day of salvation. That day is not far, I assure you. Through prayers of repentance and forgiveness Israel must become pure before the Lord will give me the order to redeem the Holy Land. The sooner this happens the sooner you will be saved. I am touched by your reception but now you must clear the way for my party to proceed. We are very tired. God Bless you all."

They obeyed and fell to the ground in total devotion. Pleased with the magnificent ovation Sabetay put on a gleaming face and requested: "Children of Israel! Lead me to my brother's house."

Eliyah welcomed Sabetay with open arms. For the first time he wasn't just welcoming his beloved brother but a holy man who belonged to the people. Sabetay's first request was to ask his brother to call in eight[2] demonstrators from outside to say the words of the *Quadish*, the prayer for the dead, in memory of his father and mother who had died in his absence.

Benefiting from the few days of calm and rest, Isaac Silveira came to see Sabetay in his private quarters guarded and managed by the new rabbis of Jerusalem. He asked to speak to him in private. He was allowed to see his childhood friend, who was now a man of the people and a man of God.

"Isaac, I don't get to see you anymore. What have you been doing with yourself?" he asked, busy placing his seal on a pile of letters his secretary Samuel Primo handed him.

"AMIRAH, I want to speak to you alone."

Isaac looked at Samuel with a feeling of embarrassment for having suggested that he leave the room. Samuel remained stand-

---

2. The tenets of Judaism required a minimum of ten Jewish men over the age of thirteen to form a *minyan* (quorum) in order to recite those prayers.

ing defiantly. Without lifting his head away from his task, Sabetay said softly: "Samuel, leave us alone."

A pack of papers still in his hand, and covering any expression of resentment on his face, Samuel left the room and shut the door behind him. Isaac found himself facing the man who used to be his closest and only friend. Now it was different. Powerful and officious advisors had taken over what used to be his responsibility.

"AMIRAH, can you stop for a minute? I have a confession to make."

Sabetay put aside his work and looked coolly at Isaac.

"What kind of confession?"

With that terse question Isaac felt pressed to come to the point. "I am very happy to be back in my home town. You must feel the same, I am sure," he said awkwardly. "What I came to talk to you about is me." He paused to gain courage: "I want to remain in Smyrna. I don't feel I am needed any longer. You have all the competent help you need without me. I came to ask your permission to stay."

Sabetay waited as if he knew Isaac had more to say. That silence bothered Isaac. He didn't know how to open his heart. "Is that all you want to tell me, Isaac?" he asked mockingly.

Isaac had a lot more to say but lacked the courage to initiate the painful subject which filled him with remorse. From the way Sabetay asked the question he sensed he knew why he came to see him. He blushed and choked. Suddenly feeling emotionally disrobed, he fell to his knees.

"Forgive me, AMIRAH, I will die if I am not forgiven. I feel that the Lord will strike me down if I am not atoned of my awful sin . . . ." The tall man's eyes filled with tears and his lips quivered, but Sabetay waited. "Up until . . . a few months ago, . . . I felt strong and proud because of my . . . purity and . . . devotion to you. I remember our early days at the yeshiva . . . when I wouldn't let you frighten me because you were always right. I stood my ground in dignity and I learned to love you. I never thought my soul . . . would succumb to the . . . temptations of the devil. I feel sick all over, . . . and shameful. I pray to God each day to forgive me or take my soul. But I know what the Scriptures say. God atones the sins perpetrated to another person only after that person pardons that sin. What is worse . . . I have sinned by deceiving you. . . . I have not been worthy of your greatness." He paused to see if Sabetay would spare him the trouble of going into details. Sabetay remained motionless looking Isaac in the eyes. "If you know what I am talking about, . . . please don't force me to tell you. Forgive me AMIRAH, forgive me . . . ," he repeated the last words and then began to sob like a child.

Sabetay stood up from behind the desk and came to lift him up. Isaac kissed the rings on his hand repeatedly. Cool and unemotional Sabetay answered him: "I forgive your sin. I can't do the same for the Creator. He would have to do it Himself. I know how you feel. Be assured that demonic temptations are also divine instruments sent upon us to make us stronger provided we repent and pray. I will miss you and so will my queen. Go and repent until you feel forgiven inside. That is when The All Merciful has forgiven you."

Sabetay went back to his desk without feeling anger towards poor Isaac who was torn with guilt for allowing himself to have an affair with Sarah. But as far as Sabetay was concerned, he had discharged another spiritual responsibility. He rang the bell on his desk. Samuel entered and saw Isaac in a sunken mood, wiping his eyes with his handkerchief. Isaac walked away. It was the last time he was to see his childhood friend. A week later he was found dead in his room with an oriental dagger on his chest. The police investigation showed that he had been murdered by two teenage Turkish hooligans who were seen leaving the building where Isaac rented a room. At the inquest the teenagers told the judge they were paid a large sum in gold by Rabbi Isaac Silveira himself to take his life. After showing the reward money still inside Isaac's ornate prayer shawl case, the *cadi* dismissed the youth putting the blame on the rabbi who must have gone mad. Sabetay knew the reason behind Isaac's plan. Talmudic laws consider suicide a dreadful sin. Isaac, who obviously could not find peace with himself, chose death by hired hands knowing the judge would dismiss the case when he saw his initials on the *taleth* pouch.

On December 12, 1665, two months after his arrival in Smyrna, four men resembling Moors entered the city on horseback inquiring the whereabouts of the Sevi residence. They had come from Aleppo with great news. The two men identified themselves as two of the messiah's twelve apostles: Moses Galanté and Daniel Pinto. They said they carried a letter from the prophet Nathan of Gaza. They could say no more for they didn't know the contents in the sealed envelope. The messengers were taken to Sabetay's home. The news of the messengers spread so quickly that the Jews of Smyrna wanted to know what sort of message was Nathan sending. Upon the urging of Primo, Sabetay appeared on the elevated threshold in front of the door of his house and assured the crowd that one of the two letters was from the Jewish community of Aleppo affirming their love and devotion to him. The other was from Nathan.[3] He asked Primo to read that letter aloud while the people on the street listened: The letter was a long one. Only a small part was read to the crowd.

> "I, Nathan submit to the King, Lord of our Lords, who will gather the dispersed of Israel, who will redeem our captivity, a man of sublime heights, the Messiah of the God of Jacob, the true Messiah, the Celestial Lion, Sabetay Sevi, whose honor be exalted, and his dominion raised promptly, and for ever, Amen. . . . These are the words of the servant of his servants, who prostrates himself by the soles of his feet."
>
> The Holy Light

Nathan, a distinguished rabbi, a prophet from the Holy Land was openly affirming that their own son Sabetay was unquestionably the messiah. One person in the crowd, who was later identified as a Sephardi poet, shouted: "Why are we being intimidated to call him by what he really is?" The crowd roared before the poet

---

3. See J. Kastein p. 143.

finished his statement. Loud "Shushhhh, be quiet!" followed. The poet resumed: "I have written a hymn foretelling this glorious moment. I will sing it and I am urging all of you to sing with me the second time around:"

> Upon thy suffering people let
> Thy kingdom's glory shine.
> For long before kings ruled on earth
> The kingdom ever was thine.
> Now that we stand on the steps of the Son of God,
> Let us exalt his name together: Mashiah, Mashiah.[4]

They chanted the hymn a number of times. In the end, four people forced themselves to the threshold where Sabetay stood, picked him up over their shoulders and carried him into the streets shouting *"Mashiah!, Mashiah!"* He was so overwhelmed, he told the enthralled and captivated loyalists he was breaking fast that day and abandoning it altogether. He issued a mandate that from that moment on to the end of 1665, a nineteen day period, was to be a joyous Hebrew festival he will institute in his new calendar. The crowd became ecstatic. The loud sounds of the cheers drew more followers in his neighborhood. A loud thundering shout: *"The right hand of the Lord is exalted!"* came from one corner of the street. All heads turned in that direction and saw a huge banner bearing the inscription of that sentence. More people flocked out of their homes spreading rugs in the path of the men carrying Sabetay on their shoulders. They took him all over the city and the procession lasted until late that night. Eventually, the euphoric parade got out of hand. An order for Sabetay's arrest had been issued by the Turkish authorities for demonstrating without a permit. Samuel Primo became worried, and dispatched aids to find Sabetay in the streets and rescue him.

Paul Rycaut had become famous in England for his frequent reporting about the messiah he claimed to know personally. During this new outpouring of devotion, he went to the streets re-

---

4. A poem by Israël Najara.

cording the incredible reverence the Jews of Smyrna were showing for Sabetay. Time was at an essence in spreading this special
news. By carrier pigeon he sent a short account to every part of
Europe with the following headlines: "THIS WAS THE DAY
EVERYONE WAITED FOR. THIS WAS THE DAY THE MES-
SIAH BEGAN HIS REIGN." Protestant leaders convened and
considered every aspect of this princely event including previous
reports about Sabetay's life. The staunch chiliasts, those who
believed in the millennium called on the public to go into immediate repentance. There were only a few more days left in 1665.
Sabetay had to be the one ordered by God to save Jews and Christians alike. Articles appeared in European newspapers arguing the
biblical validity of an ecumenical march to the Holy Land.

The Dutch scholar Peter Serrarius (Pierre Serrurier) and the
English theologian Duraeus took an active interest in these events
and urged other scholars to do likewise. They had received a report from Jerusalem that the Ten Tribes of Israel were already in
Arabia and had conquered Mecca by putting to death all the inhabitants in that city except Jews. Caravans ready to take Moslems to the Holy City of Mecca for their annual pilgrimage had
been canceled for fear that the city had been besieged by the lost
children of Israel. Serrarius published an urgent appeal which
appeared in many languages around the capitals of Europe[5] :

> The news about the march of our brethren, the Ten Tribes of Is-
> rael, is now confirmed to us from several places . . . . These events
> are so full of wonder, that we could scarcely believe, or give credit
> to them . . . . Now we have information that they are on the edge
> of the desert, and are moving from several places to the desert Goth
> of Morocco . . . and consisting of about eight thousand companies
> or troops, each of which made up of one hundred to a thousand
> men . . . . They have for their leader . . . a Holy Man who under-
> stands all languages and marches before them performing miracles

---

5. There are different versions of this letter and other foreign reactions in Chap. 9 of J. Kastein book and in more details in G. Scholem
pp. 341–342.

. . . . The people are of middle stature, their bodies healthy, their complexions fair: they saw no women amongst them . . . their horses are many . . . and their tents black . . . . They seem to dig in the sand where they expect to find a brass trumpet with which they will sound three times, alerting all nations to gather into one Universal Church . . . . I believe this to be true, although the matter seems strange and requires caution.

In the same long and detailed appeal Serrarius wrote that as a consequence of these reports a holy man in Holland had a vision in which God revealed himself to him and instructed him that all public worship must cease until the year 1672, after which a universal worship will be handed to the peoples of the world. The consciousness of European believers, Jews and Christians, was finally awakened and sealed. The turn of events did not escape the attention of the conservative rabbis in Jerusalem who by now worried that Sabetay and Nathan were going to destroy the old faith. The Sephardi congregation of Amsterdam sent a group of their scholars to the Holy Land to interview Nathan personally and test the validity of his prophecy that Sabetay was indeed God's messiah. They asked him for a sign of a miracle in their presence, however small, to convince them that he possessed divine powers. He refused explaining that he was not permitted to perform any more miracles without divine authority. He recommended that they should wait until they saw with their own eyes the fulfillment of his prophecy, only days away. He gave them a letter asking them to make it public in their own land.[6]

Behold we have learned that your hearts were awakened to return unto the Lord your God and bring forth heavenly fruit. May it be God's will that the work of your hands is guided by repentance. Strengthen the weak hands and give assurance to your feeble knees for thus saith the Lord, thy savior cometh, his name is Sabetay Sevi. He shall go forth as a mighty man, . . . and he shall prevail against his enemies. I pray that your eyes may behold the king in his beauty.

The Holy Light

---

6. A. Saportas, quoted by G. Scholem p. 363.

All the Jews of Smyrna had not yet surrendered to Sabetay as had been the case in Aleppo. Only a small but authoritative opposition persisted. It drew strength from the imperious encouragements of the conservative rabbis who had studied the Scriptures concerning the messiah,[7] and had concluded Sabetay didn't fit the talmudic requirements. The first coming of the messiah was said to be by a descendant of biblical Joseph. He was doomed to fail in his final mission to redeem Israel. He would suffer a violent death.[8] For one, Sabetay did not claim that lineage; he insisted he was a descendant of King David. Furthermore, the Talmud claimed that prior to his coming the Temple in Jerusalem had to be restored, a feat not yet fulfilled. According to the prophet Micah and later confirmed by two illustrious rabbis of the Middle Ages, Rashi and Kimchi, this Second Redeemer was to be born in Bethlehem, not in Smyrna. Most importantly, the prophet Isaiah had said he was to be wiser than King Solomon and greater in accomplishments than Moses. In the opinion of the talmudic rabbis Sabetay failed in both of these deeds. Also, the remains of the Sacred Temple became a Moslem mosque and what was left of it amounted to a heap of rubble. Moreover, Sabetay's wisdom was no match to that of Solomon, he did nothing but foolish things, and had not written or published anything significant. The arguments against Sabetay might have impressed a biblical scholar, but the public had already fallen mesmerized by what they had heard and read about him. It was too late for apologies. The world was expecting a messiah and Sabetay was that man.

---

7. In the *Zohar* there are different messiahs expected: the Son of Ischaï who is said to live upon the Earth but is not to be found, the Son of Ephraïm, the Son of Joseph, and the Son of David. The last two are the only mentioned in the Talmud. The Son of Joseph will suffer a violent death and the Son of David is viewed as the last hope.

8. Though the coincidence of Jesus, son of a Joseph, who died a violent death was overwhelmingly prophetic, this didn't stop Jews from rejecting him as the first messiah.

A few conservative rabbis and theologians, urged by Jerusalem, declared that Nathan's messages were in conflict with the precepts and ordinances of the Holy Writ. Among them Rabbi Benveniste and Rabbi Haim Peña of Smyrna, staunch adversaries of Sabetay, proclaimed publicly that Sabetay was a curse to Judaism and asked for his death sentence. Upon hearing this malediction Sabetay's supporters stormed their houses and forced them to rescind their charges or leave Smyrna. Sabetay wasn't finished eradicating the few remnants of the opposition. On the first day of the Hanukah festival, in December 1665, a few days before the onset of the messianic year, Sabetay went on the offensive and marched to his synagogue Neveh Shalom. He put on the royal gown he had tailored in Gaza, and went to the street throwing generous alms at the poor who ran behind him as Sabetay exclaimed: "I am the Lord your God, Sabetay Sevi." The crowd followed him all the way to the synagogue.

He entered the house of worship of his youth with the greatest of pomp sparked by an impressive entourage consisting of his apostles and distinguished benefactors. Many of the worshipers attending services had been there in his youth. Those who escorted him carried large silver bowls filled with candy and preserves. Behind him walked two men carrying vases of flowers and a third held in his hand a comb in its own sheath raised high for everyone to see. Rabbis Galanté and Pinto walked with the messiah holding the trailing hem of his white satin robe. In one hand Sabetay carried a silver staff similar to the one the high priest of the Hebrews carried in biblical days. In the other hand he held a silver folding fan with which he touched people's heads in a sign of blessing. All of these details had their equivalent symbolism in religious mysticism. Not everyone, however, understood their significance. Carrying a comb in his sheath was a symbol of faith residing in the soul, touching the head of the audience with the staff or the fan was reminiscent of a passage in the book of Esther describing her husband King Ahasuerus touching selectively the people he liked and admired.

When the procession ended, the congregation waited for him to sit at the alter with the officiating rabbis. A moment of confusion arose when the two chief rabbis couldn't decide how and when to begin the service. Sabetay didn't wait. He began the service singing in his melodious voice the prayers, psalms, and hymns of the joyful holiday. The delegation that followed him from Aleppo had been trained to respond with harmonious refrains. The congregants marveled at the creativity of this service. Sabetay had secured complete control. When it was time to read the Torah, the officiating rabbis invited him to carry the sacred scroll to the pulpit. They all stood before the tabernacle and before they opened its doors, unexpectedly Sabetay raised his staff and knocked at the doors of the tabernacle seven times, as if he was signaling the angels guarding the gates of heaven to stand ready for him. That unusual act was also symbolically interpreted in a number of different ways. One congregant saw it as an analogy to Moses striking the rock in the desert to give water to the Israelites, which in a broader sense conceived the tabernacle as the rock housing the Torah, the life sustaining water for the soul. The pair of astonished and powerless chief rabbis opened the doors to the ark and removed the ornately decorated Holy Scroll. They handed it to Sabetay. Once again, as he had done before his expulsion from Smyrna, he stunned the crowd by pronouncing the same Ineffable Name of God he had pronounced before. This time he insisted the congregants to do likewise. They followed his order. To justify his breach of talmudic law he gave the same controversial blessing he had given before: *"Blessed art Thou, O Lord, Who permittest that which is forbidden."* One by one they came to the alter, kneeled to their messiah. Sabetay blessed them as they murmured prayers and offered alms to his cause.

By talmudic ordinance the Torah is read three times a week: Mondays, Thursdays, and Saturdays. On this Thursday, however, after reading the Torah portion, Samuel Primo came forward and announced that the anointed King of Israel had an important message to deliver. Sabetay walked to the pulpit to give the sermon he had prepared for days. He began by admonishing the few local rabbis who had not come forward to acknowledge the new faith ordered by the Creator. He compared them to unclean animals. In a high level of ecstasy and illumination he preached that the Scriptures were full of prophecies warning the faithful to be ready for the call of the messiah. Why, then, did these despicable rabbis show total disobedience to these warnings and the deliberate desire to sin by inflicting injury to a wise man like him sent by the Lord to save them? He used an analogy that shocked them even more. He asked them bluntly: *"What has Jesus done that you ill treated him thusly?"*

He saw the revulsion on the faces of the followers and enemies alike for having mentioned the name of Jesus in their sanctuary. Deliberately, but also to please undecided Christians, he repeated his name again: "Yeshu (Jesus' name in Hebrew) has three of the consonants of Yehovah and the sacred letter 'shin' in the middle." To shock them further he added defiantly: "I shall see to it that He will be counted among our prophets."

Expecting criticism for his defiance, and before anyone mustered the courage to do so, he raised his hands and said he would curse anyone who dared criticize him. No one dared to speak. He ended his sermon with a warning:

"You have been blind all these years waiting for the messiah and rejecting him each time he came to save you! Sacrilegiously you have charged that the Creator had slumbered for not sending you a true messiah! That is a blasphemy! The Creator never sleeps! He simply lost confidence in your ability to accept His judgment! It is time you heed His messenger this time around!"

Since the days of the Diasporas, Jews had modified The Peace Prayer (Sim Shalom) in the middle of their morning service by adding a short blessing for the host country's ruler. In the Ottoman Empire they blessed the great Sultan. When the time came for that prayer, Sabetay stopped the service and ordered that it be modified. Jews of the world were to replace their ruler's name by his name: the messiah. He justified his order saying:

"Now that Diasporas are to be abolished and reunited in Israel in the new Kingdom of God, there is no need to bless a non-Jewish monarch."

Sabetay had made plans at that moment for ushers to rush to the aisles carrying hand-scribed copies of a substitute prayer[9]:

> ". . . . You who giveth salvation to kings, potentates and princes, whose kingdom is the kingdom of the world, . . . may God bless, protect, strengthen, uphold and exalt our Lord and King, the wise, holy, pious, and supreme Sultan Sabetay Sevi, the divine messiah, the messiah of the God of Jacob, the Heavenly Lion, the King of Justice, the King of kings, Sabetay Sevi. . . . Amen!"

After the *Quadish* congregants went home fully encouraged by the magnificent sermon lifting their spirits and alerting them to the approaching day of salvation. However, some didn't think it was wise for Sabetay to remove their Sultan's name from the prayer and place his instead. If it became known to the Turkish authorities, severe punishments could follow.

Next on Sabetay's agenda was to win Constantinople the way he had won Gaza, Aleppo, and now Smyrna. This most populous city had banned him in the past, but now, with an immense following counting approximating fifty thousand Jews, and an unknown number of Europeans Christians, his authority and power was deemed invincible. After Constantinople, establishing his kingdom in Israel by taking the land away from the hands of the mighty Sultan had to be in his view a foregone conclusion. This was a matter he refused to discuss, for he placed it in the hands of the Lord. Before leaving for Constantinople he called for a public gathering one evening at the Velvet Fortress, the top of the mountain where he had performed in his younger days the miracle of arresting the sun in its heavenly path. This time he was to perform another miracle. For Jews, Moslems and Christians the announcement was as important as a circus coming to town. People flocked to the top of the mountain. A huge bonfire had been lit and they all gathered around it. He had not yet announced

---

9. This prayer is cited by T. Coenen later translated into Hebrew by S. Rosanes, *History of the Jews of Turkey and the Levant*, Sofia, 1933. Also translation into English by G. Scholem p. 425.

the nature of the miracle. Suspense, apprehension and anxiety crested to supreme levels. Trumpets and shofars (instrument made with the ram's horn) sounded to announce the arrival of the messiah with his large entourage of followers. The sound of drums silenced the crowd waiting to catch every detail of the expected performance. Faces betraying fright and trepidation, lit by the flickering light of the fire, moved constantly positioning themselves to favorable locations for a better look. When the sound of the drums stopped Sabetay appeared on a stand in front of the huge roaring fire. He wore a long black cape over a white gown and black headdress. He lifted his arms and blessed the silent crowd. He took off his cape and hat and handed them to an attendant. He stood in front of the fire in his thin white gown praying silently. The terrified audience didn't know what he intended to do so near to the blazing fire. As they pondered, Sabetay made a quick move and disappeared. The move was so quick people screamed with terror even if they didn't see how he entered the blaze and disappeared.

"What happened? What happened to him?" were questions asked by those who missed the event entirely.

"Oh God, he jumped in the fire. I saw him, I saw him!"

"Jumped in the fire? He will be burned to death! Impossible!" retorted someone.

"I saw him, I tell you! I saw him run into the fire," was the reply.

Moments lapsed when no one knew Sabetay's fate, in an incredible move, he came out from the back side of the fire smiling and appearing unharmed. His white gown didn't show any sign of burns or even a blemish. The public roared with excitement at this great miracle. The Jews screamed "*Mashiah, Mashiah!*" The Turks clapped and yelled: "*Allah! Allah! Allah Akhbar!*" and the Christian Greeks joined in the ovation yelling: "*Panayamou, Panayamou!*" Pleased with the response, while all eyes fixed on him, he plunged towards the fire a second time followed by a considerably louder public reaction. He repeated the same move a third time and the crowd went mad; this time they all screamed: *Mashiah!, Mashiah!* Not a hair in his head or body had been touched. Fearing a surge of public euphoria, his attendants whisked him away before the crowd swarmed towards him wanting to touch him. Most of all they feared the Turkish police would storm the grounds to arrest him for giving a public performance without a permit.

Many of his well-to-do supporters wanted to know if Sabetay was loosing sight of his mission. The messiah was to redeem the people of Israel dispersed around the world, not perform miracles in public to terrify them. He was beginning to show outbursts of anger, abolishing ancient and respected talmudic laws, instituting shocking customs, and eating fat among other things. There were also rumors he was ready to appoint his brother Eliyah high priest and King of Turkey. These actions seemed to go beyond the realm of salvation and even reason. That was not all. He was beginning to attract Moslems among his audiences. If he ever stepped outside a thin line drawn by the government and attempted to convert a single Moslem he would be hung in public square. If he ever announced it publicly that he was appointing his brother Eliyah Turkish King, he was doomed to run into serious trouble with the authorities who would see the move as a provocation of the Sultan.

As it was, unbeknownst to the Jews of Smyrna, the Turkish authorities had begun to take note of these defiances. They appointed a task force to focus on Sabetay's future moves. The *cadi* of Smyrna ordered Sabetay to his office to warn him about the seriousness of his recent activities. This encouraged a few of his enemies to demonstrate in the streets demanding Sabetay to produce an heir of the messiah. They ridiculed Sabetay as impotent and that Sarah remained a virgin since the wedding. Sabetay became outraged and had to think of a response. He couldn't very well tell the demonstrators that Sarah wasn't a virgin when he married her. That information would have given his enemies more ammunition to ridicule him. If he thought of leaving his native city with a perfect record, he had to put this matter at ease. To dispel the malicious rumor of his wife's virginity and his impotence, he appeared one day at the balcony window and threw down at the mob a blood-stained sheet. His followers rushed to where he threw the blood-stained sheet fell on the street and fought to tear a piece as a memento of the historic event. Then he announced that Sarah will soon carry a child. That bold gesture seemed to neutralize the small opposition. Pleased with the expected reaction Sabetay said a few words from the balcony window.

The jubilation didn't last long. A few days later it was announced that Sarah had a miscarriage.

CHAPTER

14

ॐ

Jews in the city of Smyrna had finally fallen under Sabetay's spell. Elder rabbis were summoned in his court to form a synod of priests to discuss the framing of new religious canons for the new faith. He was so confident about the future, he requested a study for the peaceful transfer of political power from existing governments to the messiah. As current kings and emperors yielded their thrones to him, a momentary void in political leadership was expected. To prevent this from happening, the synod approved a list of new royal appointees Sabetay had been considering through the years, adding new names and removing others as he judged the sincerity and importance of the candidates.

It would appear to a rational mind that such an exercise in global planning by a few powerless religious men inexperienced in government would be foolish, futile, strictly academic, and very dangerous to say the least. But Sabetay and his disciples never doubted for a moment the colossal powers the Creator would wield to them. The magnitude of that power was equal to none on earth. All these years Sabetay prayed and waited for the *Shehinah*, the halo of glory, was thought not to be in vain. Like Moses who waited on top of Mount Sinai for the Lord's instructions, so did he. As an arch-pious mystic, he developed the conviction that not only the Lord's redemption would happen, but also that he was the only one on earth singularly qualified to carry out His will. With that unfaltering faith he had a masterful way of infecting his disciples who, in turn, went out on the streets to preach.

The 29th of December 1665, the day before he left for Constantinople, he revealed publicly a preliminary list of twenty-three kings and princes he would appoint in due time and had it mailed to Diasporas around the world. Accompanying the list was a directive that there would be more appointments forthcoming and that these appointments were to be respected and would go into effect as soon as final victory was at hand. Jews in the Diasporas were not accustomed to the privilege of being ruled by one of their own. This announcement drove rich followers to seek and buy slots in the forthcoming list and even buy appointments from announced candidates in the royalty list which read as follows:

1. To Isaac Silveira, his devoted childhood friend and earliest disciple who did much to plan the messianic itinerary from the day I went into exile from Smyrna, I bestow posthumously the title of KING DAVID who reigned 1000–962 B.C.E. I never forgot that Isaac supported me courageously, from the very beginning when I had no other partisan.

2. Abraham Yachini was the preacher from Constantinople who produced the copy of the first page of a parchment, written centuries before, prophesying in advance that I had been designated the Hebrew messiah. Yachini remained a believer until death. To him I bestowed the title of KING SOLOMON, king of Israel in the tenth century B.C.E. and son of DAVID.

3. The rabbi of Aleppo, Solomon Laniado, did much to enhance my rise to holiness, especially at the launch of the movement after having met Nathan of Gaza, my prophet. He, too, maintained his faith in me until the end of his days. To him I bestowed the biblical royal title of KING ZOBA.

4. I bestow the royal name of KING UZZIAH, King of Judah 791–739 B.C.E. and son of AMAZIAH to my disciple named Joseph Cohen. (This person remains undocumented in the historical accounts.)

5. I am much indebted to Moses Galanté, one of the few rabbis from the Holy City who joined the movement in defiance of the fierce initial opposition from that city. To him I bestow the royal title of KING JEHOSHAPHAT, King of Judah 873–849 B.C.E. and son of KING ASA, king of Judah.

6. To another faithful disciple, Daniel Pinto, who was first to prophesy in Smyrna that he had been visited by the prophet Elijah telling him that I was the messiah, I bestow the royal title of KING HEZEKIAH, king of Judah 715–686 B.C.E.

7. To Abraham Handali, a distinguished rabbi, I bestow the royal title of KING JOTHAM, son of UZZIAH and king of Judah in the eighth century B.C.E. (There were many of his followers who worked diligently for the movement but had kept in the background and away from publicity. This rabbi was one of them.)

8. To the Polish preacher Rabbi Elijah, who came from abroad to be at my service and accompanied me to Constantinople, I bestow the title of KING ZEDEKIAH, King of Judah 597–587 B.C.E. and son of JOSIAH.

9. One of the wealthy Sephardi leaders in Smyrna who played a personal and active role in my movement was Abraham León. To him I bestow the title of the biblical KING AHAZ, King of Judah 735–720 B.C.E. and son of KING UZZIAH.

10. Ephraim Arditti was another wealthy leader from Smyrna who, with Abraham León, provided much of the finances of the movement. To him I bestow the title of KING JORAM, King of Israel 849–842 B.C.E. and son of AHAB and JEZEBEL.

11. Solomon Carmona was another wealthy leader from Smyrna who claimed to have seen the prophet Elijah, and had sponsored many banquets on behalf of the movement. To him I bestow the title of KING AHAB, King of Northern Israel 874–853 B.C.E. and son of OMRI.

12. Rabbi Mattathias Bloch Esquenazi, Rabbi of the city of Mosul, Iraq, met me in Jerusalem and became my personal messenger. I award to him the title of KING ASA, King of Judah 915–875 B.C.E. and son of REHOBOAM.

13. To the rabbi of the city of Constantinople, Meir Alcaire, brother-in-law of an important (wealthy) follower, I name KING REHOBOAM, son of SOLOMON and last king of the old kingdom of Israel.

14. To the pious (with less notoriety) rabbi named Jacob Loxas, I bestow the title of KING AMON, king of Judah in the seventh century B.C.E.

15. To another leading merchant of Smyrna by the name of Mordehay ben Isaac Yeshurun I bestow the title of KING JEHOIAKIM, King of Judah 609–598 B.C.E., second son of JOSIAH.

16. To one of my strongest supporters, Rabbi Hayim Peña, I bestow the title of KING JEROBOAM I, King of Northern Israel 922–901 B.C.E. (This controversial rabbi was at the onset a fierce opponent of Sabetay when he returned to Smyrna. He changed his mind and became a staunch supporter).

17. A rabbi from Andrinople, Joseph Carillo, joined my movement and came to Smyrna to help me. To him I bestow the title of KING ABIAH, King of Judah, and son of REHOBOAM.

18. To Nehemiah Conforte I award the title of KING ZERUBBABEL, governor of the Jewish exiles and rebuilder of the Temple, sixth century B.C.E. (Another lesser known supporter.)

19. My most devoted and supportive of followers and benefactor from Cairo, Tchelebi Raphaël Joseph is awarded the title of KING JOASH, King of Judah 837–800 B.C.E. and son of AHAZIAH.

20. Eliakim Haber, who joined my movement, is awarded the title of AMAZIAH, ninth century B.C.E. priest of the an-

cient shrine of Beth-El. (A lesser known supporter, possibly one of the Ashkenazi rabbis.)

21. A pious beggar, Abraham Rubio, will become KING JOSIAH, King of Judah 640–609 B.C.E. and son of AMON. (He, more than others, received cash offers to sell his title.)

22. To my elder brother, Eliyah, an ardent and devoted supporter until the end of his days, I give the title of KING of the KING of KINGS. (The title meant King of the Ottoman Empire because the Sultan ruled over the kings in the lands he conquered. The reason this was not spelled out in writing is obvious. The ruling Sultan would have hung Sabetay and his brother and cut their bodies to pieces in a public square had he spelled out the exact meaning of the appointment.)

23. To my younger brother, Joseph, I award the title of KING of the KINGS of JUDAH, with the subtitle of Emperor of the Romans. (It is difficult to say why he deserved this lofty title for he is not mentioned in historical accounts as having an active role in the movement.)

This was the first list made public. Modifications were made in subsequent days as new allegiances were formed.

On December 30, 1666, Sabetay finally sailed for Constantinople. His victory had not come easy. During the eighteen years of his mission there were scars inflicted on him by his enemies, and those inflicted by him on opponents and even followers who were unhappy and disappointed by the shabby manner in which he treated the respected rabbis opposing him. He had been vengeful of them, an attitude not exactly perceived of the love and forgiveness they expected from the messiah. He and his most trusted disciples rented a large private *caïque* (Turkish sailboat) equipped with essential conveniences for travel to Constantinople. A second group of advisors left a few days earlier on coaches and horseback to join him in the big city. The land travelers arrived a few days earlier than their leader to prepare the field for this new crusade. Sabetay's plan contemplated that once the opposition in Constantinople was eliminated, the Jews and Protestants of Europe would be ready to accept him. The status with the Catholic Church was a different matter. The Church had become so powerful, evangelical and militaristic, and so distant and detached from the spirit of the Old Testament that reconciliation with Judaism was out of the question. Was it premature for Sabetay to think this far in advance? Not in the least. He believed earnestly that God had shown him the way to success this far, and without a doubt He would show him the rest of the way to universal salvation.

The day after sailing from Smyrna the wind blew from the northeast. The captain informed Primo that this was a bad omen. The vessel was bound in the northerly direction, and sailing against the wind was nearly impossible. He had experienced difficulties maintaining his ship on course. The navigation plan was to follow the coastline until they entered The Dardanelles Straits. The wind kept pushing the small vessel away from shore into the open sea. He warned there would be delays if the wind didn't change its course. He recommended entering a nearby cove and remain anchored until the weather improved. Primo reported the problem to Sabetay.

"No delays! I don't want any delays!" ordered Sabetay as he pulled his eyes away from his prayer book.

Primo needed to explain the problem in more details: "You realize, my Lord, that a ship cannot sail against the wind. We risk being thrown in the open sea and into a distant western island. We must listen to the experienced captain. He is a veteran sailor. He must know what he is doing. I have already insinuated that you wouldn't mind if we entered an uninhabited cove."

Sabetay had to shout to be heard. The sound of the wind over the sails competed with the sound of his voice. "How dare? You speak as if you and the captain are the final experts. You seem to forget that I rely on the highest authority there is, and with power much superior to the wind. That power has not let me down yet. I said no delays!"

Samuel returned to the captain and told him about Sabetay's unequivocal refusal. The Turkish captain threw his hands in the air and defiantly refused to obey: "Allah is my God! I don't know anything about the God your leader speaks of. As long as Allah has been protecting me all these years from storms, pirates, and warships, I don't intend to risk my ship and my life on account of a misguided advice from a *gyahur* (non-Moslem heathen). I have already instructed my crew to steer into the cove. Now leave us alone. We have much to do."

Meanwhile, as the *caïque* struggled to gain distance, the city of Constantinople awaited him with mounting tension and with split and divergent emotions. If the reported events in Smyrna were an indication of things to come, the city fathers feared they would succumb to the same turmoil. At one of the many rabbinical meetings searching for ways to combat the impossible odds against Sabetay, one wise rabbi asked: "Are we focusing at the heart of the problem?"

Another rabbi asked: "What do you mean by that?"

He explained: "I don't deny that as far as the Ottoman Jewry is concerned, he will have no trouble gathering the remainder of our brethren. It appears to me that this is the only concern we seem to have been focusing on. I have been studying carefully every move Sabetay has made. All his efforts seem to have been concentrated on one important problem: his quest for what he thinks is a universal takeover of Jewries in the world. Mind you, brothers! He aspires spiritual conquest larger than Jesus whose teachings created the most powerful religion on earth. He intends to unite Jews, Christians, Moslem, and others. To convince yourselves that I am right, read the prophetic epistles from him and from Nathan . . ."

His colleagues weren't in disagreement so far. But what did the speaker have in mind that they hadn't already considered? An attending rabbi interrupted: "Come to the point!"

"Sabetay has been focused on the biblical concept of universal redemption. Without a Hebrew Holy Land his dream of redemption wouldn't have any meaning in his mind. He has three important choices to surmount if his influence is to survive. I list them in order of importance." He used the fingers in his hand to enumerate them. "First, he must confront the Sultan if he hopes to win an ultimate victory, or some accommodation at best. This I imagine, is what he hopes for. Without the Sultan's defeat or approval there will not be a Hebrew Holy Land. His second choice is becoming a martyr as Jesus did and let an ardent following create his new religion. Lastly, for the first two choices to succeed he needs to win the hearts of the large population of Ashkenazi Jews, who, I might add, are known to have certain prejudices against Sephardis. Without their acquiescence he will not accomplish total Jewish compliance. I don't know how the events will play themselves out, but as far as I am concerned I am recommending we hold firm and wait for him to stumble trying to overcome anyone or all these three difficulties. He is known to make immature and even stupid moves. My conclusion is that we should stop assuming we hold his destiny in our own hands. Not so! Let the other players resolve this for us."

There was a quick response from one of his colleagues: "Your reasoning makes sense. But experience tells me that logic and reality don't always go hand in hand. At the beginning nobody thought Sabetay would come this far in his plans to destroy traditional Judaism. Yet he did! Is he capable of making stupid moves? Yes! But universal opinion seems to be on his side. He has many strengths, among them: a charismatic personality and profound knowledge of the Scriptures, monies from the rich and donations from the multitudes; all these are in his favor. Nathan is unequivocally on his side, as are the majority of Sephardi rabbis. These facts don't stack up unfavorably against him, my friend. At this stage of events Sabetay and his advisors must have a master plan. Is that plan bold enough to confront the Turkish Sultan to hand over his immense military and spiritual power in the Middle East? We don't know, and that is what makes me very nervous. We have just entered the year 1666, and the pressure will begin to mount on him and his planners to force a realization of the mission. Europe and the Middle East stand waiting with great anxiety and in some cases with desperation. The Sabatians," he laughed, "as his followers have been called, have to make a decisive move. It certainly isn't in Sabetay's temperament to abandon his dreams. The events have advanced to such a level, it is a make or break situation."

When they finished debating, the consensus seemed to be to wait for the time when Sabetay will make a wrong move and then, hopefully, get in trouble with the authorities. That would be the most opportune moment for the conservative rabbis to use their influence and make things worse for him.

That resolution, full of wisdom, appeared to have been playing itself out. Unbeknownst to the general population, government officials had already sent investigators to Smyrna to find sufficient evidence to arrest Sabetay. But they were late in arriving. Sabetay and his entourage had already embarked for Constantinople. Friends of the movement in Constantinople urgently sent a messenger on horseback to intercept Sabetay's ship as it crossed the narrow Straits of Dardanelles. They carried a warning for him to be very cautious in his speeches and actions while visiting the city. There were rumors that on orders of the Sultan Mehmet IV, authorities were to monitor his moves very closely to find the slightest excuse to arrest him. The messenger stood by *Kumkale*, at the narrow entrance of the straits, waiting for Sabetay's *caïque*. When he finally saw it, he intercepted it by boat and gave Sabetay the message. In return, confident Sabetay sent word to the community of Constantinople to exhort to prayers and repent their sins continually. In the meantime, the Chief Rabbi of Constantinople, upon learning that the Sultan was considering to put an end to Sabetay's movement, went to see *Vizir* (Viceroy) Ahmet Köprülü. He stated that a deranged Jew was on his way to the capital pretending to be the messiah. The Jewish city fathers did not support him and they would not object if severe measures were taken against him. The *Vizir* thanked him for the information but did not divulge that, under orders of the Sultan, he had already issued an arrest order. The investigators who carried the order to Smyrna, when reaching that city late, rode back as fast as they

could to intercept the sailboat in the Dardanelles or somewhere
before the boat reached Constantinople.

Meanwhile a frantic spirit began to build among the Jews of
Constantinople awaiting the messiah's arrival. A French Catholic priest in the city described his impressions of that anticipation in a letter to a friend in Marseille as follows[1]: "*Un transport
d'une joie qu'on ne comprendra pas si on ne l'a vu.* (A transport of
joy that wouldn't be comprehended unless it was seen)." He wrote
further that the "Masses expected miracles as soon as their messiah arrived, and I saw myself threatened with dire disaster if I
failed to join them as soon as possible." Also in the city of Bursa,
the birth place of Samuel Primo, located approximately 150 miles
south of Constantinople and inland across the Sea of Marmara,
which Sabetay had yet to cross, a young rabbi by the name of
Moses Suriel had a vision and declared himself another prophet
of the messiah. He publicized his prophecy in the same phenomenal terms as Nathan had done:

> "At night time notable rabbis gathered around me . . . and we sing
> hymns of praise to Sabetay Sevi to the accompaniment of musical
> instruments. I danced until I fell to the ground. Then I fell into a
> trance . . . and began to reveal infinite mysteries in our ancient Ara-
> maic language. . . . Two scribes wrote everything I said . . . Sabetay
> is our king and messiah, our righteous redeemer, he and none other
> . . . I did this every day and night at six hours intervals. . . ."[2]

This new revelation and the long wait for the arrival of Sabetay's
ship drove the Jews of Constantinople and Bursa increasingly
ecstatic, giving speeches about the rise of the Star of David and
the fall of the Crescent. Suriel aroused many wealthy Jews in the
lucrative silk trade of his city to follow the words of their messiah. He vowed to deliver every Jewish soul in Bursa to Sabetay
when he would eventually meet him.

---

1. Consult G. Scholem p. 435.

2. Translated by G. Scholem, p. 436, from the eighteenth century
Yiddish writer Leyb b. Ozer.

It took messiah's *caïque* a little over a month to reach the Sea of Marmara, nearly three times the required sailing period under favorable weather. Sabetay and his advisors were cautioned about their moves but were totally unaware of the arrest order awaiting them. Eventually on February 8, 1666, the *caïque* was intercepted by two government patrol boats in the Sea of Marmara soon after it emerged at the northern end of the Straits of Dardanelles. He was arrested and brought to Constantinople in chains. A group of Jews who had flocked to the seaport to welcome him were dumbfounded and terribly distraught when they saw their divine savior in chains.

During the preliminary inquest at the police headquarters the authorities asked a local rabbi to act as an interpreter because the prisoner was unable to communicate in Turkish. The interrogator asked Sabetay: "What took you this long to travel the distance by sea? Perhaps you stopped somewhere. Tell the authorities where you stopped and what you did." Although the question seemed irrelevant to Sabetay, it was of paramount interest to the military. The Strait of Dardanelles was the most strategic and guarded military defense in the whole empire. It was heavily fortified and the emplacements of defenses all along its fifty-mile length was a top military secret. The Venetians, enemies of the Ottoman Empire, would have given anything to have information about these defenses. To the enemy, crossing the straits meant the immediate surrender of Constantinople.

Nonchalantly Sabetay replied in *espagnol*: "The winter sea raged one tempest after another. In each case I calmed it down by ordering my companions to recite verse 29 of Psalm 107: 'He maketh the storm calm, so that the waves thereof are still,' and I recited after them verse 16 of Psalm 118: 'The right hand of the Lord is exalted: the right hand of the Lord doeth valiantly.'"

When the interrogators realized that answer after answer their prisoner had no other thoughts in mind but religion, they became convinced Sabetay was not a military threat. But the *Vizir* remained very concerned about the disruption of normal life among the Jews who controlled much of the commerce in the big cities.

He had been appraised that rich Jewish merchants were closing their businesses and were readying themselves to leave for Jerusalem in anticipation of the rise of the new kingdom. If for no other reason, the *Vizir* had decided to bring Sabetay before the national tribunal presided by him. Now, under arrest, everybody expected Sabetay would be hung in a public square. This time he wasn't confronting a bribe-hungry *cadi*, it was the *Vizir*, the spokesman for the powerful and merciless Sultan Mehmet IV. There weren't enough monies in possession of world Jewry to measure up to the wealth of the *Vizir* and certainly that of the Sultan. Dirty, unshaven from the long boat trip, and in chains, Sabetay was brought in to face three judges who ruled cases of national importance such as royal assassins, spies, revolutionaries and the like. The *Vizir* asked the first question. "Who are you? What is your name?"

Sabetay spoke through an interpreter. Concerned and worried, not knowing yet the charges brought against him, he answered meekly: "My name is Sabetay Sevi, a rabbi traveling to your city as an alms collector for the poor of Jerusalem."

The chief judge, irritated by what he thought was a devious excuse, asked him harshly: "Did you not call yourself the messianic king? Didn't the Jews follow you and offered you great sums of money?"

Reassuming a cautious and careful stance, Sabetay refused to admit to the charges implied in the judge's questions. He said: "I did nothing like that."

Each time they asked him a question he answered lowly, submissively, and evasively. In the end, the judges and the *Vizir* went into private consultation concluding that the man had none of the actions anticipated from a revolutionary they were accustomed to try in that courtroom. In fact, they thought of Sabetay as a coward and a comical simpleton who did not fit the description given to the *Vizir* by the Chief Rabbi. The fact still remained that he was considered a troublemaker for the nation. They ordered him confined to a comfortable and minimum security prison in town from where they could observe him and his followers until they were able to cool the euphoria the Jews of the city had developed.

He was given comfortable quarters and was free to meet and speak with advisors and followers with special visiting permits. But comfort or not, a prison was not a place for a spiritual leader who had been sent by God to redeem the world. Besides, his advisors feared that the government might also have plans to take action against them and the Jews of the city. They did not discount the possibility that, as was customary among government officials in the Orient, the *Vizir*, himself, might have been opening the door to a big bribe from the rich Jewish community before he released Sabetay.

Accordingly, Sabetay's advisors raised the sum of 60,000 German silver thalers for a bribe to assure against molestation of them, and another 40,000 thalers for permission to anyone who wished to visit Sabetay freely. When the clever *Vizir* saw an opportunity he expected to enrich his coffers, he offered the community a third choice. With an additional 100,000 thalers he would do what was asked of him and set Sabetay free. Joyful, the heads of the movement went to announce the good news to Sabetay who, to their great surprise, instead of being thankful, went into a fit of anger upon learning the size of the bribe,[3] and, more importantly, the lack of confidence the community displayed in God's ability to extricate him from prison. He refused to leave the prison, saying: "I would not resort to such outrageous means since only in a few days great things are about to happen and I will be freed anyway."

His dramatic refusal greatly enhanced his reputation among his followers and enemies alike, but the *Vizir* was not amused. He would not tolerate such an arrogance directed at him. He issued an order to transfer Sabetay to filthier and darker quarters. In this new environment Sabetay led a life of total deprivation. Locked in the dark and dirty cell, it was the first time he began to experience the feeling of martyrdom. In the past none of the two dozen or so avowed messengers of God escaped martyrdom, except

3. The large silver coin issued by many of the German states was valued at approximately 10 US cents of a gold dollar.

Moses who, according to biblical accounts, died joyful at the age of 120 years. The others died at the prime of their lives. He prayed and meditated hoping to understand how and when his ministry will triumph.

Days went by when his visiting disciples watched him become emaciated and feeble in the dismal prison. They couldn't make themselves accept a man of God, the hope of Israel, locked in a filthy prison with criminals. They begged him to reconsider his obstinacy and allow them to pay the bribe. Sabetay wouldn't change his mind. The jailer, acting on orders from the *Vizir*, applied his cunning talents at breaking the will of the stubborn prisoner. Treatment of Sabetay became gradually harsher until he resolved that martyrdom by slow death was unbearable. He didn't ask to be rescued but ceased to object to the bribe. The disciples met with the *Vizir*, who had not forgotten Sabetay's insult when he refused his generous offer. They begged him to be more lenient in his punishment until they found a way to raise the sum of money in his offer. He issued new orders to move him to a more comfortable cell. This time, the vindictive *Vizir* planted a rumor that Sabetay had already been sentenced to die in a singular manner designated for political revolutionaries. The Ottomans treated religious revolutionaries worse than the Romans did. The clever Viceroy must have sensed that, like all such prisoners, a fear had been gnawing at Sabetay's heart.

Primo thought of himself as a politician par excellence. His arguments and judgment always inspired confidence. He was not a physically appealing person, but what he lacked in physical demeanor he made up in his charming and inviting presence. He arranged an audience with the *Vizir* to offer him the 200,000 thalers demanded to set Sabetay free. The *Vizir* knew this would happen. To vindicate the bruised feelings Sabetay had inflicted on an important man like him, he agreed to take the money for commuting what had been a rumored death sentence to a life imprisonment in a more comfortable prison away from the city. Thus, the Vizir had the last laugh for having outsmarted the Jews. The comfortable prison he spoke of was the ancient fortress of Abydos, halfway in the Dardanelles on the Asian side near Canakkale. The town was rich in ancient Greek history and literature. It was the birth place of *Leander*, the legendary lover who swam nightly to the town of *Sestos*, across the Straits (Hellespont), to the European side to visit *Hero*, a priestess of Aphrodite, the goddess of love and beauty. One night *Leander* drowned in the cold and choppy currents streaming from the Marmara Sea to the Aegean Sea. In grief *Hero* cast herself into that sea to meet her death and be with her lover.

Soon after Sabetay was moved to Abydos the Venetians sent their fleet around the island of Crete to occupy the island from the Turks. The *Vizir* went with his armed forces to repel the offensive. There wasn't a Jewish community within hundreds of miles of Abydos. Because the Straits of Dardanelles were off-limit to unauthorized personnel, travel to the region required special permits from the Department of Interior. The closest large city to the fortress was Gelibolu, near the northern end of the Straits. From there, the distance to Abydos was about twenty miles by ship.

The fortress provided luxury quarters for high ranking prisoners such as kings of conquered lands, princes of deposed Sultans, rebellious poets, nobility who spoke against the regime, and the like. Primo discovered that the local authorities were also accustomed to receive bribes from these prisoners in exchange for permitting certain liberties in the confines of the prison. He wrote to Sabetay's brother, Eliyah, who bought the best treatment and accommodations available. With special permissions, advisors moved in town and began to plan the future of the movement from Abydos. It was assumed that once the *Vizir* came back from the Venetian war victorious, wealthy supporters would be able to extricate Sabetay to freedom. With the messiah far from reach, rumors began to flow that in reality Sabetay was not in prison; the archangel Gabriel descended from heaven and quickly assumed Sabetay's body in Abydos. The true and real Sabetay, the one and only messiah, was still traveling around the world spreading the word of God. But a few rich followers, accepting reality,

dismissed the idea of a divine salvation, returning to the only salvation they knew: managing of their wealth.

Through generations of practice, Ottoman officials became
masters at extorting bribes from the rich minorities of Jews and
Christians they called pejoratively *tchifut* and *gyahur* (heathens).
From the highest office of the land to the local official they played
the conning game of bribes in return for infringements of civil
and criminal laws. There was no crime or law that could not be
circumvented with a commensurate bribe. At Abydos prison officials began to sell privileges to Jews in the Empire and abroad
to visit Sabetay. An Armenian poet from Constantinople wrote:

> The Vizir left for the war in Crete.
> The Jews, men, women and children,
> took themselves to the Straits.
> Our city was full of pilgrims,
> from Poland, the Crimea, Persia, and Jerusalem,
> as well as Turkey and the Frankish lands.

The maritime custom officials in Constantinople organized paid
pilgrimage tours to Abydos running on a regular basis. Sabetay
desired very much the company of his wife, Sarah, who up to this
point, remained in Smyrna. Ordinarily women were not allowed
in the fortress unless they were prisoners. With the proper bribe
Sarah came to Abydos two weeks before her husband's birthday,
which coincided with the second anniversary of the couple's coro-
nation. Dervishes[4] were invited to the celebration. During their
ritualistic swirling dances in a state of constant trance they prophesied the fall of the Ottoman empire and the return of the kingdom of the Jews. This further angered the Sultan and the Turkish clerics whose patience with Sabetay was wearing very thin.

From the day Sabetay was sent to Abydos, a number of representative Ashkenazi rabbis from Poland and Germany began to
arrive to pay homage to the messiah, but more exactly to examine

---

4. Dervishes are Moslem mystics considered by the Islamic clerics
to be a rebellious group within the religion.

him critically for his authenticity. The flow of visitors became so extensive that they had to wait days in Constantinople or in Gelibolu for an audience with Sabetay. Schedules had to be changed, modified, or postponed because of Sabetay's unpredictable state of mind and because of the severe headaches. In every case, access to him was made only after his most trusted disciples interviewed the visitors and determined they were serious and especially with good intentions. On one occasion a group of Polish envoys came to Abydos. They were interviewed first by the young visionary and prophet from Bursa, Rabbi Suriel, who finally met Sabetay when he delivered, as he had promised, the entire Jewry in his native city. He climbed to the rank of one of Sabetay's most trusted advisors. Suriel went to meet the Polish rabbis at the town of Gelibolu. Assuming that the foreign envoys came to pay homage to the Redeemer, he shook their hands and asked politely: "What brings you to Constantinople from such a far away distance?"

"We desire to see Rabbi Sevi, the man who calls himself the *Mashiah*. Please take us to him," was the answer.

Suriel suspected that the group might have belligerent intentions. Changing his allure he asked again: "You haven't told me the purpose of your visit. Would you elucidate before I am able to comply with your request? You see, we cannot permit people without honorable intentions to crowd our Lord's busy schedule. I am sure you understand that."

"Are you close enough to him?" asked one rabbi.

"You may rest assured about this. I am as close as they come," answered Suriel with a cynical smile.

"Our congregations have selected us to come, test, and examine your leader who claims to be the messiah."

Suriel finally understood the primary intention of the Polish rabbis. The bluntness of the assertion shocked him. He was not able to contain his diplomatic composure. He answered: "You clever Ashkenazim! You think you have come to test us! Who do you think you are, pretending to be wise enough to test My Lord Sabetay? . . ." He saw them ruffled by his remark. Before Suriel allowed them time to respond he shocked them again: "Never mind what I said, I know who we are! To prove that, I want you to know I am able to read through your eyes who you are. If you don't believe me, come back tomorrow and I shall give you a list of the sins you have amassed through the years."

Surprised and appalled, they vowed to come back the next day if for no other reason but to discredit the challenge of this stranger calling himself prophet. It was the first time they had ever seen him, and how could Suriel claim to know all about them? They came back the next day anxious to embarrass him. They sat around a table and, to heighten the suspense, confident Suriel asked: "Which one of you wishes me to make known to the others the sins you have committed?"

The Polish rabbis looked at each other in disbelief. The young rabbi they faced was so cocky and confident they couldn't wait to prove him wrong. Defiant, the oldest in the group agreed to be interviewed.

"Are you sure, rabbi, you want me to probe into your soul with my keen eyes?" asked Suriel in a threatening manner.

Defiantly he answered with a grin on his face: "I am sure!"

Suriel asked him to sit by the window and to look straight into his eyes without blinking. With a mean smile on his face he added: "The procedure won't take very long unless you sinned all your life." No one in the group laughed at that arrogant smut.

Suriel sat across him, closed his eyes, murmured a few inaudible sentences, and opened his eyes again with a magnificent brilliance looking deeply into the old man's eyes. His eyelids vibrated ever so slightly in a continual fashion. Drenched in perspiration, Suriel suddenly collapsed in his chair. The visitors brought a glass of water and sprinkled a few drops on his face. He slowly came out of his trance, picked up the glass of water and drank a few sips. He spoke slowly and hesitatingly: "Rabbi, I was only able to have a glimpse at one incident in your lifetime. For some reason I lost contact after that. If, however, you are not convinced of my visionary powers after I relate that single incident, I will repeat the performance again and read your entire life. It is up to you."

"Go ahead!" the Polish rabbi answered mockingly. Suriel began: "Now before the Chmielnicki revolt in Poland, didn't you manage Count Zwoblocki's lands and collected rent from the peasants in and around the town of Pinsk?"

Surprised but not startled the interviewed rabbi said: "Yes, but what of it? The Scriptures do not forbid it," reminding Suriel the fact that collecting rents was not a sin.

"Oh, I know that. Let me be more specific. Did you by any chance manage the property leased by a Ukranian family named Nichodemus, Peter Nichodemus?"

Now the interviewed rabbi wasn't as quick at answering that question. He paused and after reassuring himself he said: "Yes I did. I repeat: What of it? You said you were going to read sins I had committed. To my knowledge I know of none, and if you are lucky enough to find one, you must have been reading your own." Now the visitors laughed at the clever remark by their elder.

"Are you sure you want me to continue?" asked Suriel.

"Sure, go ahead."

"The land Peter Nichodemus leased was not among the most fertile in the area. The sale of his meager crop never matched the amount assessed for his lease. Unable to pay the annual fees he sent to your office his lovely daughter with partial payment and to plead for deferment of debts in arrears. As a compassionate man, you felt sorry for her who cried and begged for forbearance. You covered yourself for their debts a number of times. This was a noble gesture in our talmudic laws . . . ."

That statement turned the interviewed rabbi's face so pale that his colleagues noticed it right away. Suriel paused to add more drama by allowing the Polish rabbis time to reflect. The war in Poland and the suffering of the Jews was a touchy subject for them. Many crimes were known to have been committed by Jewish collaborators during that war. Now if Suriel was a true seer the other visitors wanted to hear the kind of sin their leader could have committed during that infamous period of the war. One among them said: "Please continue Rabbi Suriel. Now I want to know."

Suriel still waited for a reaction from the man he faced. "Stop!" interrupted the examined Polish rabbi.

Suriel remained silent. But the others became drawn with curiosity and ordered Suriel to continue. He obliged: "When Chmielnicki's gang burned Peter's house and stole the beasts of burden she came to you, fell in your arms in despair, and told you that they could no longer pay what they owed. Lodged in your arms you felt so warm and close to her. She kissed you in gratitude. The feeling you felt was like a passion you never experienced before. Your feelings were aroused and you caressed her lovely white skin as she came even closer to you . . . ."

"Stop! Say no more, I order you! I can no longer bear the burden of that heinous sin," he yelled falling to his knees begging forgiveness from God.

Suriel stopped. He clutched the man's head in his two hands and prescribed him a recipe for penitence while the others remained watching incredulously not only at their esteemed leader, but more so how Suriel was able to read like an open book what was in his soul.

"You follow my prescription and the Lord will forgive you, I assure you," said Suriel. He removed from his vestment a letter written by Sabetay addressed to the group. He handed it over to another rabbi who read it aloud. In it Sabetay said that he had knowledge of their coming and apologized for not being able to see them sooner. Would they stay a little longer? The Polish rabbis were so impressed with what had taken place they decided to remain in town until Sabetay was ready to see them. A few days later they were invited to the fortress and were overwhelmed with honors and with awe. They wrote back a long letter to their congregations in Poland:

"He sat in his fortress . . . in red garments. The Torah scroll which he held in his [arms] was also draped in red . . . . The walls of the room were draped with golden carpets, and the floor was covered with rugs made of gold and silver. It was a princely room. . . . He ate and drank from gold and silver vessels inlaid with jewels. Later, he held a golden staff in his right hand . . . and a fan with a silver handle in his left hand . . . . When we entered we bent our knees and prostrated before him. He asked: 'Were you here during my festival and the Great Sabbath?' We answered: 'Yes, Our Lord.' He then asked: 'And did you have any doubts because I changed the Law?' We said: 'God forbid' . . . . We told him of the tribulations and massacres of the Polish Jews, but Sabetay said: 'No need to tell me. Behold the book *The Troublous Times*, written by one of your rabbis, telling of the massacres is open here with me all day long. Why do you think I am dressed in red and my Torah dressed the same? Because the day of vengeance is in my heart, and the year of my redeemed has come . . . .' He quoted from Deuteronomy: 'I will make mine arrows drunk with blood' . . . . He ordered everyone in his court to leave the room, and alone with us, he revealed great cabalistic mysteries . . . . We begged: 'Our Lord and King! May it please you to let us be servants at your gates,' but he answered: 'This is not necessary. Go in peace and bring glad tidings to your brethren.' We asked him for a written message to bring with us to our congregations. He wrote a letter to our Rabbi David ha-Levi and signed it . . . ."[5]

As he did on other occasions with other visitors, Sabetay gave each of them copies of favorite cabalistic writings specifying how events related to the messiah were to take place. Before they left, the Polish visitors submitted to him totally. They returned to Poland and assured their congregations that the man they visited was indeed endowed with messianic powers.

The year 1666 was far advanced and a universal rash of anxiety and apprehension reigned throughout Europe and the Middle East. Most Jewish congregations obeyed Sabetay's orders issued from Abydos. Beginning with summer of that year, prophesied as the Year of Salvation, until December there were considerable preparations for the big event. Shops were closed and sold. People flocked to rabbinical courts to confess their sins, receive penance,

---

5. Both Scholem and Kastein quote this passage from Leyb B. Ozer's memoirs written in Yiddish in Amsterdam.

and give alms to the poor. The zeal of becoming pure was so pronounced that many Jews submitted themselves to stricter improvisations of the four kinds of Judaic capital punishments. The four acts of stoning, burning, strangling and beheading were only imitated. None of these were carried out literally, but the penitents emulated them through creative mimicries. Some penitents went as far as burying themselves underground up to their chin, remaining in this mock grave for a few hours praying and repenting. It was like a contagious disease spreading everywhere. Many deaths were reported from these excessive mortifications of the flesh.

15

The flow of visitors to Abydos continued. Shortly after the group of Polish rabbis returned to their communities commenting with great delight their experience of meeting the *Mashiah*, a maverick Polish rabbi named Nehemiah Kohen came to visit Sabetay. He was from the city of Lwow in Galicia. Having declared himself an independent prophet, he convinced the people in his town, who were ready to join Sabetay, to withhold acceptance of him until he had an opportunity to conduct his own investigation. In his learned opinion there were important inconsistencies in the manner and the timing of the rise of this messiah residing in Abydos. He maintained that his colleagues who preceded him had been shallow in their inquiries. Kohen enjoyed a high degree of reputation in Poland, Germany, Holland and Sweden and his words were taken seriously. One had to be careful in such matters he said. They had to be absolutely certain about the authenticity of this oriental man calling himself messiah. Several North European communities collected funds for Rabbi Kohen's trip to Abydos, hoping he would return with the same zeal and passion as the preceding rabbis.

Nehemiah Kohen's mystical schooling was different than Sabetay's, whose prime sources of knowledge and beliefs were deeply rooted in the relatively more modern and surely more profound divinical literature of the *Cabala* and the *Zohar*. Nehemiah's

messianic knowledge came from an older folkloric and legendary
source of writings called the *Midrash*, composed in part by such
writings as the *Haggadah* which embrace historical traditions,
stories, legends, parables and allegories. These books were inspired
by the prophetic and poetic writings of the Old Testament. In
contrast, Sabetay's ideas and concepts were more structured into
a systematic mystical philosophy belonging to a rigorous school
of thought nurtured by centers of cabalistic studies. Nehemiah,
somewhat pedestrian in his understanding of the messianic advent, subscribed to the notion that the messiah was a descendant
of the tribe of Joseph, not David as Sabetay claimed. His messiah would be drawn into the wars known as *Gog and Magog* (of
evil empires) from where he would emerge victorious but, alas,
will fall at the gate of Jerusalem. As a consequence of this unfortunate failure, Jews will be so scattered and isolated in the wilderness that each individual will think he is the only survivor. In
due time, the prophet Elijah will appear and announce a second
messiah, a descendant of the sons of David who will reassemble
the scattered Jews and lead them this time to Jerusalem. Only
then redemption will take place. The Christian early model of
Jesus' second coming was said to have been derived from these
haggadic legends. Nehemiah was anxious to determine how
Sabetay would reconcile his claim in the light of what he had found
faulty and defended staunchly.

Nehemiah arrived in Constantinople at the end of August,
1666. Projecting himself as a representative of many communities in Northern Europe, he requested an audience with Sabetay.
Word was sent to Primo and Suriel at Abydos about the credentials of this avowed prophet. Primo warned Sabetay: "My Lord,
he is an important visitor. Many of the communities he represents
have already declared their intentions to join our movement. If
this man's impressions, after meeting you, turn out to be as positive as the previous visitors from Poland, you will have the backing of all the Jews of Europe."

"Let the prophet Rabbi Nehemiah directly come to me with
rejoicing and jubilation," answered Sabetay confidently.

Having demonstrated his contempt for Ashkenazi rabbis in an earlier encounter with a Polish delegation, Suriel was of the opinion that bringing him in without a preliminary investigation would be a mistake. He had inside knowledge that Nehemiah had a personal reason for discrediting Sabetay. He harbored his own intentions to declare himself the messiah. He insisted that Nehemiah should be given and audience only after his preliminary screening: "My Lord, forgive me if I surmise to question your decision. Nehemiah is an old fashion Haggadic cabalist and, I might add, not a very good one at that. He has antiquated ideas about the process of redemption. He is not a schooled individual. He is a self-taught and self-proclaimed man of God. In other words he is a radical maverick. I suggest we look him over and prepare him before you grant him an audience, exactly the way we proceeded with the previous visitors."

Sabetay, feeling intoxicated with the sequence of past successes, did not heed Suriel's advice. There are moments in history when a simple and single decision can well determine the success or failure of any mission. Sabetay's over confidence was one such moment. He said to Suriel:

"My dear Suriel, what do you think I have been doing ever since I was banished from Smyrna twenty two years ago? I have been confronting one Nehemiah after another wherever I went. Some were easy to convince; others required perseverance and even threats to make them see the divine light. As I said earlier let him come directly and speedily with rejoicing and jubilation."

So on the second day of September Nehemiah met Sabetay and his court at the fortress of Abydos. After a few polite exchanges and praises, Nehemiah, who had been tense during the introductory greetings, blurted crudely: "Rabbi Sevi, let it be known that I came here to challenge you and your messianic pretensions which I believe are based entirely on false premises . . . ."

The sound of the crash of a Turkish coffee cup on the marble floor interrupted Nehemiah. All faces except Sabetay's turned towards the distracting sound. It was Suriel who had dropped the cup which broke into pieces. Primo was ready to order a couple of attendants to escort impertinent Nehemiah out of the room if Sabetay had shown any sign of displeasure. Instead, with a smile on his face, Sabetay apologized: "Rabbi Kohen, I apologize for the distraction which interrupted you as you were about to register a challenge. Would you please take the time to explain the theological basis of this challenge? I am sure you will be kind enough to give us time to respond. I will be glad to explain any historical, biblical, Cabalistic, mishnaic, zoharic, or talmudic interpretations you might have misunderstood about the divine event."

Sabetay's overconfident response was like a dagger in Nehemiah's heart. Sabetay had enumerated slowly and deliberately the battery of references he had at his disposal and was ready to utilize them in a counter argument. Nehemiah was not the kind of man who would be intimidated with a few fancy words. He was a fanatic fundamentalist who grew up in a Galician Ghetto and had suffered extreme hardships during most of his lifetime. Death, poverty, starvation, and sickness were daily problems he surmounted with the help of none other but an absolute faith in the Scriptures. Unlike Sabetay, he did not emerge from a spoiled and relatively well to do family and community who could afford the cost of schooling and the idle time for intense cabalistic studies. Nehemiah's withered face reflected all the pain and suffering of the Polish Ghettos.

"As I was saying, Rabbi Sevi, you are greatly mistaken. You could not be the son of David. The son of Joseph has not appeared yet and has not begun his ministry. The *Mishnah* specifically alerts all Jews to this important precondition. Since you have not declared yourself as the son of Joseph, it is my spiritual duty to challenge you for proclaiming yourself prematurely as the Davidic messiah. I urge you to admit your sin and go into repentance for the rest of your life before you lead our innocent and suffering people to great disappointments. I also urge you to fall on your knees while I am standing here and beg the Lord for forgiveness."

What a blunt, disrespectful, and impertinent response from a man calling himself prophet! Sabetay's court members looked outraged and dumbfounded. They couldn't believe what they had heard from this ignoramus from the north. How dare he challenge their holy man, the man whom the whole world expected to be their savior? By his bluntness, he was also challenging the conviction of the true prophet Nathan, and the numerous learned rabbis who supported Sabetay and his movement. If the matter was left to Suriel, he would have grabbed the man by the crotch of his pants and would have thrown him out the room. In previous times Sabetay had been successful with his charisma and authority to convince skeptics like Nehemiah. He lectured Nehemiah on many aspects of theology attempting to bring him into his camp. No matter how hard he tried, he failed to penetrate the mental block of his opponent. Stubborn Nehemiah wouldn't yield an iota. He kept repeating the same logic about the sequence of messianic events he believed to be true. To recover from this awful deadlock, Sabetay's advisors set up meetings for the following three days, to wrangle and argue in the hope of proving Nehemiah that he had been wrong.

Nehemiah agreed to meet again and returned the following days. During those sessions they opened one reference book after another trying to bring sense into the visitor's bullheaded mind. It didn't work. But it became obvious during these lengthy discussions that Nehemiah had intentions of proclaiming himself messiah of the House of Joseph, and begin his ministry as the avenger of Jewish blood upon the gentiles of the world. Sabetay was standing in his way, for no one would accept two living messiahs at one time. In the end Sabetay became intolerant and accused him of being an illiterate. Nehemiah saw himself outnumbered and outsmarted, and in defense he took a quarrelsome attitude and charged Sabetay with vanity, fraud, and ignorance. He accused him of placing Israel into danger with his lies and deceits. Never before had Sabetay confronted such a belligerent visitor.

When Nehemiah left the fortress, three of his disciples followed him to the inn without Sabetay's knowledge. Samuel Primo was of the opinion that they had been uncharitable to this Polish rabbi who despite his lack of scholarship, was proud and closed-minded.

If only Sabetay had been a bit more patient, sympathetic, and understanding perhaps the deadlock would have been resolved. Perhaps, as they had done a number of times in the past, awarding him a title with an important assignment in the movement could have softened his position. Sabetay should have never accused him of being an ignoramus. Now the man appeared reckless and capable of doing considerable harm. They had to do something to mend the damage. At the inn Primo knocked at his door: "Good morning, Rabbi Kohen. We come in peace. If you permit us to come in, we would like to correct an unjust impression we might have left with you. Can we come in?" he asked smiling and showing his pearly teeth contrasting against his black mustache and beard.

When he saw three rabbis standing at his door, Nehemiah hesitated to let them in. Apprehensive he said: "What is there to say that we didn't say during the past three days? I will be getting ready to leave after my prayers. If you come to change my mind, you are wasting your time." He put on a frown on his ugly face. As he appeared to be ready to shut the door, Galanté and the young Suriel pushed it open and forced themselves in. The room was a mess. Chairs and the divan were cluttered with carpet bags and clothing. Primo's intention was to be sociable. He waited for Nehemiah to clear chairs and offer them a seat. When that didn't happen, impulsive Suriel became resentful. In an angry tone of voice he said: "Rabbi, if you were a Sephardi you would have been considerate and made room for us to sit and be comfortable. We told you we came in peace . . ."

He was going to say more but Primo interrupted him. Nehemiah didn't oblige. Still standing, Primo began to deliver the message of conciliation he had prepared: "Rabbi Kohen, we come here in peace as messengers of Our Lord Sabetay Sevi. We come to tell you that we are sorry and regret the way the events unfolded at our lengthy discussions. We don't see that we have a serious difference of opinion and for that reason we don't think we should let you go with an unfavorable impression. Looking at God's mission broadly we are all children of Israel and we all believe in the

sanctity of salvation prophesied by our wise ancient prophets. All
of us, including you, said it was time for our messianic mission.
Our Lord Sabetay has already proven to most Jews of this continent that he is the one who has been called to divine duty by
prophets and angels, regardless of which of the biblical houses
one thinks the messiah belongs. Let us keep our differences on
this point and work together for the same divine cause. Our Lord
Sabetay had shown you a list of royal appointments he had bestowed to pious and noble men who will assist him in creating
the new Kingdom of God on earth. He has authorized me to offer
you the royalty title of King Manasseh, son of Hezekiah and king
of Judah. You will be the twenty-fourth royal appointment he has
made. You have to agree that he must respect your abilities very
much for him to award you this most distinguished royal title.
Rabbi Nehemiah, I urge you to forget what has been said during
the past days and join us as brothers. Our Lord Sabetay wants to
see you once again and confer this blessed title personally. We
have arranged for you to come back to the fortress tomorrow."
Primo extended his hand and said: "What do you say?"

Primo and his associates waited for Nehemiah's reaction while
they stood in the small room reeking with nervous perspiration.
Nehemiah lifted the prayer book he held in his left hand and kissed
it. Then with the other hand he pointed at Primo's face, shouting: "What I say now is what I said yesterday to this man who calls
himself messiah. He is an impostor and I intend to expose him
wherever I go. Now leave my room and I don't want to see you
again. Is that clear. Now, go!" Shocked by the rebuke, biting their
lips Primo and Galanté left the room insulted but not totally surprised. They had anticipated that possibility, and therefore had
designated young Suriel to remain in the room and give him the
final message.

"I thought I told you to leave!" yelled Nehemiah to Suriel who
refused to acknowledge his order to leave.

"Not before you hear what I have to say," began Suriel with a
threatening voice. "You are not a holy man of God, you are an *hijo
d'un azno*." He had to translate into Hebrew what this meant in

espagnol. "A son of an ass and I will treat you as one! You listen to me carefully! We are assuming that you have intentions to shoot your filthy and sinful mouth bragging about the disrespect you showed towards my Lord. Under no circumstances can we permit that. Unless you change your mind this last time I am asking you, better still I am advising you to be very careful when you leave this filthy and disgusting room. One never knows when God's hand will strike you down in these remote places so far away from your homeland. I leave you with this macabre thought. I will count to three, waiting for a change of attitude, and I will leave the room after that; not before!"

Nehemiah didn't speak. Suriel counted to three, walked to the door and slammed it behind him. He rushed to meet his associates who waited in the vestibule of the inn, leaving Nehemiah pale with fear presuming he had been threatened with his life. Aghast, he got dressed quickly and, with his Turkish speaking aide, went to see the inn-keeper. He asked for directions to the *cadi's* house. Shaking and following the instructions, he ran down the street to seek refuge in the magistrate's house and ask for his help. He knocked at his door furiously. A clerk opened the door and Nehemiah launched himself inside. He asked to see the *cadi* immediately; it was a matter of life or death. The clerk told him to wait in the vestibule but Nehemiah wouldn't listen. He followed the clerk, who in despair raised his voice and ordered him to wait. Upon hearing the commotion, the *cadi* came out of his private quarters to see what the trouble was. In a desperate tone of voice Nehemiah told him through his aide about the threat he had received. Figuring it was a personal dispute among Jews, the *cadi* answered that the case was not in his purview. Then he added that if he were a Moslem, no Jew would dare to threaten him with murder, especially if it was on account of religion. The murderer and his accomplices would be hung on public square the next day.

Nehemiah, who still trembled with fear, found genuine comfort in the *cadi's* words. Shrewd as he was, he figured he had to save his life at any cost. He reasoned that he will save his life first, and when he returned home safely he will take the matter up with the rabbinical council and reconvert to Judaism. He instructed the *cadi* to call the local *Imam* (priest) as he was ready to seek conversion to Islam in front him.

Nehemiah converted to Islam a few hours later. The Turkish magistrate sensed from the beginning an opportunity to provide the Sultan with an ironclad case against Sabetay. He asked Nehemiah if he would go to Edirne to meet the ruler of all Islam and denounce Sabetay's fanatical revolutionary movement. Now Nehemiah saw himself in the reverse role of issuing a death threat to Sabetay. Out of vengeance he agreed to do it. The *cadi* sought and obtained a royal audience. The only way the ambitious *cadi* could have arranged this meeting was to give the assurance that Nehemiah was ready to testify, swearing as a new Moslem on the Koran, that Sabetay's ultimate plan called for deposing the Great Sultan and making his brother Eliyah King of all Ottoman lands. He had seen the list of royal appointments Sabetay had conceived. Nehemiah was summoned to Edirne and traveled to the royal palace under the protection of royal guards. When Primo heard the news, he became very concerned. What a pity that a stupid blunder on their part and an insignificant visitor should suddenly create havoc for their otherwise triumphant cause. They should have let Nehemiah go and shoot his mouth to his heart's content in the small town of Lwow from where he came.

Like his predecessors, Sultan Mehmet IV attended important trials of revolutionaries without physically showing his presence at the court. He sat behind a latticed wall with a view of the whole courtroom without being seen. As planned, Nehemiah, now a Moslem, testified that Sabetay was more a dangerous revolutionary than a man of God. To inject drama and fear, he said that before the end of the year Sabetay planned to call for a revolt of his followers and march against the Sultan. The moment the Sultan heard the words of the translator speak of a revolution to depose him, his heart began to race and anger enveloped his body. No one except him understood the agony of the bitter feeling of a rival wanting his throne. It didn't matter that Sabetay wasn't a political anarchist or that his followers didn't bear arms. The simple thought of knowing that in his empire a revolutionary leader had so many followers with a social and political agenda different than his was threatening enough. There was a very good reason for his anger. Historically[1] since the day of the first Ottoman Emperor, every Sultan dreaded the thought of a living pretender to his throne, even if that rival was incarcerated in a prison from which he couldn't escape. There were already too many of his sons and sons of previous Sultans now imprisoned who would kill him if they were able to set themselves free. He knew it because he had lived in that awful prison for many years. Sitting behind the latticed wall, in anger and fear, his thoughts went back to those dreadful days.

ᘺ

Harems filled with favorite wives and concubines had always been a part of the *Padishah's* (Sultan's) retinue. By the seventeenth century a *Padishah* was more distinguished by the size of his harem than by the conquests he made. If they had to go to war, they demanded female companionship in the battle field which at times consisted of one-third of their harem or nearly 100 women. With favorite wives and not so favorite concubines there were also favorite children and not so favorite ones. Succession to the throne became by necessity an on-going sinister plot of murders and massacres of the male children. These plots were ordered not only by the *Padishah* himself, but by zealous wives and concubines, by jealous brothers and sisters who stood to benefit from the death of the first male child in the royal line. Succession was literally survival of the fittest. The present Sultan lived through this terrible fear. Royal children were kept in a *kafes* (cage: literal translation). The well-guarded and secluded quarter was not a cage with bars, but a residence inside the Seraglio with high walls, opposite the rooms of the First Sultana (favorite wife). That resi-

---

1. E. S. Creasy, in his *History of the Ottoman Turks, Vol. II*, gives an excellent description of the lives of the Sultan's children. (See Bibliography.)

dence had no windows on the first floor, impeding a daring escape. The only entrance to the cage was bolted without access to the world. To protect heirs to the throne from murdering each other or by being murdered by jealous wives, they were incarcerated in individual plush cages from the age of two until they were either called to the throne or slaughtered by a rival successor. The only companions the princes had were the deaf-mutes servants who could not speak to the outside world and a modest harem of concubines rendered barren by the removal of their ovaries or by medication. If for some reason the medication failed and the concubine became pregnant, she was immediately drowned with the fetus.

Mehmet IV had been in the *kafes* since the age of two. He lived in it in mortal terror for twenty-two years. When officials came to announce his father the Sultan had passed away and he was to succeed him, he refused to believe them. He was sure it was a trick destined to murder him. Dragging all the furniture with the help of his sterile concubines, he barricaded the main door refusing to come out. The *Grand Vizir* had to think of a clever way to convince Mehmet that his father Ibrahim I, the previous *Padishah*, was indeed dead. He had his cadaver brought into the courtyard of the Seraglio asking Mehmet to look at it from the upstairs window and convince himself that indeed his father, the butcher, was truly dead. The idea worked and he came down the stairs through the unlocked front door of his cage, screaming at the top of his voice: *"The butcher of the Empire is dead at last!"*

He, like other surviving princes, had one thought in mind: to sentence the other brothers and half-brothers to death and make up for lost time! Now it was his turn to carry out that yearning. His blood was said to boil when he heard of a move to depose him.

ॐ

Now, at Nehemiah's inquest these awful thoughts surged into his heart. The Sultan had heard enough from Nehemiah. He sent a note to the head judge with his ruling and instructions. Barely ten days after Nehemiah met Sabetay, four armed guards from the royal palace arrived in Gelibolu. Their first duty was to reprimand the mayor Mustafa Pasha for conspiring illegally and permitting the prisoners in the fortress to organize worldwide subversion and conspiracies against the state in return for bribes. Then the royal guards went to Abydos and arrested Sabetay. All the other members of his court who had enjoyed regal quarters were chased out of town, nearly clubbed to death. The prisoner and the guards arrived in Edirne on September 15, 1666.

The Sultan had all the proof he needed about a plot to overthrow him. Because Sabetay was a religious leader, before bringing charges against him, the *Grand Mufti* (Turkish Archbishop) was consulted. The Mufti, who was also an overseer of all minority religions in the land, advised caution so as not to do anything that would immortalize Sabetay as a saint. He advised against the death sentence the Sultan had already put in his mind. He argued that such an act would turn the Jewish population in the empire to revolt, causing serious economic and political troubles in many parts of the empire. He reminded the Sultan of the martyr Jesus whose sentence created great turmoil in the Roman Empire. Life imprisonment, he argued, was the wisest solution.

Because no public charges had yet been issued against Sabetay, the puzzled Jews of Constantinople, unaware of what had taken place, began inventing all sorts of stories about their messiah's fate. As the year of salvation was coming to an end, the Jews who had readied themselves spiritually, if not economically, for the triumphant march to Jerusalem, spread the news that Sabetay had finally extricated himself from jail in Abydos and was currently meeting with the Sultan to ask for the surrender of his crown. The Jews of Edirne, the city where the royal palace was, upon hearing these rumors began to spread carpets on the pavements of the city for Sabetay to walk on after he came out of the palace victor and king of the world. Indeed, that was how strong the conviction was that Sabetay was the messiah and that the inevitable blessed event of redemption was a few days away.

Sabetay was brought for questioning by members of an especially selected Privy Council. Mehmet IV sat at his private loge behind the latticed wall. The council was composed of the chief Islamic leader, the sultan's chief chaplain, his personal chaplain, the mayor of Edirne, and the Sultan's physician, an apostate Jew who acted as a translator. The charges were read by the chief Islamic leader:

"You, Sabetay Sevi, are charged with messianic pretensions which, according to Hebrew Holy books, you plan to challenge the Sultan, take his crown and make Palestine an autonomous Jewish State. To promote your cause, you had received extortion moneys from many victimized and deceived followers. Moreover, according to plaintiffs who have already made depositions, you have threatened a Moslem (Nehemiah) with his life and abused your prisoner's rights at Abydos. Among these abuses you had guards bring in Moslem virgins into your company, etc. . . . ." The charges went beyond Nehemiah's testimony. Prison guards at Abydos and officials who had set up the touring trips, in return for a reduced punishment for having received bribes, had been questioned and testified under oath to a multiplicity of crimes the movement had committed. The Sultan's physician translated the chief Islamic leader's words asking how he pleaded: "All of these charges are punishable by death. How do you plead?"

Sabetay didn't know what to say. The interpreter asked in *espagnol*: "Our Great Emperor wants to know how you plead: Are you guilty or not?"

He stood terribly confused not knowing who the judges were or that his accusations were that serious to require the attention of the Sultan. He had never been in such a confrontation with the authorities before. For Jews in the Ottoman Empire, the only court they ever knew was the rabbinical court, run by Sephardis according to Talmudic laws and conducted in *espagnol*. If a case had to go to Turkish court it had to be, as the judge said, involving a Moslem. Confused and shaken, not exactly knowing who and what had brought this calamity upon him, he answered the physician meekly:

"I deny all the charges. Never had I proclaimed myself messiah. In fact I have always condemned my people for suggesting it. The truth of the matter is that I had been duped into this role by Nathan of Gaza, the instigator of the idea. From that day on, the Jews in the Empire forced me into the messianic role against my will. As long as I remember I felt swept by an irresistible wave of public clamor for divine salvation. I couldn't possibly escape the force of that wave . . . ."

Sabetay choked as the words flew out of his mouth uncontrollably. He sensed the resurgence of his illness. His head started to pound and his cheeks became inflamed with pain. He stopped a few moments to collect his thoughts. Was he, for the first time in his life, being truthful about himself and his faith? Did all those years of suffering, praying, meditating, dreaming and hard work amount to a simple indictment of the cause he believed in? He was very troubled. Could the words that fell out of his mouth been true? But then, if he had admitted to the charges he would have surely be hung and become a martyr. His disposition and deep-rooted faith in his Creator would not permit him to accept that admission! He had to plead for continued life and further struggle. Yes, it had to be that way! As long as the Creator took His time to reveal Himself to him, he had to stay alive at any cost! He stroked his aching face with the palm of his hand and decided: Yes, this had to be the way. The Creator was testing him at this moment of terror. Yes, it had to be that! He composed himself as well as he could and continued:

"I admit collecting money for the poor but I had given it all to them. All the other charges are lies advanced by my enemies."

He thought he had answered all the questions. He stopped and waited to see what would follow in the courtroom. The members of the council appeared to be touched by his innocence and meekness. The Sultan, too, reassured himself that the accused was far from being the kind of cut-throats imprisoned in the cage. While the members of the court spoke silently to each other, an aid to the Sultan came out from behind the latticed wall with a written message to the inquisitors. The message was written in the form of a set of questions. Sabetay followed with his eyes the aid delivering a message to the judges. He quickly surmised that the Sultan had to be behind the latticed wall. The Chief Islamic leader opened the folded paper and read loudly to Sabetay. The physician translated to Spanish. He began with the first question.

"His majesty Our Sultan and Caliph of this Empire wants to know if it is true that you claim to have performed miracles. Have you?"

Sabetay didn't know how he should answer that question. Was it directed in his favor or against him? He hesitated a moment and when he was pressed to answer he said meekly: "Little ones."

Laughs filled the courtroom. Then the head of the council read the second question: "I would like to attract your attention to your right side and in the corner of this courtroom. There!" He pointed with his forefinger and continued: "Our Great Sultan has ordered a royal guard to stretch his bow with a deadly arrow pointed at your heart. I have been asked to warn you that he is the best marksman in the land . . ."

He stopped to allow time for all heads, including Sabetay's, to turn in that direction. As soon as Sabetay saw the stretched bow and the deadly arrow pointing at his heart, he turned pale and began to tremble. He didn't understand why the investigation had turned so brutal so suddenly. The head of the council holding the Sultan's message in his hand read further:

"Our Supreme Sultan and Caliph of all Islam is ready to test your messianic powers. He is ready to make a bargain with you. In his proposition he stands to lose considerably more than you. It is very commendable on his part, indeed. He is ready to order the guard to release the arrow. Now, if you are endowed with the divine gift of making miracles as you have admitted, you can pro-duce another one in his presence and deflect the arrow before it reaches your heart. The moment you succeed at doing that, you save yourself from certain death and our Omnipotent Sultan will not only give you his crown and become your servant, he will ask you to convert him to Judaism and he will order us to do like-wise . . . ." To heighten the suspense, the speaker paused. Then he added slowly, lowering the pitch of his voice: "If you fail, you will meet your death, assuredly!" With a smile on his face, the head of the council waited for his statement to be translated. While Sabetay listened and trembled in his seat, the Islamic leader added: "Rabbi Sevi, it seems to me that having admitted to producing miracles, you have nothing to lose but all to gain! Now we all wait to hear your decision. The arrow waits to be released. What is your decision?"

What a test of wills? Why were they doing this? Sabetay asked himself. Suddenly a flash came to his mind that this might be the moment the Creator had arranged and would whisper in his ear: "Go ahead, do it, Sabetay! This is the moment you have been waiting for! I am speaking to you as I spoke to Abraham and Moses! I will deflect the arrow and you will be my servant. I will make the evil Sultan bow to you and hand you the crown that subjugates the land I promised to your ancestors."

In these few seconds of introspection he thought how marvelous and sweet that would be! Just as the Holy Books said it would happen. The Sultan's crown would be his, and as prophesied from the days of antiquity, the Jews would begin their march to their Promised Land. Everything he imagined about himself since childhood would come true! In those short but nervous moments, he waited with great anxiety and anticipation for those reassuring words from Heaven. He waited with his ears tuned finely. Alas! there was no voice, not a whisper. As the silence grew deeper and his accusers waited for a reply, his eyes filled with tears. He felt choked and couldn't breath easy. There was no way he would accept that deadly challenge without the divine approval he sought so desperately. Everyone watched in suspense, including the Sultan who wore a nervous grin on his face. Being a religious man himself, there was always a chance, however minute, that Sabetay would produce a miracle. The judges and the Sultan couldn't waited any longer. The guard with his bow extended at maximum tension couldn't keep his fingers tight any longer holding the arrow. Then suddenly and unexpectedly Sabetay leaped out of his seat, ran to the bench of the interrogators and fell to their feet pleading for his life. It was truly one of those historical moments, shared only by a few privileged witnesses, that would remain incomprehensible for generations. No one could understand the awesomeness of the test of wills between the Sultan and his Allah, and Sabetay and his Adonay. The stakes in that gamble were incredibly phenomenal. The only difference between the two men in confrontation was that the Sultan had been thoroughly accustomed to expect death any day, while Sabetay was facing it for the first time.

The court ordered Sabetay to his seat. Another royal message was issued from behind the lattice wall. This time it was handed to the apostate physician who acted as the interpreter. Sabetay wished he could see the mysterious authority that was issuing these orders from behind the lattice wall. The physician asked Sabetay to stand up and hear the verdict. He pointed to the lattice wall and confirmed that the Sultan was behind it and waited for an answer to the following royal statement. He translated as he read:

"You have proven to us that you are not the messiah nor that in your heart you were sufficiently convinced of it to accept death under challenge. Therefore the All Merciful Sultan concludes that, having agreed to convert to Judaism in case you had deflected the arrow, you should be willing to convert to Islam in order to save your life. His verdict is the following: Conversion to Islam or death."

Silent and with quivering lips Sabetay looked up to the ceiling and in a muted voice he implored his Creator: "Oh, God my Savior and my Redeemer: All my life I saw myself at Your service harvesting sinners and souls lost from Your Kingdom. Now I am forced to sell my soul to an evil Sultan or face death. You have guided me all through life to this moment of decision. Tell me what I should do." He waited again to hear the voice of the Lord. There was no answer. But hadn't he fallen to the floor minutes ago to save his life? In the absence of a divine message, it seemed to him that his plea had already been answered. He fell to the floor again and pleaded for his life. The Islamic leaders stood up in awe and now they praised Allah for this miracle. On the spot, they performed the religious conversion ceremony. In Sabetay's case it was a simpler matter. The normal process required lengthy preparations for a circumcision before the conversion ceremony. But Sabetay had already been circumsized as a Jew. By order of the Sultan, who was amused by Sabetay's frailty, he demanded Sabetay's baptismal name to be Aziz Mehmet Effendi. The Sultan, being a religious man, gave his name to the convert to make it known in the eyes of Allah that he was personally responsible for bringing Him another converted soul. Sabetay was to live under the watchful eyes of the royal guards and was given the honorary title of keeper of the palace gate *kapici bashi*. He was awarded a pension of 150 piasters per day from the royal treasury. Immediately after this decree, he was led to the special bath reserved for the palace servants where he was blessed and changed into Muslim clothing, this time literally wearing the turban, the symbol of Islam.

The terse and cruel news about the *Mashiah* converting to Islam broke out. Shattered and suffering, Sabetay wished he could tell his people the way it really happened in those agonizing moments in the courtroom. How was it ever possible to make them understand if he had agreed to succumb to this new faith it was because more prayers and sacrifices were needed. It had to be that God had enlarged the scope of his mission. There was more work to be done. He was entering a new realm of assignment whose divine significance would surely be clarified in time. There was no other explanation. But his deceived and confused followers didn't see it that way. Total chaos and pandemonium reigned inside the Jewish ghettos. How could that be? They demanded explanations from the apostles. Before the movement risked falling apart, Samuel Primo and Daniel Pinto invented a divine purpose to this conversion. There were plenty of references in the Scriptures and cabalistic books to justify the seemingly devastating news. To abate the awful disappointment of the followers, and the ridicule by the opponents, they issued the following proclamation:

As soon as it became known to the Turks and the Christians in the city of Edirne that the Sultan sent for Our Lord, they assumed he would be beheaded immediately and the Jews would be killed . . . . Our Lord arrived in the city two days later than expected. When he arrived in the evening it was too late to go to the Sultan. The next morning he appeared before the Sultan who greeted him: 'Peace be with thee,' and Sabetay replied in Turkish: 'Upon thee, peace.' Soon after a royal attendant brought him a robe which the Sultan had worn, and another attendant brought one of the Sultan's turbans, and they clothed him with these and called him Mehmet, in the name of the Sultan. The Sultan ordered that he be given a large sum to him every day. That was how the rumor got about that he had apostatized, but instead there was great deliverance to the Jews. Our Lord requested the Sultan to reverse the orders of wrath and anger to destroy all Jews in Constantinople . . . and no Jew suffered any harm because of this . . . ."[2]

The hopes of the world Jewry had been so highly kindled that few saw in this published message a clever deception. It hinted only by inference that their messiah converted in order to negotiate the terms of the Sultan's surrender. However, the small opposition seized the moment and spread their own version that Sabetay had fallen pray to his own miscalculated design. By this time the number of followers approximated 100,000 in number and most didn't know what to believe. They searched senselessly for honorable answers. To accept the truth was accepting a messiah without divine powers. If they rejected the words of Pinto's proclamation, then Sabetay had indeed turned Moslem, a servant of the Sultan and not of their God. In that case, what had gone wrong when everything was going so well? They would not allow to be swayed so easily that the divine cause evaporated and disappeared by a single command of the Sultan who was supposed to hand over his crown to Sabetay. No war, no fights, no aggression of any kind had taken place; just a vanishing act like the smoke

---

2. Archival documents belonging to Dr. Alfred Freimann and quoted in part from G. Scholem p. 683.

of a magician. But didn't the prophet Nathan's letters insist that their Lord Savior was likely to do things that looked strange and incomprehensible and that they should not try to judge him on appearances? That their Lord was likely to act in a manner beyond understanding? That attempting to comprehend his acts would lead into fallacies and disappointments. Yes! The answer had to be hidden in Nathan's warnings. There had to be a divine purpose mortals were unable to comprehend. Their messiah had to come out victorious or die as a martyr. Since he had done neither, the hand of God had to be still at play. That was it! Hymns and poems were composed to give homage and praises to Sabetay.

A few days after his apostasy, Sabetay sent a short note to his brother Eliyah. The note was terse, and in a melancholic tone suggested he had apostatized under God's will:

> "Now let me alone, for God has made me a Turk, your brother Mehmet. For he spoke and it was done; he commanded, and it stood fast [Psalm 33:9]."

The note was passed on to the apostles who hadn't seen him since his apostasy. They meticulously analyzed it and concluded God, in his larger design, assigned Sabetay temporarily to loftier aims. Since it was popularly assumed that the messiah had to conquer the abode of the demons before redemption, then it had to be that he was asked to apostatize to an evil religion to meet the devil and destroy him. The historical precedence was found in Psalm 34:1 when King David had also acted ungodly by changing his behavior before Abimelech, the King of the Philistines. There was another historical precedence in this. Christian apostles had to go through the same disappointment when redemption did not take place after Jesus' crucifixion.

Fear overcame some followers in many cities, blaming themselves for putting their faith in an apostate messiah. Some members of the movement turned their attention away from Sabetay and unto his prophet Nathan who remained at his home in Gaza. On November 20, 1666, after learning the fate of Sabetay, Nathan traveled to Damascus and in no uncertain terms made it known that Sabetay was still the living king and that he, Nathan, remained his servant of servants. He sent a letter to the once supportive rabbis of Aleppo and to other cities telling them that he was about to go and meet the Lord King. He beg them not to let their hearts become faint on account of the seemingly discouraging news. That all things in time would become clear. The messiah had to enter a period of penance.

Nathan's promised trip didn't materialize. He changed his plans learning of the growing opposition against him in Smyrna, Salonica and Constantinople. He waited for late January, 1667, to travel with six followers to Bursa. Incensed by his audacity to arrive as the prophet of a man who had apostatized, the rabbis of Constantinople who now went on full offensive, sent orders to the rabbinate of Bursa to excommunicate him. The order included a ban for any Jew speaking to him. When he arrived in Bursa, surprised Nathan was warned to keep quiet and leave the city or else they would deliver him in the hands of the Turkish authorities. Frightened, he turned back and headed for Smyrna were he was instructed in the same manner. He stayed in the suburbs of Smyrna trying to assess the mood of the city. A delegation of followers came to seek from him religious clarifications concerning the apostasy. Nathan had none to give beyond what he had written in his letters. Discouraged, the delegation left saying:

"May God save us . . . and send us relief and deliverance from another place."

Nathan roamed from town to town, island to island in the Aegean Sea seeking ways to pull the movement together. He traveled the entire year of 1667 only to find an utter discouragement, and contempt against Sabetay and him. He was never able to see Sabetay who resided in Edirne at the Sultan's palace. But, many fanatic followers, disoriented and confused, from communities all over the empire, some as far as Babylon and Jerusalem, began to arrive in Edirne to apostatize as their messiah had done. This was the only way they knew how to remain with their Savior.

Sabetay's life had changed drastically. His title of keeper of the palace gates was strictly honorific for he had no training or any idea about the gardens or flowers for which he was supposed to care. He occupied the ornate gate house with his wife Sarah, who had also converted to Islam. He enjoyed the friendship and protection of the Sultan's chaplain, Vani Effendi, who spent much of his time educating him on Islamic Law; from time to time Sabetay was permitted to draw parallels in Jewish rites. His mentor and teacher was sufficiently liberal to allow him considerable freedom, including meeting with his previous followers. This, however, was permitted only in the hope that he would be instrumental in convincing them to apostatize to Islam.

Sabetay began to nurture the idea in the minds of the few converts that he as their messiah will emerge vanquishing Islam from within. Any followers who remained faithful to him will be on his side marching to victory. The new breed of covert Moslems, calling themselves Dönmeh (converts in Turkish), believed that Sabetay apostatized only upon a divine order and not because he was forced by the Sultan. An historical comparison was made to the times of Jesus. Sabetay's converted followers were compared to Jews turned to Christianity when Jesus was crucified. Jesus' early disciples overcame the tragedy of the crucifixion by dwelling and cultivating the image of the resurrection: the hope of a Second Coming. The comparative reasoning was not difficult to accept.

The Jewish remnants of Sabetay's movement remained opposed to traditional Judaism for a while, upholding the new order and doctrines. Redemption remained postponed. They, too, developed a reassuring concept that his apostasy was only an intermediary step in the overall mission of the messiah who "sitteth alone in silence as he hath borne it upon himself." The good books warned that the messiah had to descend into impurity; and for a while good had to assume the form of evil. The hope that Sabetay will return to them after vanquishing evil didn't falter.

In a book Paul Rycaut[3] wrote about Sabetay he described those difficult days in the following manner:

> Sabetay passed his days in the Turkish Court, as Moses did in the time of the Egyptians; and perhaps in imitation of him, cast his eyes often on the afflictions of his brethren, of whom, during his life, he continued to profess himself a deliverer, but with that care and caution of giving scandal to the Turks, that he declared, unless their nation became like him, that is renounce the shadows, and imperfect elements of the Mosaical Law, which will be completed by adherence to the Mohammedan, and such other additions as his inspired wisdom should suggest, he should never be able to prevail with God for them, or conduct them to the Holy Land of their forefathers . . . . Many Jews flocked in, some as far as Babylon, Jerusalem . . . casting their caps on the ground . . . voluntarily professed themselves Mohammedans. Sabetay, gaining ground in the esteem of the Turks, had privileges granted him to visit familiarly his brethren . . . [avoiding] the danger of excommunication from one, and the gallows from the other.

In the year 1667 a son was born to Sabetay and Sarah. They called him Ismail Mordehay. No one was more rejoiced than his ardent followers and especially Nathan, who by this time had fallen out of grace. This birth was like a renewal of the faith and a redeeming news for Nathan who had prophesied the event, the name of the child and the year of his birth. As Sabetay's ups and downs continued, he acted both as the pious Jew and the missionary Moslem. He convinced the chaplain Vani Effendi that if he was allowed to move freely in Edirne and Constantinople he would attend services at the Sephardi synagogues during the Jewish holidays and in sermons he would ask the congregation to submit to Islam.

After the debacle caused by the last Polish envoy Rabbi Nehemiah Kohen, who in the meantime backslided into Juda-

---

3. Sir Paul Rycaut, *The History of the Turkish Empire from 1623–1677*. London 1680. Also in French, *Histoire de l'empire Ottaman*, Paris 1709.

ism and campaigned in Northern Europe for his candidacy, another visitor by the same family name, Rabbi Solomon Kohen from Volhynia appeared in Edirne wishing to meet with Sabetay in order "to see the face of Our Lord." This man was not just any rabbi. He had been a rabbinic judge for over a dozen years in the city of Budapest. After meeting with Sabetay he became so spiritually enthralled that he put his feelings in an open letter:

> I give thanks to God for having met [in Edirne] the messiah of our righteousness and the true prophet Rabbi Nathan and other leading scholars who are still with Our Lord. And I saw the face of the king in his shining radiance on the great festival of his birth. . . . He is without a doubt the true redeemer. . . . I can testify that when the great light is upon him he has no regular sleep, though he occasionally dozes . . . . Now we hope that soon all things will become clear and evident, and what is yet unknown will become manifest and they who use their tongue against the righteous will be put to shame. . . . I also spoke to the brother of our messiah, a very learned and extremely wealthy man who is several years older than Our Lord. He told me all that had happened to his brother from his childhood to this very day, and I wrote down everything his brother said . . . ."[4]

This euphoria of faith and disappointment bewildered and frustrated many Jews in European Diasporas. Members of the movement reproduced copies of Solomon Kohen's long letter to send to all congregations in Europe. To avoid severe repercussions from the Sultan from such controversial publicity, a few days later Sabetay went to the same Portuguese synagogue in Edirne where Solomon Kohen, and independently Nathan, made speeches to uplift the hope of that congregation. In his sermon he declared that there were many contradictions in the Hebrew Scriptures and only he, as the messiah, could explain them. He pulled out a copy of the Koran and read a few passages. In the end, he asked the

---

4. This abbreviated letter is attributed to two different sources discussed in Scholem p. 844.

congregation if they were ready to apostatize. Twelve men and five women came forward and he led them to the imperial council chamber where they were converted by his friend Vani Effendi with the Sultan watching from behind the lattice wall. The Sultan was so pleased, he came out of his hiding place to offer a reward of pensions to the new converts. Sabetay threw a fit and asked the Sultan indignantly not to reward them for they had embraced Islam willingly and as a matter of pure faith.

ᴣᴫ

On March 6, 1671 Sabetay decided to divorce Sarah. They had been married seven years. He claimed that she had been unfaithful, and that he felt like a Hebrew slave suffering for seven years in the hands of that wretched wife. He charged that she tried to poison him twice without success. Vani Effendi told him that in Islamic tradition all he had to do was to say in her presence: "I divorce you" three times, and that was it. Thusly, he divorced Sarah and under Islamic law she could not keep the boy Ismail. He asked Vani Effendi if he would be allowed to circumsize his own son. The Imam was utterly delighted that Sabetay was taking so much interest in his new religion. He approved his request with great enthusiasm. He scheduled at the same time the circumcision of the son of a follower who had been converted to Islam. At that ceremony he renamed his son Israel and passed the name of Ismail to the other boy. No one understood the reason.

Vani Effendi asked Sabetay one great favor: to convince his prophet Nathan to apostatize before the Sultan. Sabetay agreed and issued an order to Nathan to come and visit him. Nathan learned the truth why he was being summoned. He agreed to come but begged Sabetay not to ask him to give up Judaism. As it was, on the day the two were to meet at the palace, Sabetay lapsed into a severe depression and the event never took place. When he came out of his illness a few days later, he claimed he didn't remember having asked Nathan to apostatize.

ᴣᴫ

The long war between The Republic of Venice and the Ottoman Turks was over. It lasted twenty-five years and accomplished
little. The dispute was over the control of a few islands in the
Mediterranean and Adriatic seas. The *Vizir* came back from that
war but had to rush to a new war against the insurgents in Poland. This time the Sultan went to war with him. That war lasted
three years and in 1672 they returned victorious, discovering that
Sabetay had been imprisoned by the police charging him of conducting Hebrew services in the Portuguese synagogue, seeding
discord among Moslems and Jews, wearing phylacteries and a skull
cap instead of a turban, excess drinking and womanizing, and
worse yet, uttering blasphemies to Islam as witnessed by a few
Moslems ready to testify against him. The *Vizir* and the Sultan
were angered by the troubles he had been fermenting in their
absence. The disappointed Sultan was about to pronounce the
death sentence on Sabetay when Vani Effendi and the Sultan's
mother begged him to reconsider. They asked him to reconsider
the death sentence for they thought Sabetay was a truly holy man
who suffered many physical and mental afflictions. The Sultan
acquiesced but decided to send him this time on life imprisonment without pardon to the farthest and remotest location in his
empire, a place where Jews would not be allowed to visit. The
location of the imprisonment was to be kept a secret. He didn't
want a repeat of what had taken place at the fortress of Abydos.

Sabetay was shipped in great secrecy to a province on the Adriatic
Sea, near the border between Albania and Yugoslavia. There stood
an old medieval fortress which the Turks converted into a prison
for dangerous political inmates. Before the Turkish occupation, the
fortress was known by the Italian name of Dulcigno.[5] Since the
occupation its name had been changed to Ulgün. The published
decree made no mention of the place where he would spend the
rest of his life. In spite of the fact that Sabetay had divorced Sarah, she, out of commitment and hope to remain the messiah's

---

5. The contemporary name of the village is Ulcinj.

wife, requested the Vizir to allow her to join him in exile. She never lost hope that somehow Sabetay's divine connections would make her a queen. In exile Sarah gave birth to a daughter.

In isolation and total misery, two years after his incarceration Sarah died in 1674. Sabetay was now forty-nine years old. Lonely in a prison where no Jew was allowed to visit, he wrote to one of his admiring scholars in Salonica named Joseph Filosoff for the hand of his daughter. Filosoff agreed provided Sabetay agreed to his terms. He asked to be proclaimed the incarnation of Saul, the Jew of Tarsus christened as Paul, the father of Christianity. Sabetay agreed. He sent his daughter accompanied by her brother to Dulcigno where the wedding took place in Hebrew tradition. Appropriately Sabetay renamed his new bride Michal, the name of Saul's natural daughter. His young wife adopted Sarah's son Israel and daughter, and a bastard son forced upon Sabetay by an Islamic woman who claimed to have had intercourse with Sabetay. In return, Sabetay adopted Michal's younger brother Jacob as his son and his only rightful successor. Thus Jacob Filosoff became Jacob Sevi. The sacrifice Joseph Filosoff seemingly made in giving his considerably younger daughter to Sabetay had many rewards. Filosoff's son stood to become the Son of the Messiah.

Sabetay began to fall ill from the dampness and unsanitary conditions in his cell. He also developed an acute form of colitis which at times made him suffer from severe intestinal obstruction. As days went by his illness worsened. For the first time, sensing he may die before the day of salvation, during the Passover holiday in 1676 he wrote letters to many of his loyal followers, Jews and converted Dönmeh. One letter, without question, sounded convincingly that he had been true to his claim and devotion in the role of the messiah and was about to leave the sinful world as a martyr. In the letter he wrote:

> My brethren and dearly beloved . . . . Behold I send an angel before thee to announce and tell you all my glory in Egypt and some of what he has seen. Beware of him and obey his voice, provoke him not in anything he says unto you in my name, for I shall not forgive your transgression when God arises to judgment and the

Lord of hosts shall be exalted in judgment . . . . Thus saith the man who is raised to the heights of the Father, the Celestial Lion and Celestial Stag, the Anointed of the God of Israel and Judah."

Sabetay Mehmet Sevi[6]

His original movement had split in two factions: a new Hebrew order with new canons and modified holidays, and the new converts into Islam who saw themselves as Jews but temporarily Moslems until their messiah was released by God from his mandatory suffering. In the Ottoman Empire it was a crime punishable by death to renege Islam. Jacob Sevi, the adopted son and brother of Sabetay's new wife was made the rightful leader of the Islamic Dönmeh who called themselves by Hebrew names. On September 5, 1676, two weeks before the Day of Atonement, one of his most devoted followers and apostate Joseph Carillo, who had been a rabbi in Andrinople and was elevated by Sabetay to the title of King Abiah, arrived in Dulcigno disguised as a Turk. He brought Sabetay's adopted son Jacob and a Moslem cleric who had been converted to Islam by Sabetay. They came upon an invitation by Sabetay, who felt the need to divulge before his death a most sacred secret he harbored in his chest for nearly thirty years.

Sabetay took them for a short walk on the isolated beach and addressed them by their original Jewish names, and said in a despondent mood: "*Return every man to his house. How long will you hold fast to me?*"

"*Forever!*" was the response the three men gave.

Feeling the end of his days, he divulged to them the secret of The Mystery of the Godhead, the Divine Structure, he alone had known, among all living men, and had understood from the readings of the *Cabala*. This way he was passing on to them the thread that held his mission together. Deeply inspired, the visitors returned to Constantinople as the patriarchs of the new faith.

---

6. As G. Scholem explains in p. 915 this handwritten letter from Sabetay pasted with great care on strong paper was obtained from the Dönmeh archives. Other sources are also mentioned.

What made the most profound impression on the remnants of Sabetay's followings was the news that he died on September 17, 1676, during the closing hours of the Day of Atonement when many synagogues chanted the *Nehilah*, a moment considered to be the most solemn of the year. The Moslem guards said they heard voices from the firmament singing the chant which sounded like a holy military march. All they could catch from the Hebrew words was a striking refrain: *"El norah alilah . . ."* repeated over and over. It was quickly revealed by his followers that the patriarch Moses also died at that very same moment.

ॐ

Afterword

The news of Sabetay Sevi's death remained a secret for a year in the hope of eluding a religious upheaval between the Sabetian followers and conservative Jews. More importantly, the Grand Mufti didn't want any belligerence between traditional Islam and the Dönmeh, the Sabetian Jews converted to Islam who in spirit remained Jews but outwardly had to abide by the strict codes of Islam. For them there was no choice of returning to Judaism. Reneging Islam was heresy and was punishable by death. The followers who remained Jews and had accepted a reformation of Judaism found themselves without leadership. Their only remaining leader, Nathan, the messiah's prophet, was immediately excommunicated after Sabetay's death. The Egyptian rabbis also excommunicated Sabetay posthumously together with his wealthy patron Raphaël Joseph who had apostatized to Islam. Traditional Judaism began a systematic drive to extricate the image Sabetay had built all these years from the minds of the Jews of the Diaspora across Europe and Asia. A short phrase taken from the edict of excommunication was ordered to be displayed at all synagogues:

". . . traitor who by his apostasy had shown his true colors."

In a generation or two there were no longer remnants of Sabetian Jews. Traditional Judaism brought them back into its fold.

On January 11, 1680, Nathan roamed through Europe trying to recover the last remnants of Sabetay's movement. He died in Üsküb, Macedonia, a town very near Dulcigno, where his messiah had died. Before his death he came to visit Sabetay's grave. In an entranced vision connecting his spirit with that of Sabetay he suffered a severe stroke. He died before his associates could bring him to town for treatment. The population of Dönmeh remained very active with successive new leaderships, beginning with Jacob Sevi, his last wife's brother whom Sabetay had adopted as his son. Those of the reformed Christians of Europe who had vested great hopes on the messianic appearance in 1666 as hinted in the book of Revelation, quickly lost interest after Sabetay converted to Islam.

Now, as the twentieth century has closed, more than three hundred years after this tragic event, the population of Dönmeh is very much alive and numbers approximately 15,000 to 20,000 followers. They live primarily in the northern cities of what used to be the Ottoman Empire, the cities visited by Sabetay: Izmir (Smyrna), Istanbul (Constantinople), Edirne (Adrianople), Sofia, and other towns in the Balkans. After the Greco-Turkish War of 1921–22, when Salonica returned to Greece, fearing the intolerance of the Christian Greeks, the large Dönmeh community of Salonica moved to join their brethren in Istanbul. With the revolution of 1908 and the abolition of the monarchy in Turkey, the new democratic government abandoned its ties with religion and became a secular state. Since then the new found freedom permitted all religions to worship freely in the dominantly Moslem land of the Turks. The Dönmeh of today are free to practice their brand of Islam. They lost the initial connection they had with Jews and many times resisted Jewish attempts to assimilate them into

Judaism. They still believe that the conversion of Sabetay Sevi was a step in an attempt to fulfill the messianic prophecy of the bible. They remain apart from Jewish and Moslem communities and practice various rites and customs, such as marriage and burial, with reminders of a past Judaic influence. They have some knowledge of Hebrew and call themselves by Hebrew names. They maintain the tradition of singing many of Sabetay's songs. However, their doctrine is closer to Islam than Judaism and yet they do not marry traditional Moslems or Jews. In the past three centuries they broke into various sects reflecting social distinctions and disputes over the legitimate successor to Sabetay Sevi. To date the largest collection of Sabetay's letters, memorabilia, and historical documentation about the movement is in the hands of the Dönmeh.

Bibliography

Beck-Busse, G. *Sephardica: Rome Tremble, & les Cardinaux, and tous les Evesques*. Bern, Switzerland: Peter Lang, 1996.

Cohn, N. *The Pursuit of the Millennium*. New York: Oxford University Press, 1970.

Creasy, E. S. *History of the Ottoman Turks, Vol. II*. London: R. Bentley Pub., 1856.

Enrique Saporta y Beja, *Refranes de los Judíos Sefardíes*. Barcelona: Ameller Ediciones, 1978.

Encyclopedia Britannica, Eleventh Ed. 1910–11.

Evelyn, J. *The History of the Three Late Famous Imposters*. London: The Savoy, 1669.

Feldman, W. A. *Rabbinical Mathematics and Astronomy*. Boston: Hermon Press, 1978.

Franco, M. *Essai sur l'Histoire des Israelites de l'Empire Ottoman*. Paris: Centre Don Isaac Abravanel, 1980.

Kastein, J. *The Messiah of Ismir*. London: John Lane The Bodley Head Ltd., 1931.

Nehama, J. *Histoire des Israélites de Salonique, Vol. 5*. Salonica: Molho, 1980.

Potok, C. *Wanderings*. New York: Fawcett Crest, 1978.

The Book of Psalms. London: Cresset Press, 1989.

The Jewish Encyclopedia, (1901). Funk and Wagnalls Co.

Scholem, G. *Sabbatai Sevi*, Bollingen Series XCIII. Princeton, NJ: Princeton University Press, 1973.

Waite, A. E. *The Holy Kabbalah, A University Book*, New York: Carol Publishing Group, 1990.

Weiss, R. L. & Butterworth, C. eds. *Ethical Writings of Maimonides*. New York: Dover Publications, 1975.

ABOUT THE AUTHOR

Retired Emeritus Professor from Syracuse University, Salamon Eskinazi received his doctorate from the Johns Hopkins University. He has lectured throughout Europe and the U.S. Twice a Fulbright Scholar he was decorated by the French Ministry of Education with the Chevalier des Palmes Academiques. He is listed in *World's Who's Who of Authors*, and *Who's Who in the East*. *The Reluctant Messiah* is his second historical novel concerning the saga of the Sephardis, or Spanish Jews, since the beginning of our current era. He currently lives in Rockville, MD, with his loving and supportive wife, Terry. They have two children, David and Ruth, and three grandsons: Matthew, Michael, and Andrew.

www.ingramcontent.com/pod-product-compliance
Lightning Source LLC
Chambersburg PA
CBHW020657110726
47901CB00001B/219